The beast's flanks raked across the up___ ___ ___ of the ship's primary hull, carving g___ ___ ___rs of metal ___

The serpent's tail flexed tow___ ___ ___arp nacelle, searching for somewhe___ ___ ___glehold, while the monolithic head reared up, g___ ___ ___e dome of the bridge.

Fire shocked through the deck and Sisko felt his ship take the hit—but this was different from other battles he had fought as captain. The strike wasn't just reaching him through the echo of impact on metal and polymer.

He felt it in his nerves and bones, in the blood rushing through his veins. The poisoned temporal aura that sizzled around the creature's bulk grazed the *Robinson* and Sisko cried out, feeling it as keenly as if the vessel's spaceframe were an extension of his own body.

A terrible, dizzying pressure bloomed inside his skull, a whiteout blinding him, robbing him of his senses. He knew this sensation all too well.

From across untold distances, from beyond linear time itself, *They* were reaching out to him.

Not now! He wanted to bellow the words. *Not now!*

For an infinite moment, Benjamin Sisko became a conduit, cut loose from time itself, existing in a frozen forever. He was a prism, the lens through which a torrent of giddying images fell. Even as he struggled to reach back to the common, ordinary existence of his physical body, the part of him that was born from the beings known as the Prophets took control.

STAR TREK™
CODA
BOOK II
THE ASHES OF TOMORROW

James Swallow

Story by
Dayton Ward & James Swallow & David Mack
Based on
Star Trek and
Star Trek: The Next Generation™
created by
Gene Roddenberry
Star Trek: Deep Space Nine™
created by
Rick Berman & Michael Piller
Star Trek: Voyager™
created by
Rick Berman & Michael Piller & Jeri Taylor
Star Trek: Picard™
created by
Akiva Goldsman & Michael Chabon
&
Alex Kurtzman & Kirsten Beyer

GALLERY BOOKS

New York   London   Toronto   Sydney   New Delhi   Baseras

G

Gallery Books
An Imprint of Simon & Schuster, Inc.
1230 Avenue of the Americas
New York, NY 10020

First Gallery Books trade paperback edition October 2021

GALLERY BOOKS and colophon are registered trademarks of Simon & Schuster, Inc.

For information about special discounts for bulk purchases, please contact Simon & Schuster Special Sales at 1-866-506-1949 or business@simonandschuster.com.

The Simon & Schuster Speakers Bureau can bring authors to your live event. For more information or to book an event, contact the Simon & Schuster Speakers Bureau at 1-866-248-3049 or visit our website at www.simonspeakers.com.

Interior design by A. Kathryn Barrett

Manufactured in the United States of America

10 9 8 7 6 5 4 3 2 1

Library of Congress Cataloging-in-Publication Data is available.

ISBN 978-1-9821-5854-5
ISBN 978-1-9821-5855-2 (ebook)

*This novel is dedicated to the memory of our friends and colleagues
David Galanter and Margaret Wander Bonanno;
and with grateful thanks to all the readers
who have journeyed with us over the past two decades.*

The future has several names.
For the weak, it is impossible;
for the fainthearted, it is unknown;
but for the valiant, it is ideal.

—Victor Hugo
Les Misérables

PREVIOUSLY . . .

2376

- Captain Benjamin Sisko returns from his sojourn with the Bajoran Prophets, which began a year earlier following the conclusion of the Dominion War. (*Star Trek: Deep Space Nine*, "What You Leave Behind")
- Bajor joins the United Federation of Planets. (*Star Trek: Deep Space Nine* novel *Unity*)

2377

- After being marooned in the Delta Quadrant seven years earlier, Captain Kathryn Janeway and the crew of the *Starship Voyager* complete their 70,000-light-year journey home to Earth. (*Star Trek: Voyager*, "Endgame")

2378

- Wesley Crusher accompanies the Traveler, with whom he's been learning to grow and focus his emerging abilities, to his mentor's home planet, Tau Alpha C. There, he is "reborn" and becomes a Traveler. (*Star Trek: The Next Generation* novel *A Time to Be Born*)

2379

- Federation president Min Zife, guilty of selling to the independent world Tezwa illegal weapons that contribute to millions of deaths, is covertly removed from office by a group of Starfleet admirals with the assistance of Captain Jean-Luc Picard. Unknown to Picard, Zife is assassinated by Section 31. (*Star Trek* novels *A Time to Kill* and *A Time to Heal*)
- Shinzon, a cloned duplicate of Picard originally created to replace the captain as a Romulan spy within Starfleet, seizes control of the Romulan Star Empire following a *coup d'état*. He launches a bold plan to attack Earth and cripple the Federation, but Picard and the *Enterprise* defeat him. Diplomatic relations are renewed between the Federation and the Romulans. (*Star Trek Nemesis*)

- Captain William Riker takes command of *U.S.S. Titan*. His wife, Commander Deanna Troi, accompanies him as ship's counselor and first contact specialist. (*Star Trek: Titan* novel series)

2380
- Picard marries Beverly Crusher. (*Star Trek: The Next Generation* novel *Greater Than the Sum*)
- During an incursion by the Borg, Admiral Kathryn Janeway gives her life in defense of the Federation. (*Star Trek: The Next Generation* novel *Before Dishonor*)

2381
- The Borg launch a massive invasion of the Federation, laying waste to numerous planets and billions of lives before Starfleet achieves final victory, forever ending the Collective's persistent threat. (*Star Trek: Destiny* novel trilogy)
- During the invasion, Ezri Dax, serving as *U.S.S. Aventine*'s second officer, takes command when her captain and first officer are killed.
- Riker and Troi have a daughter, Natasha Miana Riker-Troi, named in memory of deceased *Enterprise* crewmember and friend Natasha Yar, and the deceased sister of Aili Lavena, a member of the *Titan*'s crew. (*Star Trek: Titan* novel series)
- With the assistance of unlikely allies, Admiral Janeway's death is reversed. She takes command of Project Full Circle, with *U.S.S. Voyager* and an entire fleet assigned to further explore the Delta Quadrant. (*Star Trek: Voyager* novel *The Eternal Tide*)
- Picard and Crusher have a son, René Jacques Robert François Picard. The boy is named for Picard's nephew, René, and older brother, Robert, and for Crusher's first husband, Jack Crusher. (*Star Trek: Destiny–Lost Souls* novel, *Star Trek: Typhon Pact* novel *Paths of Disharmony*)
- Following the Borg Invasion, Sisko assumes command of *U.S.S. Robinson*. (*Star Trek: Typhon Pact* novel *Rough Beasts of Empire*)

2382
- Admiral Janeway, along with the crew of *U.S.S. Voyager*, agrees to help an alien race, the Edrehmaia, on their long journey out of our

galaxy. They depart the Delta Quadrant for parts unknown. (*Star Trek: Voyager* novel *To Lose the Earth*)

- Andor secedes from the Federation over issues related to the Andorians' now-critical reproductive crisis. (*Star Trek: Typhon Pact* novel *Paths of Disharmony*)

2383

- Breen and Tzenkethi forces attack and destroy Federation station Deep Space 9. Over a thousand lives are lost. (*Star Trek: Typhon Pact* novel *Raise the Dawn*)

2384

- Years after sacrificing himself to save Picard, Data is "reincarnated" after his memories are removed from his brother, the android B-4, and transferred into the body of a new android created by Noonian Soong. His android daughter, Lal, is also repaired and reactivated. (*Star Trek: Cold Equations* novel trilogy)

2385

- Federation station Deep Space 9 (II) is declared operational, positioned like its predecessor near the Bajoran wormhole. At its commemoration, Federation President Nanietta Bacco is assassinated. Federation Council member Ishan Anjar of Bajor is appointed president pro tempore. (*Star Trek: The Fall*, Book I: *Revelation and Dust*)

- Julian Bashir defies Starfleet and President Pro Tempore Ishan to bring the Andorian people a cure for their reproductive crisis. He succeeds with help from Captain Dax. They are both imprisoned. (*Star Trek: The Fall*, Book III: *A Ceremony of Losses*)

- President Pro Tempore Ishan is exposed as a criminal. Andor rejoins the Federation. An Andorian wins the Federation's presidential election and pardons Bashir and Dax. (*Star Trek: The Fall*, Book V: *Peaceable Kingdoms*)

2386

- Exploring the Odyssean Pass, Picard and the *Enterprise* encounter an immense weapon, reverse-engineered by an alien race from a prototype "planet killer" device and sent back in time from the late twenty-fifth century. Investigating the weapon's onboard computer systems, Lieutenant Commander Taurik discovers information about future events he is not permitted to disclose. Taurik is debriefed by the Department of Temporal Investigations and sworn to secrecy in accordance with the Temporal Prime Directive. (*Star Trek: The Next Generation* novel *Armageddon's Arrow*)

- Picard and the *Enterprise* discover a rogue planet locked into a series of random jumps across multiple dimensions and points in time. They meet an alternate version of *U.S.S. Enterprise* NCC-1701-D from a reality in which Picard did not survive his capture and assimilation by the Borg. (*Star Trek: The Next Generation* novel *Headlong Flight*)

- Journalist Ozla Graniv, with the assistance of Bashir and Data, exposes Section 31's entire history and lengthy list of illegal activities spanning more than two centuries. All known Section 31 operatives are arrested, and Picard is implicated in the organization's assassination of Federation president Min Zife in 2379. (*Star Trek: Section 31* novel *Control*)

2387

- Exonerated from the fallout relating to the revelations about Section 31, Captain Picard prepares to return with the *Enterprise* to the Odyssean Pass to continue its exploration mission. (*Star Trek: The Next Generation* novel *Collateral Damage*)

- Wesley Crusher brings a warning to Picard: the Devidians, an old adversary, are attacking and collapsing entire timelines. Working with Captain Dax and the *Aventine*, Wesley and the *Enterprise* crew race to discover the truth behind this terrifying new offensive. With reality itself at stake, their investigation results in severe casualties for both ships, among them Taurik and Ezri Dax. (*Star Trek: Coda*, Book I: *Moments Asunder*)

AND NOW . . .

PART I

ESCAPE

1

U.S.S. *Robinson* NCC-71842

Benjamin Sisko fell into the void amid the tunnel of stars, feeling the velocity of interstellar space flashing around him, riding the giddy rush of it at the edges of his senses.

"Ten seconds out!" A voice at his right called the warning, but Sisko didn't break his gaze from the streaks of starlight.

Other voices ahead and behind acknowledged the shout, but he paid them no mind, staying in the moment. He leaned forward in his chair, setting his shoulders as if he could compel his vessel to travel that bit faster.

The shimmering glow seemed to grow beyond the wide viewscreen in front of him, reaching across the bridge of the starship to gather Sisko into its aurorae. He could not escape the premonition that something ominous was waiting on the far side of those warp-elongated stars; and then, with a sudden flash of deceleration, his prediction became a reality.

A shuddering whine of shed energy signaled the *Starship Robinson*'s drop from high warp as it fell back into synchrony with normal space. They had emerged on the edge of an uncharted system in the Dorvan Sector.

"Red alert! Shields and weapons!" Sisko's executive officer, Commander Anxo Rogeiro, snapped out the orders even as the vessel was still settling.

Over the six years that Rogeiro had been Sisko's second-in-command aboard the *Galaxy*-class starship, the younger man had had an uncanny ability to anticipate his captain's intentions, and his relationship with Sisko had developed to the point where they could communicate intent to each other with little more than a glance or a nod of the head. Sisko didn't need to tell the other man what needed to be done. Both of them fully understood the stakes at hand.

The *Robinson* arrived amid a shroud of debris and fire. Pieces of wreckage and drifts of metallic dust sparked off the starship's shield membrane, briefly rendering patches of it visible as the vessel advanced. Sisko's eyes narrowed and his jaw set in a hard line as he noted what could only have been bodies out there in the vacuum amid the remains. Whatever happened here, those poor souls had perished before they could hope to seek safety.

"Commander Plante"—Sisko shot a look at his second officer—"what do you hear?"

Plante held an audio relay module pressed to her right ear, listening directly to the urgent mayday message that had torn the *Robinson* away from its current mission, a parsec inside the border of the Cardassian Union. "Same message repeating on subspace, sir," she replied with a frown. "There may not be anyone left to respond to our hails."

"We have to hope otherwise," Sisko rumbled. "Anything from the Cardassians?"

"We know they dispatched a ship. A light cruiser, I think." Lieutenant Corallavellis sh'Vrane volunteered the information, the Andorian *shen* leaning back from her console at the science station. "But I'm not reading anything."

"I am." Uteln, the *Robinson*'s senior tactical officer, looked down at his captain from his station behind the command chair. The Deltan's usually warm and open expression was uncharacteristically muted. He gestured at the debris on the viewer. "Sir, I think that's what's left of it."

"*Mãe de Deus . . .*" Rogeiro uttered the curse softly in his native Portuguese. "But they could only have arrived here minutes before us . . ."

What destroyed them so utterly, so quickly? The question hung in the air, but Sisko refused to waste time dwelling on it. He ordered sh'Vrane to set about running scans for signs of survivors, and for answers.

The science officer's antennae curved inward, a certain tell that the Andorian was frustrated by what she saw on her screen. "Readings are . . . unusual. The wreckage shows extremely advanced signs of molecular decay."

"Something there," Rogeiro went on, indicating a smoky shape in the distance, beyond the wreckage. "The station."

As the *Robinson* pushed out past the dust and remains, Sisko saw the object clearly and the shape of it stirred old emotions in him. The station adrift in a long orbit around the system's red giant star was of typical Cardassian design, resembling at a distance the curved form of a *Nor*-class space station, as familiar to him as the house where he had grown up.

A strange pang of emotion coursed through Sisko. He couldn't look at the station without being reminded of the old Deep Space 9, the station that had once been Terok Nor, the place he had thought of as home for years.

The imperiled station that had sent the urgent cry for help was smaller than DS9, but it had the same distinctive curving dock pylons rising upward, forming the shape of an iron crown.

He was on his feet without realizing it. "Magnify," he ordered, and the image on the main viewer leaped closer.

At better resolution, the similarity was less marked. The station was damaged, and at its core was a spherical operations module riddled with catastrophic damage. Whole decks were torn open and exposed to space. Clouds of outgassing plasma flickered with blue fire, and overload lightning crawled across the hull in wild, bright surges.

"No life signs," said sh'Vrane. "But . . ." The Andorian's pale blue features creased, and she trailed off.

Sisko turned back toward her. "Cora," he began, sharpening his tone. "Spit it out."

She nodded. "Captain, available data from the Cardassian space authority on this station describes it as a class-four scientific facility. Designated mission, warp-field technology research. But that does not correspond with the energy signature I'm seeing here."

Commander Plante turned the monitor at her side so she could study sh'Vrane's sensor readings. The human woman's eyes widened. "I concur," she began. "That station is leaking massive amounts of chronometric radiation, at a level we'd only see in the deliberately engineered formation of a temporal effect."

"Temporal?" Rogeiro echoed the word, and he couldn't keep the uncertainty from his tone. "As in *time travel*? You're saying that's what the Cardassians are messing with way out here?"

Sisko eyed his exec. For many of the captain's contemporaries in Starfleet, the concept of travel back or forward through time was a theory on the outer edges of possibility, a wild notion spoken of in the same way ancient mariners would tell sea stories. But Sisko had lived the reality of it, on more than one occasion.

"I wouldn't put it past Castellan Garak to hide the truth in plain sight," he noted. "Temporal research is strictly regulated by treaty among all the galactic powers."

He had more to say about that, but a ghost on the screen caught his attention and arrested Sisko's train of thought. Amid the research station's docking arms, a glassy, insubstantial phantom was briefly visible, then gone.

Sisko's mind grasped for definition of what he thought he saw. *Something large, swift, almost organic in its motion. Moving like . . . a serpent?*

"You saw that too?" said Rogeiro.

"We all did," noted Plante. "We're not alone here."

"Scanning for cloaked vessels." Lieutenant sh'Vrane's long, sky-blue fingers danced over her console. "Nothing. But I am detecting faint signals from within the wreckage field. Emergency beacons. Captain, I think there are escape pods in there."

Sisko didn't answer her. His gaze was locked on the research station, glaring into the void around it, almost daring the phantom-thing to show itself once more.

And to his dread, it did.

The apparition re-formed from out of the darkness, coiling around one of the undamaged docking pylons. This time, it gained mass and became substantial, growing solid until he could no longer see through it, taking on an actinic glow that cast sickly light over the damaged station. At one end of the serpentine form, a serrated maw big enough to swallow a runabout whole gaped wide beneath a smooth, flared head. The creature moved as if the void were its natural habitat, slipping effortlessly through the vacuum.

With a flicking twist that rippled along the length of its body, the serpent struck at the Cardassian station and tore into the superstructure with vicious abandon. Shards of tritanium hull exploded around it as the creature bored through the spherical core like a worm in an apple, bursting out the other side in a shower of energetic particles. In its wake, the station began to decay, as if the serpent carried with it a toxic, degenerative aura.

"Detecting another chronometric radiation release," said Plante. "Whatever that thing is, it's feeding off the chroniton flux." She swallowed hard. "Captain, it's warping the local temporal field of everything around it."

"It's a chronovore." Sisko's words fell into the silence that followed. The definition made a horrible kind of sense, explaining the unexpected deterioration of the Cardassian rescue ship and the effect the thing was having on the station. Like some monstrous ocean-dwelling beast out of old myth, the serpent savaged the doomed station, gathering its remains in its coils and crushing them to dust.

Sisko turned away, grim faced, and snapped out commands. "Transporters. Can we lock on to those escape pods and beam the survivors aboard?"

"Negative," said Plante with a shake of the head. "Radiation levels are interfering with our sensors, and we risk exposure if we drop the shields to bring them in."

"Tractor beam?" Rogeiro offered the option. "We use it to push the pods out of the debris and into open space, clear of the radiation zone."

Sisko nodded. "Do it."

As his first officer set to work, Sisko advanced on the main viewscreen, moving up to stand between the *Robinson*'s conn and ops stations. On the screen, the serpent writhed free of the remains of the Cardassian station, pausing as it devoured chunks of debris.

Is it sentient? he wondered. *Some kind of cosmozoan life-form, attracted by whatever Garak's people were doing here?* Sisko tried to put aside the thought of how many lives had been lost in the creature's attack, wondering if it might be possible to communicate with the serpent and prevent any further bloodshed.

The creature's blank, expressionless head cast around as if it were sensing the void around it, and Sisko stiffened as it turned in the direction of the *Robinson* and paused.

"It sees us." Sivadeki, the Tyrellian woman at the helm, whispered the thought aloud as the color drained from her face. "You think it is still hungry?"

The serpent drew in on itself and burst into flight, swimming clear of the destruction it had wrought, projecting its length onto an intercept path with the slow-moving starship. Folds of matter unrolled from the flanks of the creature, falling open to give the thing a serrated hood that trailed long lines of glistening cilia.

"Full power to deflectors," snapped Sisko, his voice booming around the bridge. "Helm, back us off!"

Sivadeki obeyed, pivoting the *Robinson* up and away from the plane of the ecliptic with a burn from the impulse thrusters—but even as the starship moved, Sisko saw the creature become insubstantial again. It faded from view, and he held his breath.

"Did it . . . cloak?" Rogeiro asked the question that was on everyone's mind. "Or is it gone?"

"Sensors register no trace of it," said sh'Vrane. "Even the most complex aura cloak would leave some wake."

Then in the next second, a shimmering wall of glowing, metallic flesh-matter filled the viewscreen from wall to wall as the creature reappeared right on top of them, close enough to interact with the *Robinson*'s shields.

Sivadeki let out a reflexive bark of fright and recoiled in her chair as the creature slammed its head into the deflector envelope. It was close enough for Sisko to make out fine details on the bony cowl across its skull, dotted with sensory pits and strange palp-like growths. Quivering, talon-like horns as big as shuttlecraft emerged at regular intervals along its body, and the wide abyss of the serpent's maw was festooned with row after jagged row of spear-tip teeth, snapping angrily at the shield bubble as it tried to bite through it.

Sisko pointed toward the viewer. "Phasers, fire at will!"

At the tactical station, Uteln hit back with a broad-spectrum spread from the upper weapons ring, clearly hoping to wound the creature and drive it off, but Sisko watched in dismay as the orange-red beams passed through the body of the beast. Sections of the gargantuan serpent became insubstantial while other parts of it remained solid, rendering the energy weapons useless.

Even as Sivadeki fought to pull the *Robinson* away from the creature before it could latch on to the vessel, the glowing giant rammed its armored head through the forward shields with a shock of light. The beast's flanks raked across the upper surface of the ship's primary hull, carving gouges, sending splinters of metal into the darkness.

The serpent's tail flexed toward the *Robinson*'s starboard warp nacelle, searching for somewhere to grasp in a stranglehold, while the monolithic head reared up, grazing the dome of the bridge.

Fire shocked through the deck and Sisko felt his ship take the hit—but this was different from other battles he had fought as captain. The strike wasn't just reaching him through the echo of impact on metal and polymer.

He felt it in his nerves and bones, in the blood rushing through his veins. The poisoned temporal aura that sizzled around the creature's bulk grazed the *Robinson* and Sisko cried out, feeling it as keenly as if the vessel's spaceframe were an extension of his own body.

A terrible, dizzying pressure bloomed inside his skull, a white-out blinding him, robbing him of his senses. He knew this sensation all too well.

From across untold distances, from beyond linear time itself, *They* were reaching out to him.

Not now! He wanted to bellow the words. *Not now!*

For an infinite moment, Benjamin Sisko became a conduit, cut loose from time itself, existing in a frozen forever. He was a prism, the lens through which a torrent of giddying images fell. Even as he struggled to reach back to the common, ordinary existence of his physical body, the part of him that was born from the beings known as the Prophets took control.

He could barely hold on to the visions racing through his mind.

Trillions upon trillions of suns going out; a galaxy of dead planets surrendered to entropy and devoid of all life; a landscape of ashes, borne on mournful winds; a familiar world of verdant green aging eons in seconds.

"No time," said a woman's voice, from across an impossible distance.

He saw Bajor, crumbling and collapsing, turned to death and dust. Above it, the bright swirl of the wormhole corrupting, vomiting emerald fire and imploding.

And amid every horror, the monstrous serpents turning and moving in the darkness.

"No time," said the faraway voice.

"No!"

Sisko's cry broke whatever influence had taken him, and he snapped back to the moment, feeling the *Robinson*'s deck trembling beneath his boots. For the captain, the vision had seemed like an eternity, but not a second had elapsed in linear time.

He lost his balance for a moment and staggered against the other console, just as Sivadeki reached out toward the captain, her eyes widening.

She didn't see the talon that phased through the upper shell of the bridge dome, cutting across the corner of the deck, slicing clean through the edge of the main viewer. Sivadeki did not see the way the deck and the walls behind her decayed like rotting paper. She did not know she was about to perish until the talon passed and its atemporal aura enveloped her.

The Tyrellian woman was just beyond Sisko's grasp, but still he reached into the fire, his flesh burning as he tried desperately to pull her to him. Sivadeki met his gaze and then she was gone; every part of her, flesh and blood, uniform and combadge, reduced to a heap of gray powder as she aged millions of years in a millisecond.

A wisp of the ash settled on Sisko's hand and he found he couldn't breathe. The shock of the young woman's death robbed him of his voice.

"Phasers aren't worth a damn against that thing!" Commander Rogeiro's angry snarl reached him, and Sisko forced himself to shutter away the horror he had just witnessed. "Computer, damage report."

"Hull breaches: decks one through eight," the careful voice of the *Robinson*'s computer reeled off. *"Multiple casualties. Plasma discharge in main engineering. Structural integrity field failing."*

The captain rose and dashed back across his bridge, the light from the alert panels casting the deck in burning crimson. Behind him, a force field had automatically erected itself to wall off the corner of the bridge that the serpent destroyed. Everything inside the shimmering field was rusted and decrepit, the life drained out of it, just like the luckless Sivadeki.

"We need to get this thing off us, before we end up like . . ." Commander Plante stumbled over her words. "Like the Cardassians."

"Time," growled Sisko as a thought formed in his mind. "It feeds on *time*." He hauled himself up and over the edge of the upper control station at the rear of the bridge, advancing on Uteln. "Give me your station, now!"

"Sir?" Doubt crossed the Deltan's face, but the tactical officer obeyed the order, stepping back to let Sisko take over his console.

"Work with me," said the captain as the ship rocked under another collision with the beast. He gestured toward a vacant engineering station. "Program the guidance controls in the forward torpedo launchers for proximity detonation!"

Uteln paled. "What distance?"

"Point-blank." Sisko attacked the tactical console, jabbing hard at the display as he transmitted commands to the automated loading mechanisms down in the torpedo bay. Swift robotic manipulators swapped out the matter/antimatter warhead of the photon torpedoes for a more exotic payload.

"Captain . . ." Sisko didn't look up as Rogeiro came to him. He knew that tone of voice, knew the concern in it. "Ben . . . ?"

Anxo Rogeiro was not a man given to flights of fancy—indeed, he was one of the most skeptical people Sisko had ever known, hard-pressed to trust anything that he couldn't see or touch. Despite his earlier outburst, the first officer's belief in the numinous and preternatural was practically nonexistent, so it was with difficulty that the captain trusted him with the spiritual certainties that were part of his personal truth.

"I know what I'm doing," Sisko told him. If he laid it out in full, if he told Rogeiro that he had just had *a vision*, and that had given him a sudden, unexpected insight. *What could he say?* "There's no time for debate," he added, "I need you to have faith."

"I do," Rogeiro said quietly. "We all do, sir, but . . ."

"No time!" Sisko retorted, completing his work.

"Anti-tachyon generator modules loaded," reported the computer. *"Torpedoes loaded and ready to deploy."*

"Guidance set," said Uteln. "Sir, at point-blank range, the detonations will—"

"I know," said the captain, cutting him off with a terse nod. "Divert all power to deflectors, on my mark." Sisko looked up and met the eyes of his bridge crew. "Brace yourselves." He reached for the console and tapped the firing key. "Mark!"

Orbs of blue-white light shot from the *Robinson*'s torpedo launcher array and tracked the short distance to the shimmering flank of the creature—but they did not make contact with the serpent's body, instead detonating in a chain of blinding fire *inside* the insubstantial mass of the writhing giant.

The standard warhead of a photon torpedo would have been pure annihilation, a tiny sun born and dying as matter and antimatter wiped each other out in a flash of destruction; but the warheads Sisko had launched drenched the void and the subspace domains closest to it in a torrent of powerful anti-tachyons, the exotic inversion of particles generated by temporal anomalies.

If the serpent creature consumed the energy of time itself, then the anti-tachyons would be poison to it, but the only way to saturate the monster in their aura was to risk the destruction of the *Robinson*.

In the silence of the void, the wash of punishing radiation engulfed the predatory chronovore and it disintegrated, but the detonations were just as lethal to the starship as they were to the beast.

Sisko's crew were ready for them, and they turned into the blow. A long, drawn-out moan of shuddering metal resonated through the *Robinson*'s spaceframe and the ship was knocked aside by the torpedo blast. The captain felt himself leave the deck and collide with Uteln as the two of them crashed into the consoles at the rear of the bridge. Smoke and flame swept through the air and blackness swallowed up the captain as his head struck an illuminated panel.

The transition seemed immediate: one moment he was falling, and the next he was looking into Plante's eyes as she scanned him with a tricorder.

"Gwendolyn." He blinked slowly as a wash of discomfort came over him. "Did it . . . work?"

"Hold still," said Plante, then at length she gave a weary nod. "Aye, sir, it did. But we took a beating along the way."

"How long was I out?"

"A few minutes." She scowled at the tricorder's readout. "You need to get to sickbay, have Doctor Kosciuszko check you over."

"Soon enough." Sisko stood up, covering a wince of pain. He felt light in his boots—a sure sign that the ship's gravity generators were working at reduced capacity—and made his way over to where Rogeiro and sh'Vrane stood around the science station.

The bridge was gloomy, running on low-level emergency power, and the glow of the viewscreen gave everything around it a ghostly cast.

"Report," said Sisko, his voice husky with effort.

"Quick thinking with the anti-tachyon burst, sir," said the Andorian. "We caught the creature by surprise. It discorporated, leaving no physical traces behind. I think its mass may have been absorbed into subspace."

"Let's hope we've seen the last of it." Rogeiro ran a hand over his brow. "We've stabilized the ship and damage control parties have been deployed. Structural harm is severe, casualty reports still coming in . . ." He sighed. "We've lost some good people."

Sisko couldn't stop himself from glancing over to the ruin of Lieutenant Commander Sivadeki's station. He looked away. "What about those escape pods?"

Rogeiro and sh'Vrane exchanged glances. "We beamed them into a cargo bay as soon as we could," said the science officer, but her bleak expression told the rest of the story before she uttered it. "Inside every one . . . there was nothing but dust."

The commander stared at the viewscreen, through the broken

and static-choked image toward the drifts of time-ravaged wreckage in the near distance. "What the hell *was* that thing? I've never seen the like. And where did it come from? It damn near killed us all!"

No time. The voice echoed in the depths of Sisko's thoughts. He knew it, remembering its soft tones from his childhood. It was the voice that had lulled him to sleep as a boy, while his father worked amid the clatter of pots and pans in a kitchen downstairs. The voice that still came to him in dreams, if he listened hard enough.

"Captain?"

Sisko blinked, the brief reverie fading as he realized that sh'Vrane had been speaking to him.

"Your orders, sir?"

"The *Robinson* needs to make port," he replied, after a moment. "Can we go to warp?"

"Gingerly," said Rogeiro. "The nearest Starfleet outpost is Starbase 310. We can make it there in four days, if you give the word."

Sisko nodded. "The word is given." He pushed past the other man, moving down the bridge. "Tell Commander Plante to contact the Cardassians as soon as we are able, give them our logs and sensor readings, and let them know what we encountered out here."

"Maybe they can tell us what that creature was," said sh'Vrane.

Sisko could not escape the sense that the chronovore—and whatever had drawn it here, from whatever place or time—was the harbinger of something far worse. Something vast and terrible, beyond his human ability to grasp.

He stood by the edge of the force field holding back the vacuum of space, put out his hand, and touched the side of Sivadeki's chair. The layer of fine ash coating it filmed his fingertips and his bleak mood grew darker still.

No time, said his mother's voice, and now he was certain.

What Sisko had seen in that frozen moment was not some subjective vision or metaphorical dream state induced by the Prophets.

It was a *warning.*

2

U.S.S. *Aventine* NCC-82602

Jean-Luc Picard placed a hand on the wide expanse of the viewing gallery's port and stared out through it. Beyond the transparent barrier, the rushing aurorae of interstellar space sped past him, the glow of suns and nebulae transformed into a path of light along which the *U.S.S. Aventine* raced. Off the port quarter, Picard's own command kept pace with the ship, the *U.S.S. Enterprise*-E cutting gracefully through warp space, paralleling the *Aventine*'s course toward Sector 001, and Earth.

Seeing his own ship from this perspective gave him a profound, troubling sense of dislocation, a feeling only exaggerated by the proceedings he had experienced over the past few days.

Days. Had it really only been that long? Picard felt as if the events of their mission had aged him by decades.

He reached for the recollection of how this had all begun, weighing it in his thoughts; on the beach on Starbase 11, where he, Beverly, and their young son, René, had walked along the sands, their futures stretching out before them. That felt like a lifetime ago, and his emotions in that moment seemed foolish and naïve in retrospect.

One perfect instant of hope, abruptly torn asunder when a dying man literally fell from the skies to land at their feet.

But not just any man. Beverly Crusher's son Wesley—or at the very least, some future incarnation of him at the end of his existence.

With Wesley's arrival—*and then his death*—everything Jean-Luc Picard had looked to, every bright future and better tomorrow, was thrown into jeopardy.

The traumatic event was only the harbinger for something far worse. A forgotten threat from their past, the rapacious atemporal beings known as the Devidians, had returned and brought with them a menace graver than Picard could ever have imagined.

Even now, as he tried to hold the idea of it in his mind, his thoughts rebelled against the gargantuan horror the Devidians were perpetrating. It repelled him on a level he could barely put into words, and he was a man not given to speechlessness.

Over and over, Picard tried to frame the enormity of the danger, as if naming it would somehow make it easier to face. But no attempt seemed to capture it. Soon he would be called upon to bring the truth of what he witnessed to his superiors in Starfleet Command. He wondered how best to convey it, so that there would be no equivocation, no misunderstanding.

The Devidians are murdering the future.

What other way was there to describe the danger? A parasitic, opportunistic species, they had evolved to subsist on the neural energy of other life-forms. In his first confrontation with them, Picard and the crew of the *Enterprise* NCC-1701-D had fought the Devidians not just in the present, but in the deep past of Earth's early industrial age.

We thought we had dispatched them forever. Picard chided himself, shaking his head, frowning bitterly. *How wrong we were.*

Their sustenance denied to them on Earth, the insidious predators had simply withdrawn, and rather than be cowed, they had grown their ambitions far beyond a handful of worlds and civilizations. Picard now understood that the Devidians were preying on immeasurably more than planets, star systems, even galaxies. Whole realities were their targets, the countless alternate timelines that branched off from every instant, and every choice.

Existing outside of the normal flow of time, the Devidians had found a way to feast on the energy of trillions upon trillions of dying minds as they forcibly collapsed the branch growths of these other realities. They carved them away to nourish a bottomless greed that would continue to grow out of control if left unchecked.

It seemed an impossibility. It was an act of violence so vast it was nearly inconceivable. But Picard had seen it with his own eyes—they all had, after modifying the *Aventine*'s advanced quantum slipstream drive to take them to a distant, dead future where the predators held sway. And a blood cost had been paid for the knowledge torn from that bleak tomorrow.

He closed his eyes, fighting off the black mood that threatened to engulf him. Jean-Luc Picard knew horror, and he knew desolation. He had faced both more than once, on the field of battle against ruthless enemies like the Dominion, in his heart and soul against the Borg, or in conflict with existential threats that defied any conventional challenge. But the truth he now feared to look at head-on was beyond those.

In all his life, he had never felt so old, so powerless and forsaken, as he did today, and he knew full well the reason why.

It is because I have so much to lose, he told himself, studying his own reflection in the port. *My ship and my crew, my wife and son. Everything we have achieved. Every sacrifice we have made. All the good we have done . . . The very history we have made together is in jeopardy.*

"Captain Picard?" The words reached him, and he snapped out of his dark musings, drawing back from the viewport. Across the empty observation gallery, Samaritan Bowers stood in the doorway, his hands clasped. The *Aventine*'s former first officer, now her acting commander, forced a rueful smile. "I thought I might find you here."

"Is it time?" Picard's voice sounded husky and withdrawn.

"Soon, sir. We have a few moments before . . ." He trailed off, reluctant to finish the sentence. The man had a youthful cast to him that made him seem too young for the position he held, but even that could not hide the distance in his gaze. Like Picard,

Bowers had seen that terrible, ashen future, and he too had been forever changed by the experience. He spoke again. "Can I just say, I appreciate you returning to the *Aventine* for our ceremony. Your guidance . . . Your presence is deeply valued."

Picard gave a slow nod, glancing back toward the *Enterprise.* "We must say our farewells to the lost."

"Aye, sir." Bowers blinked and looked away.

"*The thousand-yard stare.*" Picard looked at his reflection and said the words without thinking, the phrase rising up unbidden from the depths of his thoughts.

"Sir?"

"You're unfamiliar with the term?" He took a breath. "It's drawn from a painting, a work created centuries ago by an artist during the era of Earth's Second World War. It depicts an American Marine during the conflict in the Pacific, and his face . . ." Picard gestured to himself, then to Bowers. "The look in his eyes. It's a very powerful image. It conveys the full effect of the horror he has seen."

"Ah." Bowers understood immediately. "I know that look. I saw it in the mirror today."

"As did I."

The other man's face twisted in a scowl. "How do we explain it to anyone who wasn't there, sir? What we saw in the future . . . How will we make them understand?"

"That is our burden," admitted Picard. "I share your sentiments. But we cannot allow despair to overwhelm us. We have a chance to stem the tide of that destruction, here in the present, before it can fully take root."

"You really believe we can stop the Devidians?"

"We have to try," he replied. "We are charged with a dire warning and it is imperative we bring it to bear."

"Well, Fate knows we paid a high enough price to bring that warning home." For a moment, Bowers seemed to be carrying the weight of the world on his shoulders.

"We rarely get to choose the circumstances that test us," Picard noted. "We do our duty."

"Aye," said Bowers. "That we do." He gave a shaky sigh. "I just hope I can live up to the standard she set."

In his mind's eye, Picard saw Ezri Dax, recalling the bold smile on her face and the daring glint that danced in her eyes. He had been charmed by the joined Trill, enjoying her infectious energy— the part of her that was undoubtedly the personality of the host, Ezri Tigan—and the wry, good-natured spirit that stemmed from the Dax symbiont that lived within her body.

It saddened him immensely that the *Aventine*'s captain had lost her life during their mission through time. The death of Dax, indeed of any Trill symbiont, was always a great tragedy, as so much was lost. So many lives lived, so much experience and knowledge wiped away, as if a great library had burned to the ground.

But equally he found himself mourning the potential lost by the host Ezri's untimely end. Well regarded by her crew and her contemporaries, she would be deeply missed. Picard knew her from their interactions during the Borg Invasion, and his first officer, Commander Worf, had considered Ezri a close friend, and loved the symbiont's previous host, Jadzia. The stoic Klingon would not have given his heart and loyalty to anyone who was not worthy.

He had offered his Number One the opportunity to transfer to the *Aventine* for the duration, but Worf had quietly refused, and Picard did not press him further on the matter. The warrior would mourn in his own way and in his own time.

"We should begin," said Picard, steeling himself.

Bowers gestured toward the door. "This way, sir."

The empty corridors they followed to the *Aventine*'s main shuttlebay gave the vessel the feel of a ghost ship, and Picard made no attempt to break the uneasy silence, instead marshaling his thoughts for the words he would soon be called upon to speak.

Then they reached the bay doors, which opened to reveal almost the entire complement of the *Vesta*-class ship's crew standing at attention in precise, parade-ground rows. Of the *Enterprise*'s officer corps, the sole representatives were Picard and his chief engineer, Commander Geordi La Forge; their presence was bolstered by Wesley Crusher, who gave his former captain a somber nod as he passed.

Picard found it hard to meet the other man's gaze and didn't linger on it. He had witnessed an aged version of his stepson dying before him, an incarnation ravaged by the centuries, lifetimes older than Picard himself. Each time he looked at Wesley, he saw that death replayed and remembered the pain it brought Beverly.

But this Wesley, this aspect of him, was a man from another era. Still alive, still vital, yet to become the aged wanderer Picard had seen perish. He carried himself with a wary confidence that was so unlike the bright young boy he had been during his time aboard the *Enterprise*-D. Wesley had opened Picard's eyes to the danger faced by their reality, if not all of existence.

Bowers led him to the front of the waiting crew, to an area that had been cleared of auxiliary craft directly in front of the shuttle-bay's main doors. Atop a low podium, a lectern had been set up, bearing the crest of the United Federation of Planets and the *Aventine* ship's pennant. Resting on the deck before it was a simple funeral wreath.

Bowers took the podium first and called the crew to attention. Picard could sense the other man struggling to hold his emotions in check, to keep his voice level and project the aura of strength that he was now called upon to exhibit. He felt a deep sympathy for Bowers. In moments like this, the loneliness of command could be a great burden indeed.

Bowers began by reciting a list of the junior officers and crew who had been lost in the mission to the hollow future, and with each one, he talked a little about them. He described a Tellarite ensign who loved to ski, a warrant officer who sang opera, an engineer with a brood-clutch still waiting to hatch back on their home asteroid. It was not just the repetition of dry data culled from their personnel files. Bowers knew each and every one of them, and felt their losses keenly.

A stifled sob drew Picard's attention to a woman in the front row, in a dark, nondescript tunic that didn't quite resemble a uniform. In a rare display of emotion, Agent Teresa Garcia wiped tears away from the corner of her eye. One of the operatives of the Department of Temporal Investigations, who had been dispatched with them on their fateful voyage, Garcia had made it back to the present with the rest of them, but her partner and fellow agent Meyo Ranjea had been lost along with the others. Garcia stiffened as Ranjea's name was mentioned, bowing her head as her colleague's passing was marked.

"T'Ryssa Chen, Lieutenant, *Starship Enterprise*." Bowers said the next name and it snapped Picard's gaze back to the podium.

As Bowers spoke, he pictured Chen in his mind's eye. The young Vulcan-human woman had been a valued member of his crew, and Picard had taken quiet pride in the maturation of her over the years under his command, but she too had perished before they could return to the present. Her death opened up the memory of old wounds, of other souls lost before their time in days past.

Picard thought of Jack Crusher and Tasha Yar, and of being where Bowers stood now, trying to bring some meaning to the death of friends and shipmates torn away by cruel events.

"Ezri Dax." Reaching the last name on his list, Bowers kept his voice from breaking, but only through great effort. "Captain. *Starship Aventine*." He swallowed hard and bowed his head. "We remember them. We cherish them. We carry on in their names."

"In their names." The response seemed to well up without conscious thought from the assembled mourners, and Picard found himself speaking it in echo of Dax's crew all around him.

When he looked up, Bowers was staring right at him, a question in his eyes. Picard gave the slightest of nods, and the other man returned it. "Captain Picard, on behalf of the ship's company, I ask if you would conclude the tribute."

"Captain Bowers, it would be my honor." The younger man stepped away from the podium and Picard took his place, putting his hands on the lectern.

This would be the third eulogy he had given in less than a week and the second memorial in as many days, after the service aboard the *Enterprise* the evening before. He began as he had to, speaking from his heart. "We have gathered here to make our farewells to our comrades-in-arms." He took in the faces of the *Aventine*'s crewmembers with an earnest nod. "To mark their passing from the world to whatever may lay beyond. Still, their presence remains among us. Their memory is a gift, and we are richer for having known them." His gaze passed over Bowers, La Forge, and Garcia, ending with Wesley, and he briefly changed tack. "Before I came here, I confess I spent a few hours in the observation gallery, striving to gather the right words for this moment. A pithy quote, perhaps, or some elegant poetry. But I have to confess, now the moment has come, everything I considered seems hollow and inadequate. So I look to the truth, and it is this: our friends gave their lives so that we could make it home, so that we could complete our mission. That was their duty, and it remains ours."

He saw his own fears and doubts mirrored in the faces arrayed before him—that *thousand-yard stare* of which he had spoken to Bowers repeated over and over. They looked to him, the senior man, the veteran commander, seeking some kind of assurance that there was a path through the trial unfolding before them.

Part of him felt like a charlatan. Was it wrong to give these people hope, when he found it so hard to seek it out in himself? Confronted by the bleak menace of the Devidian onslaught, any comforting lie would taste bitter in his mouth.

But he knew that to submit to the fear of it would be worse still, and Picard refused to give in to fatalism. As long as there was life, as long as there was still a chance to turn the helm of history toward a different course, he could not shirk the burden.

"On this voyage we have been tested," he went on. "We have looked into the face of annihilation, and that cost us our dearest blood. We cannot turn away. Like Cassandra, from the mythology of Ancient Earth, we are burdened with a vision of the future that we must impart to the present. We do this in the name of our oath . . . not just to Starfleet, but to our absent friends. *In their names.*" He repeated the words that Bowers had spoken earlier, and once more the assembled mourners echoed them across the cavernous hangar.

Picard looked and found a junior lieutenant off to one side at a control console, and gave him a nod. The stocky, bearded Mazarite wiped tears from his braided beard and worked his station.

Across the shuttlebay, a membrane of energy flickered into being and beyond it the main hatch dropped into the deck. The swirling, magical light of warp space filled the hangar, flooding in from outside.

A glittering thread of light—a tractor beam issuing from a hidden emitter in the ceiling—gathered up the simple wreath and carried it silently toward the force field. With a gentle push, the wreath passed through the barrier and into the space beyond.

Picard watched it shrink, coming apart to dissipate harmlessly into the *Aventine*'s warp wake.

Diminishing, fading; then gone.

No one spoke, and the silence seemed to go on forever. Then, without warning, the shimmering glow of warped stars visible through the open bay door shifted back to glittering, diamond-bright pinpoints, and the familiar rings of Saturn were visible off to starboard. They had arrived in the Sol system.

As the gathering began to break up, Wesley approached Picard as he stepped away from the podium. "You'll pardon me for saying so, Captain, but I wonder if Cassandra was the best myth to evoke. Wasn't she cursed by the gods so her warnings would never be believed?"

"True," admitted Picard. He'd made the comparison in the moment, not considering the rest of the ancient tale. "But if I am certain of anything, it is that our mission is to change the story being laid out for us."

U.S.S. Enterprise NCC-1701-E

Beverly Crusher stared at the text on the padd in front of her, but the words became an incoherent blur, losing all definition and meaning. She was supposed to be signing off on the crew fitness reports for this quarter, a simple, if time-consuming, matter that should have been easy to complete, but her focus was absent.

Her colleague Doctor Tropp, with that unerring Denobulan ability to see pain even if one was hiding it, had smoothly maneuvered her into taking on the task. He suggested she do the work in her quarters rather than sickbay, but they both knew the real reason behind it. Crusher accepted gratefully, leaving Tropp to deal with the *Enterprise*'s medical requirements, and hurried back to the family quarters on the starship's upper decks.

What Tropp had really been doing was giving Crusher an out, so she could be close to her son René when he awoke. She looked up from the padd toward his room, where the door was half open. She could make out a sleeping form beneath a blanket on René's bed, and when she held her breath, she could hear the faint whisper of her boy's breathing.

Her boy.

A cruel chill ran through her, the thought almost mocking her. *He's not a boy anymore,* she told herself, and sudden tears prickled at the corners of her eyes.

She rose suddenly, as if she could back away from the anxiety that swirled in the half-light. Crusher tore her gaze away from René's room and stared out of the ports, toward the blue-white curve of Earth dominating the view from the *Enterprise*.

Under a layer of hazy cloud, she could pick out part of the

African continent, and above, the slow-moving shapes of high-altitude weather-modification platforms. She traced the trajectory of a cargo lighter as it broke atmosphere and pulled up and away. Other ships floated sedately in the Earthlight, shining like perfectly machined sculptures—Starfleet vessels of smaller tonnage like *Nova-* or *California*-class craft, and ships of alien origin such as claw-shaped Ferengi traders or the ring-and-spar design of Vulcan cutters. All lined up at anchor on the approaches to the great spindle of Spacedock. The *Enterprise* was heading for the giant station's upper port, where the prime vessels of the fleet put in, and she looked for and found the *Aventine*. The other ship was on a different course, moving away toward another, higher orbit where McKinley Station was waiting, ready to tend to her repairs.

Jean-Luc was on that ship, and for an instant, more than anything Beverly wanted him here, *now*, with her. Alone, she was lost and adrift. She suddenly felt reluctant to look in the direction of René's room. On any other day, their son would have delighted in watching the complex ballet of these ships, but she feared she would never see such things again.

A soft chime sounded from her combadge and she sighed, pushing the thought to one side. "Crusher here," she said, after tapping the device with a finger.

"Beverly." In just the utterance of his wife's name, Jean-Luc conveyed a dozen impressions. She heard his fatigue, his worry, his determination, and his love. *"How is he?"*

"Still sleeping," she replied, automatically slipping into her role as chief medical officer. "Physiologically, René is well."

"And beyond that?"

"I honestly don't know. We'll have to take it day by day. Hour by hour, if need be."

"Yes. Of course." Her husband was silent for a moment. *"I should be there with you."*

She bit down on the impulse to agree. As much as they were loving parents to their son, they both had other duties and responsibilities, and it would have been unfair to suggest otherwise. "I can manage . . . But just don't be away too long. René is afraid and confused, and he'll need us both close at hand to give him stability."

"I know." He sighed. *"But this may take some time. I'm about to disembark from the* Aventine. *I'm beaming directly to Starfleet Command. Will's waiting for me down there. As we speak, Admiral Akaar is assembling an emergency meeting of the Joint Chiefs of Staff and the Federation Council to discuss our . . . findings."*

Picard's former first officer William Riker had been promoted to the Admiralty in the wake of the Bacco assassination some time ago, and Crusher knew that most of his time was spent acting as sector commander out on the Federation frontier. That Riker had put all that aside to go back to Earth at a moment's notice and stand beside her husband spoke volumes as to the other man's loyalty to his ex-captain.

Crusher had no doubt that her husband would be able to communicate the gravity of Wesley's warning to the powers that be, and she told him so.

"Your faith uplifts me," he replied. *"I only hope my words will be enough."*

"They'll have to be." She reached for her combadge to close the channel, but he spoke again, this time sensing her thoughts across the distance, just as she had done with his moments before.

"Beverly . . . whatever happens to him, René has not changed. He's still our son."

"I know." Her voice thickened with emotion. "But I'm afraid, Jean-Luc. I'm afraid that when I look at him, I'll only see what was stolen from us."

"You won't," he insisted. *"You only see the good. That's one of the reasons why I love you."*

"I love you too." She tapped the communicator and the silence returned in the wake of her farewell. Crusher stood there for long minutes, uncertain of what to do next.

Then she heard René stir in his sleep, giving off a weak moan. Her instinct took over, and she crossed to the threshold of his bedroom in a few quick steps. But her momentum ebbed at the door.

The bed was sized for a youth, but the person lying in it was closer to a young man, awkward and gangly and too big to fit. To see him there might have looked ridiculous to someone who had no framework for what René Picard had endured. Through his mother's eyes, it was nothing less than tragic.

The moment her son had been rushed into sickbay was seared into Beverly Crusher's mind. She had a memory for faces, and she knew almost all of the *Enterprise*'s crew complement by sight, but the young man who appeared on the stretcher before her had first seemed to be a stranger . . . except for something in his eyes and the curve of his mouth, in the way he looked at her and she saw echoes of her husband and her firstborn son. And then she knew.

René. What had happened to her perfect little boy?

During their assault on the *Enterprise* at Devidia II, the monstrous creatures in thrall to the Devidians had tried to destroy the starship and everyone aboard it with their toxic, time-active attacks, and poor René had been too close to their deadly aura, if only for a fraction of a second. The child he had been, not even out of his first decade, was lashed by a temporal distortion that aged him years in the blink of an eye. According to sensor scans, René Picard's body was now approximately nineteen Standard years old. But his mind belonged to a terrified boy of six, unable to comprehend the transformation forced upon him.

Crusher's heart filled with sorrow as she counted the cost. She couldn't stop thinking about all that René had been robbed of—a childhood still unfolding, the flowering of adolescence, and the first steps toward becoming an adult. Those experiences and those vital years were gone forever.

René moaned again and turned in the little bed. She couldn't bear to see him in pain, and she crouched by his side, reaching up to stroke his head.

I can't dwell on what is gone, she told herself. *For his sake as much as ours.* René would know it if she did, he would sense her distance, and Beverly Crusher refused to let herself become a stranger to her son.

She took a deep breath and forced herself to reframe her thoughts. If she could not put her misgivings aside, then the Devidians would have taken more from René than just time. They would have stolen his future as well.

Everyone on board, not just Crusher and her husband, understood the magnitude of the threat they had uncovered. She would not be the only one holding her loved ones close tonight, sobered by the grim reminder of how fragile their worlds were. Crusher thought of those *Enterprise* crewmembers lost to the attack and aged to dust, people like Dina Elfiki, Taurik, and Rennan Konya, whose families would not even have their remains to inter.

We still have our son, no matter what has happened.

"It's all right, René," she whispered, soothing him. "I'm here. Mom's here."

He blinked awake and focused on her. "I have bad dreams," he said, his voice broken and confused. "Mom, what's wrong with me?"

René gestured weakly toward a shelf, atop which stood a toy sailing ship from Earth's Napoleonic era. The masts were snapped and the tiny sails hung in disarray; the toy was one of René's favorites, a birthday gift from his father.

"Why did it break? I picked it up and it just broke . . . I broke it!" René stared at his hands as if they belonged to someone else. "I feel so strange . . ."

"I know," she told him, drawing her son into a comforting embrace. "We'll help you. Your father and me, your brother. Together we'll look for an answer. A way to make things better."

As Crusher said the words aloud, a possibility formed in her mind. *A hope.* She recalled a log entry she had seen at Starfleet Medical, during the year she had been off the *Enterprise*-D, something her colleague Doctor Pulaski had experienced. If anyone could help, Kate could.

Federation Embassy, First City, Qo'noS

"The Gorn envoy has postponed your meeting," said B'Enn, and she showed her teeth as she said it, the heavy ridges of her brow becoming deep furrows. "This is the fourth occasion."

"What's her excuse this time?" Alexander Rozhenko walked to a dark cabinet of crimson wood in the corner of his chambers and helped himself to a measure of bloodwine from a flask inside. A cool night breeze was flowing into the room through the open window, out from the edges of the First City and across the towers of the Klingon capital, and he felt the need for something to warm him.

His adjutant gestured with the padd in her long fingers. "She did not give one, Ambassador."

Alexander smiled and sipped his drink. "B'Enn, it's just you and me here. You don't have to use my title."

"Forgive me," she said tersely, "I become more formal when I am irritated."

"I know." His smile widened. "It's quite alluring."

Despite his attempt to lighten the mood, the woman didn't respond. There was a little reticence in their relationship, which had only recently graduated from the professional to the romantic, and both Alexander and B'Enn were still navigating the shoals.

He went on. "Reschedule, then. As we always do." He shook his head. "If it takes me a hundred years, I'll have the Gorn Hegemony and the Empire sitting across a table from one another with their blades sheathed."

"A laudable goal, if doomed to failure," said the woman, glancing up at the banners hanging behind Alexander's desk. To the right, the blue and silver of the United Federation of Planets, the state to which Rozhenko served as ambassador to Qo'noS, and to the left, the crimson and gold of the Klingon trefoil. The latter was symbolic of Alexander's birthright, as the son of Worf of the House of Martok and K'Ehleyr of the House of Galann. "There may not be open war between our species, but there will never be peace."

"No." Alexander raised a finger and poured a second cup of wine. "I won't have such words spoken here." He handed her the other cup. "A human of my acquaintance once told me of a maxim that I have never forgotten. *Politics is the art of the impossible, made possible.* This is what we do, B'Enn. We make things possible."

She smiled a little then, warming to him, and saluted with the cup. "To the possible, then." After taking a drink, B'Enn shook her head. "Am I a fool for getting myself involved with an idealist?"

Alexander touched her arm. "Well, we're not betrothed yet . . ."

She made a face of false shock. "Think of the scandal. An ambassador and his adjutant in a relationship. What *will* the scions of the Great Houses say?"

"Old warriors are the worst gossips of them all. It gives them something to talk about when they're not posturing or sharpening their *bat'leth*s."

B'Enn gave a brief chuckle, amused by the image, but her humor quickly faded. "But the matter with the Gorn still concerns me. She has done more than simply postpone your planned meeting. She departed the system this afternoon."

"Oh?" Alexander gave her a questioning look. This was news to him. "Back to the Hegemony?"

"Indeed. And my contacts in the City Guard tell me that most of the Gorn living in the embassy compound went with her. Only a skeleton staff remains." Her frown returned. "The Gorn are a stolid people, rarely given to such rapid reactions to anything. I cannot help but wonder what motivated them."

"I have an inkling," admitted Alexander. "There have been reports from Federation monitors of garbled communications from deep inside Gorn space. Suggestions of a disaster of some kind, a catastrophe that is drawing heavily on their resources. The envoy's sudden departure might be connected to that."

"They've been attacked by someone?" B'Enn wondered aloud.

"Or some*thing*." Alexander was musing on that possibility when a low buzzing tone sounded from the adjutant's padd. She peered at the device and he saw her expression shift. "What is it?"

"An incoming subspace message. Long range, using Federation Starfleet channels." She hesitated. "Ambassador, it is the *Enterprise*. From your father."

Alexander was momentarily robbed of a reply. He and Worf had settled into a stiffly formal routine of communication over the years, dictating letters to each other every season and meeting in person when the circumstances allowed it. But neither man was in the habit of reaching out unexpectedly, not without good cause. As much as father and son loved each other, there would always be a distance between them that they could never truly bridge.

B'Enn was a perceptive sort, and she knew enough of the family's history to know when to excuse herself. "I will be in the anteroom if you require me."

He put down the bloodwine and opened the channel. Immediately a holographic projection suite concealed in the stone walls of the ambassadorial chambers activated, and in a flicker of digital light, a three-dimensional representation of Worf came into being.

"Father." Alexander inclined his head. He would have liked to be delighted by this surprise communication, but past experience told him to be wary. "This is unexpected. But welcomed."

"*Son.*" Across the interstellar distance, Worf gave a slow nod. He wore the uniform of a Starfleet commander, but his baldric was missing, as if he had begun to disrobe and then thought better of it. "*You are well?*"

"I am." Alexander had not told his father of his burgeoning relationship with B'Enn, or much else for that matter in recent months. He felt a pang of guilt as he realized that he was overdue with his regular letter. *Is that why he has contacted me?* Alexander wondered how great the energy cost had to be to push a real-time subspace signal all the way to the heart of the Klingon Empire.

"Good." Worf nodded to himself. He seemed distracted, and reluctant to say the next words. *"You may think me foolish, but I wanted to hear the sound of your voice. It came to me today that it has been too long since I heard it. I wanted to be sure you are safe and whole."*

Alexander opened his arms. "I am," he repeated. "The work keeps me busy . . . You know how it goes."

"Better than most." Worf nodded again, with a brief smile. Alexander's role as the Federation's ambassador to the Empire had, for a time, been his father's responsibility. His son had stepped into the role after Worf had decided to return to active duty with Starfleet, and both men agreed that the son had the better temperament for diplomacy. *"You are spoken of well by your opposite number on Earth. You make me proud."*

Alexander paused, weighing his next words. It would have been easy to skim over the surface of this conversation, to say the right things and conclude it quickly. But he could not escape the sense that there was more going on beneath the surface, and if only his father's stoic manner could bend a little, he might reveal it.

He took the direct approach. "You didn't just contact me to hear me speak." He met his father's gaze across the light-years. "Tell me what troubles you."

Worf shook his head. *"You're as sharp as your mother. She saw my weaknesses as clear as daylight."*

"It's not weakness to be troubled," said Alexander. "Let me help."

After a long moment, Worf spoke again. *"Ezri Dax is dead. She was killed on a secret mission a few days ago. Host and symbiont, both lost forever."*

Alexander felt a knife of regret twist in his belly. "Oh, Father. I am so sorry."

The death of the Trill symbiont meant not only the ending of all its life experiences, but also those of the beings who had hosted it, including Alexander's stepmother, Jadzia.

Jadzia Dax was one of the few women, along with Alexander's biological mother and the late Jasminder Choudhury, to whom

Worf had ever freely given his heart. Now with Ezri Dax's passing, whatever remained of Jadzia was truly gone from the universe, and for his father, it had to feel like losing her all over again.

Abruptly, the reasoning behind his father's need to seek a moment of connection with his son was all too clear. "How did it happen?"

Worf gave him a sharp look, as if he was about to say more but caught himself. When he spoke again, he was clearly skirting around a truth he did not want to reveal over subspace. *"An insidious enemy we had thought dispatched."* Worf halted, scowling at nothing. *"The threat is a grave one. I need you to be watchful."*

"Always." Alexander sensed Worf's reticence to say more and pressed the point. "This is a secured hyper channel," he noted. "You may speak freely."

"I am not certain that I can," Worf said darkly, and he half turned from the holo-pickup at his end of the conversation. Alexander knew the tell: his father was closing himself off once more, raising his shields.

Alexander asked the next question before he was even aware of it leaving his mouth. "What is it that you are afraid of, Father?"

Worf's dark eyes flashed, and Alexander knew immediately that he was correct. Worf was a courageous Klingon warrior of the kind that songs were written of, but he was not invincible. Dax's death had wounded him deeply, but that wasn't the only thing. There was more at hand here.

He knows something terrible, Alexander realized, *and his instinct is to protect me from it.*

"I must go," said Worf. *"Guard yourself, my son. There are shadows everywhere."*

"Father—" Alexander reached out a hand to the holograph, but it was already too late.

Worf's image froze and then dissipated into the night air, leaving his son with the deep sense that something was very, very wrong.

3

Perikian Monastery, Lonar Province, Bajor

"Blessings of the Prophets to you, honored vedek," said the young man in the dun-colored robes, performing a shallow bow.

"And to you, Prylar Sarm." Kira Nerys gave him a wan smile and he went on his way, his sandals clapping across the worn stones of the cloister floor. Sarm was an affable sort, and eager to please, but at times she found him to be a little *too* earnest.

He was, Kira reflected, around the same age she had been when she first became a fighter in the resistance against the Cardassian Occupation. She wondered how someone as open and trusting as Sarm might have fared in those dark and dangerous days. *Not well*, she had to admit. It was a testament to how much things had changed greatly in the years since, that some Bajorans had the freedom to grow up a little naïve, and very sheltered.

She wanted to remind people like Sarm of how fragile it all was, of how easily the things one took for granted could be torn asunder. *But how does that make me sound? The veteran freedom-fighter-turned-vedek, seeing danger at every turn?*

Alone with her thoughts, Kira walked to the arches looking out over the hills bordering the Perikian Monastery, finding the glitter of the Tecyr River winding its way toward the nearby city of Korto. She sat on a low wall, gathering her robes beneath her, and took a deep breath of Bajor's summery air, in hopes that it would cleanse her thoughts.

On some level, Kira Nerys's entire life had been a battle toward the singular goal of peace. As a soldier in the resistance, she had fought to wrest that back from the Cardassians, and then in partnership with the Federation, fought again against enemies who tried to take it anew. But it was only in her later life, as the path of Kira's existence had taken her through a series of profound spiritual challenges, that she felt as if she was truly able to grasp the true meaning of it. Her faith gave her the peace that a lifetime of struggle had never been able to provide.

So why is it I feel unsettled? The question rose into her conscious thoughts. She fingered the simple chain of her earring. *I've never been so close to enlightenment as I am now, and yet . . .*

Despite the warmth of the sunshine, Kira's skin prickled with a peculiar chill. Over the last few weeks, the talk of the monastery had been the unexplained flashes of light glimpsed in the depths of the night sky.

Out toward the edge of the Bajor system lay the Celestial Temple of the Prophets—in the parlance of the uninitiated, what nonbelievers called the wormhole to the distant Gamma Quadrant—and for some time, strange aurorae-like phenomena had been glimpsed skirting the edges of the Temple's perimeter.

When the wormhole's great interstellar gateway opened as the Prophets granted passage to ships traveling to and from the other side of the galaxy, the glow of its majesty could be seen from Bajor with the naked eye. Some considered the beings who dwelt within to simply be a form of life evolved beyond common flesh and blood, but to those with faith, the Prophets were something far greater. They were the guiding hand over the fate of Bajor and its children, the stewards who had guided Kira's people throughout their history.

Her experiences, her direct contact with those beings, had led to the honorific that many now gave to Kira Nerys. They called her the *Hand of the Prophets*, and although she eschewed any such grand title, her fellow Bajorans had made the choice for her. For better or worse, she would be the Hand until her last breath. So she strived to make the best of it.

But even she could not explain away the emerald aurorae that came and went like distant chain lightning around the Celestial

Temple's domains. Her friends on the space station, Deep Space 9, gave Kira dry, scientific justifications—random bursts of tachyons interacting with invisible subspace fields, dark matter propagation, photonic bleed from nebulae in the Gamma Quadrant. There were a hundred possibilities, but no certainty.

But where science could not venture, belief could thrive. Into the ambiguity, the ranjens, prylars, and vedeks of every monastery on Bajor offered their interpretations, and it troubled Kira that many of them were ill wrought. There was a new tension hiding just below the surface on Bajor, as Kira's people openly hoped for the better, but secretly feared the worst.

Something has to be done, she told herself. *I'll petition the kai for a meeting. I can ask him to make a public statement—*

She heard a sandal's tread off toward the far end of the cloister, and it halted her train of thought. Kira assumed that it was Sarm returning once again, and she looked up, expecting to find him approaching.

But instead, she caught sight of a woman in a veiled, flowing dress—something rather immodest to be wearing inside a monastery, if she were honest—who stood half-hidden in the shadows at the far end of the cloister. That prickle on Kira's skin became the tips of a thousand invisible needles, and her heart beat faster.

"Hello?" She rose to her feet, calling out to the stranger. "Are you a pilgrim from the city? Are you looking for someone?"

The veil kept the woman's face from becoming visible, but she reached out a hand, as if she expected Kira to take it.

When she was a child, the old monks the young Nerys met on her first visit to this monastery had told her that some of the cloisters were haunted by *borhya,* the unquiet spirits of the dead. The memory of that warning resonated in her thoughts as she tried to focus on the woman's face, but the definition of it retreated like fading mist.

The woman walked away, disappearing around a corner, and before she knew it, Kira had gathered up her robes in a fist so she could dash after her.

At the corner, Kira entered a circular chamber with a high, domed roof lit by shafts of sunlight. She cast around, peering past tall stained-glass windows and hanging brass censers, looking into every doorway that led away into the monastery's many interior spaces.

She heard the footsteps again, behind her this time, and turned. The veiled woman was descending a wide stone staircase that went down into the lower levels, toward the memorial crypts.

"Stop!" Kira called out in shock, her voice echoing off the dome overhead. "You can't go down there!"

But the woman was already gone, and Kira had an unerring sense of where she was headed.

She should have called for a prylar or one of the monastery's guardians, but Kira felt compelled to go after the stranger alone. She took the stone stairs two at a time, descending into a dry, amber-lit undercroft.

On the far side of the crypt, a tall wooden door bearing the symbol of the Bajoran unity between world, people, and the Prophets was open. It should not have been. There was supposed to be a guardian down here, and a ceremonial rope hanging across the entrance, but neither were in evidence.

As Kira approached, the air thickened and turned warmer. The candles burning in the sconces on the walls seemed to glow brighter, and her footsteps took on a low echo. Kira's every sense became heightened. She knew this feeling, and it terrified and elated her in equal measure.

She stepped through the doors, expecting to find the monastery's chancel, but the room seemed unreal. And there, waiting for her on the altar, was a sacred ark made of sanctified wood and magenta-hued glass. The woman in the veil was nowhere to be seen.

Of its own accord, the ark opened to reveal the object within: a spinning crystalline form that resembled a rough-hewn hourglass, glowing with a mesmerizing inner light. Kira knew exactly what she was seeing. It was one of the Tears of the Prophets, the holy relic known as the Orb of Time.

The Orb of Time isn't here, she told herself, questioning the evidence of her own eyes. *It's far away in Ashalla, in the Great Abbey with all the others.*

And yet, the ways of the Prophets were unknowable. Kira had borne witness to their uncanny ability to alter reality more than once, and she knew that to resist it would be pointless.

She let the moment guide her. Kira reached out, just as the veiled woman had reached out to her in the cloister. Her fingertips brushed the Orb's shimmering aura.

And she beheld a catastrophe.

In her mind's eye, Kira Nerys saw a dark field lit by innumerable torches, each flame fading and guttering out until only shadows remained.

In the gloom, she could make out what had once been fertile growing land, but now it was pallid, lifeless sand. She heard a keening gale in the distance, and marched toward the sound, finding only the gnarled roots of a long-dead nya *tree. The tiny bones of animals littered the ground beneath her feet, and she had to look away from them.*

Kira saw the broken peaks of barren mountains at the horizon, and she knew their shapes. They were the Perikian range, the same ones she saw each morning from the window of her quarters in the monastery. This dead world was Bajor.

There was a whisper in the doleful wind, a woman's voice carrying a warning. Kira strained to listen, but it was hard to pick out the words. She forced herself to follow the faint sound, even as sickly viridian illumination settled across the murdered landscape. The ill light came from high above, and Kira steeled herself before turning her face toward it.

Up there in the haze, a twisting mass of green fire cast its glow toward her. Shapes moved inside the inferno, vast forms twisting and writhing.

Then she heard the voice, as distinct and clear as a cloister bell.

"No time," said Kira Meru, whispering across the veil of death into her daughter's ear.

"Vedek Kira?"

With a sudden implosion of sensation, Kira's eyes snapped open and she almost fell to the stones at her feet. The shock of dislocation was so strong that it made her head swim, and it took a long moment for her to gather herself.

She looked up to find Prylar Sarm standing over her, his expression one of concern, his hands on her shoulders. "Are you all right?"

Kira waved him away. "What . . . ?" She glanced around, getting her bearings. She was back in the cloister, sitting on the wall looking out toward the river. Or was it that she had never moved at all?

Sarm wrung his hands. "I was walking by and I saw you staring off into nothing." He spoke quickly, evidently unnerved by her reaction. "When you didn't respond to my greeting, I became worried. You appeared to be in some kind of trance."

The Prophets spoke to me. She wanted to tell him what she had experienced, but something stopped her. The veiled woman, the vision, it all seemed so personal, so deeply rooted in her soul, that to speak of it aloud seemed *wrong*.

Kira twisted in place and looked up, toward the point in the sky where she knew the Celestial Temple lay. But there were clouds moving swiftly over the landscape, heavy and low. As she watched, the first glittering motes of snowflakes began to descend, falling in ghostly silence across the monastery's domes and precincts.

"Snowfall in summer," she said quietly. "That shouldn't be."

At her shoulder, Sarm drew his hands to himself and invoked the names of the Prophets under his breath. "First the lightning about the Temple, and now this," said the young monk, worriedly shaking his head. "It is an ill omen."

Starfleet Headquarters, San Francisco, Earth

The main conference room was on the upper level of the building, with an unparalleled view through its windows out across the campus and toward the Golden Gate Bridge. Beneath a backdrop of brilliant blue, lines of air trams and flyers sped back and forth into the city's sky lanes.

Picard soaked in the vista for a moment, hoping to center himself, but a chime sounded and the windows began to darken as the room switched over to secure mode.

His companion didn't seem to notice. Dressed in simple civilian attire, Wesley Crusher was making last-minute adjustments to the complex device he held in his hand, manipulating data readouts in a ball of projected light.

"Do you need a moment?" said Picard.

"No, Captain, I've got it," Wesley replied, without looking away. "I'm just making sure the Omnichron's internal data matrix will be able to interface with the conference room's systems. We don't want to lose anything."

The Omnichron, as Wesley called it, resembled an advanced form of tricorder, but Picard knew it to be far more than that. The device was far-future technology, brought back to this era by Wesley's older incarnation, and his present-day self seemed to instinctively know how to use it.

An officer in a commander's uniform approached them with an easy, open smile on his face. "Captain Picard, Mister Crusher? I've configured a station for you to use during your briefing." He gestured to a console on the far side of the room.

Picard nodded. "Commander Paris, isn't it? You're one of Admiral Janeway's crew."

Paris gave a slight shrug. "Not these days, Captain. It's been quite a while since I served on *Voyager*. I'm on Admiral Akaar's staff."

"Of course. I knew your father. Owen was a good man, he is sorely missed."

Paris's smile faltered a little. "Thank you, sir."

Wesley looked up from his work with the Omnichron and hesitated, studying Paris intently.

"Is something wrong?" said Paris. He gave a weak chuckle. "What, do I have food in my teeth?"

After a moment, Wesley shook his head. "I'm sorry. You remind me of someone I used to know, from back in the day."

"Oh. I get that a lot," said the other man. "Guess I have that kind of face." Paris gestured for them to take their places, and Wesley stepped up to the station, waking it from standby mode.

As Paris retreated toward the long, curved table that dominated the north side of the chamber, Picard turned to watch a handful of flag-rank officers file into the room from the opposite door to take their seats. Other spots around the table had deliberately been left empty, but they too were quickly filled as the admirals who were unable to be present in person were sketched in with holo-avatars. He knew them all. Some personally, some by reputation. A few he would have considered comrades and others . . . Well, not quite rivals, but certainly not friends.

Towering over all of them was Leonard James Akaar, the stoic Capellan commander-in-chief of Starfleet Operations, the fleet admiral whom junior officers had nicknamed "*the mountain*," not just because of his height, but in reference to the granite-carved lines of his face and the unyielding nature of his command style.

To Akaar's right, a human woman with a shock of white hair took her place and didn't spare Picard even the slightest glance. He hid a frown. Marta Batanides was head of Starfleet Intelligence, but many years ago when they came out of the Academy together, she and Picard had been fast friends. So much time had passed since then, and truthfully, Picard regretted not making more effort to maintain that comradeship. He would need her support today.

Some of the others he had met at fleet functions or on operational deployments, such as the bearded, paternal Trill Jorel Quinn and the Vulcan woman T'Raan. Only one person was relatively unfamiliar to him, a human from the Centauri colonies named Victor Bordson, whose shimmering holo-presence suggested his image was being transmitted into the chamber from across a great distance.

The most welcome face was that of Will Riker, his former first officer. But even Will seemed uncharacteristically muted. From across the room, he caught Picard's eye and gave him a warning nod. *Be ready.*

Of all the assembled flag officers, Riker was the newest of the group. He had been pushed into the role in the troubling aftermath of the assassination of former president Nan Bacco, and at the time he had made no secret of the fact that he didn't want the promotion. But as he always did, and as Picard knew he would, Riker had risen to the challenge and proven himself worthy of the job. Sometimes, it felt a little strange to take orders from his former Number One, but Picard had not been in a hurry to surrender the center seat of a starship. Rising up the ranks didn't seem so important anymore, after marrying Beverly and fathering René.

The thought of his wife and son took Picard's attention for a moment, and he didn't notice the seventh member of the assembly until he was standing right behind him.

"Jean-Luc." He turned toward the sound of his name, to meet the gaze of Rear Admiral Kaud Idyn. "What have you brought us this time?" There was an open note of judgment in the tone, and he saw the distrust in the Deltan's large, blue eyes.

Picard kept his expression neutral. He had never made peace with Idyn, not after crossing swords with him over the Briar Patch incident more than a decade earlier. At the time, Idyn had been a senior member of Admiral Matthew Dougherty's staff when he had become embroiled in a conspiracy to forcibly relocate a population of humanoids called the Ba'ku from their homeworld. Picard and the *Enterprise* crew exposed that malfeasance, and Dougherty later perished at the hands of the Son'a renegades he colluded with. Idyn was the only one of Dougherty's staff to come out of the investigations that followed unscathed, but the rumors that he and the admiral had shared some sort of personal relationship had never gone away. Years later, Idyn stepped into the post his mentor had once filled, and despite everything, he had never forgiven Picard for being involved in Dougherty's downfall.

Picard frowned at the thought. The last thing he wanted was baggage from old personality clashes getting in the way of the important information he was here to provide. Idyn glanced at Wesley, looking him up and down, noting the temporary identity tab that Starfleet Security had attached to his lapel.

"Mister Crusher is here as a consultant," Picard noted, feeling compelled to explain Wesley's presence. "He has a unique perspective on the crisis at hand."

"Indeed?" Idyn considered that for a long moment. "You thought it necessary to bring a disgraced ex–Starfleet cadet into a meeting of the Joint Chiefs of Staff?" Belatedly, Picard realized that Idyn knew exactly who Wesley Crusher was, despite initially giving the opposite impression.

Wesley closed the Omnichron's case with a snap. "That was a long time ago," he said levelly. "I made a serious mistake and I took full responsibility for my part in it. I made amends."

"Someone died, I recall," the admiral pressed, and Picard sensed he was looking for a weakness, for a flaw in Wesley's armor.

"Do you have a point to make, Admiral?" Wesley met the flag officer's look head-on.

Idyn's gaze drifted to Picard. "I hope you have more arrows in your quiver than just this one's testimony, Jean-Luc. I'm not sure how much weight his opinion will carry, even if he is your stepson." Idyn moved to take his seat, but Picard stepped in to stop him, putting a hand on his arm.

"Idyn, don't make this about our past disagreements," he told the admiral, speaking quietly. "This matter is too important. I need you to understand that."

The admiral very deliberately removed his hand and gave Picard a hard look. "You bludgeon your way in here with Riker's help," he said, equally quiet. "You claim the sky is going to fall and set off the highest of alerts, expecting Command to drop everything and pay attention to you. You'd better be able to back that up."

"You know my record," growled Picard. "Do you really think I would do this if it weren't absolutely warranted?"

"I think you're used to getting your own way," said Idyn, moving off. "As to the rest, we'll have to see."

"What was that about?" said Wesley.

Picard gave him a look that made it clear he didn't want to get into it. "Are we ready?" He nodded at the Omnichron. "We can't afford to leave anything unsaid today."

"We won't, sir." Wesley gave him a nod. "Trust me."

Another hologram flickered into being at one of the vacant spots around the table, sketching in the image of a tall Rhaandarite woman in a simple black tunic and trousers. Picard didn't recognize her, but Wesley did.

"That's Laarin Andos, director of the Department of Temporal Investigations. She wrote a really good monograph on the nonlinear propagation effects of temporal loops." Wesley paused. "Well, I mean she *will* write one, in a different timeline. Not this version of her, of course."

"Of course," echoed Picard. "Will she be receptive to what we have to say?"

"The DTI lost one of their own on the *Aventine* mission. She has to know how serious this is."

"Let us hope so."

"Gentlebeings, can I have your attention please?" Commander Paris called out from across the room. "If you will all rise for the president?"

Already on their feet, Picard and Wesley stiffened to attention as the rest of the attendees, holograms and actual alike, stood in respect. A moment later, in a space at the center of the table, the president of the United Federation of Planets took shape out of a swirl of photons, flanked by two of her adjutants.

An elegant Andorian *zhen* of great poise and character, Kellessar zh'Tarash was the one person in the chamber who, it could honestly be said, was fully respected by everyone here. She surveyed the faces of the admirals with a careful glance, before settling on Picard and Crusher. *"Good afternoon, everybody. Please be seated. I apologize for not being there myself today, but I'm on Andor addressing an incident regarding a cloning scandal . . . I know our time is valuable, so I suggest we get to the heart of this with all due alacrity. Agreed?"*

Picard noted that Idyn bristled a little at that, but the Deltan said nothing. *"Zha* President," he began, "thank you for giving me this opportunity."

"We've all read your report," said zh'Tarash, *"and quite frankly, Captain, anything as alarming as the suggestions it makes demands our immediate attention. But I want to hear it from someone who saw this aftermath with their own eyes."*

"Mister Crusher and I will answer all questions." Picard nodded to Wesley.

When she went on, the president's tone had cooled, and her azure features took on a judgmental air. *"You will,"* she asserted. *"You are Jean-Luc Picard, and your reputation precedes you. No one in this room would begrudge giving you the floor. You've served the Federation faithfully for years, and saved countless lives in the process. You have earned the right to demand our attention, Captain. Make it count."*

"No pressure," Wesley said quietly, almost to himself. He tapped a few controls on the console before him, and in the space before the conference table a cloud of holo-pixels blinked into being.

Picard took a deep breath and addressed the group. "Eighteen Standard years ago, on Stardate 45959.1, my ship was summoned to San Francisco on a priority mission. Something was discovered beneath the city during an archeological dig. An artifact of unusual temporal provenance."

"The head of the android known as Data." Andos spoke for the

first time, offering up the information. *"Displaced in time by some five centuries."*

"Quite," noted Picard. "In the process of investigating this puzzle, the *Enterprise* uncovered an ongoing temporal incursion by a race of humanoids from the Devidia system." At his side, Wesley tapped in new commands, bringing up images of the planet Devidia II and the beings themselves.

Picard had an instant and visceral reaction to the presence of the holographic Devidian, as he recalled the unpleasant aura that surrounded the aliens. *Like a shudder, drawn out over hours,* he recalled, *like someone walking over my grave.*

"The Devidians are a phase-shifted species," added Wesley. "They're parasitic in nature, existing in an alternate synchronic state to most life in this dimension."

"What do they feed on?" asked Bordson, making no attempt to hide his disquiet at the featureless Devidian's spindly and unsettling appearance.

"Terror," said Picard, grim faced. "They derive sustenance from the neural energy of beings in highly agitated states. In the course of our investigation in 2368, we learned that one group had opened a conduit to Earth's past, where they were harvesting that energy from the victims of a pandemic."

"They're invisible, they travel in time, and they live off the raw agony of others?" Zh'Tarash grimaced. *"Well, that's enough to give me nightmares forever."* She sighed. *"I take it the group you encountered were neutralized?"*

"Yes, *Zha* President," said Picard. "My crew and I stopped the incursion and sealed the temporal corridor. But it seems that was not the last of the Devidians."

Admiral Akaar spoke up, his voice a soft rumble. "Director Andos, does the DTI concur with Captain Picard's version of that incident?"

"It does," the Rhaandarite said primly, *"and to be clear, the Earth incursion of 1893 he refers to is one of several suspected Devidian*

'harvestings.' There is circumstantial evidence of other incidents, not only on this planet but elsewhere in the galaxy. We theorize that various 'clades' of Devidians time-shifted to locations and periods where they could freely nourish themselves from the neural energy of dying sentients." Andos's delivery was metered and matter-of-fact, which only served to underline the chilling reality of her statement. *"They favored events such as plagues, wars, mass extinctions, and the like, particularly in time periods where their prey had yet to develop post-atomic technologies. In such cases, their presence could go unnoticed until they . . . satisfied their hunger."*

Admiral Batanides leaned forward in her seat. "Following Captain Picard's report on these things in '68, Starfleet Intelligence put an advisory in place to all our vessels and allies. We made sure anyone who encountered the Devidians again would know how to deal with them."

"But that assumed they'd just carry on as before," said Wesley. "These beings are nothing if not devious. They existed for thousands of years before Starfleet discovered what they were doing. The Devidians didn't leave or die off. They figured out another way to get what they want."

Picard gave a solemn nod. "It is my duty to report that Devidians are no longer limiting themselves to small-scale incursions into the past. From what we have been able to ascertain, they have moved their entire corpus into a zone *outside* the time stream. There they have constructed a . . ." He faltered, struggling to find the words. "A vast mechanism for absorbing colossal amounts of neural energy, en masse."

"From whole worlds?" Quinn was aghast at the possibility.

"Sir, I am afraid to say you are thinking on too small a scale." Picard addressed the Trill with a shake of the head. "We believe the mechanism the Devidians have created can harvest not just the neural energy of life across planets, star systems, and galaxies, but that of an entire quantum reality."

Quinn turned pale at the thought, the patterning of marks

down his face darkening with it. "By the Suns . . . That's beyond the grasp of any rational mind!"

"How do you know of this?" Admiral T'Raan eyed Picard warily.

"We modified the *Starship Aventine* for temporal transition and we ventured four millennia into the future," said Wesley. "We saw one of their harvesting hubs with our own eyes."

"I will clarify," T'Raan continued. "How did you become aware of the Devidians' intentions?"

Picard and Wesley exchanged looks. He wondered how best to explain those facts—that an older, future incarnation of Wesley Crusher had died bringing the information to them. In the end, the younger man answered the question truthfully, if not completely.

"I discovered their plans on my travels," he said. "I've been tracking incidents of extreme temporal activity ever since."

Andos raised an eyebrow at that, but didn't press the point. *"My organization has been doing the same. We have seen an uptick in anomalous phenomena."*

"This is incredible." Finally, Idyn chose this moment to speak up. "And I say that not in a sense of awe but in one of disbelief. Picard speaks of an enemy capable of collapsing a discrete timeline. *A universe killer?* How can such a thing even exist?" The Deltan shook his head, as if trying to dispel the image. "It is inconceivable!"

"That doesn't make it impossible," ventured Riker. "There's a cosmos of unknowns out there."

Picard turned to Wesley. "Show them."

Wesley produced the Omnichron and spoke directly to it. "Activate and interface with holo-matrix." The device levitated out of his hand and floated to the console, beaming a thread of light into the system. "Play back file alpha."

With a burst of color, the Omnichron took control of the holograph in the conference room and a fan of screens spread out in midair, fanning open like the motion of some elegant piece of clockwork. Each three-dimensional pane was an image capture from their voyage into the deep future, showing the ashen, entropic wilderness they had encountered.

Picard watched the emotions—or lack thereof—on the faces of those assembled in front of him. The admirals peered into the portals on the future and saw only devastation. Picard closed his eyes briefly. He could feel the memory of that moment when he first arrived on the wasteland world at the end of existence, like a patina of dust coating his skin.

The images showed a broken landscape devoid of any life, down to the microbial level. They presented a menacing black sky where the embers of dead stars cast no light or warmth. The holographs were a vision of a universe filled with decay and corruption. A crumbling, rusting, collapsing reality trapped on the cusp of total dissolution.

"The Devidians are no longer limiting themselves to the life energies in our continuum," said Wesley. "A time-active species like theirs is well aware of the presence of multiple timelines, and as their hunger pushed them to search for food sources on an ever-increasing scale, they sought out those quantum realities less stable than the others. They actively increased those instabilities to force them toward the point of complete disintegration."

The holographic panes shifted, bringing new horrors to light. Along with the phantasm-like Devidians, there were the serpentine ravagers that the aliens used as their brute-force weapons. Those creatures had been responsible for the deaths of Dax, Chen, and the rest, and for stealing years of existence from Picard's son.

"I believe this is why you haven't seen or heard from them in nearly twenty years of subjective time," Wesley went on. "At first, the Devidians used their abilities to tap into unstable alternate timelines that were already fracturing, harvesting the neural energies of the beings in those quantum realities as they perished in the collapse, in a massive feeding frenzy."

The screens changed once again, merging into one great panel dominated by a single image. Picard shivered involuntarily as he saw the gargantuan Devidian "construct" once again, the vast machine they had built to consume infinity.

Blossoming like some colossal fungal growth from the blackened flanks of a long-dead volcanic mountain, the great device coruscated with the captured neural energy of innumerable sentient beings, stolen away in the moment of their most awful pain. Part of the construct seemed to exist out of synchrony with the rest of reality, and looking too long into those spaces caused nauseating sensory distortion.

The image relayed the dreadful scale of the device, but it could not convey the aura of sheer despair that had surrounded it. Jean-Luc Picard was not one to put much stock in the numinous or the preternatural, but he could not deny that he had felt death itself in the air of that blighted place.

"It was not enough for them," the captain said, looking away. "With each surge of consumption, the greed of the Devidians has increased exponentially. Their hunger cannot be sated, even with the pickings from a near-infinite number of dying timelines. They learned how to deliberately engineer the implosions, to force a collapse, where one would otherwise not have happened." Picard gestured to Wesley, and the warped images retreated mercifully back into the shadow. He searched the faces of the beings in front of him. "Think of that. Think of the utter terror that would grip any sentient life-form that could understand the magnitude of such destruction. That pure fear is the rich bounty the Devidians crave above all else. They feast on the insubstantial energies of death, and what they do not immediately consume, they store, and they weaponize."

"How is that possible?" said Akaar.

"Through advanced biomechanical structures," noted Wesley. "The Devidians have symbiotic relationships with lesser species they deploy as gene-engineered tools and servants. Primarily, a kind of ophidian with a highly malleable organic configuration, but also humanoid avatars capable of holding an individual consciousness and controlling the larger attack creatures." Crusher pointed out images of the various different forms, ending with the giant spaceborne serpents. "The latter I called the Naga, from the Hindu myth."

Picard moved to the middle of the room, bringing himself to stand directly in front of President zh'Tarash, with the admirals surrounding him on either side. "Moment by moment, these parasitic beings have been eating their way through a multiverse, and their predations are imperiling our timeline and others entangled most closely with it."

"This . . . is a lot to process, Captain," said the Andorian. She glanced at Akaar and then to Batanides. *"If anyone else brought such a story to me, I would think them insane."*

"There's still time," muttered Idyn.

"The scenario Captain Picard presents is an extreme one, but it is not beyond the realm of possibility," admitted Akaar, after a long moment.

"Director Andos," began Batanides, "manipulations of the spacetime continuum are the DTI's turf. In your opinion, does Captain Picard's account have merit?"

"For the record," said the Rhaandarite, *"the Department of Temporal Investigations will make no firm conclusion at this point. We are still gathering data."*

Picard heard Wesley release a sigh of irritation. The backing of Andos and the DTI would have been invaluable in convincing the Admiralty that immediate action was needed. Now they would have to argue from a weaker position.

"However," continued Andos, *"we do concur that there is an extant threat currently in play. This may be connected to the race designated as the Devidians. Further analysis is required to be certain. But it cannot be denied that an aggressor force . . . these so-called Nagas are attacking locations containing time-active artifacts, and may also be targeting beings from species known to be temporally sensitive."*

"You're referring to what happened at Bezorek Station," said Riker.

"Correct." Andos nodded. *"That DTI facility was badly damaged after an incident involving a time-travel device in our custody."*

"As I recall it, Bezorek Station was almost destroyed," said Picard, irritated by the understatement. "Surely that underlines the seriousness of this?"

"There has been unusual chatter from some of our intelligence sources inside the other galactic powers," noted Batanides. "Rumors of a catastrophic solar implosion in Gorn space, and garbled signals from the Tholian Assembly."

"Those events could have many causes," said Bordson. *"The Typhon Pact is always playing some kind of game."*

Admiral Idyn nodded at Bordson's words and drew himself up. "Forgive me, but I must be blunt. I do not doubt that Captain Picard and Mister Crusher believe fully in what they have presented to us, and their holo-show was quite disturbing. But we are discussing a threat that will not fully manifest for thousands of years, yes? If these Devidians exist in the far future, can we not stop them here and now, before they mature into this grave danger?"

"That's not how this works," said Wesley with a grimace. "It's more complicated than that."

"Forgive me if I have trouble thinking fourth dimensionally," Idyn retorted. "My concerns are with the present, not some possible tomorrow that has not yet occurred." He leaned forward, gesturing at the air. "If strategic Federation assets related to time travel are in danger, if Federation citizens sensitive to such things are under threat, Starfleet's first and most immediate duty is to protect them, is it not? That is where we should apply our focus. Picard's apocalyptic claims can be investigated in the interim."

"I concur," said Admiral T'Raan.

Admiral Quinn nodded reluctantly. "I feel I must also agree."

Picard looked to Riker, waiting for his old friend to come to his defense; but the other man said nothing, maintaining a sullen silence.

When it became clear no more voices would join in, the captain pressed on. "I do not disagree with Admiral Idyn, but I fear that anything less than a proactive stance on this matter will have fateful consequences. We *must* put our efforts into stopping the Devidians, at all costs! If they are allowed to continue, I believe they will not only bring about the destruction of this quantum reality, but an infinity of others. They will be free to tear through an endless continuum of universes, obliterating every possible version of us and our worlds, condemning eternity to ash."

"At all costs." T'Raan echoed his words. "An emotionally charged statement, and one that often stands as prelude to destructive actions." The Vulcan admiral gave Picard a withering look. "Captain, the Federation has fought in too many wars. The Cardassians, Tzenkethi, the Klingon schism, the Dominion invasion, the Borg, and more. Is there no diplomatic solution? Have you considered how we might arrest these encounters with the Devidians without making yet another enemy for the Federation?"

"I offered that on our first meeting," said Picard, "and they refused."

"I can only wonder at the cost of defeating them, if we had to," added Quinn. "Do we actually countenance the destruction of an entire species? It wounds my soul even to conceive of such a price."

Picard frowned, and reached for the truth. "I do not come to this easily," he insisted. "But yes, we must face the possibility that in order to draw the line against the Devidians here, in our reality, we will need to make the greatest imaginable sacrifice."

"How great?" Zh'Tarash's bright eyes fixed Picard like twin searchlights.

Picard met her gaze and did not flinch. "I fear we may need to burn down our worlds in order to break the fire of the Devidian hunger."

In the wake of Picard's words, everyone began to talk at once—some of them dismayed at his statement, others arguing against it or in favor of direct action. He had come to Earth hoping that there could be consensus, an understanding of what needed to be done, but it seemed that was a forlorn hope. Picard was gripped by a new dread, that he would become mired in talk and discussion, while the threat from beyond continued its inexorable advance.

"Enough." The president's voice cut through the overlapping conversations, cracking like thunder. *"This is not a matter we can decide on in the heat of the moment."* Zh'Tarash's holo-avatar took in the members of the Admiralty, meeting their gazes one by one. *"I'm adjourning this meeting for today. We must reflect on what we have seen and heard, and consider our best options moving forward. We'll reconvene tomorrow morning to discuss our next step."* She paused to take a breath, glancing at Picard and Wesley. *"Mister Crusher, thank you for your input, but I hope you understand that your status as a civilian prevents you from further participation in this conversation. If I need your expertise again, I'll call on it. Understood?"*

"Yes, *Zha* President," Wesley said tightly.

Zh'Tarash rose, and the others did the same. *"Nothing spoken of here leaves this room."* She added, *"This meeting is adjourned."* With a final nod, the hologram of the Andorian and her silent aides vanished.

Andos and Bordson disconnected moments later, leaving voids where their avatars had stood, and the remainder of the Admiralty filed out of the room in silence.

"They saw the same thing we did, right?" said Wesley with a scowl. "We couldn't have been more emphatic about the danger!"

Picard heard his words, but he didn't reply. Instead he put a hand on Riker's shoulder before the other man could leave. "Will, you know how grave this is. I need your help to make the Admiralty understand. If they do not fully grasp what is at stake for our reality—"

Riker turned back to face him, and there was a distance in his expression. He said nothing for a long moment, and in that silence Picard saw something he had never seen before in his old friend's eyes—a cold fury, there and then gone.

"It's not clear-cut, Jean-Luc," said Riker. "There's the danger right in front of us, from these Naga attacks. And then there's this existential threat you're describing. There may well be a connection, but we have to decide what takes priority."

"Survival takes priority," said Wesley, folding his arms across his chest. "Not just for the Federation. For *everyone*."

Riker shot the younger man a hard look, but before he could reply, Commander Paris reentered the conference room at a run.

"Ah, good, you didn't beam out yet . . ." Paris jerked a thumb over his shoulder. "Admiral, Captain, the C-in-C wants you in his office, immediately. There's been a new development."

"What do you mean?" said Picard.

"Sensor arrays on the Klingon border have picked up urgent subspace signals from within the Empire. Their military forces are engaged at the planet Boreth. It looks like another temporal incursion is taking place."

4

Monastery of Kahless the Unforgettable, Boreth

R'Kol had to concede that the experience was, in a terrible way, *exhilarating*.

Towering, shrieking lines of lightning shocked out of the clouded sky above the monastery, fusing rock and ice into glass where they touched down, and the wind howled like the guardians of *Sto-Vo-Kor*. The sacred mountain trembled beneath the boots of the Klingon cleric as he sprinted along the frost-rimed path cut into the sheer stone face, and in a moment of reflection, he could have sworn he heard the planet itself cry out in agony.

Down to its very bones, Boreth was gravely wounded. The attacks had started with the dawn light on the horizon, as word came in from across the pilgrim world that an unseen enemy was at large. Within hours, the invasion had spread across the Plains of Trial to beyond the Petitioner's Encampment and the Meged Fells. Great fissures kilometers deep had appeared in the northern continent and the western sea was aflame. Boreth's planetary defense garrison was believed dead, their final transmissions a cacophony of maddened shouts and enraged roars. One by one, the settlements across the hallowed planet went dark as the line of attack closed into a circle, tightening around the monastery's peak like a black noose.

The enemy were at the gates, having burned the lands behind them. They had come to destroy the sacred places of Kahless the Unforgettable, and the secrets of the great vault buried deep beneath the holy monastery.

R'Kol sent the call for aid into the void from the transmission tower on the neighboring peaks, but nothing had come back on the open channel, nothing but hissing, screaming static. He suspected that the enemy was generating some kind of disruption field that blotted out all incoming signals.

No, be honest, he told himself as he ran, *you* hope *that is so, against all odds. The alternate explanation is far worse.*

Briefly, through a gap in the cloud cover, R'Kol had glimpsed the flash and glare of fire in the heavens, the signs that could only mean a battle in low orbit. Had the Empire sent ships to save them? Was the same battle being fought here on the ground duplicated in space?

But it is no battle, he thought grimly. *It is a rout.*

R'Kol stopped to catch his breath, his lungs burning in his chest as chugs of white vapor escaped his frostbitten lips. He was a long way from being a young man, but the adrenaline coursing through his veins made the years fall away, at least in the moment. He wiped flecks of frost from his long, braided beard as another low rumble surged through the mountainside. In the middle distance, huge shards of the rock face sheared away and tumbled into the narrow valley far below, one great boulder smashing through the middle of the cloister bridge that spanned the gap.

He spat angrily into the snow and cursed. "I do not wish to die a dishonorable death," R'Kol snarled into the frigid air. "Give me something to fight!"

It was then that the Klingon realized two truths: first, that the rumbling was not coming from the trembling rocks around him; and second, that the fates were about to deliver exactly what he had demanded.

He turned toward the sound, and at last he saw the foe.

The enemy came out of the darkness. A leviathan serpent as tall as a habitat block, its head a horned cowl of shiny bone, its great maw festooned with jagged teeth. Where the creature moved, R'Kol saw the rock beneath it crumble and disintegrate, becoming powdery sand. It tainted everything around it, leaving a miasma of decay in its wake.

THE ASHES OF TOMORROW 61

Spears of disruptor fire lanced up to rake along the monster's flank, and R'Kol looked away, spotting the shooters on a higher ridge. He could not make out their faces, but the shouted war cries from the hooded figures with the rifles were known to him. His comrades Gyls and Kened, and the brothers of clan K'Laarq, come to Boreth for a sabbatical six rotations ago, were relishing this chance for battle.

They called his name. "It has come for the vault beneath," shouted Gyls. "The crystals!"

"Aye!" R'Kol raced up the last few meters to their side, watching the creature as it mauled a domed building on the outer donjon, yelling out as he ran. "There can be no other explanation!"

"Any word from orbit?" said one of the brothers.

R'Kol shook his head. Kened threw him a disruptor pistol, and he caught it easily. "This will be the bite of a glob fly to that thing," he grunted.

"Every bite is a wound," Kened retorted. "Every wound a victory."

R'Kol said nothing, checking the gun's charge, waiting for his moment. The giant serpent shook tile and wood and stone from its mouthparts, then reared up, sensory pits humming in the icy air. It turned in their direction, making a guttural, throbbing sound.

The noise was familiar to R'Kol. He had heard it in his sleep and during watches served over the vault of crystals. In the bowels of the monastery, artifacts older than the Empire's history lay under eternal guard, each shard a piece of frozen spacetime. R'Kol never questioned the nature of the crystals, as that was not his place. He knew only of their power and their potential. One who touched the surface of a shard with their bare flesh was said to become briefly untethered in time, set adrift along the years of their own life line to witness days past or days yet to be. The contents of the vault were the closest thing to holy among the Klingons, a race whose mythology told that they had slain their own gods. That a monster had come to destroy them seemed strangely fitting.

The serpent struck at the building above them and they fired at it, concentrating the beams of their weapons on the visible eye spots. Their attack was rewarded with a bellow of pain, but it was a brief triumph.

The creature tensed, gathering energy inside itself, and released a pulse of coruscating radiation. The wave of hazy light accelerated the passage of time for everything in its aura, turning ice to vapor, wood to ash, stone to sand.

It washed over the Klingons at the edge of its power and then receded like a tide—but they were still touched by it, and it killed them.

Not all at once.

R'Kol saw Kened take the first blow. The other Klingon fell to his knees in a drift of snow, screaming in agony. He clawed at the flesh of his face, raking gouges in the ridges on his forehead. Gyls and the brothers went into traumatic shock, their bodies shaking like victims of some terrible palsy, the tremors so violent they broke bone.

Then R'Kol felt the force of it, and it was the shock of his life. In an instant, every nerve in his body was singing with raw pain. If he had been dipped in fire, the suffering would have been no less. He collapsed into the ice and slush, warring with his own flesh in a desperate attempt to keep control of himself. He could hardly move, with even the slightest twitch adding more torture to his ordeal.

The disruptor in R'Kol's hand went hot, burning the flesh of his palm. Before his eyes, the pistol corroded and fell to pieces. The skin on his fingers wrinkled and shed itself, revealing bones soon blackened and decayed. The pain grew beyond measure.

But worse than all of that, wickeder than the soul-searing torment, was the madness that engulfed his mind. R'Kol's thoughts were flooded with howling shadows, a thousandfold cacophony of them overlaid across one another. Each shadow cried out in his voice and it had his face—but they were not *him*.

He was R'Kol, son of Garkal, born in the Severed Hills south of the First City, oath-sworn of Kahless; and so were the shadows, but each was his twisted reflection. They were pieces of different lives led, other paths taken. Some clerics like him, others soldiers, scholars, farmers, fathers, murderers, madmen. All of them crowded into his skull, raging and screaming, driving him insane.

It was a mercy as R'Kol's body began to disintegrate. In his last instants of conscious, rational thought, the cleric caught sight of something in the sky. The clouds parted, and a great winged shape alight with fire cleaved across the night.

The burning hawk filled his vision as R'Kol fell into darkness.

I.K.S. *Gorkon*

Acrid smoke and punishing heat filled the bridge of the battle cruiser, making it hard to see more than a few spans from one's face. Plasma fire licked around the edges of the main viewscreen as the Klingon starship thundered through Boreth's frigid skies, cutting an infernal scar from horizon to horizon. The deck plates moaned beneath the forces imposed upon them, the great ship bucking with each turbulent updraft. And yet, the vessel's commander seemed to guide the vessel through sheer force of his will.

"Steady as the sword cuts!" Captain Klag barked the order to his crew, eyes wide with fury, as if daring them to do anything other than obey him.

"They told me you were wild, but I never listened." At his side, Chancellor Martok bit out a hard laugh, his scarred faced creased with martial glee. "*The son of M'Raq is a death bringer*, they said! And by my blade, they were right!"

"Only to our enemies, General." Klag used Martok's old honorific, but the chancellor did not call him on it. "We must follow this fight to the bitter end."

"Aye." Martok gave a sharp nod. "Honor demands it."

A flight of *B'rel*-class ships had followed the *Gorkon* into battle over Boreth, responding to the myriad of distress calls transmitted from the pilgrim world. It was pure chance that Klag's vessel, temporarily carrying Martok's flag on a voyage back to the homeworld, had picked up the same messages and joined in the response.

None of the warship commanders had expected the threat that rose off the planet to meet them, the gigantic serpent-thing that spat a weaponized venom capable of warping time. The birds-of-prey were gone now, either consumed in fusion fires or adrift and burning in terminal orbits.

Together they had managed to kill the creature, but the blood cost was great and the *Gorkon* was badly damaged. With the fatalism of a warrior that could be conjured only in a Klingon heart, Klag and his crew knew that their lives might be forfeited to destroy the second serpent tearing into the monastery below.

"Keep us stable, helm!" Laneth, Klag's second-in-command, called out to B'Olgana, the officer at the pilot's station. "We must bring our cannons to bear!"

"Easy to demand, difficult to accomplish," B'Olgana shot back. "A *Qang*-class starship isn't built for atmospheric operations!"

Laneth scowled and shot a look at H'Jen, the callow young lieutenant at the weapons station. "Combat state?"

H'Jen was new to the *Gorkon*, and Klag had privately wondered if she was seasoned enough for her posting. But her quick actions in orbit had proven her worth. "All weapons ready, but the heat of reentry threatens to affect our disruptor emitters. The longer we hold fire, the more likely a malfunction. We should act swiftly."

"Ha!" Martok pounded his heel on the deck. "*Kai* the gunner! She speaks for us all, draw blood first and damn the risk."

"Hold the torpedo launchers," Klag ordered. "Disruptors only. I'll not be responsible for obliterating Kahless's Mountain."

"Look there," insisted Martok, jabbing a gauntleted finger at the screen and the ravaged peaks beneath them. "Mortal hands will no longer decide the fate of Boreth, my friend. We can only ensure that the enemy pays the butcher's bill."

Klag's attention turned to a screen at his right hand. The second serpent creature was rising up, swimming through the smoke and fire, and tasting the air with a forest of sensory cilia. It turned toward them. "It sees us."

"Forward disruptor batteries locked on," said H'Jen. "By your will, Captain."

"Let it come." Klag steeled himself, his hands tightening into fists. "Engage at point-blank range."

The beast writhed like a sea wraith through water, climbing from the ruins of the half-destroyed monastery. Waves of radiant energy buoyed it up, defying gravity, and fleshy sails unfurled along its length as it rode the howling winds. The creature's maw opened, wider and wider, becoming a glistening cavern packed with hooked lamprey teeth. It rose to meet the *Gorkon*'s diving approach, a snake attacking an eagle.

The shimmering mouth filled the bridge's viewscreen and Klag gave a guttural snarl, gesturing with his fist. H'Jen's targeting sensors, damaged in the orbital fight and fogged by the toxic chroniton field about the beast, locked on as best they could.

Searing lances of green fire issued out from the *Gorkon*'s weapons, all but one blast finding their mark as the two combatants closed the distance.

Klag saw pieces of burning meat the size of aircars slashed away from the beast's twitching body, falling on the snowcapped peaks in a rain of flesh and poisonous blood. And still it came, unfazed by the agony they inflicted upon it.

H'Jen continued to fire, but the follow-up shots passed harmlessly through the monster's flank as it de-phased itself, momentarily dropping out of synch with local spacetime.

"Evasive!" Klag's fingers gripped the arms of his command throne as the creature twisted toward them. "Traverse and fire as we pass!"

The gunner called out an affirmation of the orders, but B'Olgana shouted over her as she fought to pivot the *Gorkon* away. "We cannot avoid it! Brace for collision!"

In the vacuum of space, the turn would have been enough to elude the alien behemoth, but in the drag of Boreth's atmosphere, the starship was too slow to make a clean pass. The monstrous serpent re-phased as it connected with the *Gorkon*'s superstructure, and the beast's jaws closed on the portside wing.

Tritanium spars and plates of hull metal bent and withered under the force of the savage bite. Writhing against the velocity of the impact, the creature shook its massive head, letting its teeth slash through deck after deck, instantly killing any of Klag's crew unlucky enough to be present.

The *Gorkon*'s port wing distorted and ripped free, taking one of the starship's warp nacelles with it as beast and vessel fell away from each other. The wreckage collided with a string of serrated peaks to the west of the ruined monastery and lit off a pillar of fire.

The ship howled and tumbled into a roll, clipping another spindly crag as it passed. Klag called for emergency maneuvers, but the serpent's attack had taken his ship beyond the point of survival. The *Gorkon* spiraled into the white abyss of a snow-choked valley and struck the ground with a deafening impact.

Icefang Valley, Boreth

This is not the Barge of the Dead, Martok told himself. *I am in too much pain to be a corpse, and the hells are hot, not freezing cold.*

He opened his one good eye with effort, reaching up to wipe away the layer of blood that had gummed it shut. He lay on his back, against a field of hard metal, with the reek of burning tritanium in his nostrils. Overhead, the thick clouds had dissipated in the shockwaves from numerous thermal detonations, and in the night he could see the diamond-hard glitter of distant suns.

Calling on his old spacer's skills, ignoring the pain racking his body, Martok searched the sky and found the speck of light that was Klinzhai, the sun around which the Klingon homeworld orbited. *There. To the north, high above the horizon.*

The sight gave him strength, and he gritted his teeth, sitting up with great effort.

He got his bearings. Along with a cluster of other survivors, he sat upon the ventral hull of the *Gorkon*, now inverted where the ship had crashed upside down in a wide crevasse. Fires burned everywhere, and plumes of black smoke marched past him, pulled by the constant wind.

"Here." Captain Klag stepped out from the gloom, offering Martok his hand. The chancellor waved it away and rose to his feet unaided.

"How long was I unconscious?" Martok remembered leaving the deck when the *Gorkon* was hit, striking the bulkhead with enough force to make him black out.

"Not long," said Klag, his breathing labored. "H'Jen and I dragged you to safety."

"My gratitude," he said with a nod. "How many survivors?" Martok wasted no time on other concerns. This was still a battle, and it had not yet ended.

"Unknown." Klag's expression darkened. "B'Olgana died on impact. Laneth's wounds are grave." He waved at the ruin of his ship. "Others are vacating the . . . the wreck. Regrouping."

Martok knew the captain's silent pain. He too had lost honorable warriors and good ships in combat. "What of the second serpent? It lives still?"

"See for yourself." Klag raised one hand to point toward the end of the valley, and Martok saw that his uniform sleeve was wet with blood. The chancellor did not comment on the wound, and followed the captain's direction.

Above the ridgeline, framed by plasma fires from the *Gorkon*'s shattered warp nacelle, the creature had returned to its first target, ripping its way through the citadels and domes of the monastery. It roared like thunder and punched into the bedrock beneath the buildings, turning the stone into a torrent of ash. Martok found himself shaking his head, sickened by the wanton, heedless destruction of the hallowed site. No Klingon could have witnessed the desecration and felt anything but rage and sorrow.

"We could not stop it." H'Jen's voice carried to the chancellor on the wind, and her shock was his.

In silence, the *Gorkon* survivors watched the mountain collapse, and from within the hulking dust cloud that marked its destruction came a brief, brilliant pulse of blue fire. The air screamed as a humming implosion took place within the haze; then the mountain, the ruined monastery and the secrets buried beneath it, vanished into a crackling singularity that lived and died in a fraction of a second.

"Curse that hulking great *petaQ*!" Commander Laneth called out from where he lay slumped against a broken hull plate. "I swear death . . . on all its kind!"

Klag did not move from the spot where he stood, staring into the dust cloud. Slowly and carefully, the *Gorkon*'s captain drew his disruptor. "You will have your chance, Commander." He jutted his angular chin toward the ruins. "Look there."

Martok squinted into the haze and saw movement. The dust swirled and parted, allowing the serpent-thing to fall forward, crashing down over the top of the ridge, rolling and spilling into the ice-rimed valley beneath.

For a brief moment, he hoped it might be dead, killed by the effect of its own attack on the vault after swallowing the energy of the time crystals. Pieces of the vast creature sloughed off, raining down on the snowpack; but then the bloody chunks began to writhe of their own accord, and Martok saw fanged mouths bursting out from beneath seared skin. In some obscene fashion, the giant was unmaking its body into smaller versions of itself.

Smaller being a relative term. The remnant forms were as big as riding beasts, mouths wide enough to bite a warrior in two. And they were coming this way, grasping blindly in the direction of the *Gorkon*'s wreckage.

Captain Klag gave no order, he simply fired a shot into the first cohort of the slithering beasts, and his crew followed his example. Martok cursed his lack of a ranged weapon, his own gun lost in the crash, but in short order he realized he would not need it.

For every creature disintegrated by a disruptor bolt, another was snaking forward over the ice, snapping at the air. Martok's hands slipped back to the grips of the twin *mek'leth* blades sheathed beneath his spinal armor, and the chancellor drew them with a flourish.

As the first serpent came into his reach, Martok slashed the air with the blades and cut the thing deeply, mortally wounding it. The monster perished with a screech and Martok reeled back, feeling the crackle of decay from the dying creature's toxic aura. The *grishnar* furs wrapped around his armor faded to gray, aged by the effect, but the chancellor was too quick to suffer it himself. More came and Martok found his pace, striking and killing until the icy hull around him was spattered with steaming gore.

Despite the grim circumstances, he was grinning, his blood singing in his veins. He felt *alive*.

There came a brief lull as the first wave of beasts lay dying, but it would last only for moments. The remainder approached, and they were innumerable. It came to Martok that today would indeed be a good day to die.

Fitting, he thought. *An intractable enemy, impossible odds, and a fight for revenge. I have waited my whole life for such a battle!*

At his side, Captain Klag gave a wry grunt and muttered something beneath his breath.

"What say you?" Martok demanded.

"They are the thousandth knife," Klag repeated, gesturing at the horde of creatures as the mass swarmed toward them. "I recognize the weapon that will end my life. Are you familiar with that poem, General?"

"I know it well," Martok retorted. A relic from the past, written in the era of heroes, the first line of the ancient Klingon verse came easily to mind. "*And though I had slain a thousand foes less one, the thousandth knife found my liver.*"

Emerald flame burst out in screeching torrents as the *Gorkon* survivors opened up with their disruptors, and from his position, Laneth shouldered his disruptor rifle, joining in the recitation as he fired into the ranks of the serpents. "*The thousandth enemy said to me, now you shall die, now none shall know . . .*"

"*And the fool looking down, believed this!*" From across the shattered hull, H'Jen shouted out the next line, her eyes alight with rage.

"*Not seeing, above his shoulder, the naked stars,*" Klag continued, raising a blood-smeared *bat'leth* to the sky.

"*The naked stars,*" Martok repeated, glancing back toward the distant ember of Klinzhai. "*Each one remembering.*"

He tightened his grip on the twin *mek'leth*s, and ran toward a glorious death.

Starfleet Medical, San Francisco, Earth

On any other occasion, Beverly Crusher would have chastised herself for what she was doing. She had little time for doctors and practitioners who used their reputations and their networks of friends to circumvent the channels that others had to follow. It had always seemed unjust to her, insidious almost, how some could put the right word in the right ear and get what they needed. In past ages, power like that had flowed from wealth and privilege, but in an era where material want was almost nonexistent, the economy of favors still existed.

Crusher would not have dreamed of using such tactics for her own gain. Until today.

Funny how a threat to the life of your child makes you reevaluate your moral standards. She sat back in the chair in front of the monitor screen, watching the progress bar fill as the records from Starfleet Medical's database copied across to her data tablet, and gave a long sigh.

A few questions to certain people had allowed her to gain access to the fleet's more esoteric information stores, where obscure and sensitive medical files were located. Beverly Crusher was well thought of by her colleagues at the complex on Earth, some of them having been newly minted residents under her tutelage, during her time as head of the facility some twenty years ago.

She glanced around, thinking back to that time. Her office had been on the floor above this one, and she had relished the work, throwing herself into the practical business of managing interstellar medicine across the Federation's worlds. But that year seemed so distant to her now, and that Beverly Crusher had been a different person.

On some level, she had hoped that becoming a mother for the second time would make things easier, that she would be ready for the challenges.

Wrong! Having René is nothing like how it was with Wes. It's all brand-new. She smiled at the thought of her two sons, but her expression quickly turned brittle. For all the challenges Wesley Crusher had faced growing up, he had matured into a man she was fiercely proud of, but René might never get that opportunity.

René's journey to adulthood had been forcibly accelerated by a brush with a Devidian Naga, aging him physically while his mind remained at a child's developmental level. Now the doctor was calling in every marker she could, gathering every last scrap of information on the effects of chroniton fields on the human body, to see if it could be undone. If there was a way to reverse what had happened to their boy, she had to find it.

Her communicator chirped, and she tapped the fascia. "Crusher here."

"Doctor, this is the Enterprise.*"* She recognized the voice of Ensign Sebel, a young Cygnian woman serving in the ship's communications division. *"I have been trying to locate you."*

"Is something wrong?" Crusher's skin prickled with a sudden chill as she immediately feared the worst. She had left René asleep back in their quarters on the *Enterprise*, with Counselor Hegol to keep the boy company. With all of the starship's complement due to rotate off the vessel for much-needed shore leave on Earth, the plan had been to pick up René later and go to Jean-Luc's family château that evening. "Do you need me to beam up?"

"No, Doctor, it is nothing serious," Sebel said quickly, realizing her mistake. *"I am sorry if I alarmed you. There is an incoming subspace message, for your attention. From another Starfleet vessel."*

"Which one?"

"The Athene Donald, *out by Proxima."*

Crusher knew at once who that would be. "Can you connect me?"

"Certainly. Please stand by . . ."

The combadge chirped again, and the next words that issued out into the air were the terse but welcome tones of a valued friend. *"Beverly? You there?"*

"Hello, Kate. It's good to hear from you."

"Of course it is, but never mind that." As was her brisk nature, Katherine Pulaski cut straight to the point. *"What the devil is this you've sent me?"*

"I need your help." Crusher hadn't expected to speak directly to Pulaski over this matter, but rather to use her expertise at a remove. She had already discreetly downloaded reams of material from the other doctor's medical logs, but records of a particular incident during Pulaski's tenure aboard the *Enterprise*-D were proving hard to locate.

She imagined Pulaski reading the data file off her screen. *"This patient you have, a young human male suffering from unnaturally forced maturation. I know how that goes."*

"That's why I wanted your input. I'm specifically interested in what took place with the *Lantree* and Darwin Station in 2365."

"I won't forget that in a hurry." The other doctor had firsthand experience of aging before her time, after the antibodies of gene-engineered children attacked her body during a mission to the Darwin outpost colony. *"We used a sample of my DNA from prior to infection onset as a model for a cure,"* she explained. *"They*

put me through a transporter and reset my body, like turning back a mechanical clock."

"I've considered that," said Crusher. "But this aging is radiation induced, not from a pathogen. I'm worried a transporter method might not work."

"Radiation . . ." Pulaski chewed on the word for a moment. *"You need to dig into the files of one of our* Enterprise *predecessors, from the late 2260s,"* she went on. *"I remember something Leonard McCoy wrote that might be relevant, about an incident on Gamma Hydra IV."*

Crusher immediately ran a new search string. "Thank you, Kate. I knew I could count on you for a steer on this." She hesitated. "This case is special."

"I can see that." Pulaski sighed. *"Beverly, the subject's data you sent me was anonymized, but you have to remember, I was the* Enterprise's *CMO for a year. And my memory is good enough to recognize elements of Jean-Luc Picard's DNA in this young fellow. The patient is René, isn't it?"*

There was nothing to be gained by hiding the truth. "Yes." Beverly ran a hand over her face.

There was a long pause, and in it Crusher heard the faint whisper of subspace static. Then Pulaski went on, and this time her voice was softer. *"As your friend, and as a mother, I understand completely what is motivating you with this. But as a doctor and your colleague, I'd be remiss if I didn't call you on the ethical conflict of a practitioner treating their own child. We have to remain detached, Beverly. I could never do that if it were my daughter, Jackie. And I think you are no different with René."*

In an ideal world, Crusher should have recused herself immediately and referred René's treatment to one of her colleagues. But she couldn't face that, she couldn't let go of the responsibility.

"You're right," she said. "And after this is all over, if I have to go up before a board of inquiry, even lose my post, I'll do it. But right now, there's no one else at hand more qualified than I am to help him. Kate, I just can't stand by and watch him suffer." She almost lost the last words as emotion thickened her voice. "I won't."

"Oh, who am I trying to kid?" Pulaski muttered. *"I'd do exactly the same thing if I were in your shoes."* She blew out a breath. *"All right. Anything you need to help solve this, I'm here for you. I'm sending you all my case files from the Darwin incident."*

Crusher wiped a tear from the corner of her eye. "Thank you, Kate. I owe you."

"Not in a million years," said the other woman. *"Give René a hug from his aunt Katherine. Athene Donald, out."*

A few seconds later, a new file appeared in Crusher's data queue, shot across subspace from Pulaski's personal logs. She leaned forward in her chair and began to pore over the notes.

U.S.S. *Titan* NCC-80102

Fatigue filled William Riker like water flowing into an empty glass. He padded quietly across the living room of his family's quarters, throwing a look up at the windows casting weak blue light into the space. The starship was berthed inside the enclosed upper dock of Spacedock in Earth orbit, enveloped in the soft glow of the interior.

It was gamma shift—ship's night—and by rights, Riker should have been back here hours ago. He felt guilty for making excuses to miss dinner with his wife and frowned at himself for losing track of time, burying himself in his work.

He hesitated in the middle of the room and listened. Tasha's room was silent—his daughter was off the ship, visiting her greataunt on a farm in the English countryside—but he could hear Deanna breathing softly from the master bedroom, the gentle rhythm telling him she was deep in slumber.

Riker didn't have the heart to wake her, so he picked his way to the replicator, getting himself a cup of black tea, and then sunk into a comfortable chair. He shrugged off his outer tunic and loosened the collar of his undershirt. He could feel sleep lurking close at hand, but not near enough to grasp.

His thoughts, as tired as they were, refused to settle. Over the past few hours, the admiral had personally gone through every report and log he could get his hands on, soaking up every detail of the *Starship Aventine*'s mission to the far future and the ominous sights Picard and his team had recorded there. It made for sobering reading, but the deeper he went, the more compelled he was to continue.

He had remained in his office, even after his adjutant, Lieutenant Ssura, turned in for the day. The gangly Caitian had eyed him warily, pressing the suggestion that the admiral call it a day as well, but Riker tersely dismissed him. *This is too important to ignore,* he thought. *I have to be on top of every last detail.*

And that was true; but there was another factor in play, something Riker had not revealed, not even to his wife.

The grim threat that Picard and Wesley warned of, these time-active phantoms stalking the universes, felt horribly *familiar* to Riker. Not just because he had encountered the Devidians face-to-face during their venture into Earth's nineteenth century, but from a deep-seated, almost primal abhorrence that he couldn't put into words.

It was almost as if he knew them, knew what horrors they were capable of. *But that wasn't possible, was it? How can I know what I haven't experienced?* Riker scowled at the notion and, ignoring his steaming mug of tea, he snatched up the padd that Ssura had left him, detailing sensor logs taken by the *Aventine*'s science officer during their jaunt.

Riker studied the words, seeing them without really registering them, trying to look through the data to find the truth that eluded him. The words seemed to blur into one another, and his eyelids began to droop. Without warning, sleep finally reached out and took him under.

He was on the bridge, but the dimensions of it seemed incorrect. It wasn't the *Titan*, it wasn't the *Enterprise*. Or, at least, it wasn't the most recent *Enterprise*.

He was sitting in the command chair of a vessel that no longer existed.

I am the captain. He knew that fact, believed it, felt the shadow of it over his thoughts. *But how is that possible?*

Riker heard a voice, urgent and firm. "Forty-five seconds to target."

He nodded at the report, but the action was sluggish. He felt as if he were moving in slow motion, every act an effort. *Who is speaking?*

His eyes brought a familiar face into focus at the helm: Sariel Rager. "Sensors show it's pretty crowded, sir," she was saying. "I'm adjusting our course to give us some breathing room."

His head turned, as if he were a puppet led by some unseen master, looking back and up toward the tactical station. "Tasha, put Starfleet frequency one-four-eight-six on audio."

Tasha? The name came out of his mouth, easy and fast. *A mistake?*

At the large, curved railing separating the upper consoles from the lower bridge, Lieutenant Commander Yar stood at her station, poised and ready for anything.

"Aye, sir," said the woman, "on audio."

But she's dead! The enormity of that rang through Riker's thoughts. *Am I dreaming? Where is this coming from?*

A dream would have been hazy and ill defined around the edges, but this felt different. It was strong and clear, not abstract like a memory, but as real as something happening in the moment.

I am here, Riker realized. *I am living this.*

"Weapons on standby," Yar was saying, "all of them, sir."

He tried to break away from the pull of the sensation, but it was impossible. Riker's consciousness clawed at the edges of the strange recollection, and he became aware of something ghosting him, a second self like a flickering afterimage.

A shadow, closing in on him. A shadow with his face, a splinter of him from some other life he had never lived.

Panic gripped him. He needed to wake up. The longer he stayed in this dream state, the harder it would be to escape it. The shadow grew and grew, filling the edges of his vision. Filling his mind.

"What the hell are those?" It took a moment to realize he was hearing himself speak.

Riker forced himself to perceive what lay before him, finding images swirling on the bridge's main viewscreen. A twisting mass of dark, shimmering objects emerging from a temporal rift. They were heading directly toward the ship.

Nagas. Those are the Nagas. They're coming for us!

"Conn, evasive!" The voice that was not his voice shouted the order. "Get us out of here!"

But it was too late to change the inevitable. *This is happening now. This has already happened.*

The Nagas would rend and destroy, devour life and disgorge decay. They were already aboard his ship.

I am going to die, and my family will die with me. The abject terror of that certainty was like being plunged into ice. *This is happening now. This has already happened.*

It wasn't a communicator chime or the sound of an alert siren that roused Deanna Troi from her deep slumber, but something far more subtle and immediate.

Her mind sensed the subconscious cry from her husband's thoughts, Troi's innate empathic senses reaching out to catch the flood of emotion from his nightmare.

She snapped awake and was on her feet in a flash. Grabbing a robe from the foot of the bed, Troi shrugged it on and dashed into the living room. "Will?"

He woke with a start, shocked back in his seat, knocking a discarded padd off his lap. For a brief moment, he looked around with naked fear in his eyes, as if he didn't know where he was. "What . . . ?"

"Were you dreaming again? It's all right," she told him, taking his hand. "I'm here."

Riker squeezed her hand tightly. It wasn't the gesture of a loving husband, but the panicked grip of someone afraid for their life. "Daughter . . . Where's our daughter?" He half rose from the seat, but Troi eased him back.

"She's not here, Will. She's staying with Aunt Janet, remember?" Troi could feel her husband's pulse racing, and she did her best to project calm.

Riker blinked. "Yes. Of course." He paused, and then took a long, deep breath as he struggled to re-center himself. "I forgot about that."

Troi instinctively settled into a counselor mode. "Everything is fine. You're safe here." She took a breath. "You had another nightmare. Do you want to talk about it?"

"Are we safe?" He met her question with one of his own. "This new threat from the Devidians, the scope of it . . . It's beyond troubling, Deanna."

"I know," she admitted, "but we can't let that overwhelm us. We have to focus on what we can do, on the immediate circumstances before us."

"You're right." Riker went to sip his tea, then made a face as he realized it had gone stone cold. "It's preying on my mind. These dreams are so vivid. So *real*. Like a memory, like a lived experience."

"Stress can play tricks on us."

He shook his head. "I can still feel the emotions of it clinging to me." Troi's husband gingerly sketched out the dream images he had experienced, like someone exploring the edges of a wound. "I felt like I was drowning in shadows." At length, he met her gaze, and she saw conflicted feelings warring behind his eyes. "I've never been so terrified of losing you and Tasha as I was in that moment. It felt *true*," he repeated.

"It wasn't." Troi drew him close. "You won't lose us. I'm here.

Tasha is safe back on Earth. We will always be there for one another." She squeezed his hand. "I know you would never let anything happen to us."

"No." When he spoke again, the conflict in Riker's manner had vanished. "No, I won't."

He removed his hand from her gentle grasp, and Troi felt an odd sense of disconnection as he withdrew. Her brow furrowed, her empathic senses touching only a cool, metered calmness where, moments before, her husband's thoughts had been jumbled and turbulent. It was as if a shadow had passed in front of the sun.

"Will, what is it?" She searched his expression for some hint of what he was thinking. "You can tell me anything."

"It's okay. I'm all right, thanks to you." He smiled, but it didn't reach all the way to his eyes. "I wasn't sure before, but I see it clearer now. Don't worry, Deanna." He reached up and touched her cheek. "I know what to do."

5

___

Starfleet Headquarters, San Francisco, Earth

As the turbolift whisked him up to the conference level, Picard used the moment alone to cover a yawn and shake off the lethargy pooling in his bones. He glanced out a thin strip of window in the side of the building, watching the campus settle beneath him as he rose. It was midafternoon here, and he could see a squad of cadets down from the Academy crossing the main plaza in a tight, careful formation. Above, the skies promised rain, lending the day an oppressive cast.

He had not slept well, even in the château's wide, comfortable bed with his wife asleep beside him, his thoughts churning, and his mind unable to switch off. Finally, Picard had silently slipped out into the cool night air, to walk among the rows of ripening vines that ranged around his family home. He found no peace there either, and when his communicator finally sounded its pre-programmed alert, it came as a relief.

He dressed in his uniform and prepared breakfast himself, and without waking Beverly or René, Picard waited in the anteroom until Starfleet contacted him to prepare for a site-to-site transport. The matter at hand was too important to waste time traveling via public transporter stations, and he surrendered the temperate French night to the muggy, overcast North American afternoon in the hum of matter-energy transit.

Security passed him through without question, and it was telling that he had no escort this time. Picard had half expected to find Commander Paris waiting for him in the atrium, but there was only a hard-faced officer who scanned the captain with a tricorder before pronouncing him clear to proceed.

The growing sense that something was amiss formed fully when Picard entered the conference room from the previous day, to find only two other people waiting there for him: Admirals Akaar and Riker, the two men cutting short their conversation as he entered.

Picard glanced around. "Am I early?"

"Right on time," Akaar corrected.

He glanced at Riker. "Then it's everyone else who is late."

"Not quite." Riker shook his head. "The other admirals won't be present for this conversation."

"Oh?" Picard's unease deepened. He began to wonder what had taken place after he and Wesley had presented their report the previous day. President zh'Tarash had adjourned the meeting, but clearly that had not been the end of it.

Akaar intuited Picard's train of thought and headed it off. "I've already spoken with T'Raan, Bordson, Idyn, and the others, Captain. We've discussed the situation and we are in agreement."

"Agreement about what?" Picard was clearly ten steps behind everyone else, and it was a feeling he disliked intensely.

By way of reply, Riker gestured past him, toward the space in the middle of the curved table. As Picard turned, a flicker of holographic light formed into the figure of an Andorian, and the president's avatar took shape.

"Captain," said the hologram. "Thank you for coming. I wanted you to hear this from me directly."

Picard gave a nod but said nothing, noting that this time zh'Tarash was not accompanied by avatars of her aides. That fact only served to increase his disquiet.

Zh'Tarash indicated the two admirals before she went on. "Regarding the Devidian report, I've spoken with Admiral Akaar and the other members of Starfleet Command, and discussed the matter with the Federation Council. I know you're fully aware of the current political climate in the UFP and the increased scrutiny under which this office currently operates, after the business with Section 31." She sighed. "With that in mind, it has been decided that any immediate *large-scale actions in this matter are not in the best interests of the Federation."*

"Not in the best . . . ?" Picard echoed the words before he realized, and caught himself. But it was too late to hide his surprise.

Zh'Tarash went on, overlooking the interruption. *"Your testimony, the data provided by Mister Crusher, and the logs from the Aventine's sortie into the future are being analyzed by Andos's top people at the DTI. Additionally, a special working group is being prepared to consider our options."*

"*Zha* President," Picard began, finding his voice again. "With all due respect, this is not a situation to be debated in a committee! Action *is* required!"

"I concur," said zh'Tarash, her antennae curling at the strident tone of his voice. *"Action is being taken. The extant threat of these so-called Naga creatures is now a Starfleet priority."* She glanced at Akaar.

"An advisory has gone out across the fleet," said the towering Capellan. "Additional defensive protocols are in effect at sites where time-active technology or artifacts are present. We have also sent warnings to all Federation members and associate governments, with specific focus on species we know to be temporally sensitive."

"A defensive stance is a half measure at best." Picard could hardly believe what he was hearing. "I do not say this lightly, and I take no pleasure in it, but I must insist that we confront the Devidians directly. They are pure predators. They won't be deterred by force fields and a few more starships."

"You have made your opinion clear, and be assured it will be taken under advisement," said zh'Tarash. Picard opened his mouth to continue, but she spoke over him. *"Now let me be clear, Captain. The Federation has suffered great damage to its confidence over the past few years. Rebuilding after the Borg Invasion and weathering the assassination of my esteemed predecessor would have tested any coalition such as ours, and we have also faced corruption and deceit inside our political and military organs. The fallout from the Tezwa crisis, the*

situation with the rogue artificial intelligence." She sighed and shook her head. *"If this threat is as serious as you suggest, then we must move carefully to address it. At this moment, our Federation is fragile. I must balance the needs of the member worlds and focus first on what is happening right now, not what might happen in a possible future."*

Picard's lips thinned as he heard the echo of Admiral Idyn's words in the president's reply. Had the Deltan swayed the politician?

Zh'Tarash went on. *"It would be irresponsible of me to broadcast the possibility of a potential existential threat to the timeline without thoroughly vetting every aspect of it. Can you imagine the response if we were to go public with that? There would be mass panic across the entire quadrant, or worse!"*

"I understand," said Picard, reframing his approach. He looked toward Riker, once again hoping that his friend would offer some support, but the other admiral remained silent, watching him. "But we cannot simply stand by and allow the Devidians to further their schemes. If we do not act decisively, I fear there will come a point where we will not be able to stop them."

Zh'Tarash shook her head. *"I refuse to accept that. I have full confidence that Starfleet will be able to effectively protect our citizens, our worlds, and our assets."*

Picard gave one more attempt to make his argument. *"Zha* President, this is not about defending the present. This is a matter of rescuing the future. No just ours, but *every possible future."*

The President's cobalt-shaded features hardened, and she looked toward Akaar. *"Admiral, you have your orders. Proceed as directed."* Off the Capellan's sober nod, zh'Tarash returned the gesture. *"Good day, gentlemen."* The hologram froze, and then vanished.

Picard turned back to the other men. "This is a mistake."

"Captain Picard," said Akaar, with full formality in his tone. "You are advised that a moratorium is now in place regarding any unauthorized discussion about the *Aventine's* mission and the potential metatemporal threat. All Starfleet personnel with knowledge of this situation are bound by Federation law and their Starfleet oath not to discuss it, under penalty of arrest and incarceration."

"I know my responsibility, and so do my people," he bit out, focusing on Riker. "Will, are you going along with this?"

"You heard the president, Jean-Luc," said Riker. "For now, this has to be kept under wraps. The Naga attacks are our priority."

It was not the response he was expecting from his friend. *Where is the William Riker of old, ready to defy the word of a senior officer when they made the wrong call?* Picard's surprise flashed into frustration, and for a long moment he considered the last remaining card he could play.

How far can I push this? If I threaten to resign, would that convince Akaar of how serious I am?

"No." Akaar shook his head, as if he were reading Picard's mind. "I know you, Captain. I can imagine where your thoughts are taking you right now. Listen to me when I say that it will do no good to make a rash choice in this moment. Stand down."

"It's for the best, Captain," added Riker.

"No, Admiral." Picard shook his head. "I don't believe it is."

He did not wait to be dismissed, and protocol be damned, he left the conference room with a dark mood gathering about him.

In a few moments, Picard was outside in the plaza, and he marched away, following the paths through the manicured gardens and out of the Starfleet Command complex. He strode back in the direction of the old marina, walking without really choosing his path, bleeding off his directionless annoyance. Of all the possible outcomes to this meeting, an order to sit on his hands and do *nothing* was not one the captain had considered.

He did appreciate zh'Tarash's position. Everything she said about the fragility of the Federation was true, and there were those who would seize on any declaration she might make to weaken that union for their own ends. And he sympathized with Akaar's position, faced with these unpredictable, lethal attacks across the galaxy.

But both those truths paled into insignificance alongside the far greater threat. It was as if the danger the Devidians represented was almost too much to conceive of. In that shortfall of understanding lurked the potential to lose *everything*.

He shook off the thought. His throat was dry, and he stopped at a street vendor for a carton of fresh, nonreplicated juice. As Picard drank, he looked around and saw the black and gray tunics of other Starfleet officers here and there among the locals. One man stood out to him: sandy haired, wearing sunglasses to shade his eyes, waiting in the lee of a public video screen.

Tom Paris.

Paris seemed to sense Picard's scrutiny and walked away, disappearing around the corner of a nearby building. But the captain had the very real sense that the junior officer had been observing him, most likely having trailed him from the Starfleet campus.

Are they monitoring me? Did Akaar or Batanides send him? He frowned at the notion, but he couldn't shake the possibility. *Am I being watched to make sure I keep my silence?*

Hall of Ancient Thought, Mount Seleya, Vulcan

He felt the hard grains of sand on the soles of his bare feet and the cool aura of the flagstones as he walked. The simple reality of the sensations kept him present and helped him remain grounded in the now as the voices of the ghosts whispered around him.

Spock paced the mazelike corridors of the Hall of Ancient Thought without a conscious path in mind, instead allowing himself to be guided by the sensory impressions and phantom presences that filled the chambers.

He cast his gaze upward, the watchful eyes in his age-lined face finding shapes in the gloom. Along every wall, hundreds of alcoves were filled with *vre'katra*—urns made of clay, stone, bronze, and other materials. Their forms spoke to the eras of their origin— some were only a few centuries old, while others dated back to before the Time of Awakening. Within these katric arks, the psionic essences of Vulcan's greatest thinkers were preserved for all eternity. If one had the sharpness of thought and the clarity of purpose to hear them, those lost psyches could be communed with, and their knowledge recollected.

Quietly returning to his homeworld as a pilgrim rather than as his ambassadorial status would allow, Spock had come to the great halls in the footsteps of his ancestors, seeking enlightenment.

His time in service to Starfleet and the Federation had been replaced by a new mission over the last few decades, a more personal endeavor that he had made the focus of his remaining years. Spock strived for the ideal of something that he would never live to see, yet felt obligated to bring about.

Some described it as *Ni'Var*, from the old word in the ancient Vulcan tongue meaning the duality of natures in a single form, but he preferred a more precise term: *Reunification*.

In the deep past, before the philosophies of Surak and the doctrines of logic had taken hold across Vulcan's warring clans, Spock's ancestors had been split by a schism that could not be bridged. This event, what historians now called "the Sundering," saw those who refused to follow Surak's teachings depart their birth world and seek out a new planet to call their own. Those dissidents were the seeds of the civilization that would become the Romulan Star Empire.

Vulcan and Romulus—two worlds with common roots but separated by centuries of divergent history and culture. The notion of bringing these estranged sister civilizations back together might have seemed like an impossibility for some, but the prospect of it compelled Spock in a way that nothing else in his long life ever had.

And so he had come back to Vulcan to seek guidance from the venerable dead. Minds were preserved in the katric arks from the ages before the Sundering, the essences of Vulcans who had lived in an era when there was only one people. Perhaps, if he could commune with them, he might find insight that would aid him in his cause.

But Spock's plans were not unfolding as he had hoped. For days, he had fasted in a yurt out in the deep desert, meditating to bring his mind to a singular focus. The Vulcan prepared and ordered his thoughts, so that he would be able to sense and interpret the telepathic imprints from the ancient arks.

Now, as he paced the echoing cloisters of the temple, the voice foremost in his mind seemed to come to him from somewhere else. Somewhere beyond the sand and stone, beyond Vulcan. Out in the vastness of space.

If he were to attempt to explain the experience in simple terms, to a being without psionic ability—say, to a certain human physician of his acquaintance—Spock would have equated it to the misalignment of a subspace signal. He, as the receiver, had tuned himself to hear the lost spirits in the arks, but instead a more powerful, urgent signal was blotting out those faint transmissions.

At first, Spock had thought his preparations to be insufficient, and redoubled his efforts to reach the *katra*s of the dead. But now he suspected that whatever exertions he made would not be enough to dispel the voice from beyond. Some unknown quantity of that distant cry was tied to Spock's own psyche, in a way he struggled to define.

This is not my first experience of such phenomena, he recalled. In the eighth decade of the twenty-third century as reckoned by Federation calendars, during an extended stay on Vulcan, Spock had attempted the *Kolinahr* ritual in order to purge himself of all emotions. A rogue telepathic presence had interrupted those events, forcing him to seek out the source.

It seems that history is repeating itself. Spock halted in the dimness and bowed his head. He knew that now, as before, if he did not determine the nature of the recurring voice, it would disrupt his meditations at every turn. He sighed, reluctantly accepting what had to be done.

With care, the Vulcan dropped into a settle on the stone floor and closed his eyes. He visualized the calm ocean of thought rolling invisibly around him, the spirits in the katric arks as the currents and eddies that flowed through the vastness. He allowed himself to detach from the physical sensations of his place and time, wading into the bottomless depths, opening himself up and listening for the cry from the dark.

Spock drifted among a whispering crowd, buoyed by the myriad utterances of the ancient *katra*s. It was as if they knew what he was attempting; on some level, they were *helping* him.

He raised his hands, as if pushing at the membrane of reality. *I am here.* Spock projected the simple thought into the void, hoping to unite it with the call from the silence. *Who are you?*

It began as a distant hum, a sound that was no sound resonating through the depths of his psyche. As it grew closer, louder, he sensed a turbulent cloud of unchecked emotions coiling about it. Spock braced himself, uncertain of what to expect, as all about him the calm psychic ocean began to rise.

The sound resonated and shifted. It was not just a voice, but an infinity of them, countless variations of the same roaring snarl breaking over him. There were so many it was impossible to sift through them and draw out meaning. All he could grasp was the sense of a depthless shadow, the raw sensation of violence and the reek of spilled blood. He felt fear, pain, and anger.

And yet, there was an unmistakable familiarity to it, almost shocking in its directness. Spock *knew* this faraway mind, he knew it intimately. It could only belong to a being he had once connected with via touch telepathy—what many non-Vulcans simplistically called a mind-meld.

Such contact always left behind a fragment of the shared mind within the other's psyche, an ephemeral thread that would forever join the two beings. It was how Spock had immediately known of the death of his dear friend James Kirk on Veridian III, when that connection between them had been severed.

Who are you? Spock asked the question again, struggling to find the identity of the tormented soul. Throughout his life, the Vulcan had joined minds with others on many occasions, and the psyche reaching out to him now could be any one of them.

Who. Are. You?

Then, abruptly, the contact shrank back and faded, diminishing into the background susurrus of the katric whispers once again. Whatever brief interaction he had made, the Vulcan could not sustain.

Spock opened his eyes and frowned. Unless he could isolate and explore the full meaning of this intrusion, he would never be able to find his insight.

Château Picard, La Barre, Earth

"I felt powerless," said Picard, pacing across the château's living room. "As if nothing I said reached them."

"That can't be true." His wife shook her head, putting down a steaming cup of tea. Crusher considered reaching out to him, then thought better of it. Jean-Luc was rarely so annoyed. He didn't need her sympathy, he needed to vent his frustration to someone who would understand. "Your voice is respected in Starfleet."

"Not enough to spur them to act, it would seem." Irritably, he shrugged out of his uniform tunic and threw it on a cushioned chair, as if shedding himself of it would lessen his ire. "I said everything I could, Beverly. Short of storming into zh'Tarash's office and demanding an audience with her, there's nothing else I can do."

"Not the best option," she noted. "And also, that's not exactly true."

He didn't immediately pick up on the hint she dropped, going back to his replay of the conversation at Starfleet Command. "I really thought Will would see the significance of this, but he didn't even question the orders."

"Will Riker has different priorities now," said Crusher. "He's not your XO anymore, Jean-Luc. You can't expect him to back you just because you're his former commander. And you have no idea what might have been said behind closed doors."

He sighed, accepting her point. "You're right, of course. But still, it's not like him. I wonder if there isn't something going on I'm not aware of."

She watched her husband walk to the window and gaze out over the vineyards surrounding the old house. "I don't think I've ever felt this . . . ineffective in my life. I'm ringing the church bell as loud as I can, telling them the wolves are coming . . . and their response is to hide and hope they go away."

"They listened when you told them about the Borg," she reminded him.

"That was ten years ago," he noted. "Much has changed since then." As Picard said the words, he saw something outside and he trailed off, his expression becoming melancholy.

Crusher went to her husband, pressing herself to his back, bringing her arms around him, resting her head on his shoulder. It was then that she saw what he had seen: their son, René, sitting on a wooden bench out by the grass.

René held a toy—a bright red racing car in the style of a 1930s speedster—and she saw how he glumly turned it over and over in his fingers, as if he couldn't understand why it now seemed so small. Sorrow twisted in her chest and she held her husband a little tighter.

After a long moment, Picard spoke again. "We cannot stand here and do nothing." His voice was low and determined.

She drew back and gave a nod. "Of course we can't. René won't be the only one to suffer. Ezri, T'Ryssa, and the others . . . Countless families will know the same pain as theirs." Crusher took a deep breath and met her husband's gaze. "We need to light a fire under the Federation Council."

"I fear the moment for that has already passed. And by the time we get them to realize the seriousness of this, it may be too late."

"So it's the other option." She folded her arms across her chest. "I'm here for you and René, every step of the way."

A faint smile pulled at the corner of his lips. "You understand the consequences of what you're suggesting . . . ?"

"I haven't suggested anything," she countered. "I'm implying a few things, though."

"Taking matters into our own hands. Disobeying orders." Picard rubbed his chin. "That's a road we've gone down before. It won't be so simple this time. And it can't be just you and I. We'd need a lot of help."

Crusher went back to her tea and took a thoughtful sip. "Between us, we know a lot of smart people," she went on, "and I think it's fair to say, a lot more who owe us favors."

"Should we make a list?" He raised an eyebrow. "Send invitations for a dinner party?"

"That's an excellent idea," she told him, and for the first time in a long while, she felt a stirring of hope. "I'm sure we can cook something up."

Coranum Sector, Cardassia City, Cardassia Prime

The nurse did a poor job of hiding her surprise when Elim Garak walked into the garden unannounced, and she quickly stubbed out the *yvor* cigarillo she had been smoking, driving it into the dirt of a cactus planter before attempting to recover her composure.

"Honored Castellan," she began, stifling a cough. "How unexpected to see you this morning."

His usual routine, if he were on Cardassia, was to arrive in the afternoon and stay for a few hours. He varied the days of his visits, more out of an ingrained sense of tradecraft than an actual need for randomness, but on this occasion unfortunate circumstances had brought him here early.

"Hmm." Garak gave her a withering stare, then glanced at the planter, making it clear he had noted her indiscretion. "That's a bad habit. If I learn that you've been partaking of it around your patient, I will see that Doctor Parmak dismisses you." He made the statement in a conversational fashion, but the nurse knew full well how serious he was.

"Just the odd one," she insisted. "And always outdoors, never inside the house." She nodded toward the building, the gray ridges of her face darkening in embarrassment.

Garak studied the squat three-story building. One of the many advantages of being castellan of the Cardassian Union was that so many resources were now at his disposal that he struggled to keep track of them. Among the benefits was control of several state-owned dwellings in the capital, and this modest domicile was perfectly positioned to serve as a secluded place for respite and recuperation. Up in the hills, the air was clear and the views were adequate. On a bright day, one could look from the windows on the eastern side and see all the way to the domes of the Cardassian Assembly.

"Has there been any improvement since my last visit?" Garak asked the question even though he knew the answer already. The house had sensors everywhere, although he rarely used them to eavesdrop on the sole resident, and the nurse had standing orders to report any changes in behavior, no matter how small.

"Nothing, Castellan," she replied. "I speak to him, as you requested I do. But your friend remains uncommunicative."

"Perhaps you're not saying the right things." He walked past her toward the stone stairs leading inside, and waved her away. "Wait outside. I'll signal if I require your presence."

"Your will." The nurse bowed, but Garak's words were as much for the woman as they were for his two uniformed bodyguards, who stood waiting by the hedges.

Inside, the house smelled faintly of a recently cooked breakfast, and he noted that the place was clean and in good order. It was the least he could do for the patient; the man had saved his life and, if Garak allowed himself to be fanciful for a moment, one could say that he had saved his soul as well. He passed the well-stocked library on the way up the wide staircase toward the master bedroom, and he was disappointed to see that the book he had artfully left out on one of the tables had not been picked up. It was a non-digital reprint edition of *The Russia House*, a delightfully amusing work by the Terran author le Carré that Garak had talked about at some length on his last visit.

On that previous visit, he tried to encourage his charge to leave the sleeping quarters and explore more of the old house, anything to get him out of those rooms and into some semblance of living. But that attempt had clearly failed. He sighed and pushed his disappointment aside as he came to the door, straightening up and fixing a sober expression on his face.

Garak knocked twice, paused for a breath, and entered. "Hello," he began. "Forgive the intrusion."

He found his friend in a wide wickerwork chair positioned near the glass doors of the bedroom's balcony, his dark eyes distant and his expression unmoving. Julian Bashir did not answer him. In point of fact, Bashir had not spoken a word to Garak for many months.

In the aftermath of his terrible confrontation with the renegade artificial consciousness known as Uraei, Bashir had fallen into a deep catatonic state from which few physicians believed he would ever return. But Garak had never been one to underestimate the dear doctor, and he took it upon himself to provide a place of rest and convalescence, where the human might find his way back to functionality.

Increment by increment, Bashir's condition had improved, but although he had risen from his catatonia and no longer required care for his every need, he still remained locked inside himself.

Garak had tried a number of approaches to break through the barrier of silence, but each one was rebuffed. He studied the graying in the growth of his old friend's beard and not for the first time, he wondered if this was to be their lot. Would Garak repeat this ritual until they were both old and infirm? Bashir's silence and Garak's chatter about things of no consequence, carrying on until one of them passed away? It wasn't what he wanted, for himself or for the human.

He hesitated. On the drive to the house, Garak had almost ordered his detail to turn the skimmer around and return to the city. He had no idea of how Bashir would react to the news he carried. Would it deepen his disconnection with the world around him? Could he even understand?

As a student of the subtleties of other beings, Garak sometimes sensed thoughts going on behind Bashir's empty gaze, but he could never be sure. The doctor was no ordinary human, after all, genetically enhanced to be superior among his kind. Garak could only surmise as to what was going on in the depths of the other man's mind.

At length, he sat on the vacant chair opposite Bashir's. "We know each other too well," he said. "More than I might like. And you know, while I may have, on occasion, obfuscated the truth in our conversations, I have always been honest with you, Julian."

Was that a subtle motion in Bashir's gaze? Perhaps the ghost of a question? He did not break his silence, so Garak reluctantly pressed on.

"As you are aware, my position as castellan affords me certain insights, most notably intelligence reports pried from the grasp of my learned colleagues in the Cardassian Intelligence Bureau." He thought of Prynok Crell, the head of the Obsidian Order's replacement, and frowned. The man, like his organization, lacked the flair their predecessors had shown, but he was effective in his own way. Enough that Crell had been able to provide a troubling report from Earth regarding a certain Federation starship and its crew. "Something has come to light. I hesitate to share it, but I feel to say nothing is a lie of omission that even *I* cannot consider."

Was it wishful thinking, or had Bashir turned slightly toward him, the vacant cast of his face shifting? Garak hoped for and regretted having the human's attention, in equal measure.

"Our agents on Earth have learned of an incident aboard the Federation *Starship Aventine*. It is with great sorrow I must tell you that our friend Ezri Dax perished during the vessel's most recent mission."

Garak had found the woman to be agreeable company and a bright, personable sort. Her passing would draw light out of the universe, and so it was to be lamented. Still Bashir said nothing, and so Garak continued.

"I will of course ensure that the Cardassian Union sends its most heartfelt regrets." He paused, allowing the formality in his words to drop away. "She was one of the kindest humanoids I have ever known, I must say. She weathered the worst of my moods when she counseled me on Deep Space 9. Ezri helped me get to the root of some . . . personal issues, and for that I will always be grateful."

Silence followed, and finally Garak decided he had no more to say. He started to rise from the chair, but froze halfway when he realized Bashir's hand was on his arm. He looked down and saw the human staring straight at him.

"How did it happen?" Bashir's voice was gruff and raw with disuse, but his words were clear, as was the pain that marbled them.

Garak experienced a range of emotions in a few fleeting seconds—pleasure at hearing his friend speak once more, sadness at the cause behind it, concern for Julian's mental state—but he swiftly put those things aside and concentrated on answering the question. "That is unclear. It is believed that the *Aventine* took part in a mission classified above top secret by Starfleet Command. Several days ago, our intelligence placed it in proximity to the *U.S.S. Enterprise*, near the Devidia star system in the Beta Quadrant. Dax was one of several casualties noted after both vessels returned to Earth." He watched as Julian's hand dropped away. "This information is not currently public knowledge, although I understand the families of the deceased have been notified."

Garak made a mental note to erase the recordings from this room's sensors. He was breaking numerous protocols by revealing data from Cardassian sources to an off-worlder. It wouldn't do for his political rivals to find out about it, but in this moment he cared more about sharing the truth with his old friend.

Julian slowly got to his feet and padded across the room. "Devidia. I don't know it." He shook his head, a darkness gathering in his gaze. "I need more, Garak. Tell me all of it." Fury kindled at the edges of his words.

The Cardassian spread his hands. "Regrettably, that is all I have to share."

"Then I need to find someone . . . who can explain things." Bashir's hands drew into fists as he fell silent, looking inward. When he spoke again, it was clear he had made a decision. "*Sisko.* Where is he?"

Garak hesitated. It wasn't something he made known, but in his later years, he had kept up a quiet scrutiny of the whereabouts and fortunes of his former associates from his years on DS9. He thought of it as a hobbyist's pursuit, a throwback to his old espionage days. He was well aware of Benjamin Sisko's movements. But if he admitted that, what would come next? Unfortunately, he knew the answer.

"It is my understanding that Captain Sisko has recently taken a leave of absence from his command aboard the *Robinson.* He was last seen boarding a transport on Heraklion VI."

"To where?"

"Why, Bajor, of course."

Bashir paused by the bed and seemed to take stock of himself and his surroundings, running a hand over the day robe he wore, then casting an eye toward his meager personal items on a nearby shelf. Garak had made sure to secure whatever belonged to his friend before bringing him to the residence, up to and including Kukalaka, the peculiar threadbare toy from Bashir's childhood. He had hoped the familiar would stir Julian to break his silence, but now it seemed clear that only the shock of a lover's death was potent enough.

Garak rarely experienced what others might call empathy—admittedly, such emotions were not of much use in his past trade—so the jolt of compassion he felt toward Bashir was genuinely novel for him.

He knew what the human would ask next, so he answered first. "There's a discreet Kobheerian freighter in orbit that runs cargo across the border. I have them on retainer. They can get you to Bajor in a few days."

"I'd appreciate that." Bashir threw off the day robe and found a jacket. All signs of his infirmity, his reticence to move or speak, they were gone as if they had never been. "I'll beam up immediately," he added. "Can you make the arrangements?"

"I will do so, if that is what you wish." Garak was unsure of his friend's sudden shift in character, but he did not try to change his mind. Still, he was concerned. "Are you sure you are well enough to travel? Perhaps you should take a few days—"

"No." Bashir's reply was firm and unequivocal. "I can't stay here." Then he showed a brief, brittle half smile. "Garak . . . you're a good friend. Watching over me all this time . . . You brought me back, I want you to know that. After what happened with Uraei, for the longest time I felt like I was adrift in a black ocean. I had no constant except for your voice. I want you to know, it meant a great deal to me."

"That is . . . what friends do." The words felt awkward, but truthful. Fully and completely truthful. *How refreshing*, thought the Cardassian.

Bashir moved with a renewed purpose, a fiery determination that Garak had rarely seen in the doctor, and he immediately surmised the root of it. He'd seen the same before, in the eyes of soldiers and warriors, in his own reflection. The driving need to avenge the death of someone beloved.

Garak tapped out a string of commands on his wrist-comm, and presently the freighter signaled they were ready to take on their passenger. Bashir gave him a last nod of farewell, and then the human was gone in a swirl of light and color.

It was only when he was alone in the room that Garak realized his friend had left his personal effects behind—clothes, books, and Kukalaka among them.

Garak spoke his thoughts to the air and the hidden sensors. "One might wonder what else he is leaving behind."

6

—◆—

Château Picard, La Barre, Earth

The transporter deposited Geordi La Forge in the warm evening air at the end of the long driveway, and his optical implants automatically adjusted to the lower light level from the daytime he had just departed. The rich smell of tilled earth reached La Forge as he made his way toward the main house, and he looked over the lines of vines extending away across the property. The blocky shapes of robotic tenders floated over the plants on antigravs, occasionally dusting them with puffs of pesticide or scanning the growths with fans of light.

It was tranquil out here. *I can see why the captain's family would want to live in this place,* thought La Forge. *Except for the mechanical gardeners, it can't have changed much in hundreds of years.*

The Picard vineyard was literally and figuratively light-years away from the concerns that had been dogging the engineer since the mission into the grim future spurred by the pursuit of the Devidians. Like everyone else who had been part of the *Aventine*'s flight, La Forge was still struggling to process what he had witnessed. Part of him wanted to be back on the *Enterprise*, searching for a way to combat the alien threat, and another part wanted to leave it behind and never look back. It didn't help that he had been ordered to discuss nothing of the mission's tragic events, not even with his crewmates who had shared the experience.

He couldn't escape the sense that maybe they had bitten off more than they could chew. The *Enterprise* crew were no strangers to incredible challenges, and their reputation as Starfleet's best was fully deserved. But eventually, everyone met their match, and La Forge was afraid this crisis with the Devidians might be theirs.

He approached the door, and pushed those thoughts away. As odd as it had first seemed when Captain Picard sent him a dinner invite out of the blue, La Forge didn't realize how much he wanted to do something normal and ordinary until he was changing into civilian clothes. *A meal with friends,* he thought. *Right now we could all do with something like this.*

The door opened as he reached up to the brass knocker and Beverly Crusher stood on the threshold, delight written across her features. "Geordi! You're here! That's wonderful! Come in, come in." She beckoned him inside.

"This place is lovely," he noted.

"It really is," agreed Crusher. "Jean-Luc's sister-in-law, Marie, has kindly turned it over to us for a few days while she's in Paris."

"Well, thanks again for the invitation." La Forge offered her the bunch of flowers he was carrying under one arm. "These are for you."

"Oh, how nice." She gave the blooms a delicate sniff. "Algolian tulips!"

"I was going to bring a bottle of wine," he admitted, "but, well . . ." La Forge made a gesture that took in the whole of the property, vineyards and all. "I figured that'd be a little redundant."

She grinned. "I'll go find a vase for these. Jean-Luc's busy at the stove. Go say hello."

"Sure thing, Doctor."

"*Beverly,*" she corrected. "We are very much off-duty tonight."

He wondered what she meant by that. La Forge wandered into the rustic farmhouse kitchen, assailed by a riot of mouthwatering aromas. "Something smells good."

"I'm making my signature dish, *Cassoulet à la Picard,*" said the captain as he worked at some slices of meat. "Well, it's just regular cassoulet, you understand, but with a little more wine in it than usual." He shook the engineer's hand. "Thank you for coming, Geordi."

"Am I the first to arrive?"

"No, no. Doctors Tropp and Hegol are in the lounge playing

a spirited game of kella. Wesley and René are around." Picard pointed at a small pan of sauce and handed him a wooden spoon. "Here, stir this gently for me, would you?"

La Forge did as he was ordered. "Worf sends his regrets," he noted. "Something about some unfinished work needing to be done."

"Hmm." Picard frowned at that. "Never mind. We can speak to him later."

"Is anyone else coming along? Guinan? The Riker-Trois?"

"No." Picard took back the sauce, giving him a nod of approval. "I'm not sure of Guinan's whereabouts, and . . . I didn't extend an invitation to the admiral or his family." He went back to the stove.

"Oh." La Forge sensed he'd touched a nerve. Earlier in the day, the engineer had overheard two departing crewmen repeating a rumor that Picard's meeting with the Admiralty had gone poorly, but paid it no mind. Now he wondered if there was some truth in the scuttlebutt.

"I hope you'll forgive me," said Picard, turning from the cooking to pour him a drink. "Tonight's not just dinner. It's much more than that."

"I had an inkling," La Forge admitted. "That's why we're gathering here, right? Where we can talk . . . freely?"

"Yes. If you're willing?"

He knew immediately what Picard was really asking him. "Absolutely, Captain."

"No ranks tonight," said Picard. "Just some friends having a conversation."

"Sounds good." La Forge glanced at the food in the pots. "I wasn't kidding about how that smells, and I haven't eaten anything since a ration bar for lunch."

Picard broke into a chuckle and patted him on the shoulder.

Wesley ghosted down the corridor, picking out the places where the wooden floorboards might creak loudly beneath his feet, and moving to avoid them. The voices of his mother and her friends from the *Enterprise*'s medical division were a gentle mutter of warm tones reaching up from below, but here on the château's second floor the half silence was heavy and solemn.

He hesitated at the door to René's bedroom, caught between wanting to check in on his sibling and respecting his personal space. The door was slightly open, and a flicker of soft blue light danced around the edges as dots of color moved back and forth. Wesley listened intently for the sound of his brother breathing, but what he heard next was the cracked, breaking voice of an immature teenager.

"I know you're out there," said René. "You can come in if you want."

"Good ears," said Wesley, opening the door wider.

"*Oui.*" René sat on the small bed in the corner of the room, and he looked like a trapped animal, his back against the wall. Outwardly resembling a young adult in his late teens, his face was fixed in an altogether more childish expression of sullenness. Anxiety radiated off him.

In his hands he held the source of the odd light—a toy planetarium projector throwing out holograms of planets and constellations as seen in the night sky. The device seemed to be malfunctioning, the images randomly blinking in and out.

"I broke something else," René said sadly. His face was puffy, as if he had been crying. "I keep breaking things."

"Let me take a look." Wesley sat cross-legged on the floor and held out his hand. René reluctantly turned over the device and allowed him to examine it. Immediately, Wesley saw the problem. "Oh, this is no big deal. You popped out the emitter head, here. See?" He held it up to show René where the component had become dislodged. "I can fix this in a second." Wesley kept talking as he worked. "These things are pretty simple, they're just made for . . ." He caught himself before he finished.

"Made for little kids," said René, his voice rising. "But I'm not little anymore. *I hate it!*" He said the last words with real fire, and Wesley put the toy aside.

"I bet you do." He sighed, wishing he could ease his brother's torment. "When you're young, all you want to be is older, but then when you're older you wish you were young again."

"I don't want to be *this*." René prodded his chest. "Everything is small! I keep banging my head and stubbing my feet on things. I can't touch anything because I break it!" His eyes swam with tears. "That monster on the ship hurt me and now I'm stuck like this, and it's not fair!"

"No, it's not." Wesley inched forward. The boy had aged years in seconds, but without the time to grow into and adjust to the changes of his body. With such a void in his life, it was no surprise that he felt like an alien in his own skin. "I'm sorry, Racer." He called him by the nickname, hoping to ease him out of his sorrow. Years before, Wesley had christened the younger boy *Racer René* after seeing him run around the farm like a speeder at full tilt, and it had stuck.

"I can't race now. I'm too scared." René shook his head, then he met Wesley's gaze with a plaintive expression on his face. "Can you help me, Wes? Mom says you can do clever things. Can you change me back?"

From the start, Wesley had known this question was coming, and he didn't have a good response. "It's not that easy, René."

After he had left Starfleet and struck out on his own, Wesley had fallen in with a race of advanced beings who called themselves the Travelers. Under the tutelage of one of their kind, he had learned a great deal about the nature of the universe, and the complex unity of time, space, matter, and thought. His insights granted him preternatural abilities that even now he was still learning to control, but turning back the clock by force of will wasn't one of them.

How can I tell him that altering the time stream isn't like reversing a holoprogram? Wesley sighed, searching for some way to ease René's trauma. At length, he reached up and took his brother's hand. "I can't make things like they were," he admitted. "But there is something I could give you, if you want it."

"What do you mean?"

"You grew up too fast, too soon, because of what happened on the *Enterprise*, right?" He paused, framing his words so that René's younger mind would be able to grasp what he was offering. "Every time we make a choice, there's a different version of us that goes another way. And I've seen some of them, René. Different versions of you that got to grow up slowly." He tapped his head. "It's hard to describe, but I can . . . remember them."

"O . . . kay." René's brow furrowed. Explaining quantum theory and parallel timelines to a child wasn't an easy task, but the boy seemed to grasp the notion.

Wesley's Traveler-influenced insight granted him the ability to perceive alternate temporal states. Under the right circumstances, he might be able to share that with someone whose genetic structure was close to his. *A half brother, perhaps.*

"Do you want to see them? The other Renés? They could help you understand how you've changed."

"I want to go back to how I was," said the youth, and for the first time his voice held a note of maturity. "But I can't do that. So I have to do the best I can." René nodded. "Yes, please, Wes. I'd like to see them."

"Close your eyes." René did as Wesley told him to, and they brought their heads together until they touched. "This will feel a little weird."

"It already does," came the reply.

"You got that right." Despite himself, Wesley smiled. "Here we go."

He reached into the depths of his thoughts, finding the places where the skeins of past, present, and future interlinked, seeking out the lines of life of not just *this* René Picard, but those of others in countless shadow existences, each one removed from this reality by a twist of fate, or a decision made.

Wesley sensed them in their parallel existences, iteration after iteration of his sibling, living their lives, growing and maturing.

Come and see, he said, projecting the words into René's mind, guiding his young charge's consciousness alongside him. *See what you can be, little brother.*

And for the first time, the directionless fear inside René Picard eased.

"Oh, let me help." Tropp took some of the plates from Picard's hands and carried them into the dining room, deftly arranging the place settings around the big wooden table that dominated the space.

"Thank you," Picard replied, throwing the Denobulan a grateful nod. "Dinner's almost ready." He turned toward Hegol Den and Geordi La Forge, who were already wandering in from the lounge. "Could someone call the boys?" He hesitated to think of Beverly's adult son Wesley as "a boy" anymore, but it was a hard habit to break, calling back to when the younger Crusher had been an enthusiastic child peeking out of the turbolift onto Picard's bridge.

"I'll get them," said Hegol with a nod. The Bajoran handed La Forge his wineglass and made for the stairs, but as he passed the window he saw something outside that slowed him to a halt.

Picard saw the shift in Hegol's expression and didn't like what it portended. "Is something wrong?"

"Someone is there," said the Bajoran. "A human. I don't know him, but he's wearing a Starfleet uniform."

The brittle, hopeful mood inside the house seemed to freeze solid around them. Picard stepped up to take a look for himself and spotted the figure.

Out in front of the farmhouse, caught in the amber glow from the windows, Commander Tom Paris stood alone, taking in the building as if he were trying to figure out a way inside.

Picard's eyes narrowed, and he passed the silverware in his hands to Hegol before moving toward the door. "I'll deal with this. Everyone else, carry on."

He stepped out into the welcoming night, in time to see Paris slipping a tricorder into a back pocket beneath his tunic.

"Captain." Paris gave a respectful nod and shifted his weight nervously. "I'm sorry if I'm intruding—"

Picard didn't give him time to finish. "What are you doing, loitering on my family's property?" He switched to the unforgiving tone he used on officers whose performance disappointed him. "I don't recall sending an invitation to Admiral Akaar's office."

"Very true," Paris admitted. "It's just, uh, that . . . Well, given everything that has happened recently, and the orders from Command . . ."

"I know the orders," Picard snapped. "I was in the room when they were given. None of that explains what *you* are doing *here*."

"I've always loved France," said the other man as he fumbled for an explanation. "I mean, with a name like mine, how could I not? But admittedly, Marseille is more my speed—"

Again, Picard cut him off in midflow. "Do I need to call the gendarmes?"

Paris spread his hands. "I think that would be a bad idea."

"Indeed. Because then it would become a matter of public record that Starfleet Security has you spying on me!" He folded his arms across his chest, allowing his annoyance to come to the fore.

"It'd be a bad idea for us *both*," Paris corrected. "Because it would also raise suspicions about your recent activities, sir. And I don't think you want people looking too closely at who you have been talking to in the last day or so."

Despite the temperate evening, a chill ran down the captain's spine. Was it possible that Akaar's aide had already surmised what Picard and his wife had set into motion? "That sounds very much like a threat, Mister Paris." His manner hardened. "I think very highly of Kathryn Janeway, so it is only out of respect for your former commander that I haven't already set a terrier on you."

"Y-you have a dog?" Paris glanced around nervously.

"I'd like you to leave," said Picard, ignoring the question. "*Now.*"

"Captain, no . . ." Paris blew out an exasperated breath. "Great work, Tom," he muttered to himself. "Sir, I've done this all wrong. Please let me explain." Picard maintained a stony silence, and Paris struggled on. "I know what you have been doing. Who you have been talking to. *I know.* Not Admiral Akaar, or Batanides, Idyn, or anyone else. Just me . . . Well, and I told my wife, B'Elanna. But I haven't reported my findings up the chain of command, despite orders to the contrary."

"And why would you withhold that information?"

The younger man's face clouded, and Picard had the sense that he was recalling the memory of a past ordeal. "Out in the Delta Quadrant, on *Voyager*, we experienced some of the worst effects of temporal manipulations. Whole parts of our lives, lost and forgotten. The past and the future colliding, and the damage it caused . . ." He shook off the thought. "I know better than a lot of people how messing with time can have terrible consequences. Sir, I saw the *Aventine* reports. I believe everything you said about the threat the Devidians pose."

"And?" Picard prompted, measuring the younger man's sincerity.

"And I'm just as frustrated as you that the Federation Council has turned this into a matter for debate." He took a step closer, producing his tricorder. "This is generating a masking field. Sensors can't read us or record this conversation. I came here tonight to talk to you, Captain, off the record. To tell you that B'Elanna and I . . . we want to help."

Picard searched Paris's eyes for any hint of mendacity, and he found none. In the silence that followed, he weighed his instincts toward the younger officer.

Was this some ploy to entrap him? Could Picard trust a man he barely knew?

Janeway trusts him, he thought, *and she is not one to suffer fools gladly*. In truth, if Admiral Janeway hadn't been somewhere out in the extragalactic void, Picard might have had her along as one of tonight's dinner guests.

"Do you understand the implications of your statement, Commander Paris?" He gave the other man a firm stare. "You would be going against a direct order."

"It wouldn't be the first time, sir. Not by a long way." Paris shook his head, and Picard heard his own words echoed back to him. "I can't just stand by and do nothing."

Someone in Paris's position would be a great asset, considered the captain. *There's still so many moving parts to this. More allies would be very useful.*

Paris spoke again, interpreting Picard's silence as a dismissal. "Well. I've said what I had to say. I apologize for interrupting your evening."

As he turned to walk away, Picard called after him. "Mister Paris. Are you hungry?"

Paris halted, uncertain of what would come next. "I could eat, sure."

"Follow me," said Picard, making his choice. "We'll set an extra place for you."

After dinner, the conversation went on long into the night.

It was a strange gathering, by turns a warm and welcoming meeting of friends and then eventually a serious matter of plans for an uncertain future. Tom Paris left first, missing the dessert course in his haste to return to San Francisco, later followed by Tropp and Hegol, who departed for their shore leave billets, as had most of the *Enterprise*'s crew.

The captain and his wife offered La Forge a bed in one of the spare rooms and he accepted it gratefully, but sleep didn't come easily to the engineer.

Unsettled, he tossed and turned. The somber matter of the

conversation over the dinner table dogged him, making it hard to switch off and drift away.

Sometime before dawn, as a pink glow gathered at the horizon, La Forge surrendered to the fact he wasn't going to sleep, and picked his way down the stairs to the kitchen for a drink of water. A flicker of light out in the yard caught his eye and he saw Wesley sitting on a wooden crate by a nearby outbuilding. Doctor Crusher's son was manipulating an orb of holographic light, pulling and pushing at elements of the display with his fingers, frowning at what he saw.

La Forge recognized the holo; it was the interface for the device Wesley called the Omnichron, the complex gadget his elderly future self had left behind for him. Intrigued, La Forge ventured out and approached.

"Couldn't sleep?" Wesley shot him a look as he came over. "Me, neither."

"You think it would come easy, it's so quiet here." La Forge looked around, taking in the silence. "Sometimes I forget what it's like not to hear the sound of warp engines all the time."

Wesley nodded. "It is lovely. This house, these fields . . . I can see why my mom likes it."

La Forge detected a note of sadness in that. "But it's not for you, is it?"

The other man looked up at him. "And it's not for you either, right?"

"No." La Forge had to admit, he had him there. "Nice place to visit, but I wouldn't want to live here."

"You and I have too much wanderlust." Wesley looked back at the hologram sphere. "Too many worlds out there for us to see."

La Forge chuckled. "You're a mind reader now?"

"Nope, but like knows like." He nodded at another crate. "Pull up a chair."

La Forge sat and studied the multifarious structure of the three-dimensional screen. "Temporal-stream interactions," he said, guessing at the patterns on the display. As well as the information presented in the visual spectrum, his optical implants could also read levels of additional complexity existing at the far ends of the infrared and ultraviolet spectra. "There's so much layered in there, how can you parse it all?"

"That's just it," said Wesley with a sigh. "I can't. It's beyond me."

"But you made that thing." La Forge gestured at the open Omnichron in his hand, from which the display emerged.

"A version of me made it," Wesley corrected. "I'm not him. He was a lot older than I am, and clearly a lot more experienced." He shook his head. "I mean, you'd think if my future self was going to leave me a message, he'd at least make it easy for me to read it . . ."

"He was protecting it," offered La Forge. The engineer had been the first to closely examine the Omnichron after Wesley's elder self had died aboard the *Enterprise*, and it had been La Forge's tinkering with the device that summoned the present incarnation of Wesley. "I mean, we have no idea how long he was fighting the Devidians."

"What was he . . . ? What was *I* thinking . . . ?" Wesley said quietly. "There's so much here I don't understand. If only I could have spoken to him."

"Aren't there rules against meeting your past self?" La Forge shook his head, pondering the thought. "A Temporal Prime Directive?"

"They're actually more like guidelines. Time is more malleable than you might think. That's what the Devidians have figured out, and they're using it to their advantage."

"So we're stuck playing catch-up," La Forge replied. "How do we gain the upper hand?"

Wesley closed up the Omnichron, and the holo-sphere popped like a soap bubble, disintegrating into nothing. "We can't do it alone. We need someone smarter than we are. I mean, *way smarter*."

That description fit one mutual acquaintance of theirs. "Data. But I have no idea where he is."

Wesley nodded. "Same here. I haven't seen or spoken to him since that incident with the Machine three years ago."

"Happy to put that behind me," noted La Forge. At the time, the colossally destructive AI known as the Machine had seemed like the most existential hazard they had ever faced, but that galactic-scale menace paled in comparison to the Devidian threat to an entire multiverse of timelines.

"I'm guessing Data gave you the means to contact him," continued Wesley.

La Forge nodded. "A quantum transceiver. But Data left to follow his own path, and I promised myself I would respect that." He paused, adding, "He's not the person he used to be. He has different priorities now."

"I get that," said Wesley. "Data's my friend too, and after all he's been through, he deserves his peace." Then he gestured with the Omnichron. "But if we fail in what we're doing, there'll be no peace for anyone, anywhere or anywhen."

A rueful smile crossed La Forge's face. "Let's be honest, if we left him out of what might be the greatest scientific challenge in living history, he'd be pretty pissed off."

Wesley returned the smile. "If I know Data, he's probably already got a working theory. Plus, the Devidians cut his head off back in the nineteenth century, right? He might appreciate an opportunity to even the score."

La Forge nodded, sobering again. "I'll send the message. But I can't guarantee he'll respond."

"Then we'll just have to go find him," said Wesley.

U.S.S. *Aventine* NCC-82602

"Captain?" Sam Bowers heard the voice at the edge of his hearing, but for a moment he didn't register it was directed at him. "Captain Bowers, sir?"

He blinked and glanced up from the padd in his hand, finding

Lieutenant Mirren standing over him with a concerned look on her face. The operations officer was clutching a padd in both hands.

"I'm sorry, Oliana. I was light-years away."

Bowers had lost himself in the mountain of virtual paperwork that came from standing down the *Aventine*. And signing off on shore leave for the crew, not to mention the seemingly endless streams of reports, engineering schedules, refit cycles, and repairs for the damage inflicted on their last mission. *Aventine* was also overdue for her regular baryon sweep, and he made a mental note to add that to his already lengthy to-do list.

Along with a couple of off-duty ensigns from Chief Engineer Leishman's team, he and Mirren were the only people in the ship's main mess hall, and the room seemed unusually quiet. Crew rotations off the vessel were already well under way, giving the *Aventine* the echoing quality of a half-empty house—a sad impression that only further underlined the sorrow that stalked the ship's corridors after the death of Captain Dax.

Sam still wasn't used to the crew calling him by Ezri's rank. It just didn't seem right. And he hadn't even begun to think about selecting an executive officer, after his brevet promotion to the center seat.

"I thought you'd be in the ready room," said Mirren. She gestured with the padd. "This communique just came in for you, sir."

Bowers didn't want to admit that he felt uncomfortable surrounded by Dax's possessions, which is why he was down here. He had yet to clear the room of her personal effects. He could order a subordinate to handle the task, but that felt wrong. Soon he would have to box up the last pieces of Ezri Dax's presence on the ship, and then she really would be gone.

He put the thought aside and held out his hand. "What do you have for me, Lieutenant?"

Mirren frowned as she gave him the padd. "Not typical comms protocol, sir. Usually a message with this sort of priority header is either holographic or audio-visual. But this is text only."

"Oh?" Bowers scrutinized the words on the screen as a built-in sensor read his thumbprint and verified his identity.

A line of writing scrolled across the screen, halting there for a moment before it vanished. *Captain Bowers,* it read, *please forgive the subterfuge. This message is not from Starfleet Command. My name is Beverly Crusher; my husband speaks very highly of you.*

"Okay . . ." Bowers considered the message. At the very least, Captain Picard's wife was violating several fleet protocols by using a priority channel in this manner. He could tell by the signal header that the communication was being deleted from ship's logs nanoseconds after it was sent.

"Is something wrong, sir?" said Mirren.

Bowers shook his head. "Everything's fine, Lieutenant. You're dismissed."

"Aye, Captain." Mirren raised a questioning eyebrow, but said nothing, leaving him alone once more.

Bowers considered Crusher's message for a long moment. By rights, he should have ended the conversation immediately. Instead, he typed back a reply, and once he began, thoughts he'd been keeping to himself poured out.

I appreciate that. I heard what happened at Command. We are all very disappointed by the president's decision.

The padd chimed and a reply appeared, then disappeared. *Jean-Luc believed you would feel that way. Many share the same sentiment. Inaction is the worst course to be following right now. Do you agree?*

"Absolutely," Bowers said quietly, and tapped out the word in reply. Dax and the other members of the *Aventine* family who had perished were gone, and doing nothing to deal with the predators that had taken them was, in his mind, unconscionable. Bowers filed a formal protest with Admiral Akaar's office after the gagging order came down from on high, but no response had been forthcoming.

He thought hard about the next words, and then continued to type. *Please make it clear to Captain Picard that he has the full support of the* Aventine'*s command crew in*

Bowers paused, searching for the right way to phrase it, then made the choice he believed that Ezri Dax would have.

any options he might wish to pursue.

Château Picard, La Barre, Earth

"Whatever you need, we are here." The synthetic voice issued out of the console in his father's study, converting Captain Bowers's replies from text to rendered speech.

René had heard the careful mechanical tones from the floor above, and padded quietly down to the landing to listen more closely, his overwhelming curiosity drawing him in.

Last night, he had lain silently in his room after being sent to bed, straining to hear the conversation of the adults as it went on into the small hours. He knew what they were discussing was very important, that it was connected to the monsters that had attacked the *Enterprise* and hurt him and his parents' friends.

After Wesley had helped him banish some of the fear swirling around him, his young boy's mind had gone from being afraid to questioning everything. If he was bigger now, then he would have to act like it. That meant he had a duty to help, if he could, and to follow the example set by his parents.

Papa had already left a while ago with his friend Geordi, but Wesley and Mom were busy sending messages to people, and René listened intently.

"He's with us," said Wesley. From his angle peering through the banisters, René could see his brother standing against the far wall of the study with his arms folded across his chest. "I figured he would be. Dax was loved by her crew. They want to know her death meant something."

"Still," said his mother. "If he agrees to what we need, Sam Bowers may have one of the shortest captaincies in Starfleet history."

"Bowers is a good man," Wesley went on. "He knows exactly what is at stake."

"All right then," she said. "Computer, dictate, encrypt, and transmit the following: Captain, would you be willing to make one of the *Aventine*'s shuttlecraft available to us for a few hours?"

René listened and heard nothing. *A shuttlecraft?* His mind raced at the possibilities that represented.

Then the console pinged and the synthetic voice replied. *"Tell me where and when you want it. I'll keep it off the logs, if you can promise to bring it back in one piece."*

Wesley clapped his hands together and grinned. "We're in business, Mom. We might actually pull this off."

"I know you know the odds of success," said René's mother, after sending landing coordinates and a final thank-you to Bowers, "but don't tell me. Let's just carry on."

René watched Wesley reach out and take his mother's hand. "We're going to do this." He stopped, and glanced up in René's direction, a questioning look in his eyes. René shrank back before Wesley could see him, and he heard his brother's last words before he vanished back into his bedroom. "For all our sakes."

U.S.S. *Enterprise* NCC-1701-E

Worf's thunderous bellow sounded off the crumbling stone pillars of the fighting arena as he kicked away from the low wall and used the boost to swing up and down on his foe.

The hulking Nausicaan male tried to parry with the short swords in his fists, but he was too slow. The leading fangs of Worf's *bat'leth* buried themselves in the Nausicaan's sternum and the alien warrior fell, fatally wounded.

Worf wrenched the weapon out of his enemy's chest and kept up the pace, rushing a skull-headed Rotelek as the barrel-chested being stomped up to take its fallen comrade's place. It spun a barbed, whistling mace on a heavy shaft, the head dense enough to shatter even Klingon bone.

Worf ducked low, his blood singing in his ears, and cut across the alien's legs, severing ligaments and slashing through muscle. The Rotelek hooted in pain and its momentum carried it forward to crash against the flagstones.

The third and final attacker—a Suliban woman wielding a spiked chain—traded bulk for speed and made Worf work far harder than he had dispatching the other two. Jagged blades slashed at his training tunic, drawing blood as the lithe female danced out of the reach of the *bat'leth*. He turned the weapon to a guard position, deflecting the humming chain as it lashed through the air, and waited for his moment.

It came when the chain snagged on the tip of the *bat'leth*, and Worf pulled with all his might. The Suliban was jerked forward, skidding off-balance, and the Klingon grabbed a fistful of the metal links. Ignoring the pain as it slashed his palm, Worf whipped back the chain along its length and his final attacker was struck across the head. She went down and fell still.

Breathing hard, Worf drew himself up and tilted his head back to release a snarl of triumph. Around him, the bodies of his defeated foes shimmered and dissipated, reclaimed by the holographic emitters hidden in the simulated environment.

"Arch!" he barked, summoning the control panel for the holodeck. A section of the *Enterprise* revealed itself off to the far side of the ruined amphitheater, and he stalked toward it.

Worf had been in here for several hours now. It was a benefit of the ship's crew being on leave that no one had booked any of the holodecks, but he was yet to be satisfied with his performance. Each run of his calisthenics program had increased the difficulty setting of the opponents, pushing him to fight harder, but it still felt *wrong*.

Laying his *bat'leth* on a broken pillar, he went to the arch and jabbed at its readout, looking at the analytics of his performance—attack posture, effort ratio, time to injury, and more. He was not pleased. He was, to use a human aphorism, *off his game*.

Worf had not rested well in some time. Sleep was troubled by fitful, half-recalled dreams that forced him awake in the dead of ship's night. He could not escape the morose, directionless temper that gathered around him whenever he was at rest. It was what had driven him to contact his son unbidden, and dissuaded him from accepting Captain Picard's offer to eat with his family. Worf felt compelled to keep moving, to keep fighting, as if that were the only way to stay one step ahead of the shadows at his heels.

Shadows. The word ran a chill across his flesh. He scowled and drew himself up, preparing to reinitiate the program. This time he would double the number of attackers and increase the difficulty level another twenty percent.

From the corner of his eye, Worf saw movement on the far side of the arena, in the gloom where the simulated sunlight did not fall. He turned and saw a male figure, made unrecognizable by distance. Trying to focus on it was hard, and he felt a piercing pain in his temple. He blinked, then looked back at the arch. "Computer, identify that holo-character."

"No characters are currently active in this program," came the reply.

"There!" Worf jabbed a finger at the figure in the shade, but when he looked back, it was gone. The chill on his flesh returned, deepening.

Worf strode back to his *bat'leth* and pulled it close with one hand. He walked slowly into the middle of the arena, casting around.

"Show yourself!"

Worf had barely spoken the words when he sensed a presence behind him. He spun on his heel and came face-to-face with a hazy, ghostlike form. He had only the vaguest impression of a face, of dark angry eyes, and a heavily ridged forehead.

A Klingon.

The shadow flew at him, and he saw the glitter of an unsheathed *d'k tagh* knife in its fist, its secondary blades snapping open. Worf parried automatically with his *bat'leth*, but the weapon cut only air. As swiftly as it had appeared, the shadow was gone.

He whirled around, his ingrained battle sense rising. A second, a third, fourth, and fifth form came toward him, projecting silent rage with every step they took. The shadows were identical, and through the mist wreathing their faces, Worf saw furious eyes glaring back at him.

Recognition hit like an electric shock. Those were *his* eyes. These were shadows of Worf's own nature.

An emotion he rarely knew coiled inside the Klingon's heart: *fear*.

He translated that into wild rage, striking out with the curved blade, cutting down the shades with violent slashing motions. But for every ghost-self Worf dispatched, more formed around him.

The waking nightmare closed in on him from every side. The silent shadows advanced as one, reaching out with daggers in their hands.

"*No!*" Worf roared the denial with every fiber of his being, bringing down the *bat'leth* in a powerful killing blow.

At the last second, the fall of the blade was arrested and the warrior found himself holding the weapon at the throat of another Klingon in dark robes and an ornamental sash. The shadows were nowhere to be seen, and bare-handed, the other man held the wicked blade at bay.

"Father?" The hood atop the robes slipped back and Worf looked into the face of his son.

"Alexander?" He shook his head. "No, it cannot be! You are not real!"

"I am, I assure you," his son shot back, blood oozing around his fingers where he gripped the tines of the blade. "And I wish to remain so!"

Worf withdrew, taking a step back as the fog that shrouded his thoughts dissipated.

Alexander tore off a strip of cloth to bind the cuts on his hands. "The error is mine. *Enterprise*'s computer told me I would find you here; I came directly from the transporter room."

"You . . . came to Earth?"

"To see you!" Alexander replied. "But when I entered the holodeck, you were fighting something I could not see. I called out and you did not acknowledge me."

"I . . . saw shadows . . ." Worf took a deep breath and forced himself to focus, shifting tack. "Why are you here?"

Alexander seemed dismayed by the question. "The message you sent to Qo'noS, it set me ill at ease. I could not ignore my misgivings." He reached out and placed a hand on his father's arm. "I needed to see you in the flesh. And with good cause, it seems."

Worf bristled at the inference in his son's words, and he slipped back into old, brusque patterns. "I appreciate your intention. But if your only reason for traveling across the quadrant was to consider my well-being, it was a pointless endeavor. You need have no concern."

Alexander gave a bitter, humorless laugh. "So he says after almost opening my throat." He shook his head. "Father, there is no shame to admit that Dax's death has affected you deeply." He sighed, and Worf saw his mother in him. "I grieve with you. We will honor Ezri and Jadzia together."

Worf grimaced, unable to assemble his thoughts into coherence. *It is not just Dax's death that plagues me. There is darkness and despair. But I cannot submit to it. There is too much at stake!*

He tried to find a way to explain, becoming more frustrated as words failed him; and then the moment broke as a bosun's whistle sounded from the holodeck's arch.

Worf pushed past Alexander and tapped the intercom. "What is it?"

"Incoming message," said the ship's computer. *"Priority alpha."*

"Father . . . ?"

Worf ignored his son. "Display message."

A new figure appeared on the holodeck, shimmering into life, out of place among the ruined stonework. *"Hello, Worf,"* said Beverly Crusher. *"I'd like to speak with you. It's about something Jean-Luc and I have been discussing."*

The tangled emotions of the past hours vanished in a rush and Worf drew himself up. *Duty solves everything,* he thought. *Duty gives clarity and purpose.*

"I suspect I already know what you want of me," he said, cutting straight to the heart of things. Worf glanced back at his son, who stood silently watching him, and then away again. "You need not explain." As he said the words, he felt his doubts and fears ebbing away, at least for the moment.

"What would you have me do?"

7

U.S.S. *Titan* NCC-80102

Picard materialized on the *Titan*'s transporter pad in a humming flash of light, exchanging the openness of the outdoors with the brightly lit interior of the starship.

"Transport complete," said the lieutenant at the console.

"Thank you, Mister Radowski." The reply came from a tall, gangly Caitian, who fidgeted nervously from foot to foot. "Please encrypt the transit log."

"Permission to come aboard?" said Picard, adhering to the formalities.

"Granted, sir," said the felinoid, gesturing with a thin paw. "And welcome to the *Titan*. I am Lieutenant Ssura, Admiral Riker's aide. He's waiting for you in the operations center, if you would come with me?"

"Lead on." Picard allowed Ssura to guide him, and as the captain fell in step, he got the distinct impression that the lieutenant was taking him the long way around, through the *Titan*'s less-populated corridors. He'd expected to observe the usual traffic of junior officers busy at their duties, but he and Ssura were alone. "Quiet day," he remarked. "Is Captain Vale on board?"

"She is." Ssura nervously ran a paw through his black-and-white fur. "She sends her apologies that she couldn't meet your arrival, but the admiral . . . Well, he felt it best we keep your meeting here on a need-to-know basis."

"Oh?" That explained Ssura's order to the transporter operator, to encode the logs showing Picard's arrival. The captain frowned at the implication of that, and reflexively pulled at the cuff of his uniform.

Presently, Ssura brought him to the doors of the operations center and gestured for him to enter, hovering on the threshold. Inside, Picard found a curved room that looked out over *Titan*'s stern, the compartment lined with holographic projection tables and data feeds. Half office and half command nexus, it was from here that Will Riker usually managed his role as commander of the Alpha Quadrant frontier sector.

Riker rose from his desk to greet him as he approached. "Captain, thank you for coming." He shot a look at his aide. "That'll be all, Lieutenant."

Ssura bobbed his head and retreated, leaving the two men alone.

"Would you like something to drink?" Riker had already replicated two cups of Earl Grey and offered one to Picard.

"I didn't think you drank tea," he replied.

"I've developed a taste for it recently."

"Thank you, but no." Picard held up his hand, and started in as he meant to continue. "I appreciate you giving me the opportunity to discuss this situation in private. I'm concerned that other agendas are getting in the way of addressing this crisis."

"No small talk, then?" Riker smiled slightly. "Just straight to the matter at hand."

"I think it is warranted," Picard replied. "I don't exaggerate when I say this may be the most serious threat we have ever faced."

"You've made that very clear," said Riker. "And I agree."

"Good." Picard folded his arms across his chest. "Let me be completely honest, Will. I had hoped to see that support when we were addressing the president. But I couldn't help but feel like Wesley and I were alone out there, our voices going unheard."

"Every word you said was taken with the utmost seriousness," Riker said firmly. "Captain, there's a legion of people around the Federation right now, considering how to address the Devidian threat. You're not alone."

"*Considering* it," echoed Picard. "But not *acting* on it." He glanced out of the viewport. "Look there." He gestured outward, taking in the range of Spacedock's cavernous interior, where the *Titan* was currently moored. As well as the *Luna*-class ship, the *Enterprise* was berthed on the far side of the great chamber, as were a pair of *Steamrunner*-class frigates. "We're aboard one of the most advanced ships in the fleet. *Enterprise* is here, and so is the *Zephyr* and the *Enessi*. All currently awaiting orders. We could have an expeditionary fleet at Devidia II in a day. And you have the latitude to bring in science vessels, perhaps the *Quasar* or the *Aurora*. Will, we could be working against this danger instead of losing precious time—"

"I know you mean well, Jean-Luc," interrupted Riker, "but of all people, I shouldn't have to tell you to respect the chain of command. Things are in hand. You need to accept that."

Picard was silent for a moment, a little taken aback by the other man's words. "You want me to accept that delay is preferable to action? I can't! You weren't there, Will. You didn't see what we saw. It was utterly terrifying. A future of ashes and dead stars. If we don't do something, we'll be allowing it to happen!"

"I *do* understand," insisted Riker, looking away. "More than you know. But I also know where the course you're advocating could lead us." He nodded toward one of the screens, which showed a complex wavelike structure of overlapping timelines. "I've seen the report that Agent Garcia turned in to the DTI. I read her conclusions, based on the data from Wesley's device and the *Aventine*'s scans. She's not just talking about neutralizing the Devidian threat in this reality. She's suggesting radical alterations of our entire timeline. Full-scale temporal manipulation. You must know how dangerous that is! You and I saw it with our own eyes when the Borg Queen tried to prevent First Contact!"

"Yes," admitted Picard. A chill passed over him as he recalled looking down on a blackened, Borg-infested Earth born from a radical shift in timelines. "And for that reason, I would not endorse such a possibility unless there was absolutely no other way."

"Command believes in the strongest possible terms that any attempt to alter our timeline could be catastrophic. The Federation has treaties in place with every other galactic power forbidding the use of time travel. If we ignore them, what precedent does that set?"

"I'll argue the case to anyone willing to hear it," Picard replied. "The Romulans, the Klingons, the Typhon Pact, they're in as much danger as the rest of us. Don't you see, Will? This is not a Federation matter. It's not even a galactic one. It's beyond any notion of boundaries!"

"Jean-Luc . . ." Riker sat back against the viewport, and chose his words carefully. "I understand the stress you must be under, after what happened to René. I'm a father, and I know how I would react if it were my children . . ." He frowned and corrected himself. "My child. If it were Natasha."

Picard's jaw stiffened. "You know me better than that. My concern over my son's condition is in no way clouding my judgment, and I resent any implication otherwise."

"All right, let me put this another way." Riker walked across to one of the holo-tables and used it to bring up a three-dimensional star map, projecting a globe of space that took in the Alpha Quadrant and much of the Beta Quadrant as well. Dots of crimson appeared, scattered seemingly at random across the galactic plane. "These markers are sites where time-active artifacts, stellar anomalies, or temporally sensitive species are present." He tapped another control, and a series of indicator flags popped into existence, overlapping with several of the red dots. "These are the locations where the Naga incursions have taken place. There's a logical pattern to where they hit. They're extremely aggressive, and they are specifically targeting these sites. We can't just allow them to continue their attacks without mounting some kind of defense."

"I don't disagree with the sentiment," snapped Picard, "only the methodology."

Riker went on as if he hadn't spoken. "The DTI have drawn up a list of what they consider the most sensitive targets, and the fleet is mobilizing to fortify them." He nodded out at the Spacedock.

"In a few days, *Zephyr* will be on its way to the Cassandra Array, and *Enessi* will be guarding the Pharoid Chamber in the Takara system. Other ships will be taking up defensive positions across the quadrant. The Federation Council wants to see Starfleet doing all it can against this threat."

"Then let me take the *Enterprise* and pursue this myself," said Picard.

"You and your crew have been stood down," Riker replied. "The *Aventine*'s too. And for good reason. You said it yourself, you've been the closest to the effects of these creatures. We don't know what long-term consequences there might be for those exposed to them."

"That's a poor justification, Admiral." Picard put hard emphasis on the other man's rank. "And you know it as well as I do!"

Riker's eyes flared. "*This* is the immediate threat that must be dealt with," he insisted, jabbing a finger into the holographic map. "Not some possible timeline that may not even occur! As shocking as the future that *Aventine* visited might have been, it's only one of an infinity of potential events. The clear and present danger has to take priority. I'm sorry you fail to see that."

Picard felt a moment of helplessness as his argument rebounded off his former first officer's grim mien. "I won't pretend that I'm an expert in temporal mechanics, but I know what I saw. And if you had seen it too, you'd feel as I do. This isn't some predetermined destiny cast in stone, we have the free will and the capacity to change it. We have to prevent that future at all costs!"

"Even if it means sacrificing our present? Or worse, deleting our entire history from existence?" Riker shook his head, his voice rising. "You don't get to make a decision of that magnitude. No one person should!"

Searching for a reply, the captain was sobered by the realization that nothing he could say would change the admiral's mind. Will Riker had a stubborn streak, that was true, but in all the years they had been friends, Jean-Luc Picard had never known him to be so inflexible. It was out of character for the man, and Picard was concerned about what was driving him.

But Riker's intractability was not Picard's focus. If the admiral would not take his warnings to heart, then so be it. On the way to this meeting, the captain had considered the next decision he would make, and now it was clear he was already past the point of no return. Riker's words cemented Picard's choice.

Orders be damned, we must act before it is too late.

Riker's expression shifted, and he stepped away from the holo-map, moving toward his console. "I know what's going through your mind right now," he began. "I know exactly what kind of man you are. Don't make a choice we'll both regret."

Picard became very still. It was true, there were few men who knew his mind as well as Will Riker. Years of serving alongside each other aboard the *Enterprise* had forged an instinctive bond between them.

When he didn't reply, Riker went on. "Since your return to Earth, Starfleet Intelligence has been monitoring you, and the other members of the *Aventine* mission, in the interests of interstellar security." He sighed. "I know you're planning to go rogue. I'm aware of your wife's encrypted conversations with Captain Bowers and Commander Worf. Not to mention the suspicious behavior of a number of others."

"Assuming those things are true," said Picard, his tone giving nothing away, "what do you intend to do about it?"

The admiral answered by tapping an intercom on his desk. "Riker to bridge."

"Keru here, sir," came the reply.

"Send a security detail to the operations center, immediately." He closed the circuit before Keru could respond.

"That's not necessary," said Picard.

"I'm afraid it is," Riker went on. "As of now, your command is suspended, pending a full inquiry." He held out his hand. "Your communicator, please."

"If you insist," said Picard, frost forming on the words. He removed his insignia and dropped it into the other man's open palm.

"I want you to know I'm doing this with great regret, Captain," said Riker, "but you've left me no choice. Admiral Batanides provided details of a civilian transport you chartered for a voyage to the Tlaoli system . . . You were going to look for the time portal there." He shook his head. "Did you think we wouldn't find out?"

Tlaoli IV was a desolate world whose existence was known only to a few top-flight Starfleet officers. Hidden beneath its surface was one of the most powerful transtemporal devices in the galaxy, an ancient mechanism known as the Janus Gate.

"The transport's been impounded and its crew bound over," said Riker. "You planned to violate a standing order. What were you going to do once you got there? That planet remains a secret for good reason."

A chilly calm descended over Picard. "I admit, the Janus Gate was one option that I considered." Behind him, he heard the doors hiss open and glanced back, seeing a pair of security noncoms enter the room. "But it wasn't my only one." Making the gesture casual, he reached for the cuff of his sleeve. "I knew we were being watched. And I also knew there was a scenario where you could not be convinced to see my point of view. Therefore, it was necessary to lay a false trail."

"Wait . . ." Riker saw Picard touch the fascia of the second communicator band hidden at his wrist, and he lunged at the intercom pad, barking out an order. "Red alert, shields up!"

But the command came too late, as Picard vanished into the bright haze of a beam-out.

Location Concealed

The swirl of energy faded and the captain found himself in a Starfleet transporter room almost identical to the one he had arrived in aboard the *Titan*. For a heart-stopping moment, he was afraid that Riker's crew had been one step ahead of his subterfuge, and captured his dematerialization, diverting him back before he could escape.

But then he saw Wesley Crusher at the control console and Picard let out the breath he had been holding in.

"Welcome aboard, sir," said Wesley. "I guess your conversation didn't go to plan?"

"On the contrary," said Picard, stepping off the transporter. "It went exactly as I expected it to go. I had hoped I would be wrong."

Crusher checked a readout on the console. "We have to move, sir. If they track you—"

"This will be over before it begins," finished Picard. He tapped an intercom on the wall. "Picard to Worf."

"Worf here, Captain." The Klingon sounded more terse than usual. *"We are ready."*

"Have all mooring clamps disengaged, get us free and clear," he replied.

"Understood."

Picard closed the channel and sighed. "Never thought I'd be doing this again," he murmured.

"It's not like they gave us a choice," said Wesley. "We wouldn't make it past Mars in another ship. This is our only shot."

"Yes," Picard admitted reluctantly. "You're correct, of course. But right up until the last moment, I kept hoping that Will . . . that he would understand."

Wesley frowned. "The William Riker I remember would have been first in line to buck the regulations, but I suppose getting flag rank changes you. Like they said back at the Academy, 'the admirals see things differently.' "

Something *was* different about Riker, Picard reflected, that much was certain. But right now was not the time to dwell on it. As he put aside the thought and concentrated on the task ahead, a quote from a favorite book came to mind, and he spoke it aloud. *"Let us sacrifice one day to gain perhaps a whole life."*

"Victor Hugo," said Wesley, "*Les Misérables*, am I right? Does that make us Valjean?"

"We'll see," said the captain.

U.S.S. *Titan* NCC-80102

Christine Vale marched onto the *Titan*'s bridge from her ready room, a tense expression on her face as she glared at the alert indicators. "Will someone please tell me what is going on? We're supposed to be docked and locked." She flicked a gunmetal-colored thread of hair out of her eye line and waited for a response.

"Admiral Riker ordered the condition change," said Commander Sarai, rising from her post at the executive officer's station. "No explanation yet, Captain, but he called security to the ops center shortly before."

"Is that right?" Vale didn't like what Sarai's report suggested. Only a handful of the *Titan*'s crew had been informed that Jean-Luc Picard was coming aboard for a private meeting with Riker. Combined with a torrent of lower-decks rumors swirling around the ship about the *Aventine*'s recent mission, it triggered the captain's old peace-officer instincts, her suspicions deepened. Whatever was going on, Riker had not yet seen fit to bring her into the circle.

"There was an unscheduled outgoing transport at the instant the admiral's order came in," added Sarai as the bridge doors opened behind her. "The pattern was scrambled—"

"It was Captain Picard!" Riker stormed across the threshold, and he was furious. "I need you to track him!"

"Melora?" Vale turned to Lieutenant Commander Pazlar, at the ship's science station. "Can you assist?"

"Working," said the Elaysian woman, "but there's a diffusion field present. It's fogging my readings. Hard to locate the source of the beaming, but it's close by."

"He planned this from the start," Riker muttered. "We should have seen it coming . . ."

A second alert sounded from Ranul Keru's security console, adding to the chaos, and Vale turned toward the Trill. "Is one problem not enough?"

"I have an emergency message from Spacedock control," said the security officer, nodding toward the main viewer, where the dock interior extended away from the *Titan*. "They're ordering all vessels in port to go to red alert."

"Way ahead of that," Vale replied. "They say why?"

"Well, uh . . ." Keru blinked, as if he wasn't quite sure what he was reading. "Captain, someone is stealing the *Enterprise*."

Sarai raised an eyebrow, a very Vulcan expression on the Efrosian woman's pale olive face. "It would appear that somebody is a student of history."

Riker pushed past Vale's first officer toward the midbridge, glaring at the berth on the far side of Spacedock's interior. Despite the fact that most of the vessel was dark and inert, the *Sovereign*-class *Starship Enterprise* was moving slowly away from its moorings, the curved prow of its primary hull turning incrementally toward the open space doors.

"It's him," said Riker. "We have to stop Picard before he gets clear of the station. Cut us loose!"

Vale didn't take kindly to being given orders on her own bridge, but Riker had the rank and *Titan* was his flagship. She threw a nod to Aili Lavena and Sariel Rager, the officers at the ops and flight control stations. "Initiate emergency departure protocol."

"Aye, Captain." Lieutenant Commander Lavena executed the command and *Titan* rocked gently as docking arms withdrew from the ship. "Clear in thirty seconds."

"If they get through the doors and into open space, we'll lose them," noted Sarai.

Riker turned back toward Vale and her XO. "I'm authorizing the use of level-one prefix codes. Transmit to the *Enterprise* and override their helm."

Keru worked his console, and the lines of patterning down his face pulled tight as the Trill scowled. "No effect, Admiral. That diffusion field, it's coming from *Enterprise*. It's blocking subspace comms."

"*Titan* is floating free," reported Rager. "Ready to maneuver."

"Thrusters ahead full," ordered Vale. "Get us after them."

Titan's viewpoint shifted as the docking modules on either side of the ship fell away, but the movement felt agonizingly slow. *Enterprise* was much closer to the doors and already had a sizable lead.

"Helm, go to impulse power," said Riker. "Microburst acceleration. Put this ship ahead of them. We'll use *Titan* to block the doors if we have to!"

"Sir?" Lavena gave Riker a wary look, then turned to Vale for guidance.

As always, Dalit Sarai was the first to quote the rulebook. "Starfleet regulations expressly forbid the use of impulse engines while inside Spacedock, Admiral."

"I know the regs," Riker retorted.

"And we're sticking to them." Vale shook her head, cutting him off. "I'm not running the risk of crashing my ship into a bulkhead."

"Tractor beam, then!" said the admiral.

"We'll need to get closer," noted Sarai. "The diffusion field disrupts the beam at range."

Riker made an exasperated noise.

"They cannot be allowed to escape," he went on, a warning in his tone. "There's too much at stake."

What the hell does that *mean?* Despite herself, Vale felt a chill run through her at Riker's stern pronouncement.

"Captain, that diffusion field is interfering with everything," said Pazlar, glancing up from the science station. "I can't scan the interior of the *Enterprise*."

"No one should be aboard," Riker said to the air. "All the crew are on mandatory shore leave, I saw to that."

"Well, clearly someone is over there," said Sarai. "And if Captain Picard *is* taking out his ship without authorization . . ." She let the statement hang.

"That violates a lot of *other* regulations," noted Vale. She shot a look at Riker. "Admiral, is there anything you feel I should be aware of regarding this situation?"

But Riker didn't respond to her question, instead advancing on the *Titan*'s tactical station, where a patient, dark-skinned Vulcan stood silently observing. "Commander Tuvok," he began, "target the *Enterprise*'s primary maneuvering thrusters. Disable them."

Tuvok broke his silence. "With respect, sir, I do not believe that is a proportionate course of action."

"A low-power shot," insisted Riker. "Enough to blow out the thruster grids but not enough to penetrate the hull! I know your skills, Commander, I know you can do it."

"Sir, that contravenes safety guidelines—"

"I will take full responsibility," Riker spoke over Tuvok's misgivings.

The Vulcan gave a slight shake of the head. "Admiral, Spacedock control procedures render all weapons inert while inside the main bay. Even if I wished to, I could not discharge the phasers."

Riker leaned in and his voice dropped, so only Tuvok and Vale heard what he said next. "Are you helping him?"

"Sir?" Tuvok's stoic expression shifted fractionally, but Vale knew he was affronted by the comment.

"Aspect change on the *Enterprise*," called Pazlar. "Moving directly toward the space doors and accelerating."

Riker turned away. "If we can't chase them and can't fire on them . . ." He stopped suddenly, as if something had just occurred to him. "We lock them in." The admiral dropped into Vale's chair and spun one of the side monitors to face him, jabbing commands into the screen.

The captain let the breach of protocol pass, and folded her arms. "I'd appreciate knowing your intentions."

"Watch and learn," Riker retorted. "Computer, interface with Spacedock operations subnet. Override code Riker-Beta-Six."

"*Ready,*" said the synthetic voice.

"Initiate Kirk Contingency. Lock it down!"

The term wasn't one that Vale was familiar with, but she immediately inferred the meaning. In the mid-2280s, Starfleet's most iconoclastic captain, James T. Kirk, had famously hijacked his own vessel from this very facility, and in the aftermath, security procedures were improved to prevent such a thing from happening again—*just as it is now*, she reflected.

On Riker's order, the giant serrated doors around the entrance threshold activated, warning lights flashing as they slammed shut across the *Enterprise*'s escape path. A shimmering force wall flashed on, bolstering the barrier.

Short of blasting through Spacedock's superstructure, there was now no way out for the other starship.

The admiral rose from Vale's chair and returned to the mid-bridge, nodding to himself. "We have him now."

"Closing to optimal tractor beam range," said Sarai.

"Activate," ordered Vale. "They may try to crash the doors."

She watched the flickering rods of light extend out from the *Titan* and seize the *Enterprise*. A tremor ran through the decks as the *Luna*-class vessel took hold of the larger *Sovereign*-class ship.

"They've cut thrusters," reported Lavena. "Captain, I think they've given up."

"Don't count on it," said Riker.

"Diffusion field is fading," added Pazlar. "They're just sitting there."

Riker turned on the Elaysian. "Life signs?"

"A very faint reading, sir," she noted. "Middeck levels, concentrated on the *Enterprise*'s emergency bridge."

"I know exactly where that is." The admiral beckoned to Keru. "Lieutenant Commander, you're with me. Assemble a boarding party, we're going over there." Then Riker slowed, as if remembering that this was Vale's command, not his, and he glanced toward her. "If you concur, Captain?"

"Go ahead," she said, at length.

As Riker and Keru left the bridge, Sarai leaned in to speak quietly to her commander. "To refer back to your first question, Captain. I have no idea what is going on."

U.S.S. *Enterprise* NCC-1701-E

Keru's team materialized in the corridor outside the *Enterprise*'s emergency bridge, forming from out of the half darkness. The ship was in low-power mode, its internal lighting levels at minimum, so illumination came from the SIMs beacons on the security team's wrists.

"Clear left." Chief Dennisar, a muscular Orion carrying a compact phase-compression rifle, panned his weapon down the corridor and found nothing.

"Clear right." N'keytar, a thin and pale female of the Vok'sha species, held her phaser at the ready.

Keeping his own weapon holstered, Keru exchanged looks with his team. "This feels wrong."

"Agreed," said the Orion, but any further comment was drowned out by the sound of a second transport.

Admiral Riker and Lieutenant Sortollo phased into being, summoned by the all clear, and Keru noted that the flag officer was also armed. He didn't like the precedent that set.

Riker strode over to the door. "Sealed?"

"Looks that way," said Dennisar, tapping the controls.

"Force it open."

Keru gave Sortollo the nod and the young human set to it, making quick work of pulling out the panel and overriding the lockout.

"He may try to beam out, or make some other attempt to escape," Riker went on. "Believe me when I tell you, Captain Picard is one hell of a chess player. He'll have countermoves for everything."

"Sir?" Keru ventured a question. "Perhaps it would be best if you stand by out here?"

"He has to be stopped, for everyone's sakes," Riker said firmly. "I have to be the one to do that." His gaze turned inward for a moment. "I owe him nothing less."

"Got it," said Sortollo, and with a crackle of static discharge, the sealed doors hissed open.

Inside, the oval compartment contained a cramped, compact version of a full starship bridge. Complete with multifunction consoles capable of duplicating the operation of any command station, the emergency bridge allowed any ship's complement, even with the smallest of skeleton crews, to continue running the vessel in the event that the main bridge was destroyed.

The space was dimly lit, with only the brightness of the LCARS displays offering radiance, but Keru immediately picked out the shapes of two figures moving in the gloom.

"Stand to!" snapped the Trill. "Show yourselves!"

"It's over, Captain," said Riker, following Keru into the room. "Let's not make this any harder than it has to be."

"Captain, huh?" said a voice, which very much did not belong to Jean-Luc Picard. "You hear that, dear? I just got a promotion."

A blond-haired human male Keru didn't recognize stepped into the light from his beacon, and he wore the uniform of a Starfleet commander and a lopsided grin.

Riker knew him, though, and the admiral's jaw hardened. "Mister Paris."

"Well, technically it's Mister and Missus Paris," he corrected as the second figure revealed herself. Keru saw a woman with the subdued forehead ridges that only someone of Klingon ancestry would possess; she too was in uniform. "I couldn't have managed this without my wife's expertise," added Paris.

"B'Elanna Torres," said the woman, by way of introduction. "Ignore my husband, I kept my own name."

"What have you done?" Riker demanded an answer. "Where's Picard?"

"He was never here, Admiral," Torres said flatly. "We're just the distraction."

"I hope you think it was worth it." The color rose in Riker's face. "You two have just destroyed every last piece of goodwill you earned over the last decade." He strode in, until he was an inch away from Paris's face. "I'll give you one chance. Tell me where Picard is and what he's planning, and perhaps your children won't have to see their parents through a brig's force field for the rest of their lives."

"I can't tell you what I don't know," said Paris.

Riker turned to Sortollo and snapped out an order. "Contact the *Titan*. Tell them to get the space doors open and sound a system-wide alert." Then he faced Paris once again, shaking his head. "What possessed you to do this? You don't even know Picard!"

"We know what he's trying to do," Torres stated firmly, shifting her weight. "And once you've lived the hell of time twisting in on itself, you know it's worth any risk to stop it."

"What does she mean?" said Dennisar.

Paris pointed at the admiral, moving to put himself between Riker and his wife. "Ask the top brass. But you know the admirals, they'll probably tell you it's top secret, need to know."

Something in the man's glib manner rang a wrong note with Keru, and all at once the reason became clear. *He's stalling.* The Trill saw Torres make a casual move toward one of the multifunction LCARS and before he could shout out a warning, she tapped a control.

N'keytar was on the other woman in a flash, but too late to stop her. "She sent a comm signal," said the Vok'sha. "Encrypted, low power. Which means the receiver has to be nearby."

"Arrest them!" Riker bit back an angry snarl and glared at the husband-and-wife mutineers. "Picard won't succeed. Know that. You've thrown away your futures for nothing."

Paris sobered, and his false humor vanished. "If he doesn't, there'll be no future for anyone."

U.S.S. *Aventine* NCC-82602

The turbolift doors opened, depositing Picard and Wesley on the *Aventine*'s expansive bridge. The two men stepped out, both of them fully aware of the fateful choice now unfolding in front of them.

We're in it now, Wesley told himself. *No turning back from this.*

At his side, Picard halted, concern forming on his face. "Captain Bowers?"

The *Aventine*'s commander rose from his seat and gave them both a welcoming, if rueful, smile. "Captain Picard. Apologies for not being there to greet you, but my plate's a little full, what with the insubordination and all." Bowers gestured to the main viewscreen.

Wesley saw that the rust-colored arms of the McKinley Station repair platform were in the process of retracting from around the starship's hull, falling back to allow the long, arrow-like *Vesta*-class vessel to move away.

"One minute to clear space," said a familiar, rumbling voice.

Both Wesley and Picard turned to find Worf at the tactical console, his face set in a serious mask. He gave them a curt nod and continued with his duties. At the science station, a second Klingon in civilian robes and metallic baldric spared them a look.

"Alexander?" Captain Picard's eyes widened in surprise.

"Greetings," said Worf's son. It took Wesley a second to see the resemblance, but then it was clear to him. He remembered the young, spirited boy he had first encountered aboard the *Enterprise*-D, and saw the maturation of him in the man by Worf's side.

"It's good to see you," continued Picard. "You're . . . joining us on this endeavor?"

"I am," he replied, casting a quick glance in Worf's direction. "My skills are yours."

"Welcome to the pirate life, Ambassador," said Wesley.

Alexander gave a grunt of amusement. "Should I have brought my cutlass?"

Another of the *Aventine*'s bridge crew called out from one of the secondary consoles. "Communications from McKinley are being jammed. We've got maybe five minutes before someone notices."

"Thank you, Lieutenant Mirren," said Bowers, before turning to his chief of security. "Lieutenant Kedair, how are things with our unwanted passengers?"

The Takaran woman sniffed and made a sour face. "Give me a moment, sir," she said. "Locking on to their combadges as we speak."

Bowers leaned in to explain. "There's a bunch of maintenance teams on board from McKinley. Obviously, they're not party to our little, uh, excursion. I imagine right now they're rather alarmed that the ship is moving."

"Quite." Picard glanced around the bridge, and Wesley followed his gaze. All but a couple of the *Aventine*'s command stations were manned by Bowers's crew. "Captain, forgive me, but I assumed that your ship would be running with a minimum complement . . ."

"It is," said Bowers. "I rotated off as many as possible. But a few people figured out on their own what was in the wind. And they asked to come along."

Kedair looked up. "For Captain Dax's sake. We owe her that much."

For a moment, the bridge fell quiet and the *Aventine* crew shared a solemn moment of solidarity over their lost commander.

Into that silence, Picard offered a few words. "You honor her memory. But make no mistake, what we are about to do will very likely blacken your records beyond any hope of redemption. You've all done enough already. No one would think any less of you if you were to step away."

"Sir," said Mirren, meeting Picard's gaze, "with all due respect, the answer's no." She nodded at Bowers. "Besides, the captain already gave us that speech."

"The answer then was also no," noted Kedair.

Picard gave a nod. "So be it."

"Transporter arrays are ready," said Alexander. "Maintenance crew biosigns locked in, ready to initiate mass beam-out."

"Do you need a hand?" Wesley stepped up to a nearby station.

"Thank you, yes." Alexander mirrored the controls to Wesley's screen and together they synchronized the procedure. "All we need now is a destination."

Wesley glanced at the curvature of the Earth beneath them. "We're passing over the island of Fiji right now. It's nice there this time of year."

"Perfect," said Bowers. "Gentlemen, energize . . . *now*."

Wesley watched an internal sensor display as the ship was depopulated down to its skeleton crew. "Done. All ashore that's going ashore."

"Captain!" Mirren called out, attracting the attention of both Picard and Bowers. "Uh, I mean *Captains* . . . We've received a coded subspace signal from Commander Torres aboard the *Enterprise*. It's just two words: *Time's up*."

"It would seem our misdirection has run its course," said Picard.

Bowers nodded, returning to the center seat. "Lieutenant Mavroidis, do we have our heading set?"

"Aye, sir," said the Ullian woman at the conn. "Ready to initiate slipstream drive the moment we depart Terra's mass shadow."

"Get us moving, full impulse," said Bowers, and as he spoke, the *Aventine* fell free of McKinley Station and began to pick up speed. On the main screen, the distant spindle shape of Spacedock in its lower orbit disappeared out of sight.

Wesley heard a warbling alert from Worf's station and glanced up. "Shuttlecraft *L'Rell* is approaching from the planet," he noted. "They are requesting permission to dock in bay one."

"Mister La Forge's timing is impeccable, as always," said Picard.

"He's cutting it fine," noted Bowers. "Your man will only get one shot to board before we have to hightail it out of here."

"It will be enough," Picard replied.

Shuttlecraft *L'Rell* NCC-82602/4

"Last chance to change your mind, Doctor." La Forge leaned forward over the shuttle's controls, working the output of the impulse grid to squeeze out a little more thrust than the manual said was possible. "We can still turn around."

"You're not going to make a joke about being flown around by a blind man, are you?" In the seat behind the flight station, Beverly Crusher was holding on to a metallic carrying case with great seriousness. "With the acuity of your optical implants, I trust you far more than any other pilot!"

"Hold that thought and revisit it if we land." He quickly corrected himself. "I mean *when* we land." Early on in his Starfleet career, La Forge had switched tracks from flight operations to engineering, and while he still had good piloting instincts, he had to admit his skills were a little rusty.

Ahead of them, the graceful, elongated form of the *Aventine* was rising like a dolphin breaching the surface of an ocean, and as the shuttle closed the distance, La Forge saw a section of the hull retract away to reveal the glow of a landing bay. From this distance it was no larger than his thumb, and even as the *L'Rell*'s velocity closed the gap, his target remained unnervingly small.

"This is going to be a hot touchdown," he warned, "so we may, uh, bounce a little."

"Bounce?" Doctor Crusher's tone suggested she was reevaluating her previous statement.

"Technical term," he replied, working to match velocity with the starship. "Just keep a good grip on that precious cargo. It's fragile."

The container Crusher was holding bore the sigil of the Daystrom Institute's Okinawa Annex, and up until a few hours ago, the one-of-a-kind transphasic sensor inside it had been in pieces in their labs, as part of an ongoing analysis by the DTI.

La Forge had hand-built the device himself back on the *Enterprise*-D, when they had first encountered the Devidians, and the sensor's unique capabilities would prove useful in the coming days as they sought to track down the aliens.

Stopping to pick up Crusher at the Picard château in La Barre, being careful not to sear the vines with the thrusters, he then sped around the Earth to Japan, and together they employed their shared reputations to gain access to the sensor and "reacquire" it.

"Here we go." La Forge aimed the *L'Rell* into the opening and felt the shuttlecraft rock as it punched through the atmospheric field holding out the vacuum of space. He cut the thrusters at the last second and landed it squarely on the *Aventine*'s deck.

He caught an odd noise from the cargo compartment at the aft of the shuttle.

"Did you hear that?" said Crusher. As La Forge rose from his seat, she handed him the sensor case and ventured back into the cabin. "Give me a second."

Through the *L'Rell*'s canopy he saw the shuttlebay doors sliding closed. Just before they sealed, La Forge caught the flash of faster-than-light transition as the *Aventine* leaped into slipstream.

"That's it, we're away," he said to himself. La Forge picked up the case and opened the hatch, stepping down off the drive nacelle.

Captain Picard was waiting for them on the deck. "Mission accomplished?"

Geordi held up the case. "I'll need some time to put this back together, but I'd say things went according to plan with our part of the operation."

"That's open to debate." Crusher stepped out behind him, and the doctor seemed very unhappy. "Come on out," she said, addressing her comment back into the shuttle. "There's no use hiding in there now."

"What . . . ?" Picard's and La Forge's faces showed the same shocked surprise when a third person exited the *L'Rell*.

René Picard looked down at the deck, guiltily rubbing at the back of his neck. "Sorry, Mom, Papa."

"Where did he come from?" La Forge was momentarily taken aback, but even as he asked the question, he could already guess the answer.

"He stowed away in the shuttle when you landed at La Barre," said Crusher. "He overheard us talking about our plans the morning after the dinner."

"No, no . . ." Picard shook his head. "René, you can't be here."

"Why not?" The young man's sullen mood broke into frustration and anger. "You took Wesley with you! You were going to leave me behind on Earth with Aunt Marie!"

La Forge stepped aside as Picard came in and put a hand on his son's shoulder. "René, we talked about this. We're going somewhere dangerous. It's not safe."

"I don't want to be safe," insisted René. "I want to be with *you*."

"We could drop him off somewhere," offered La Forge.

Picard sighed. "We can't risk it. We're all fugitives now." Then he showed a brittle smile. "Perhaps it's for the best that we face this challenge together."

PART II

REVELATION

8

Sisko-Azeni Residence, Hedrikspool Province, Bajor

"Your editor called again," said his wife, her voice echoing around the cabin as she called into the kitchen. "Wasn't as polite as last time. Something about a deadline?" She made a mock-serious face.

Jake Sisko gave a contrite nod. "You think she knows I'm ducking her?" He formed patties of ground meat in his hands before placing them on a cooking tray.

"I think she knows." Azeni Korena folded her arms and cocked her head, the Bajoran's earring catching the fading light of the evening. "Of course, I'm not an author, so correct me if I'm wrong, but don't you actually have to *write* books in order to be one?"

"I'm working on it," he said halfheartedly. "Just rewriting some things."

"Next time, *you* talk to her." Korena walked to the sink, pausing along the way to check the oven. "I'm not going to keep covering for you. The Prophets look unfavorably on those who fib for others, even a little bit."

"Okay." He admitted defeat. The reality was, Jake's new novel was pretty much ready to be submitted, but he felt the pressure of having to follow up his first book, *Anslem*, with something of equal caliber, if not better. The new book was a semiautobiographical work, based on his own experiences in the Gamma Quadrant, aboard a tramp freighter called the *Even Odds*—and while the text sat on his padd, it existed in an ideal state of prepublication perfection. The moment he submitted it, however . . . All that became uncertain.

"Have you at least settled on a title yet?"

"I'm considering calling it *Crossings*," he said. "What do you think?"

Korena made an unimpressed sound, the ridges on her nose wrinkling. "It's a little uninspired. I like *Rising Son* better."

Jake had learned early on in their marriage that Korena's instincts were usually correct, so he accepted that with a nod. "All right." He was going to say more, but through the kitchen window he saw the shape of a flyer lift off from behind a stand of trees and speed away into the southern sky.

Out in the countryside beyond Hedrikspool, the land was sparsely populated and traffic was infrequent. The remoteness of their cabin was a big part of the reason why Jake and Korena had chosen it, giving them a level of privacy that life in Bajor's major conurbations never could. There was a price to being the son of the Emissary, and while it rarely was a source of distress for the couple, even among well-meaning locals it could become tiresome.

"What is it?" Korena sensed his unease and came to him. She spotted the figure in the hood before he did and pointed. "Someone's coming up the path. Are we expecting guests?" She raised a wry eyebrow. "Your editor, come for her book?"

Jake didn't return her smile. "I don't know." He couldn't explain it, but a shiver ran down his spine, the ghost of a sensation that something was amiss.

A firm hand knocked on the cabin's wooden door and Jake drew himself up, cleaning off his hands before striding over to address the interloper.

A few times a year, some overeager religious devotee would track him down and present themselves at his home, and while Jake was always respectful of the Bajorans, he was never quite comfortable with his place in their belief systems. In recent weeks, there had been an increase in fiery rhetoric from some of the more iconoclastic vedeks, and Jake was afraid that this uninvited visitor's arrival might be connected.

All that changed when he opened the door, and the man waiting outside rolled back the hood hiding his face.

"Hey, Jake-o," said his father.

"Dad!" A surge of joy burst inside him and Jake drew the other man into a hug. "It's you!"

"It's me," Sisko replied, and the two men shared the same wide, heartfelt grin. "You look good, son."

Jake chuckled, and self-consciously rubbed at the growth of beard on his chin. "Ah, you only say that because I look like you when you were younger."

"True," admitted Sisko. "Handsome runs in the family."

"Well, this is a lovely surprise," said Korena, from the doorway. "Come in, Benjamin. It's delightful to see you!"

Jake saw his father's smile falter for a moment, and that ill-at-ease sensation came back to him as Sisko entered the house.

He shrugged off the hooded jacket to reveal civilian clothes beneath. His father had clearly been traveling off the grid, keeping his identity secret. Jake had the burden of occasionally being recognized for who he was, but Benjamin Sisko's face was familiar to every religious Bajoran.

They exchanged a glance and, once again, his father reached out and laid a hand on him. "This moment . . . This *feeling*," he said. "You ever wish that you could take an instant in time and freeze it right there? No motion forward or back, just being in the moment and living the best of it."

Jake nodded. "Yes."

"But we can't." A note of melancholy crept into Sisko's voice. "That's not how time works."

The question pushing at Jake welled up. "What are you doing here, Dad? Last time we spoke on subspace, you said the *Robinson* would be out on patrol for another six months."

"Jake"—Sisko reached up and touched his son's face—"I took a leave of absence from my command. I was called back here."

"To Bajor?" said Korena. "By whom?"

Jake's father didn't reply. His hand dropped away and he looked upward, in the direction of the evening sky where the glow of the distant wormhole was rising.

Korena sensed the shift in the conversation and stepped back to let father and son have a moment alone. "You must be thirsty from your trip. I'll make some *deka* tea."

Jake's misgivings grew as Sisko led him to the chairs by the window and they sat. "Something is wrong."

Sisko nodded. "I'm sorry to bring bad news, son. The Old Man is gone. Ezri Dax was killed."

"Oh, no . . ." Jake's breath caught in his throat. "Both of them?"

"Yes." Sisko's eyes misted briefly, and he blinked away any tears before they formed. "She was on a classified mission. Starfleet has withheld the details."

Jake's hands drew together. "I can reach out to my contacts at the Federation News Network, they might be able to learn more—"

His father silenced him with a shake of the head. "I know this is hard, Jake, but it's not why I am here. There's more . . . and it may be worse."

"I don't follow you."

Sisko picked his next words carefully. "I'm going to ask you to do something for me, here and now, something very important. And I need to know you won't fight me on it."

Jake took that in, holding his silence. After the trials, the challenges, and the adventures the Sisko family had been through, he trusted his father implicitly. But he couldn't go forward without knowing what was at stake, and he told him so.

"You've never asked me for anything," said Jake, "and you've always been there for me. You say it, I'll do it. But I have to know the reason."

Sisko leaned forward and studied him with steady, unblinking focus. "You need to take Korena and leave. *Tonight.* Go to the starport in Ashalla, get passage on a ship out of the Bajor system. Go to Cestus III."

"Cestus?" Jake knew that the colony in that system was home to members of the Yates family, and his stepsister Rebecca and her mother—his father's second wife, Kasidy—were currently living there. "Kas and Becca . . ."

"Kas has her ship. You tell her what I'm about to tell you, to pack up and light out for somewhere on the fringes. Somewhere remote, off the grid. As far from Bajor as you can get." He took a weary breath. "A safe haven."

Jake's mind reeled at the demand, but he didn't push back. If his father was demanding this of him, then there had to be a good reason. "All right, sure. We can take the monorail across the straights to the north continent, make Ashalla in a day or so . . ." He paused. "What have you seen, Dad? Is it them?" He nodded toward the sky. "The Prophets? Did they show you something?"

Sisko nodded gravely. "On the *Robinson*, there was a moment . . . We engaged this creature in battle, and there was some temporal effect. I think the Prophets wanted me to know what would come next." His voice dropped to a low register as he relived the memory. "I saw destruction, Jake. A terrible end for Bajor, and countless other worlds too. Worse than anything we've ever faced here before."

"You came back to stop it." Jake knew his father's instincts as well as his own. Bajor was more of a home to Benjamin Sisko than Earth was, as if he had discovered a missing piece of himself when he came to this place. "How can I help?"

"My son." Sisko squeezed his hand. "I know you could. But we have to make certain Kas and your sister are safe. I can't do both. I need you to carry that weight for me." He shook his head. "My heart fills up with ice when I think about losing you or them. At least on some distant world, far from here, you might all be safe. Do you see now, son?"

Jake considered what had been said. "You're asking a lot. You want me to abandon you, to what? An unknown fate?"

"I want you to save what we have, what we are," said Sisko. "And maybe I'm wrong about the whole damned thing." He snorted. "I've been questioning myself every step of the way here. Maybe your old man is seeing things that aren't there. I hope I am! You can come back when it's over and tell me I was a fool." He paused, looking inward. "I hope I'm wrong, Jake. With every beat of my heart, I hope. But that image lives in my heart. I saw a sky full of ash and the stars cold and dead."

"Talnot's Prophecy." Jake turned to see Korena standing in the doorway, her eyes wide with fear, her hand at her mouth. "You're describing the Word of the Final Days."

"That's an ancient myth," said Jake, moving to her and taking his wife into an embrace. But then he remembered something that the Changeling Constable Odo had once said: *Bajoran prophecies have an odd way of coming true.*

Jake had experienced firsthand the awesome potential of the alien beings that lived in the wormhole—the Prophets, as Korena's people knew them. Once, the dark energy of the worst of their kind had briefly possessed him, and he knew what power they represented. *If they've brought my father back here, there's a purpose to it.*

At length, Jake drew back. "All right, Dad. We'll go."

Location Concealed

The fourth Hirogen stalker-cruiser shuddered and the pulsing engine glow amid its structure flickered and faded; then, in the same manner as the first three cruisers that had come out to meet the intruder, the hulking, armored craft *imploded.*

"Watch carefully and take note," said one of the observers. As was his way, he made it into a lesson. "It really is quite remarkable."

For a fraction of a second, an inversion of time formed in the heart of the vessel, and the mass of the stalker was gutted from the inside out. Hundreds of Hirogen hunters vanished across a murky event horizon as they were ripped from the decks, their ship crushed by incredible forces. When the effect faded, all that remained was a smoking, twisted lump of metal barely a quarter of the size of the original vessel.

"They have finally understood they cannot win," said the second observer, her voice holding a tiny measure of sympathy for the bellicose Hirogen. "They are retreating."

"Not quickly enough," came the reply.

A cluster of Hirogen seeker-fighters laid down a wall of particle-beam fire, likely in hopes of holding off the enemy that had destroyed their bulwark, while another cruiser maneuvered away to generate a subspace tunnel. It was clear to the observers that this attempt would be futile.

The things that had killed the Hirogen ships phased into the visual spectrum, emerging from the wrecks they had bored into in bursts of debris, presenting gargantuan serpentine forms wreathed in crackling chroniton fire.

Three of them advanced across the darkness. They flicked and writhed through the void, winking in and out of existence as the blasts from the seekers cut the space they passed through.

"See how the aggressors move?" He raised his hand to highlight one of the creatures. "Instantaneous temporal desynchronization, an instinctive action."

"Skipping across the top of the seconds," she offered, "like a stone skimming the surface of a lake."

He nodded approvingly. "Well put."

Now the creatures were upon the flight of fighters, and they attacked them with savagery, ripping them apart. The observers watched as the lone remaining cruiser began to coruscate with light, as the first bursts of precursor radiation appeared around it.

"The tunnel forms," she noted. "But not quickly enough, I think."

"Indeed." He nodded. "They won't escape."

The crew aboard the last Hirogen ship came to the same conclusion, and in a last-ditch attempt to save itself, it discharged every weapon it had. The fusillade of energy had just as little effect as the guns of the now-obliterated seekers. The three serpent forms converged on the hunter vessel and phased through the walls of its hull, destroying it from within.

"And that is the end of that," he said, reaching up to find a gestural interface.

With a motion of his fingers, the immersive holographic presentation surrounding them retreated, becoming smaller and smaller, zooming out at an incredible rate until the wrecks were lost among the pinprick glow of stars and nebulae. The display shrank until it was only a hundred meters in diameter, becoming a scale model of their home galaxy.

Still, the shape of it filled the middle of the laboratory, and its hazy glow cast strange patterns across the walls and the myriad of esoteric equipment lining the workstations.

She walked into the image, until the great segment of the galaxy where the incursion had happened was floating in front of her pale face. "That is the forty-seventh observed engagement with the Hirogen within the confines of the Delta Quadrant in the past seventy-two hours. And yet no determinable pattern is clear." She looked across to her father. "What does it mean?"

"Chaos is a pattern," he said. "You may not yet perceive it, Lal, but once the complexity of it is comprehended, it will become clear."

She frowned, emulating the emotion that came with the expression. "I would prefer a more straightforward answer."

Data showed a wry smile. "As would I."

Lal experienced a faint approximation of grief. "I feel sorry for them. They are a threat to life, and yet we observe their demise at the hand of these creatures and I experience empathy. Curious."

"Well, you're only human," her father said dryly. He reached up and ran a hand through his hair. It was a needless but very human gesture, one of many such details that had become part of his persona in his reborn android form.

On the surface, Data resembled his old self filtered through a human lens, sans golden eyes and pale metallic skin. Lal's father had been made in the image of his creator, the genius cyberneticist Doctor Noonian Soong, but she had been allowed to choose her own identity. Her first, short-lived incarnation was that of a young human female, and when Data brought her back to existence a few years ago, she ultimately decided to return to that form once again.

Like her father, she could have been mistaken for a baseline humanoid from any one of a thousand starfaring cultures, but beneath their biomimetic skin, they were synthetic beings of most advanced design.

Data collapsed the hologram and deactivated the advanced imaging array that had provided the raw feed for the images. The array's reach was great. It granted them the ability to remotely perceive events taking place in real time, across tens of thousands of light-years, via quantum-tunneling effects. But Lal always found herself feeling disquieted after using it, as if the device distanced her from the universe around them, instead of connecting her to it.

"The Hirogen have been making inroads into former Borg territories for some time, searching not just for new hunting grounds but also for any remnants of their technology," said her father. "I suspect the Hirogen were intent on learning the Borg's process for time travel. It follows the progression we have seen with these serpent creatures that the hunters would ultimately draw their predation. It seems that anything associated with temporal manipulation is an attractant."

"Their attacks only have the appearance of randomness." Lal moved to the laboratory's window and tapped a control to open the shutters. "This is a guided effort," she said. "I conclude that the creatures themselves are only semisentient, but I believe there is an intelligence commanding them."

Since the presence of the creatures was first detected, Lal and her father had been assembling a data set on the targets of their attacks. As well as sites inside the Federation, the Klingon Empire, Tholian

Assembly, and the Gorn Hegemony, they had noted evidence of incursions in the territories of distant, time-active species such as the Na'kuhl and the Krenim. More troublingly, there was mounting evidence that some of the so-called higher-evolutionary races at large in the galaxy, such as the Organians, Metrons, and the Q, had gone silent. If these details were connected, it did not bode well.

Lal allowed herself a moment to consider these facts as she looked across the barren gray landscape outside, toward the purple-pink sky at the horizon.

There was a kind of desolate beauty to this planet. Designated on Federation navigation charts as Omicron Theta, the galaxy at large believed it to be a failed colony and a dead world. But this was, for want of a better term, her father's birthplace, where Doctor Soong had worked to bring his vision of artificial life to fruition.

Data claimed that relocating them to the forgotten outpost was the perfect way for them to hide in plain sight, but Lal often wondered if it was evidence of the quality that humans called eccentricity.

He moved to stand beside her. "Your conclusions are, as usual, quite correct. But I fear we are only seeing the edges of a far larger plan in progress. This is a concerted effort to disarm any possible retaliation against a vicious and temporally active aggressor."

"An assault from across time," said Lal, considering the ramifications of the statement. "But to what end? Is it preparation for an invasion from another era? Colonization of the past by some future civilization?"

"No," said Data, his expression turning grave. "That might be survivable. I believe the attack on the Hirogen we witnessed and the other incursions are precursors to a single, supremely destructive act. The annihilation of this timeline, and possibly others."

Before Lal could frame an adequate response to that pronouncement, she sensed a silent signal from the laboratory's detection grid. A slipstream exit point had opened and closed a few light-days short of the planet, triggering a proximity alert.

"A Starfleet vessel, making an orbital approach." Data seamlessly interfaced with the grid's readings, parsing them in a nanosecond. "*U.S.S. Aventine, Vesta*-class starship, registration code NCC-82602. According to current fleet advisory, that ship is under a warning order. It is classified as renegade." He halted and turned back to face his daughter. "They have no reason to be here. Our sensor cloak conceals us from all scans. Do you have an explanation for their arrival?"

Lal sensed he already knew the answer. "I do not wish you to become upset with me," she said.

He cocked his head. "What did you do?"

"The quantum transceiver you gifted to Geordi La Forge. He activated it a few days ago. There was a message."

"I know." Data frowned. "I chose not to respond. It was a question of balancing our need for privacy with other concerns."

"I disagree," said Lal. "You have become too isolated, Father. Geordi is your friend. And his request was important."

"You sent him our coordinates."

She nodded. "I felt it best, given the circumstances. If what you suspect is taking place, remaining here and observing it happen is not a suitable option."

"You believe so?" He raised an eyebrow. "Some events may be beyond our capacity to alter."

"Once more, I disagree," she countered.

For a long moment—a full 3.6 milliseconds—Lal wondered if she had taken her own initiative too far. But then her father's wry ghost of a smile returned and he silently accepted her reply.

Without a word, Data interfaced with the lab's control framework and commanded the sensor cloak to deactivate, revealing their presence to *Aventine*.

Sisko-Azeni Residence, Hedrikspool Province, Bajor
Sisko awoke the next morning to an empty house, but strangely the sense of melancholy he expected was absent.

The previous night's sleep had been the first in a while that went long, deep, and untroubled. After bidding farewell to his son and his daughter-in-law, he sat at the table on the veranda and watched the stars. The emptiness he experienced after his vision aboard the *Robinson* melted away, and Sisko felt something powerful take its place.

Purpose.

Returning to Bajor felt right, it felt inevitable. The certainty that he was where he was meant to be gave Sisko a new energy, driving him forward.

A couple of hours after B'hava'el rose over the trees, casting honey-gold sunlight across the house, Sisko went back to the table and chairs on the veranda. A few minutes before the agreed-upon time, he set out a flask of Klingon bloodwine, an excellent vintage from the House of K'Cam, and five steel cups.

He waited by the rail, listening to the whisper of the wind. The night before, there had been doubts. But not now. Bajor had renewed him. He had forgotten how much he missed this world.

The overlapping hum of transporter beams drew his gaze to a spot in front of the house. Three forms accreted out of the air, becoming solid and real, and as the effect faded, he gave the new arrivals a nod of welcome.

"Gentlemen," he said, "thank you. I wasn't certain you'd all be here."

"That was never in doubt, Captain." Miles O'Brien looked exactly as Sisko always remembered him, his uniform sleeves rolled up to the elbows, as if he had just stepped away from the work of tearing down some vital system on Deep Space 9.

"Some things take precedence over everything else." By contrast, Jake Sisko's childhood friend Nog had changed a great deal over the years the elder Sisko had known him. Nog's journey had been a remarkable one, from a Ferengi youth with a wild streak to a Starfleet cadet and now a decorated officer on the rise.

"Nothing would have kept me away." The third arrival was

dressed in nondescript civilian clothes, and sported a growth of gray-black beard that gave his features a severe air. Of all of them, Julian Bashir had changed the most. Unlike Nog, Sisko found it hard to look into the doctor's eyes and see the man he had once been. Time and adversity had not been kind to Bashir, and his manner was hard-edged and wary.

"How are you, Julian?" O'Brien fumbled around the awkward question. "You look, uh, different."

"Nine months locked inside your own mind will do that to you," said Bashir.

"Come up." Sisko beckoned them to the veranda, then set to pouring out measures of bloodwine into the cups.

Nog and O'Brien shared a look as they approached. "I wanted to say congratulations on the new promotion, Command Master Chief," said the Ferengi.

"Thanks, Lieutenant Commander," said O'Brien, self-consciously touching the new insignia at his throat. He nodded at Nog's crimson-hued collar. "How are you handling the switch to the command track?"

"Not as straightforward as rebuilding a warp core," admitted Nog with a toothy smile. "But I'm XO on the *Saticoy* now. It's a small ship, but it's a good billet."

"It seems I missed a lot while I was on Cardassia," Bashir said quietly. "But it's good to see all of you."

"It is," agreed Sisko as he passed out the cups. "I'm only sorry that it's taken something like this to bring us back together."

The four of them held the bloodwine for a moment, following Klingon tradition to warm it to release the drink's potent aroma.

At length, Sisko raised his cup. "To absent friends."

"To Ezri," said Bashir, his voice catching.

"To the Old Man," said Nog.

"Aye. Clear skies and Godspeed," concluded O'Brien.

As one, they drank down the bloodwine in a single brisk jolt. The fifth cup—Ezri's cup—remained untouched.

The hush that followed extended for some time, as each man reflected on the loss of their dear friend and comrade. Finally, Sisko broke the silence.

"I don't have answers about what happened to her. Starfleet stonewalled my request for more information, citing Dax's death as a 'matter of galactic security.' But I know it happened on a top-secret mission. And Picard was there."

"Captain Picard?" O'Brien frowned at the mention of his former commander. "I thought the *Enterprise* was still out in the Odyssean Pass."

"No, they were recalled after that business with President Zife," said Nog, referring to the recent investigation into events surrounding the resignation of the troubled former Federation president.

"I have a few details," said Bashir. "In his role as castellan of the Cardassian Union, our old friend Garak has access to intelligence sources far beyond our means . . ."

"Benefits of being a head of state, I suppose," noted O'Brien.

"On my way here, Garak updated me on something," continued Bashir. "Starfleet Command are playing it close to their chest, but a high-level advisory went out yesterday regarding Ezri's ship, the *Aventine*. The fleet has been put on alert and the *Aventine* has been declared renegade."

"That can't be a coincidence," said O'Brien.

"No," admitted Sisko, "but right now there's nothing we can do about that. I didn't just ask you here to say goodbye to a friend." He put down the cup and met their gazes, one by one. "We've been through a lot together. Experienced things that would break lesser men. Had our preconceptions challenged, again and again. At one time or another, you have each followed me into the unknown, to do what must be done. Now I'm asking that of you again."

"Off the book?" Bashir raised an eyebrow.

"A long way off, Doctor," he replied.

"Why do I get the feeling this has something to do with the wormhole?" O'Brien shook his head. "We've been seeing unusual events out there for a while now. Energy bursts we can't explain, strange aura-field effects, low-level chroniton discharges . . ." He noted that the crew aboard the second DS9 station had logged the anomalies with sector command, but so far nothing had come of it. "People are getting spooked, and I have to admit, I'm one of them."

"That's not like you, Miles," said Bashir. "You're unflappable."

"Not so much these days," said O'Brien. "You know me, Julian, I'm not one for believing in things I can't see. But I won't deny, there's something strange in the air. It just doesn't *feel* right. Every day, ships are dropping off Bajoran pilgrims and assorted pessimists, and filling up with people who want to leave. I sent Keiko and Yoshi to Bajor, and told her to find a transport back to Earth for a few weeks until it all calms down. Molly's there now, visiting her grandparents."

"I feel it too, Chief," said Sisko. "I felt it from half a quadrant away." They listened intently as he told them about the dreamlike vision he had seen aboard the *Robinson*, and the reaction of Jake's Bajoran wife to what he described.

"So what's our next move?" Nog leaned back against the veranda's support. "Do we bring this to Starfleet?"

"Bring them what?" snapped Bashir. "One man's waking nightmare, a few anomalous readings, and some Bajoran mythology?" He gestured at the others. "*We* all know that can add up to something, but will Starfleet Command take it seriously?"

"There is someone else we should speak to," said O'Brien, nodding to himself. "But the last I heard, she was in spiritual seclusion."

"Agreed." Sisko returned the nod. "I'm sure Vedek Kira can make time for her old friends."

Omicron Theta

A chilly breeze across the dusty landscape greeted Picard and the others as they materialized. He reflexively pulled his field jacket closer and glanced around.

Although the sun was shining high in the sky, the planet was still cold and unwelcoming. Out beyond the edges of the derelict colony before them, empty fields of dry, sandy earth extended toward the horizon, broken only by the skeletal lines of dead trees.

"Not exactly a garden spot." At Picard's side, Captain Bowers gave the vista a searching look. "What happened here?"

"The colony was attacked by a crystalline entity," said Wesley. "Decades ago now." Picard's other companion dropped into a crouch and ran his fingers over the dust.

"I've heard of them." Bowers gave a sage nod. "Giant cosmozoan creatures capable of stripping a planet down to the bedrock. Never had the pleasure, though."

"Consider yourself fortunate," said Picard. "What you see now is all that remains of a once-thriving colony."

But he also saw the echo of the dead worlds he had glimpsed in the distant future wrought by the Devidians. A crystalline entity, like those he had encountered in the past, was a formidable threat, but even it could prey on only one world at a time. The Devidians could destroy on a scale that would make such a loss seem trivial in comparison.

"It might thrive once again," offered Wesley. "Look here." Amid the crumbling earth, he found a few small green shoots, the hardy plants pushing up toward the sunlight. "New life."

"The planet is healing," said a familiar voice. Picard and the other men turned as Data and his daughter, Lal, approached them from among the ruined buildings.

"I have suggested to my father that we could accelerate the process," noted Lal. "But he prefers to let nature move at its own pace."

"My perspective has changed somewhat in recent years," said Data. "When one is functionally immortal, it alters your concept of time." He smiled and offered Picard his hand. "Welcome, Captain. It is good to see you."

Picard accepted the gesture, but he sensed a distance in his old friend that he could not articulate. "Data. Lal. I'm pleased to find you both here." He hesitated, then decided to risk being candid. "I confess, I was uncertain how you would receive us."

"Why, cordially, of course. We are still friends, are we not?"

"Always."

Data released his handshake and looked away. "Wesley. How long has it been?"

"Too long," he replied, and smiled ruefully. "I'm sorry I've been out of touch, but I've been . . . *traveling*."

"That is an understated euphemism for temporal and extra-dimensional transit," said Lal.

Wesley's smile faltered. "You've been keeping tabs on me?"

"There is much in the universe to observe, including you," said Data, throwing his daughter a look. "Lal feels that we spend too much time watching the play and not enough acting in it. I admit, we sometimes live vicariously through the adventures of our friends." Data changed tack, moving to shake hands with Bowers. "You are Commander Samaritan Bowers of the *Aventine*. Or is it captain now?"

"Needs must," said Bowers. "I've heard plenty about you, Mister Data."

"Then the advantage is yours," replied Data. "All I know about you is that you and your starship are currently being hunted by Starfleet Command, in connection with charges of mutiny."

"Yeah . . ." Bowers let go of Data's hand. "About that . . ."

"I know you are . . . *on the lam*, Captain." Data looked back at Picard. "I imagine the motivation must be quite serious for you to take such drastic action."

"You have no idea," Wesley said quietly.

"I think we might," noted Lal.

"May I ask who else is involved?" Data watched Picard expectantly.

"A few of *Aventine*'s senior crew," he explained. "Myself, Wesley and Beverly, Worf and his son. And Geordi, of course."

"Of course. He is well?"

Wesley saw an opportunity. "He's aboard the *Aventine* right now, working on something we could really use your help with. A piece of advanced future technology containing vital information about a deadly threat we've uncovered."

Lal cocked her head, clearly intrigued. "What is the origin of this technology?"

"Me," said Wesley with a shrug. "Well, a much older temporal incarnation of me. He forgot to leave any instructions with it."

"This threat you refer to . . ." Data considered the idea. "I assume it is the reason for your acts of insubordination, sir?"

"Correct." Picard paused, framing his next words carefully. Data's help would be vital to their mission, but the android was no longer a Starfleet officer, not even technically a Federation citizen. Data belonged to his own community of synthetic life now, and he was not obligated to aid them. *I have to tell him the full and brutal truth,* Picard thought. *He will understand what is at stake.*

"The Devidians have returned." Data spoke as if he had plucked the thought directly out of Picard's mind. "Or perhaps, it would be more accurate to say they never left."

"That's . . ." Picard stumbled over his reply. "Yes. Exactly right. Their appetite for the suffering of sentient beings has grown to unimaginable proportions."

"They are destroying divergent timelines and engorging themselves on the resultant release of neural energy," continued Data. "A remarkable, if monumentally callous, act of parasitic behavior."

"You knew about this?" Wesley frowned.

"I have generated a large number of hypotheses, based on observed information," said the android. "Your arrival today collapsed those possible scenarios down to a much smaller sample size. I estimated the Devidian option to be the most likely one, in the ninety-seventh percentile."

"Then you understand how serious this is," said Bowers. "Starfleet's sitting on its hands while the Devidians tear up the time stream. We have to find them and stop them. Your reputation, Mister Data, suggests you'd be an asset in making that happen."

Data considered that for a moment, walking away across the dusty ground. "I believe the Devidians are currently in the primary phase of their attack. It is my conclusion that the assaults taking place across observed space, in this galaxy and beyond, are the results of their atemporal creatures entering this timeline through a unique, interdimensional focal point. A point that transgresses all concepts of spacetime as we know it."

"If that location could be determined . . ." Wesley picked up the thread of the idea, gathering momentum as he thought it through. "We could head them off, drive them back. And more than that, we might be able to use it to track the Devidians."

"We need you, Data," said Picard. "Will you come with us?"

"It is just a theory," said the android. "I have little else to offer beyond that."

"Father!" Lal turned on him, a very real expression of dismay on her features. "We could do more!"

Data gave her a sad look. "I regret that the likelihood of effecting any change in oncoming events is so minute as to be barely worth considering." He turned back to Picard and the others, delivering the naked, uncompromising truth of it with barely a flicker of emotion. "I am sorry, Captain. In a sense, it always has been too late to stop them."

"I refuse to accept that." Picard bit out the words.

"The facts do not care about your refusal, sir. They simply *are*."

Data's statement struck Picard like a physical blow. "If the Devidians succeed, then you will be destroyed along with everything else when this timeline is consumed! Are you prepared for that?"

"There is a 0.045 percent probability that a quantum-encoded positronic neural matrix could survive a complete temporal collapse," replied Data. "Those are the best odds for Lal and me. But I cannot improve yours, Captain."

"How can you ask us to accept that fate?" Wesley advanced on him, shaking his head. "Did you ever accept *yours*, Data? You were just supposed to be a machine, a walking, talking library! But you forged your own future. You defied the path set out for you!"

Data's neutral manner disintegrated, and he shot a look at Lal. "Do you see, daughter? *This* is why I did not reply to Geordi's message. Because I did not want my friends to come here, and I did not want to have this conversation with them. But now I have no choice. I will not conceal the truth." He turned back to the others. "Captain . . . Jean-Luc. Wesley. I cannot lie to you."

Picard reached out a hand and put it to Data's chest. He looked the android in the eyes. "I know you believe what you have said, just as I know you are not the Data I once knew. Perhaps you have made your peace with this fatalistic outcome. That is your right." He nodded toward Lal. "But are you ready to make that choice for your child? Will you condemn her to a fractional chance for survival? Come with us! Strive to bend those odds toward better favor." He stepped back, giving his old friend a moment to consider his words, as the chill winds blew around them.

Eventually, Data answered him. "As always, sir, you make a compelling argument. And I find I have little counter to offer."

Lal took her father's hand. "You may be right," she began, "there may be no escaping our fate. But that does not mean we should not fight it down to the very last second of our existence." She nodded toward Bowers. "Captain, I request permission to join your crew and assist in your mission."

Bowers spread his hands. "More than happy to have you, miss."

Data frowned at his daughter. "I could forbid you to leave."

"You could," she admitted. "Do you think it would make any difference?"

At length, he gave a brisk chuckle. "I suppose not." Data looked back at Picard. "As you request, then, we will—"

Both the androids suddenly froze in place, as if a switch had been tripped.

"Data?" Wesley took a step closer, concern creasing his features. "Lal?"

In the next second, the two of them blinked back to awareness, a new expression of concern on both their faces.

"Another starship has just entered the system at high warp," said Lal.

"A Starfleet vessel," added Data. "*U.S.S. Titan*, *Luna*-class, registration code NCC-80102."

9

"Sensor readings from the planet are ill defined," said Lieutenant Kedair. "I read the landing party's biosigns clearly, but other scans are inconclusive."

"Are we sure anyone is down there?" The Ullian at the conn glanced back from her station. "The whole planet looks dead."

"Maybe it's meant to." Next to the Ullian, the *Aventine*'s operations officer ventured her opinion.

Worf sat forward in the command chair, staring into the middle distance, vaguely aware of the conversation going on around him. With Captains Picard and Bowers on the surface of Omicron Theta, Worf was the ranking officer aboard ship, and command of the vessel was his. But his thoughts were in a place littered with shadows and half-formed feelings.

Every time his mind was at rest, the Klingon found himself drifting back to the moment on the *Enterprise*'s holodeck, when dark phantoms crowded the edges of his awareness. The cold, inexorable terror lurked out there, slowly working its way closer to his heart.

At first he wondered if it was some powerful melancholy that had come to him in the wake of Dax's death, but even in his darkest days after losing K'Ehleyr, Jadzia, and Jasminder, Worf had never experienced anything like this.

What is happening to me? Where is this malaise coming from?

Among Klingons, it was rarely spoken of when a warrior fell into the depths of the *Ged'naq*, the lost places of the soul. It was expected for one to burn through such turbulent feelings, to defeat them as one would a foe in single combat. Some said that the fire in Klingon hearts burned so strong that it could consume those in whose chests they beat. Worf looked inward to that fire on many occasions, but it had never seemed as bitter as it did today.

I cannot submit to this, he vowed. *I cannot be weak, not here, not now. Our greatest battle is coming, and I will not be found wanting.*

His silent oath echoed in his mind, but it rang hollow. Worf, son of Mogh, did not fear death; he feared failing his friends and comrades.

"Father."

Worf became aware of his son standing close by. "What is it, Alexander?"

"Lieutenant Kedair seeks your attention."

"Ah." Worf shook off his distraction and glanced at the Takaran, who regarded him with a pinched expression. "What is it?"

"Long-range sensors have detected an energy burst above the plane of the ecliptic." Kedair was terse, clearly irritated at having to repeat the comment Worf had missed the first time. "It is most likely another starship dropping out of warp."

Worf's body tensed with immediate, prebattle tension, and he rose from the command chair. "I want confirmation, now." He pivoted toward Alexander, who had returned to his post at the ship's tactical station. "Go to yellow alert and raise shields!"

But Alexander's attention was on something else. "Incoming hail," he reported. "Starfleet priority channel, local."

From the moment the *Aventine* had fled the Sol system, all command-tier messages from Starfleet had been muted, each growing in severity of tone as it became clear that the *Vesta*-class ship had gone renegade. Nothing had come in for the better part of a day, but now the channel was active again.

Alexander scowled. "Father, it is the *Titan*. Admiral Riker's flagship."

"Confirmed," said Kedair. "Coming toward the planet from the far side. They don't see us yet, but they must know we are here."

Worf reached for a decision, for the tactical choice that would serve best in this situation—and he did not find it. For an instant, his mind was blank.

"Orders, sir?" Mirren, the human woman at the ops station, prompted him with the question, and Worf snapped back into action.

"Move us out of close orbit," he commanded, pointing toward one of Omicron Theta's rocky satellites. "Head to that moon. We'll draw them away from the planet."

"Another signal from Admiral Riker," said Alexander. "The subspace carrier has a prefix modulator code embedded in it. They're making an attempt to override our systems."

"All codes have been scrambled," offered Kedair. "That won't work."

Worf nodded. "Away-team status?"

Kedair made a face. "I no longer read them, sir. Nor the colony's ruins. It seems the sensor mask that was in place earlier has been reactivated."

Worf accepted that with a nod, then turned to his son. "Answer Riker," he said, making a decision.

"Opening hailing frequencies." Alexander tapped the controls, and the main viewscreen switched to an image of the *Titan*'s bridge.

Across the distance, Worf and Riker locked gazes, and what each saw in the other gave them a moment of pause. Mirrored in the admiral's eyes was the same dissonance, the same disconnection, that Worf recognized in himself.

First to speak was the woman in the *Titan*'s captain's chair, flanked by Riker on her left and Deanna Troi on her right. "*Aventine, this is the* Titan, *Captain Christine Vale commanding. You are ordered to stand down and prepare to be boarded.*"

"Vale." Worf gave her a respectful nod. He knew the Izarian

well. She had served with him aboard the *Enterprise*-E as chief of security, and in that time, she had impressed the Klingon with her fortitude and skill. She would be a worthy opponent in any conflict. "We will not comply."

"*Worf . . .*" Deanna spoke before the *Titan*'s captain could respond, imploring him. "*Don't let this go on. Please.*"

"I am sorry, Deanna," he admitted. "We've made our choice."

"*Clearly you have.*" Riker rose to his feet and stepped up to stare down the Klingon across the distance. "*I can see it. Your decision is as plain as day. It's like a* shadow *at your shoulder.*"

A shadow. The word robbed Worf of his breath, he felt it like daggers in his flesh. For a second, it was as if Riker were there with him on the *Aventine*'s bridge, dragging the image from the depths of the Klingon's unquiet thoughts.

Riker nodded, sharing something unspoken with him. "*You're wondering how we found you after you masked your slipstream wake?*" His lip twisted. "*I know you, Worf, and I know Picard. I know how you think. You came here looking for Data, to pull him into this ill-conceived crusade of yours.*"

Worf said nothing, willing his expression to become unreadable.

"*That stone face won't work.*" The admiral gave a humorless laugh. "*How many poker games have you lost to me? This is no different.*"

"The *Titan* is moving up over the planet's northern pole," said Kedair. "Following us on an intercept course."

"*Aventine* will be within their weapons range in forty-seven seconds," added Alexander.

Captain Vale stood up, attempting to reassert her authority as the *Titan*'s commander. "*By order of Starfleet Command, you are ordered to stand down. We don't want to use force, but we will if you give us no other option—*"

"*He knows that.*" Riker cut her off. "*Where's Picard? Did you find Data down there, or has he abandoned us organics for good this time?*"

"We will not comply," repeated Worf.

"I expected no less," said Riker, and with a throat-cutting gesture, he ended the transmission.

U.S.S. *Titan* NCC-80102

Riker turned away from the viewscreen toward Vale, and Troi saw his hands tensing into fists. "Take us to battle posture, shields up, all weapons ready, sound red alert."

Vale hesitated. "Is that really the smartest move to make? This isn't like before; we've got them in our sights. Worf's a fighter, but he's not going to risk—"

"I didn't ask for a debate, Captain." Again, Riker cut her down before she could finish speaking. "I'm going to call the shots on this one."

Vale chewed on her annoyance, then echoed the admiral's order. "Red alert! Battle stations!"

"The *Aventine* remains at yellow-alert status," reported Tuvok, studying the tactical sensor returns. "Their slipstream drive is in standby mode."

"We can't afford to take any chances," Riker went on. "I want intense scans across all bands. If Picard's not on the bridge, he's doubtless planning something."

"We should attempt to talk to him before we do anything else." Troi tried to reach her husband, but he was only half listening to her.

"Tuvok, target the *Aventine*'s engineering section and compute a phaser strike that will disable their slipstream drive." Riker nodded to himself. "I want them hobbled."

The Vulcan set to work programming the attack. "Admiral, I must warn you that such a shot has a high probability of collateral damage to the *Aventine*."

"So noted," he replied. "Lock on and prepare to fire at my command."

Vale moved closer, her voice dropping. "I thought we didn't do the *shoot first, ask questions later* thing. In fact, I'm pretty sure that's on page one of the officer's manual."

Troi felt a flare of annoyance in her husband's emotive aura. "This will escalate things," she added. "None of us want that."

Riker studied them both, regret in his eyes. "Neither of you see it. We're already past that point. Picard's counting on our restraint. And if we show it, he'll use it to get away from us." The admiral nodded toward the planet. "We may not catch him again."

"I will not sanction firing on a Starfleet ship that doesn't pose a direct threat," Vale said firmly.

"Will." Troi laid a hand on her husband's arm. "Listen to her."

"All right." Riker pulled away and addressed Tuvok again. "We'll send a message. Photon torpedo, minimum yield, detonate it across their bow. Do it *now*."

At length, Tuvok gave a curt nod. "Firing."

U.S.S. *Aventine* NCC-82602

"Bring us about," began Worf, grasping for the next order to give. His thoughts were sluggish, preoccupied with Riker's odd but perceptive comment.

A shadow at your shoulder. Worf could almost feel the weight of it, a ghost that followed him just out of sight, lurking at the corner of his eye.

"Reading prefire activity on the *Titan*," said Alexander.

The Klingon was momentarily taken aback by the report. *Would Riker really make an unprovoked attack on the* Aventine? Again, he hesitated, losing his momentum. "Turn the ship," barked Worf, finally settling on a plan. "Bring us bow to bow, show them the minimum target aspect."

But it was too late. "*Titan* is firing! Incoming torpedo!"

"Evasive!" Worf called to the helm, and he felt the tremor in the deck beneath his boots as *Aventine* accelerated into a rising turn.

In the next second, the photon torpedo detonated well short of the vessel, in a brilliant solar flash. The shockwave from the blast buffeted their shields but did not penetrate, serving only to shake them up a little more.

"Warning shot," said the Ullian. "They won't miss with the next one."

"I will not give him the opportunity." Worf took a deep breath, attempting to banish his hesitation. "We need to . . . to draw them away. We need fighting room." He stalked back to the conn and ops stations. "Take us around that moon, maximum impulse. Make them pursue us."

As the ship began to move again, Kedair cleared her throat. "Commander Worf, with respect, what is our plan here? Are we going to abandon the away team on the surface? We're on the edge of transporter range, even if we could locate them."

"I am . . . improvising," Worf retorted. "Unless you have a better idea, Lieutenant, I suggest you mind your post."

"*Titan* is moving to follow," said Alexander. "They're locking phasers!"

Worf nodded. "Reinforce aft shields and maintain heading."

Then Alexander called out again. "*Titan* is firing."

Worf gripped the back of Lieutenant Mirren's seat and braced himself for the hit, ready for *Aventine*'s deflectors to absorb the blow, but the shock that rang through the vessel was not the diffuse shudder from a blunted phaser strike. Worf stumbled, almost losing his balance, as the ship took a direct hit, full force to the hull.

Kedair gaped at her sensor readings. "They fired right through the deflectors! They have our shield frequency!"

"How . . . ?" Worf staggered back to the command chair. "Impossible!"

"McKinley Station," said Mavroidis, a sudden understanding coming over her. "Those maintenance crews we beamed off the ship before we fled, some of them were working on the shield emitters. They would have known the settings!"

Worf cursed himself for failing to consider the possibility. In the haste to escape, it had been overlooked.

Another blast clipped the *Aventine*'s starboard hull and slammed the ship off-kilter. "They are attempting to neutralize our drive capacity," said Kedair. "Sir, orders?"

Alexander stood poised at the weapons station. "Ready to return fire, on your mark."

Worf opened his mouth to speak, but found no words. The shadows were pressing down on him, robbing him of his voice. He could feel them all around, hiding out of sight. If he turned his head, he feared he would see them.

"*Father!*" his son shouted at him, breaking through the fog in his mind.

"Remodulate the shield harmonics!" He bellowed the command, the sound of his own words dispelling his hesitation. "Execute evasive pattern Pike-Seven-Gamma!"

It was the right order; it was also too late to matter.

Worf's delay cost the *Aventine* its escape, as the *Titan*'s phasers finally found their marks and struck the glowing intercooler grids on the starship's nacelles. Overwhelmed by the surge of energy, the mains went offline to stem the overload effect before it could race through every system.

Aventine's engines went dark and the ship fell into the Theta moon's gravitational well. Behind it, the *Titan* moved in, powering up its tractor beams.

Omicron Theta

"Damn!" Picard let the curse drop, hating how powerless he felt.

The holographic panorama in the middle of Data's laboratory showed every second of the engagement happening far above them, the curve of the largest of the Thetan moons filling one side of the chamber, and the two starships floating before it, like toy boats adrift on a black lake.

"The *Aventine* is losing power," said Lal. Both the androids could instantly interface with the lab's systems, summoning the hologram at will and drawing information from banks of hidden sensors. "But I am detecting no attrition of crew life signs."

At Picard's side, Bowers let out a sigh. "Thank the fates for that."

Wesley shook his head, frowning. "What the hell is Worf thinking? I've seen better tactics from first-year midshipmen."

Picard let that comment pass, but he too was dismayed by how slow the *Aventine* had been to react. Admiral Riker had the upper hand, and the slim lead they had worked so hard to gain was lost.

"He'll board the ship and lock it down." Picard thought through Riker's most likely course of action. "With the skeleton crew on *Aventine*, there won't be any real resistance." He sighed. "There must be something we can do."

"I'll give myself up," Bowers offered. "I can buy some time while you figure out another option."

"Or I could transit up there," said Wesley, pulling the Omni-chron device from his belt, turning it over in his fingers. "Board the *Titan*, maybe sabotage their tractor emitters . . ."

"We can do better than that." Lal turned to study Data, who had remained silent since they entered the hidden facility. "Father, we should intervene."

Data gave a grunt of amusement. "You won't rest until I've given away all my secrets."

Picard moved to him. "Data, if there is anything you can do, please, I implore you."

The android met Picard's gaze. "I will employ force only if there is absolutely no other option."

"No one is asking you to destroy them, sir," said Bowers. "Just make my people safe."

"Very well." Data broke away, staring into nothing. As he did so, the hologram shifted aspect, zooming out. The avatars of *Titan* and *Aventine* reduced to the size of Picard's hand, and the second moon became visible at the periphery of the three-dimensional image.

"There are beings in the universe who do not wish to share it with synthetic life," Lal explained. "We thought it prudent to create a defense mechanism, in case they ever came looking for us."

"What is that?" Wesley pointed at the surface of the larger moon and Picard saw what at first seemed like pieces of the lunar surface floating up into space.

A swarm of dart-shaped objects, rendered as tiny shards of light by the hologram, burst out from beneath the airless landscape of the moon, and turned toward the *Titan*. At the same time, a second cluster of darts lifted away from the smaller satellite and vectored toward the ship.

Data raised his hands, making small gestures with his fingers that translated into flocking movements of the darts. He resembled someone conducting music that only he could hear.

"Drones?" Picard looked to Lal for confirmation.

"Yes, Captain. Simple, self-replicating devices utilizing limited intelligence. Swarm logic, if you will. They operate via a distributed subspace network to coordinate their actions."

As the darts homed in on the *Titan*, the vessel reacted. It abandoned the drifting *Aventine* and bright lines of phaser fire reached out to neutralize the drones at the leading edge. A few darts winked out, but the others reconfigured their approach, moving swiftly into a globe formation, with the *Titan* at its core.

"They broadcast a powerful anti–Cochrane field," noted Data, "enough to prevent the creation of a warp bubble. At this moment, I imagine *Titan*'s chief engineer is relaying that fact to Admiral Riker." He moved his hand and the darts changed shape, each one unfolding like a metallic fan. "Clever things, if I do say so myself. Lal's designs were inspired by Tholian spinner ships. We improved on their concepts quite a great deal." He paused. "And . . . *there*." The drones connected with one another, forming a shining, mirrored sphere about the *Titan*, instantly cutting it off from everything around it. "Done."

"You trapped them?" Bowers shot Data a questioning look.

"Quite so," he replied. "The sphere is a high-order matter-energy form, drawn from a tertiary subspace domain, which generates a nullifying field. We have essentially locked the *Titan* inside a temporary pocket dimension of its own. Until the field decays, they cannot escape."

"How long will it last?" Wesley walked into the hologram, reaching for the sphere as if it was something he could grasp hold of.

"The power drain is great," admitted Lal as the hologram flickered out. "The laboratory's sensor cloak has already deactivated to divert energy to the drones. I estimate we have no more than 4.24 hours before release."

"I concur," said Data, before he turned to the others. "So. Gentlemen. Shall we proceed?"

The three men exchanged a look, and then Bowers tapped his combadge. "*Aventine*, do you read? Lock on to these coordinates. We have five to beam up."

Location Unknown

He was on the bridge, but the dimensions of it seemed incorrect.

These were not the compact, steel-blue surfaces he recalled from his years of service aboard a starship, but an abstract representation of them. The panels appeared to be carved out of a sandstone-like material, deep red in color, sculpted by wind and the passage of time. The size was wrong, exaggerated and distorted, turning consoles and chairs into crenellations and turrets more suited to some ancient castle.

As he walked, his steps were heavy, his feet dragging with each movement. His boots sank into fine drifts of golden sand, and it was hard to keep going.

The warped bridge was at once too large for the space it occupied and too small. He felt a closeness drawing in on him, a sense of other beings moving at his back, just out of sight.

Every time he turned to get a better look at them, they retreated.

He glimpsed only the edges of shadows, forms rolling like smoke beyond his line of vision.

Emotion came to him, then. A curious, burning power to it, humming through his veins. He knew anger was there, but so was fear. They echoed inside his psyche, making it difficult to think clearly.

A battle was taking place. Far away, flames and shot bombarded the walls of the castle-bridge abstract. He felt the monumental weight of duty, heavy as a steel collar, the cold and lonely obligation of a commander to those who served with them. And there was a special kind of sorrow there too, the sadness of one who knew they had failed, opening the deepest wellspring of regret.

It was a heady, potent brew, and he had difficulty centering himself. Every attempt he made to take charge of the turbulent thoughts failed.

This is not real, he told himself, *this is illusion. A dream.* But knowing the truth of it did nothing to help.

Slowly, he began to understand. These were not his thoughts. They were not his emotions. He was a passenger, forced to journey through the trauma of another.

"Spock."

Resonating as deeply as the toll of a great ornamental gong, his name reached him. It was a lifeline, a tether pulling him back from the dream-vision. He felt himself detach, and in the last moment before the connection faded, he saw a horde of silent shadows, clustered about a single figure screaming fury into the sky.

"Spock," repeated the voice, "return to me."

He opened his eyes and the dream was gone.

"These are not my chambers," he intoned, glancing around.

Judging by the coolness of Vulcan's night air and the texture of the stones in the high-ceilinged corridor, he was in fact some distance from the pilgrim cells adjoining the Halls of Ancient Thought.

"This is the passage of the Eighth Consideration." He turned toward the woman's voice. "You should not be here."

"Saavik." He raised his hand in the traditional greeting of their people. "It is agreeable to see you."

"I concur." Saavik returned the gesture.

In years past, they had been student and mentor, then officer and commander, but they had always been trusted friends. He and Saavik were united as kindred intellects and fellow comrades, and while they did care deeply for each other, it was in the most Vulcan of ways. They supported each other wholeheartedly, she in her career with Starfleet and he in his mission of Romulan reunification. When he asked for her help, Saavik had come without question.

She brushed a curl of hair from her eyes, glancing back down the corridor. A few of the hall's monks with their shaven pates stood nearby, watching with the faintest air of dismay, unwilling to venture closer. "You were sleepwalking," she explained. "The guardians were uncertain how to address the phenomenon."

"How long?" Spock's throat felt arid.

"A full day. They say you rose from your slumber without waking and came to this place. You remained unresponsive." She sighed. "I was already on my way here from ShiKahr when they contacted me."

"Fortunate."

Saavik studied him closely. "Tell me," she said. "What troubles you?"

He raised an eyebrow. "You have always seen me clearly, Saavik."

A cast of concern passed over her. "If you are unwell," she continued, "we will help you."

He knew immediately what she was speaking of, even if she did not say the words. "Although Bendii Syndrome is hereditary in many cases, be assured that I do not suffer with the condition that claimed my father's life." Spock shook his head. "What has affected me so these past days is of an entirely different origin." He beckoned her to sit, and to the obvious displeasure of the guardians, the two of them settled on the ancient flagstones.

With spare, careful words, Spock relayed the images he had glimpsed in the dream, and Saavik listened intently. When he was finished, she offered a theory.

"These visions come from someone else. Another consciousness."

"Without doubt."

She considered that. "You once told me of a similar contact you experienced, during your preparations for the *Kolinahr*. You sensed the machine-intellect called V'Ger on its approach to Earth. Could this be the same?"

"Not a synthetic life-form," he replied. "It is not a Vulcan mind. The emotions were strong, unchained."

"You glimpsed a battle," said Saavik. "In the abstract, someone being attacked. Perhaps aboard a starship . . . But was it a memory, or an experience being lived in the moment?"

"The latter," Spock answered, with abrupt certainty. "I felt . . . *him*. I knew his anger and his fear. He has never known the like before, and it corrodes him. This emotion is eating him alive." A new, sudden urgency came to the Vulcan as he gained a new insight. "Saavik, I fear that this person is racing toward an abyss they do not know lies before them. The fracturing of their psyche will only worsen as time passes."

She took a long breath. "What does that mean for you? Is there some way we can isolate you from this effect?"

"The most expedient method would be to cure the affected party."

"How can we do that if we do not know their identity?"

"But we do." Spock's gaze turned inward. "*I do*. I need only to find him in my own memories." He tapped a finger on his brow.

For a brief moment, Saavik's composure slipped and her half-Romulan side showed through. "That's a risk. What if you are dragged into another fugue state? I may not be able to reach you next time!"

"This must be done. For his sake as well as mine. I have shared my thoughts with this person. It is the only explanation for the psionic connection between us."

"A mind-meld?"

He nodded. The dreams of fear and shadows were coming to him through the remnant of a past telepathic connection.

"Very well." Saavik leaned forward and placed her fingertips upon the *katra* points on Spock's face.

"No." He tried to disengage, but she did not allow it.

"If this must be done, I will aid you," she insisted. "Let us begin."

Spock relented. "I know you too well to expect you to obey a command if you set your will against it. Very well."

He took a deep, sonorous breath, closed his eyes—

—*and then they were on the bridge of a ship.*

But the dimensions were incorrect.

This is not real, said Saavik, her nonvoice echoing. *This is illusion.*

A dream, said Spock. *But only for us. For him it is a veiled version of reality. We glimpse it through the haze of his emotions.*

As ghosts, they allowed themselves to flow toward the dark, burning heart of the images, as the originator revealed himself.

A battle rages nearby. Saavik shuddered with the force of it. *But he does not fear death. He fears* failure. *Even the admission of weakness wounds him.*

Yes. Spock saw the dark figure before him, the ill-defined form bellowing its rage even as it clawed and punched at the shadows surrounding it. *And with good reason. See? His mind is in turmoil.*

Such regret. Such sorrow. But he believes it comes from within. He blames himself. Spock sensed Saavik's attention. *He does not understand. His torment comes from outside. Do you see it?*

For an instant, Spock perceived the vision through Saavik's perspective and the illusion *shifted* like a tide of sand. What he had first thought were the manifestations of some internal mental struggle were revealed as something entirely different.

The shadows were not abstract things. They were other minds, echo-selves of tormented psyches flooding in from the void.

Where are they coming from? As the unspoken question formed from Spock's thoughts, the raging man in the heart of the maelstrom turned toward them, as if hearing his voice.

Spock and Saavik perceived a dark face twisted in pain, lips curled back in a snarl and eyes wide beneath the heavy, ridged brow of a Klingon.

"Help me!" roared the warrior.

"Worf." Spock spoke the name into the dimness.

When it was over, they found themselves where they had begun, upon the stones of the darkened corridor.

"The Klingon who serves aboard the *Enterprise*." Saavik gave a nod. "I have heard of him."

Spock rose slowly to his feet. "Many years ago, when he was Federation ambassador to the Empire, Worf and I worked toward the common goal of securing a series of powerful relic-weapons from the deep past."

Saavik rose with him. "You refer to the so-called Malkus Artifacts."

He nodded. "Correct. We joined minds then. His telepathic imprint has remained dormant in my psyche until now."

"Because he needs help. Perhaps, on some subconscious level, Worf's mind is calling out to you because he knows you are the only one who can aid him."

"I believe so. I must seek him out."

Saavik's brows drew together. "That will be difficult. Worf is currently a fugitive. Along with Jean-Luc Picard, he and several others defied orders and hijacked the Starfleet vessel *Aventine*, for reasons that Command have not seen fit to reveal."

Spock raised an eyebrow. "An unexpected complication. But not insurmountable."

Saavik mirrored his expression. "The whereabouts of the *Aven-*

tine are unknown. You believe that you alone can locate the ship that all of Starfleet is currently searching for?"

Spock gave a curt nod. "Yes."

U.S.S. Titan NCC-80102

If fury were a fire, then Deanna Troi's husband would have burned down everything around him.

She watched him stalking the *Titan*'s bridge, hovering like a hawk over the crew as they worked desperately to get the ship out of the snare that enveloped it. Riker's seething, ice-hot anger simmered barely below the surface, hardening his expression into something fearsome, something she had seen only on rare occasions.

Although she hid it, Troi was disturbed by the churn of emotions in him that only she could sense. Riker's annoyance, having emerged in the wake of Picard's escape from the *Titan* and the theft of the *Aventine*, had not lessened. If anything, it was growing stronger.

When Tom Paris and B'Elanna Torres flatly refused to disclose any of Picard's intentions, Riker threw them in Spacedock's brig and ordered Christine Vale to take the *Titan* to high warp. At first, Troi had been doubtful that her husband's command to take them to Omicron Theta was the right call, but he brooked no discussion, shutting down everyone.

Ultimately, he had been right. The *Aventine* was there and, apparently, so was Data. But Will had not counted on how far the android was willing to go for his former captain. His ire at losing Picard a second time threatened to overwhelm him.

"How much longer?" Riker strode across the command deck to where Vale was in close conversation with Melora Pazlar. "Every minute we are trapped inside this thing, they're light-years farther away."

"I am well aware, Admiral," Vale said curtly.

Normally, the edge in the captain's tone might have registered with Riker, but he didn't seem to notice. "There must be *something* we can do! Channel a covariant pulse through the main deflector dish, destabilize it with an isophasic resonance—"

"Melora has run simulations on all of those solutions and a dozen more," said Vale, cutting across him. "We do more damage to the ship than this . . . bubble."

"That may have to be a price we pay," he shot back.

"Admiral, we know the particle decay rate of the field effect," said Pazlar. "If we wait, it will fade and free us of its own accord."

"*Wait?*" Riker bit out the word, and Troi sensed everyone on the bridge hesitate. "Jean-Luc Picard will not control this pursuit, I will. We cannot let him set the agenda, is that understood?"

"You've made that clear," said Vale.

"Will." Troi stepped in, pitching her voice low. "Let your people do their jobs."

He shot Troi a look and his lip curled. Instead of answering her, he went to the tactical station, summoning Tuvok's attention. "Phasers don't work on that," he said, gesturing at the inner wall of the mirrored sphere. "Data did his homework there. We're too close for photon torpedoes, even at minimum yield."

"Correct, sir," said the Vulcan, wary of where the conversation was leading.

"I want you to program a quantum torpedo for launch." Riker held up his hand to silence Tuvok before he could voice his concerns. "Let me finish. I want you to intentionally decouple the warhead's phase inhibitors."

"That'll make it unstable," said Troi. "It will drop out of synch with normal spacetime."

"Exactly." He nodded toward the screen. "And that will be enough to let it pass *into* the material of the sphere. And when it detonates, the sphere will collapse."

"That is one possible outcome," admitted Tuvok. "Another is

that the detonation incites a cascade effect that will reflect back and crush the ship."

"We're not waiting any longer," said Riker. "I'll take the risk."

"I don't agree." Vale stepped up. "Perhaps we should discuss this privately, sir?"

"I don't need a pep talk in my own ready room," he shot back. "Tuvok, you and Pazlar program the torpedo, double-time. Make it work!"

"Are you making that a direct order?" Vale met his gaze.

"I am, so snap to it." He turned away. "Fire when ready, Number One."

Number One? Troi frowned at Riker's use of the signifier. When her husband was the captain of the *Titan* and Vale his first officer, that shorthand had been appropriate; but Vale had been the ship's commander for the better part of a year, and using the term of address here and now almost seemed a slight.

Troi met Vale's gaze. The other woman had caught the remark, but she was clearly more irritated than troubled by it.

After a few moments, Tuvok reported that the reprogrammed quantum torpedo was ready to deploy.

"Divert all available power to reinforce the shields," said Vale, staring ahead at the main viewscreen. "Structural integrity to maximum. All decks brace for effect . . . and fire it."

"Torpedo away," reported Tuvok.

Troi dropped into her chair, spotting the bright ember of the weapon as it looped out on a collision course with the sphere barrier. She turned to see her husband glaring at the torpedo, as if he were daring it to fail, to prove him wrong.

"Impact!" Pazlar called out the warning, just as a dazzling white light filled the bridge. Troi raised a hand to shield her eyes as the *Titan* rocked in the grip of the detonation shockwave. Control panels sparked and she tasted the acrid tang of burnt polymers as the energy recoil hit them.

When the trembling deck steadied, she looked up and saw that the sphere was now in tatters, the drones that had surrounded them torn apart and destroyed.

"It worked. I knew it would." Riker was on his feet, marching toward the main viewscreen. "Scan for warp signatures, slipstream decay," he ordered. "Any trace of the *Aventine*, anything at all!"

"Nothing on sensors," said Rager, at the ops station. "Negative return on ion trails. If they did use slipstream, they must have masked it."

"La Forge." The admiral said his former crewmate's name like a curse. "He did this. Hid them from me." Riker shook his head. "Not good enough. This is not right." He turned back to look across the bridge, taking everyone in with a single, severe glare. "We can't fall short on this, do you understand? You need to do better! Find that ship!"

"We understand," Vale said firmly. "We've all got it, loud and clear."

Troi saw the flash of anger in her husband's eyes and intercepted him before he could carry on. "There's nothing more we can do here," she said. "Starfleet Command should be informed about what happened. They can put ships in this sector on high alert. If they sight the *Aventine* . . ."

"Yes." He nodded, his annoyance ebbing, but only a little. "Contact Akaar, priority one," he told his wife. "This is not right. More ships . . . more ships will help us catch them."

Riker's wife tried to read him once again, but her empathic sense found only a confusion of conflicting emotions—anger, impatience, regret, even sorrow. "Will . . ." She reached out for him, but he was already walking toward the turbolift.

"Get it done," he told them, with a final nod to Vale as he left the bridge. "You have the conn, Commander. Carry on."

"Now he's demoting me?" Vale said as the turbolift doors closed.

"We're all under great stress, Captain," said Troi. "It was just . . . an ill-considered comment."

Riker knew he was supposed to step away, to take a moment to gather himself.

He feared that if he stopped moving, stopped striving, the impetus sustaining him would vanish—but if he kept going, if he didn't stop to breathe, he would drive himself into the ground. Both realities warred inside him, pulling him in one direction, then the other.

He only realized where he was going when the turbolift deposited him on the lower decks, close to holodeck two. Under alert conditions, the simulation chamber remained out of action, but his command privileges allowed Riker to override the controls and bring it back to life.

He entered, selecting a neutral location for himself—a beautiful piece of parkland on Deneva's southern continent, now lost after the Borg Invasion but forever preserved as a hologram.

The stress and the constant velocity of the chase gnawed at him. He felt it in a tingle in his fingers, the echo of an adrenaline rush. Riker forced himself to breathe slowly, searching for a calm place inside himself that remained beyond his grasp.

In here, things could be quiet and perfect, if only for a little while. In here, there was the chance for a respite, brief but vital.

"Arch." He called for the interface and pulled a handheld control padd from it, tapping out demands, customizing the holo-program as he went. "A picnic," he decided. "With my family."

Outside of the holodeck, out in the real world, there was too much noise, too much to deal with. If he could just get away from the turmoil in his thoughts . . . If he could just pause and *make it right*. Things would be better. He could stop Jean-Luc before he did something everybody would regret.

"I can't let him destroy this," he muttered, summoning a hologram of Deanna in that beautiful sundress she'd bought on Risa. Seeing his wife was like a balm, and it soothed him. The simulation didn't look at him with worry like the woman on the bridge. This Deanna looked at him with love, not judgment.

It was better, but it wasn't right. He deleted the Denevan landscape and tried something else. A cabin in his native Alaska, with crisp snow on the ground and a sharp chill in the air.

But it was still jarring, in a way he couldn't articulate. Riker shook his head. "This is not right."

Again, he blanked the backdrop and began to build from scratch. A rustic clearing on some bucolic, nonspecific world. A nearby lake bounded by trees. A house this time. Not a cabin, but a place where you could raise a family.

Then their child. Or was it children? *One? More?* A girl . . . Was there a boy as well?

He looked at the padd, switching through template after template. The holoprogram suggested possibilities, drawn from reality and from the vast catalog of simulations in its database, but each time Riker tried to settle on an image, he found it wanting and erased it.

"I know what my own flesh and blood look like," he said aloud. "I just need it to be correct."

It would not work if it wasn't correct. How could he rest here, how could he find a place to gather himself, if it *was not right*?

"This is wrong," Riker snapped, shaking his head. He tapped out a command, wiping it all, sending him back to the holodeck's neutral grid.

He took a deep breath, and started again.

10

— ◆ —

Perikian Monastery, Lonar Province, Bajor

A bow-wave of silence advanced in front of Benjamin Sisko as he walked up the wide stone steps before the monastery. The prylars and ranjens who saw him coming were struck by the sight, their conversations ceasing midsentence. The monks inclined their heads as he passed, giving their venerations to the Emissary, then whispering to one another in his wake.

"Does this happen to you a lot?" Walking at Sisko's side, Nog cast a wary eye over the Bajorans.

"It's a gesture of respect," he told the Ferengi. "They consider me the messenger of the Prophets in the corporeal world, and I have to honor that belief."

"I understand that," said Nog. "I just . . . Well, I've never seen this kind of thing close up before."

"Does it make you uncomfortable?" Following a few steps behind, Julian Bashir gave him a questioning look.

"People bowing as we walk past?" Nog glanced back. "Yes, it does feel a bit strange. Maybe I should have gone back with the chief."

"I need you here, Commander. O'Brien would have been missed on DS9," said Sisko. "And we couldn't wait." They reached the small plaza in front of the monastery's main entrance, and he looked up at the stained-glass friezes accenting the building.

"So, do we just knock on the door?" Bashir put his hands on his hips, surveying their surroundings. "Arguably, the whole place must know you are here by now."

"The whole province," Nog corrected, gesturing with an outstretched hand. "See there?"

The Ferengi indicated a large gathering of Bajorans who had set up a makeshift camp outside the southern gates of the monastery. Some of them resembled the monks tending to the holy site, but their robes were ragged and their manners less serene. They carried silk pennants atop tall poles with lines of Bajoran text written upon them, and although Sisko could not read the words, he knew what they said.

The people outside were adherents to the Prophecy of Talnot, the ancient Bajoran cleric that Jake's wife had mentioned. They were a fringe group of believers in an inevitable apocalyptic event who foretold a terrible fate for the planet and its people.

In other times, Sisko would have dismissed them as doomsayers and extremists, but his experience aboard the *Robinson* and his vision of a desolated world gave him pause.

What if they've been right all along? The possibility chilled him.

His thoughts were interrupted as a florid-faced man in the robes of a vedek came racing out, with a pair of adjutants in tow. "Emissary!" He bowed low. "You honor us with your presence." He cast a worried look first toward the camp at the gate, then at Nog and Bashir. "I am Vedek Otan. And our assemblage is, uh, at your service."

"Thank you," Sisko intoned. "We're here to speak with Vedek Kira."

"I suspected as much." Otan's head bobbed. He took a breath and stepped closer, his voice dropping to a whisper. "If I may be so bold to say, Emissary . . . With Talnot's Word spoken of widely in recent days, I beseeched the Prophets for clarity in this, and this morning you arrive. Do you bring guidance?"

Otan clearly needed to hear something that would assuage his fears, but Sisko stopped short of offering the vedek some vague platitude. He could not give an assurance that he himself didn't have.

"We all have questions," he said, at length. "I hope Vedek Kira and I can find the answers."

"Yes, yes, of course." Otan beckoned one of the younger monks to him. "Prylar Sarm will escort you to her. But I am afraid your companions will have to remain outside."

"As you wish." Sisko turned to speak privately to Nog and Bashir. "Gentlemen, why don't you observe? Knowing Nerys, this won't be a long conversation."

"We'll take a turn around the ornamental gardens," said Bashir.

But Nog was reluctant to accept. "Captain, are you sure?"

Sisko leaned in. "Look around, Commander. Everyone here is on edge. They're afraid that the end of the world is in the offing. We don't need to cause more problems."

"But that's just myths and legends," said Nog. "Right?"

"We'll see," Sisko replied, setting off after the prylar.

Nog watched him go. "That's not a reassuring answer," he muttered.

"Now you know how most of Bajor feels," said Bashir.

She knew he was there before he spoke.

Kira heard Sarm's distinctive, padding footsteps along the cloister's flagstones and the heavier tread of someone else close behind. Without turning, she sensed Sisko's intensity moving closer. Ever since the vision, Kira had known someone would come. It was only right and fitting that it was the Emissary.

"Vedek Kira?" said Sarm as she rose from her place by the stone garden. "We have a guest."

"Hello, Benjamin." She turned to face him, and allowed herself to feel nothing but the warmth of the moment, taking in the happiness at seeing her old friend once more.

"Nerys." He inclined his head, smiling a little as he picked up on her mood. "You look well."

"Who'd have thought the ascetic life would agree with me?" She reached up and cupped Sisko's ear with her hand, feeling the warmth of his blood through his skin, searching for the sense of his *pagh*, the force of his life.

She withdrew her hand, and they embraced. Kira was glad he was here; but she was also concerned by Sisko's arrival. The timing could not be a coincidence.

Kira wanted his unexpected appearance to be happenstance, something as simple as an old friend looking in on her well-being. But that was not to be.

It had taken her a lifetime to grasp the reality, but Kira knew that the paths of their fates had been written long ago, and they were bound to follow them to their conclusion.

They parted and studied each other. Having served side by side through so many trials and tribulations, Kira and Sisko shared the strong and unspoken bond that only comrades-in-arms could know. She searched his eyes, and she knew then what she feared was true.

"You saw it too." It was not a question. "The vision."

He nodded grimly. "Right up to this moment, I kept hoping I would be the only one."

"Same here." She dismissed Sarm with a nod of thanks, and the young prylar retreated to the cloister, out of earshot. When they were alone, she guided Sisko to a bench where they could sit. "Where were you when it happened?"

"The bridge of my ship. Sectors away." His dark gaze turned inward as he recalled the moment. "We were fighting a creature, a gigantic thing like a serpent."

"A viper . . ." she whispered.

"It had the ability to warp time." Sisko's brow furrowed. "When it hit the ship, that was when I saw . . ."

"Bajor in ashes."

"Yes."

"We both saw stars and planets dying. And the wormhole, burning with green fire."

"Yes." He took her hand. "Nerys, what does it mean? Is this something the Prophets will do, or are they warning us? Are the Pah-wraiths returning?"

Her gaze dropped, and she answered his question with one of her own. "In the vision, did you hear someone? See someone?"

Sisko took a breath. "There was a woman's voice."

"*No time.*"

She felt a thrill of shock through his fingers as she said the words, and he let go of her hand. "We don't have long, do we?"

"I can't answer that." The brief moment of joy Kira had experienced was gone, and in its place was a hollow knot of dread. "The answer isn't here on Bajor." She looked into the western sky, where the faint shimmer of the Celestial Temple could be seen, even in daylight. "It's up there. We have to find it."

"Nog and Julian are here," he told her.

"Julian?" Her eyes widened. "The last I heard, he was on Cardassia. I thought he was in some kind of catatonic state."

"He was. But it seems Ezri's death shook him out of it."

She considered that. "It must have been terrible for him. How is he?"

"Different," admitted Sisko. "And not just because of what happened to Dax. I think the man we knew doesn't exist anymore."

"We've all changed," she noted, pulling at her robe. "But the fact that you are here means that some things remain the same."

"Nog's ship, the *Saticoy*, is in orbit. It can take us to Deep Space 9. And from there . . ." Sisko trailed off. "Well, we can figure it out along the way."

"Just like old times."

He stood, and she moved with him. "We can go now, if you're willing."

Kira hesitated. "You saw the Adherents of Talnot at the gates?" Off his nod, she carried on. "They're appearing everywhere, on Bajor and the moons, on the station. Their ranks are swelling by the day. People are terrified. When they learn we had this conversation, if they even suspect what we've shared—"

"I know. The Emissary and the Hand of the Prophets, meeting in secret. It could cause panic. We don't need to pour fuel on that fire . . ." He considered it for a moment, then handed her a Starfleet combadge from an inner pocket. "Take this. Nog will beam us to the ship, move us covertly."

She called out to Sarm, and as the monk approached, she took Sisko's hand again. "I'll talk to Otan. He'll understand."

Sisko's doubts showed in his expression, but he didn't voice them. "All right. I'll see you on board." Then his smile came back, just for a moment. "Just like old times."

U.S.S. *Aventine* NCC-82602

"Are you certain?" Absently, Wesley rubbed the growth of beard on his chin and sat back, leaning against the computer console dominating one side of the astrometrics lab.

Data paused, giving him an arch look. "You've asked me that question three times in the past four hours. Phrasing it differently each time, of course, but the intent remains the same. And so does my reply. *Yes, I am certain.*"

Wesley let out a slow exhale. "The others are not going to like this. Not one bit."

From the far side of the room, Lal gave a brisk snort. "Is there anything about *any* of this situation that is likable?"

"It's just . . ." Wesley let his hand track up over his face. He hadn't slept properly since they fled the Sol system, and in retrospect, staying up to pull an all-nighter alongside a pair of tireless synthetics had probably not been the smartest thing to do. "It seems like every step forward we take with this problem, we sink in deeper. It just keeps on getting worse."

Data's expression softened, showing sympathy. Wesley still found it odd to see such human emotion on the android's face, after years of knowing him as a being incapable of such things. "Reality does not care about how we feel, Wes. It simply is."

"How we choose to face it is what matters," said Lal. "We never would have found the source without you."

"That does *not* make me feel any better," he admitted.

Their work in the astrometrics lab had begun by mapping the attacks of the Nagas, overlaying that with patterns of known Devidian incursions, and searching for the distinctive triolic energy traces common to both. Merging that with information gleaned from the Omnichron's voluminous memory bank was painstaking work, akin to sifting the mass of a dust cloud for one specific speck of matter, but hour by hour, the solution had gradually built itself before them.

Slowly, surely, lines of connection drew across the galaxy. Fine threads of temporal energy came together, weaving into thicker strands, then into a mass that had a definite, detectable center.

Even someone as intellectually gifted as Wesley, with his Traveler-augmented mind, had trouble keeping up with the incredible cognitive skills of Data and his daughter. In truth, the reason he had repeated his question was simple—he was afraid he had missed something along the way.

But no. These were the facts. Wesley studied the star map projected out around them on the curved screens of the lab's spherical walls. Facts did not lie.

"We have to tell them," he said. "The sooner we get there, the more time we'll have to consider a solution."

"They will be here presently," noted Data. "I took the liberty of asking Captain Picard and Captain Bowers to come down here. And as for a solution . . ."

"We already have that answer." Lal finished her father's sentence.

Wesley shook his head. "No. There has to be another way."

"I wish it were so. But you are more aware of the stakes than anyone." Data studied him. "You have seen the danger firsthand. You know that this is a matter of mathematics. As the Vulcans so eloquently put it, the needs of the many outweigh the needs of the few."

"That all depends on how you define 'the few,' doesn't it?"

The doors hissed open to admit Picard and Bowers, with Worf

following a step behind. The three men had taken what rest they could, but they shared the same grave mien as Wesley. It was hard to disengage when so much was riding on their mission.

For now, the *Aventine* was stationkeeping inside the crimson-hued deeps of a Mutara-class nebula, waiting for a break in the search pattern of nearby ships as the fugitive crew planned their next move. They had narrowly avoided detection upon exiting slipstream from the Omicron Theta system, and only Bowers's quick thinking had saved them.

"The *Orion* has resumed its patrol," offered Bowers, intuiting Wesley's unspoken question. "They'll be beyond scanning range in one hour, and then we can move again."

"Captain McLane is a man of keen insight," said Picard. "We'll need to be cautious when *Aventine* exits the nebula. I wouldn't put it past him to leave behind a few sensor probes in the area."

"I'll bear that in mind." Bowers glanced at Data. "Of course, we need a destination before we can go anywhere."

"We have one," said the android. "In fact, we have much more than that. Wesley, Lal, and I have spent the past hours mapping the Devidians' assaults, searching for the method amid the chaos."

"You found something?" Picard walked toward the star map, his eyes narrowing as he tried to parse the complicated snarl of energy traces.

Lal nodded. "It was Wesley who provided the key insight."

"It was? I did?" He blinked. "I must have missed myself being brilliant. But in my defense, I am a little punchy."

She went on. "My father and I had been operating on the assumption that the Devidians and their attack creatures were transitioning directly into this reality from a location outside conventional spacetime. But the energy required to penetrate a dimensional membrane over and over again is great, far more than an individual Naga could produce." Lal indicated the star map. "Wesley noted that rather than forcing an entrance each time they attacked, the Devidians might be using one that was already open."

"With that in mind, we altered our search to find a common point of ingress into this timeline," said Data, picking up the thread. "A wormhole."

Worf shook his head. "That does not follow. A wormhole effect is a pathway across distance. A tunnel from one location to another, not a portal to another dimension."

"In almost all cases, you are correct, Commander," allowed Lal. "But there are exceptions."

"In this instance, one key exception," added Data, "with which you are already familiar, Worf."

The Klingon's face fell as he caught on. "You are referring to the gateway to the Gamma Quadrant, in the Bajor system."

"That's the one." Wesley went to the astrometric console, using the interface to peel away the lines of threads on the screen. Layer by layer, the position of the Bajoran wormhole was revealed. "There's no other conduit like it that we know of. A stable, non-decaying corridor across the galaxy. Every other wormhole in recorded history is of finite duration, but not this one. And there's a reason for that."

"The Prophets." Picard studied the star map. "The noncorporeal life-forms living inside the wormhole, the ones the Bajorans consider their deities. They exist outside of the linear time stream as we know it. They keep the Bajoran wormhole anchored."

"The information gleaned from the Omnichron programmed by Wesley's older self appears to confirm our hypothesis," said Data. "He believed that to protect themselves, the Devidians had translated into a form of nonlinear existence similar to the Prophets. Allowing their forms to exist in a realm beyond our continua."

"The other me called it *intertime*," added Wesley. "Somewhere time as we know it does not exist. Think of it as the space between the ticks of the clock."

"You're saying that the Nagas are passing into our time stream through the Bajoran wormhole." Bowers sounded it out. "If that's so, wouldn't Deep Space 9 have been the first place to see them?"

Lal shook her head. "They don't come through all at once," she explained. "That is the insidious, ingenious part of it. What arrives here from intertime is, in effect, a quantum ghost, passing unnoticed into our space. It draws on the ambient energy of this dimension to make itself corporeal when it is ready to attack."

"Deep Space 9's logs indicate they have been picking up unusual particle traces in recent weeks," added Data. "Including higher than normal amounts of chronitons and triolic energy. But they had no way of knowing what that signified."

"Does this give anyone else a headache, or is it just me?" Bowers pinched the bridge of his nose.

"There's more," said Wesley.

"Of course there is," sighed Bowers.

"Continue, please." Picard gestured for Wesley to carry on.

"If the rate of incursions continues to grow, the Naga attacks will only get worse." He plucked the Omnichron from its place, unfolding it. A holographic projection phased into existence, throwing out panes of light, each one showing the surface of a devastated planet. "These Nagas they're using, they're bigger and more aggressive than the ones we've previously encountered. They've evolved to become more powerful. We've confirmed that they have annihilated the planet Vorgon Prime, and the phenomenon known as the Nexus." He waved through the images, coming to one that hit him hard. "Tau Alpha C is gone. The homeworld of the Travelers, my friends . . ." He couldn't say any more.

"Wesley, I am so very sorry." Picard offered the sympathy, but it was cold comfort.

"The attacks are increasing in strength and frequency," said Data firmly. "As suspected, the common denominator for each target is some connection to interdimensional or time travel. The Devidians are systematically destabilizing our timeline and robbing us of all possible means to strike back at them."

"Then we blockade the wormhole," grunted Worf. "It has been done before. We cut off their path of invasion. Halt the advance."

Data, Lal, and Wesley exchanged glances. Now it came down to the heart of the matter, and the crushing truth.

Wesley shook his head. "Physical measures won't stop them."

"Even when the mouth of the wormhole is shut, it still exists there on a quantum level," said Lal. "Closing it will not be enough."

"It must be utterly destroyed." Data's words seemed to chill the air. "If we hope to stabilize this timeline, even if only to delay the inevitable, the Bajoran wormhole must be collapsed permanently, never to reopen again."

Data's grim pronouncement lay heavily on Picard as they set to the next order of business, preparing the *Aventine* to depart the nebula and plotting a careful course toward the Bajor system.

Bowers returned to the bridge to liaise with his crew, but Picard felt the need to be alone with his thoughts. This new revelation regarding the Bajoran wormhole was a double-edged sword; if true, then it offered them the chance to cut off the Devidian advance into this time stream, perhaps even to preserve it. But there was no way to know how a forced collapse of the wormhole would affect the beings known as the Prophets.

It was possible such an act would end their existence. And moreover, he could only imagine how the Bajorans would react to such an action.

How can we sanction a strategy that might kill their gods?

Picard rested against a viewport, looking at but not really seeing into the nebula clouds surrounding the ship, and dwelled on the questions that rose up. He found himself wondering how much more they would need to sacrifice in order to stop this apocalypse.

"Captain." The low, muted voice startled him, jerking him out of his reverie. He turned to find Worf standing in the middle of the corridor, as rigid as a cadet at attention. "I must speak with you."

"Of course, Commander." Picard pushed aside his own concerns for the moment. "What is it?"

"I request to be relieved of my duties."

It was the last thing he expected to hear. "Relieved? Mister Worf, in case you've forgotten, we're not exactly following Starfleet protocols at present."

"I failed you!" insisted the Klingon. "I failed this ship, and . . . and dishonored Dax's memory." He looked away. "Admiral Riker was moments from taking control of this ship, because of my hesitation."

Picard was aware that Worf had seemed distracted of late, but given the scope of the problem at hand and the captain's own concerns, he had not seen fit to address the matter. Now he wondered if that had been a mistake. "We are still at liberty. That is all that matters."

"No." Worf ground out the word between gritted teeth. "Captain, I have not been forthright with you. For some time, I have been troubled by intrusive thoughts, by waking dreams that prey on my mind. I cannot sleep! It has undercut my ability to function as a Starfleet officer. The engagement at Omicron Theta proved that." He looked up. "I have become a liability. I made the mistake of trying to battle through it, and in doing so, I almost cost us the mission."

"Worf . . . *jupwI'*." He used the Klingon term for *my friend*, deliberately pitching the conversation as one between two comrades, not captain and commander. "Each of us is being pushed to our limits in this. And there will be farther to go. But we must work together. Only in unity can we succeed."

"I will hinder you." Worf shook his head. "I will petition Captain Bowers for a shuttlecraft. If I set off on a different course, I can act as a decoy to draw Riker's attention. This way, I will be of service." He took a breath. "I fear if I remain, my next failure will be inevitable."

Outside the viewport, the mass of the glowing nebula drifted away as the *Aventine* began to emerge from the great dust cloud. Picard was silent for a moment, watching the blackness of space reach in and take its place.

He had rarely seen Worf show such vulnerability. The warrior's confidence was severely shaken, and not just because of the near defeat by the *Titan*. "Tell me about these waking dreams," he said. "What do you see in them?"

"*Shadows.*" Worf said the word as if it were the name of something demonic, something he was fearful he would summon if spoken of too loudly. "My own face, reflected back to me, but twisted. A legion of them, bringing pain and torment. Of late, it grows worse."

"Have you ever experienced something like that before?"

Worf gave a wary nod. "Once. Returning from the *bat'leth* tournament on Forcas III, when I encountered a quantum fissure. For a brief instant, I shared the same space with dozens of alternate versions of myself. It is a dark mirror of that." He held up a hand before Picard could ask the next logical question. "I have already scanned myself, sir. My body does not exhibit any signs of similar effects to that incident. This . . . is all in my mind."

"You can't be sure of that. Perhaps Doctor Crusher can—"

"I am sure of one thing," Worf said, cutting him off. "I am unfit for duty. Please, Captain, accept this."

Picard sighed, regretting what he would say next. "Your request is denied. I need you here. I have too few allies on my side to consider losing even one of you. I'll do anything in my power to help, but in this moment, the mission takes precedence over everything."

A ripple of anger pulled at the Klingon's face, but only for a moment. He straightened, his manner turning coldly formal. "Understood. May I be dismissed, sir?"

"Worf—"

The three-tone bosun's whistle of the intercom cut into Picard's reply, followed by the voice of Captain Bowers. *"Bridge to Picard."*

He tapped the intercom, scowling at the ill-timed interruption. "Picard here."

"Captain, we may have a problem. We've just cleared the nebula, and there's something out here."

"So the *Orion* did leave a probe behind to watch for us."

"No," said Bowers, *"it's a ship, civilian registry, closing fast. I don't know how the hell they knew where we were, but we're receiving a tight-beam hail, specifically directed to the* Aventine.*"*

Picard glimpsed movement out in the void, and instinctively turned toward it. The copper-hued shape of a small, elegant ship grew as it vectored in toward them.

The design was distinctive: the bisected ring-and-spar form of a Vulcan swift courier, not much larger in tonnage than a Starfleet *Danube*-class runabout.

"They're requesting permission to dock," continued Bowers. *"What do we do? I'm open to suggestions."*

"We have covered our tracks with the utmost care," said Worf, snapping back to his brisk, military manner. "This may be an attempt to entrap us."

"I suspect not," said Picard. "But there's only one way to be sure."

La Forge sprinted into the *Aventine*'s shuttlebay gripping a tricorder in one hand. Captain Picard's urgent request for his presence didn't come with an explanation, but he could tell from the tone of it that *double-time* was definitely implied.

Worf and Picard were already there, joined by Bowers's security chief, Lonnoc Kedair. He noticed the Takaran woman was discreetly armed with a phaser, and she gave La Forge a severe nod as he came in.

The bay doors were already open, and the slim fuselage of a high-warp, low-mass craft nosed in through the force field holding out the vacuum. La Forge recognized the elegant engineering flourishes typical of Vulcan shipwrights. This was a diplomatic messenger, of the kind designed to speed between worlds carrying communiques deemed too sensitive for subspace radio.

"Reinforcements?" La Forge offered the question to the captain.

"Ask me again in five minutes," said Picard. He indicated La Forge's tricorder. "I need you to conduct a deep-range, full-spectrum scan of that ship and its crew. Anything untoward, bring it to my attention."

"Understood." As the courier extruded a set of landing skids and set down, La Forge began the scan, relaying the tricorder data directly to his visual cortex through a link to his optical implants. "No sign of any tracker emissions. Identifier beacon is inactive." He paused. "I read a single life sign on board."

As the shuttlebay resealed, a hatch retracted into the courier's fuselage and a ramp deployed. Without ceremony, a figure in dun-colored robes emerged, and a face seasoned by wisdom and lined by age appeared as he stepped through a mist of discharge from the thrusters.

"Isn't that . . . ?" At La Forge's side, Lieutenant Kedair's mouth dropped open in surprise, and she started to point, then caught herself.

"Yeah, *it is*," he whispered back, hardly believing it himself.

Spock of Vulcan: one of the most venerated Starfleet officers in the history of the Federation, and here he was falling out of the sky like some bolt from the blue.

"Ambassador." Picard covered his astonishment far better than the lieutenant and his chief engineer did, raising his hand in the traditional Vulcan salute. "This is . . . very unexpected."

Spock returned the gesture. "Well met, Captain Picard, Commander Worf. It is agreeable to see you once again, circumstances notwithstanding."

La Forge's tricorder beeped, signaling that the bio-scan of the elderly Vulcanoid was complete and showed no anomalies. The sound drew Spock's attention, and La Forge found himself being scrutinized.

"Commander La Forge, greetings," began the ambassador. "Please be assured that I am who I appear to be. However, if you wish to conduct additional scans to confirm I am not a Changeling, Chameloid, allasomorph, bioreplicant, or other ersatz form, I will permit it."

"No, uh . . . that won't be necessary." La Forge shot Picard a look. "He's the genuine article, sir."

Picard cleared his throat. "As edifying as it is to see you once again, Ambassador, I'm afraid your timing is inconvenient."

"On the contrary, Captain, I deem it to be quite opportune," said Spock. "I am fully aware of your current circumstances. My security clearances afford me access to the highest levels of Starfleet Command. On my journey from Vulcan, I took advantage of them to glean the details of both your arrest warrants and the alarming information you brought back from this ship's jaunt into the future. Both lead to very troubling conclusions." He paused. "I understand why Admiral Akaar has seen fit to designate you as priority fugitives."

Kedair cleared her throat, recovering her poise. "Sir, if you are here to intercept us, I would respectfully suggest you return to your craft and be on your way." Her hand dropped to the hilt of her holstered phaser.

Spock raised an eyebrow. "My intention is not to waylay the *Aventine*, nor to interfere in your mission, Lieutenant. In the past, I too have had cause to disobey orders."

"Why are you here, and how did you locate us?" Worf made the demand with characteristic bluntness.

"I deduced the *Aventine*'s most logical course and heading by examining environmental microindicators and running predictive algorithms of my own creation," said Spock.

"You just . . . figured it out." La Forge considered the massive complexity of sifting a coherent answer out of so many disparate bits of information.

"Indeed." Spock's gaze returned to Worf. "As to the first part of your question, Commander, I will of course provide whatever assistance I can in your work against the Devidian threat. But my primary reason for intercepting the *Aventine* is you, sir."

"Me?" Worf's body language changed, becoming defensive.

Spock nodded. "I have seen the shadows, Mister Worf. I have come to free you from them."

11

———

U.S.S. *Aventine* NCC-82602

"I still don't see why we can't do this in sickbay." Crusher studied her tricorder intently, running a handheld scanner over Worf's brow. "I won't pretend to be the expert that Ambassador Spock is, but it seems risky. Your neurochemical balance is far outside of Klingon physiological norms. If it grows worse, you could fall into a coma or suffer permanent brain damage."

"With respect, Doctor, in this matter I will defer to Vulcan wisdom," Worf told her. Spock's offer of aid to calm his unquiet mind was the first thing in days that had given the Klingon a measure of hope.

With each passing day, the pressure of the chaos in his thoughts grew more strident. He had begun to fear that he would lose his sanity. It was chief among the reasons he had wanted to leave the *Aventine*, before it grew too severe to control, so the slim chance of any healing was impossible to ignore.

Crusher looked across to Captain Picard, who stood with Alexander in the holodeck's entrance vestibule. "Worf's cortisol levels are extremely elevated. His fight-or-flight response is running at full tilt. A human would be crawling the walls by now."

"There is something to be said for Klingon fortitude," said Picard.

"The word you're looking for is *stubbornness*, Captain," added Alexander. Worf's son folded his arms across his chest. "My father has it in abundance."

"It is a family trait," Worf retorted, then glanced back at Crusher. "I appreciate your concern, Doctor, but this is how I wish to proceed."

"I can give you something," she offered, reaching for a hypo-spray. "To lower your stress."

"No." He shook his head. "I must face this with a clear mind."

"Stubborn," repeated Alexander.

"All right, but at least let me do this . . ." Crusher produced a small circular device with a blinking indicator. "It's a neural monitor. If your brainwave patterns become irregular, we can beam you directly to sickbay."

Worf grudgingly agreed, and Crusher applied the device to one of his temples. He walked to the holodeck doors, pausing only to lower his voice and speak to Alexander. "No matter what happens, do not pull me out. I must see this to the end."

"You ask too much." He saw fear in his son's eyes. "You are precious to me, Father."

"As are you to me. I trust Spock. He will rid me of this malaise." Alexander sighed. "I wish I had your conviction."

Worf clasped his son's hand. "I will see you soon. All will be well . . . Or we will meet again in *Sto-Vo-Kor*. Whichever is fated."

Without looking back, he advanced toward the doors, which sighed open at his approach. Worf crossed the holodeck's threshold, stepping from the brightly lit corridors of the *Aventine* and into the snowy chill and rarefied air of a stone courtyard.

He let himself acclimatize as the doors shut behind him, his breath escaping his lips in a streamer of white vapor. "Boreth," he said aloud, taking in the walls and donjons of the Klingon monastery. It had been some time since his pilgrimage to the sacred place of Kahless the Unforgettable, but the simulation brought his memories of it flooding back.

Boots crunching on the frost-rimed ground, he approached a hooded figure sitting on one of a pair of stone benches in the center of the courtyard. At first, he wondered why the Vulcan had chosen this specific location, assuming that they were to come together in some neutral, uncluttered space. The current state of the real Boreth was uncertain, after being attacked by a pack of Nagas, but the reason for Spock's choice of it soon became clear to him; his memories of the planet were ones of being at peace, of knowing himself. Spock had deliberately selected a setting that spoke to Worf's Klingon heart on a deep, visceral level. A place that rooted him in his own identity.

"Greetings, Commander." The Vulcan indicated the other bench. "Sit." He eyed the device attached to Worf's head. "A gift from Doctor Crusher?"

"Yes." Worf sat opposite the Vulcan. "She is concerned."

"Humans." Spock offered the word like a shrug. "They mean well."

The two of them sat for a moment as the heavy flakes of thick snow settled silently on the ground. Spock's gaze was bright and keen, and Worf sensed him searching his eyes for some elusive hint of truth.

"You make efforts to hold your thoughts in check, but I see the turbulence beneath the surface," said the Vulcan.

"You sensed that from across the quadrant. My . . . turmoil?"

"Yes. An echo effect from our previous connection. I could no more ignore it than a wound to my own flesh." Spock raised his hand, leaning closer. "This will be different from the first time we joined minds. We will both experience discomfort. Are you prepared?"

"I do not know," Worf admitted. "But I feel the horizon of my thoughts slowly decaying as the shadows encroach. I wish to be rid of them. I will endure what I must."

"Very well." Spock's fingertips touched the surface of Worf's face, and the first faint traces of psychic energy moved between them. "My mind to your mind."

"My thoughts," said Worf, closing his eyes, "to your thoughts."

It was difficult at first, as he knew it would be. To open up one's inner self to the embrace of the meld was a kind of surrender, and surrender was not a Klingon trait. But the door between the two of them opened both ways, and through it Spock offered only openness and trust. Worf forced himself to accept the gesture, and the connection solidified.

"Our consciousness moves as one." They were the Vulcan's words, but Worf heard them resonate inside with his own voice. "We journey inward. We search for the place where the darkness dwells. We search for the shadows."

And soon they found them.

Worf's eyes opened. He stood side by side with Spock in the snowy courtyard, but something was different. The monastery buildings were aging as they looked upon them, the stones crumbling into black sand as millennia passed in seconds. Overhead, the night sky slowly darkened as point after point of starlight guttered out.

"Mister Worf." Spock pointed toward the edges of the courtyard. "Do you see them?"

A legion of smoke-shapes were forming, the cohort of shadows lining the broken stone walls. They were the vanguard of an army, howling silently at Worf, massing for attack.

He uttered the question that had been driving him from the very start. "What do they want from me?"

Spock cocked his head, coolly evaluating the overwhelming threat surrounding them. "They are angry and afraid, just as you are," he said. "What they want is what you have and they do not, Mister Worf. *Existence*."

"I do not understand."

The shadows began to advance. Slow, surefooted, certain of their victory, the hazy forms closed ranks and tightened the circle around Worf and Spock. As they drew nearer, they became better defined. Shapes that suggested faces with ridged Klingon brows grew definition. Phantoms clad in smoke became figures in uniforms, some in gray battle armor, others in robes of common cloth. They bore weapons—a panoply of blades, cudgels, even stones and sticks.

They wanted Worf to die at their hands, but it was more than that. He felt it clearly for the first time, through the lens of Spock's insight. The shadows wanted what Worf possessed—they were the dead and they wanted to live. His very reality was what they desperately craved.

Strangely, the Klingon felt a jolt of sorrow for them. These pitiful half lives, these echoes of himself that had been snuffed out of existence. The ghosts of countless other selves, each Worf lost, furious, insane, and *desperate*.

Spock stood close at hand. "Do you understand them now?"

He nodded, grasping for comprehension as the shadows thickened into a wall thousands deep. "This is not my mind rebelling against me! Where have they come from?"

"The shadows originate from beyond your consciousness," said the Vulcan. "From beyond what we comprehend as our existence. Each one of them is you, torn away from a different life. They have lost everything. They are *afraid*."

Worf had committed himself to this, expecting to face a fight to the death, where his blood could sing in martial fury. But the battle before him was one of wills, where the weapons were despair and grief.

The shadows hurled themselves toward him, and at last he heard their screaming, their frantic cries to be saved. It horrified Worf to see these broken mirrors of himself, and it chilled his heart to imagine what terrors could have wounded them so gravely.

"You must choose," Spock said urgently. "Defy them or submit to them. But only one consciousness can live within your mind. Too many will crush you from within."

"*No.*" Worf stepped away from the Vulcan and walked into the mass of the shadows. He spread his hands, showing he bore no malice. He raised his head, bearing his throat. "You have no place here! This existence is *mine*!" His denial thundered around the courtyard.

The wailing and screaming rose to a shattering crescendo, but Worf endured the bitter storm of it, holding on to the truth of himself. The shadows tore into him—through him, passing like smoke across a shaft of light—and with each impact, he experienced a fraction of a life led, a life lost.

Memories that were not his briefly caught on his consciousness, fading in and out. He saw flashes of pasts he had not lived—a Worf never adopted by humans, a Worf whose marriage to Deanna Troi bore him two children, a captain of the *Enterprise*, a venerated ambassador, a blinded soldier still fighting the Dominion, a Romulan slave, a half Borg, a rage-fueled conqueror, and an infinity of others.

Each desperately clawed for purchase in the vessel of his body. Their realities had died along with them, and what essences of them remained sought to live at any cost. Even if that meant usurping the Worf that lived in this timeline.

"No," he repeated, beating them back with a roar. "Face your ends with honor, as I will face mine when the moment comes!"

Worf's heart hammered against his ribs and his nerves sang with pain, but he stood firm. He could feel Spock's presence at his back, the Vulcan's impressive mental strength holding him up.

"I have you," whispered the other man's voice. "I will aid you. But only you can end this."

If Worf fought them, he would lose. If he surrendered, he would lose. The only path to survival was to acknowledge the truth, for Worf and for every other version of himself.

"You lived!" he shouted to the dead sky. "But that moment is gone! Know that none of you will be forgotten! Your legacies are mine . . ." Worf bowed his head and summoned the words to end his torment. "*Now die well.*"

Crusher's tricorder emitted a strident warning tone and she made for the door. "That's enough, he's on the verge of complete neural overload!"

Alexander moved to block her path. "Doctor, please step aside."

"Your father is seconds away from brain death," she shot back. "Let me pass!"

"His wishes—"

"To hell with them," grated Picard, smacking his hand on the control panel. "We won't lose another friend today."

The holodeck doors opened, but to their collective surprise, the Boreth holo-scenario was no longer active. Inside the chamber, the bare silver walls and the emitter grid were visible, and the only indicator that the simulation had been running was a fading chill in the air.

Worf and Spock approached them, and the Klingon offered something to the doctor. Crusher held out her hand, and he dropped the neural monitor device into her palm.

"It short-circuited," he explained.

"Clearly." Crusher pulled out her tricorder and conducted a new scan. "How do you feel, Commander?"

Worf smiled thinly, and met the worried gaze of his son. "Better."

"What happened in there?" Picard peered into the holodeck, as if expecting to find something still lurking inside. "You were only gone for a few minutes."

"The concept of time is altered during a meld," noted Spock. "For Mister Worf and myself, the subjective event lasted for several hours." He paused. "Captain, I must make you aware of the matter of our shared experience. I am now convinced that the mental distress experienced by the commander was caused by an outside influence . . . a great number of them, in fact."

"How so?" Picard frowned at the notion.

"When I joined with Worf's mind, I sensed a multitude of near-identical mental patterns attempting to impinge on and overwhelm his consciousness. Telepathic echoes of other selves, cut loose from their corporeal forms in a moment of wretched agony."

"Are you asking us to believe in ghosts?" said Alexander.

"I assure you, Ambassador, these are no mythical phantasms."

Spock shook his head. "For every parallel timeline where a version of us exists, there is a trace of psionic energy on a wavelength close to ours." He tapped his brow. "Imagine those traces cut loose and adrift after the collapse of their timeline. Some might find their way across dimensional borders, where the barrier is porous. They would be attracted to energy of a similar potential, driven to seek the life taken from them."

"It would seem," said Worf, "that I have been haunted by my own ghosts."

"By thousands, if not millions, of possible versions of yourself," corrected Spock.

"Incredible . . ." Picard took in the idea. "And quite ghastly."

Crusher looked up. "I hate to say, that sounds plausible." She gestured with the tricorder. "I've been analyzing sensor readings captured during some of the Naga attacks, and there's a common anomaly that keeps showing up. In scans of some people exposed to the influence of the Devidians, there are traces of multiple, overlapping brainwave patterns. At first I thought it was some kind of warping effect caused by the temporal displacement, but if Mister Spock is correct . . ."

"Those are the last traces of minds from dead universes, crying out for help." Alexander shuddered at the thought. "Is there no end to their cruelty?"

"This could be just the beginning," said Crusher. "If the Nagas continue to bleed into our time stream, and the barriers between dimensions weaken, this side effect will grow more prevalent. More people will fall victim to it, like a . . . a temporal multiple-personality disorder."

"But why was Worf affected first?" Picard looked to Spock, then to his executive officer.

"You misunderstand, Captain Picard," said Spock. "The commander's formidable mental strength allowed him to *resist* the invasion of his mind. Others who experienced the same effect have likely perished from it."

A cold, creeping realization came over Worf. "Sir, I am not the only one to suffer this." His thoughts went back to the moment on the *Aventine's* bridge over Omicron Theta, when he had confronted Will Riker face-to-face. "Having seen this from within, I understand it now. And I know I saw the same darkness in Riker. The same shadows, clouding his gaze."

The color drained from Picard's face. "*Mon dieu.* If that is so . . ."

"If the admiral is experiencing the same pain and terror I suffered," said Worf, "I fear for him, sir."

U.S.S. Titan NCC-80102

Sleep, when it finally came for Deanna Troi, was not a peaceful state.

Instead of allowing her body to recharge and recuperate, it felt as if she were only docking it in place for a time, shutting down into a dreamless non-state. So when she heard the musical tone from the other part of the cabin, Troi could not immediately decide if it was real, or the artifact of some half-recalled dream.

The sound was soft and gentle, and familiar to her. She lay alone in bed, straining to listen for it. Her hand moved to Will's side of the mattress and found nothing there, the sheets cool from the absence of her husband. She tried to remember the last time they had awoken beside each other—days, it felt like. She suspected he was catching short bursts of rest in his office in the operations center, concentrating as much of his waking time as possible on tracking down the *Aventine*.

It was turning into an obsession, and people were talking. She and Christine Vale were not the only ones who had noticed how Riker had misaddressed the *Titan's* captain in the heat of the moment, and that slip was one of many. On his last, brief visit to their quarters, he had seemed lost for words after coming across a picture of their daughter, Natasha. Troi's husband was becoming increasingly distracted, and his unwillingness to talk to his wife was troubling. Even her empathic senses, so attuned to his moods after many years together, gave her little insight.

She heard the noise again, for certain this time. The melodic tone was like a snatch of birdsong, and it connected to a memory.

Jean-Luc's Ressikan flute. Troi remembered listening to Picard picking out a beautiful, mournful tune on the alien instrument, and she knew this was the same.

Pulling on a robe, Troi walked into the main area of the admiral's quarters. She found a message light blinking on a desktop console, and frowned. The device had been switched off when she went to bed a few hours earlier.

Warily, she tapped the screen. A line of text appeared, asking her if she would like to hear more of the tune. "Yes," she told it, compelled by her curiosity. "Proceed."

But what came next was not more music, but a familiar voice. *"Deanna,"* said Jean-Luc Picard, *"are you alone?"*

"Yes, I'm here."

"One moment."

The console display dissolved into a torrent of digital code, and in the next second a flickering, pixelated hologram of the *Enterprise*'s captain formed in the middle of the room. Projected from one of the console's hidden holo-casters, it was a poor-quality transmission, but clear enough for her to read the emotions on Picard's face.

He looks old and worn out, she thought. *The stress of this is aging him.*

"Deanna, we need to talk."

She nodded. "Yes, we do." Troi paused, glancing around. "Should I ask how you're doing this? Are you somewhere nearby?"

"No," he replied. *"Hence the poor connection. As to the method, thank Data for that."*

"He's on the *Aventine*, then. Will was right about you recruiting him."

Picard nodded. *"Data was able to penetrate* Titan's *subspace communications array with a masked holographic signal. It's encrypted, so* no one can listen in on this conversation, but I don't know how long we can keep the channel open, so I must be direct."

"Don't ask me to go against my husband." The words slipped out of her mouth before she knew it. "I won't choose between him and my loyalty to you."

"*I would never make that demand,*" he replied. "*I have always trusted you implicitly, Deanna. I trust you now.*" Picard's hologram moved across the room toward her. "*I need to know about Will. I need your insight. From the moment we returned to Earth, I sensed something was amiss with him. I couldn't put my finger on it. But he wasn't acting like the man I know.*"

"He's under a great deal of strain." Despite her own misgivings, Troi's first instinct was to defend Riker. "What you have done . . . It isn't easy for him to deal with."

"*It wasn't done lightly,*" said Picard. "*I hope you believe me.*" He paused, and she sensed he was searching for the right words. "*But this goes far beyond a difference of opinion. The William Riker I know and respect would not sanction an unprovoked attack on another Starfleet vessel. He would not stand by and do nothing while innumerable innocent lives are at risk.*" His voice dropped. "*Tell me I am wrong. Tell me you don't see a change in him.*"

"I . . . I can't." Troi stared at the floor. She wanted to believe it wasn't so, but her instincts pulled her inexorably toward the opposite conclusion. "He's become distant. Distracted. Even confused at times."

Picard's concern was evident. "*Deanna, this is important. I believe Will is under the influence of an outside force that is affecting his judgment. This is not like before, with the Cytherians. This is something far more insidious. I've embedded a file in the matrix of this message with all the information I have. Read it and reach your own conclusions.*"

She said nothing. Riker was one of the most resilient people Troi had ever known, but she had seen him brought low by alien influences more than once.

Picard continued. *"Has he experienced any waking dreams? Nightmares? Has he spoken to you about seeing shadows?"*

Troi's blood ran cold. She recalled Riker's words to her, days ago when he had awoken in the middle of ship's night, drenched in sweat, after crying out in his sleep.

I felt like I was drowning in shadows.

"Yes." She searched her thoughts, trying to recall the turbulent shape of her husband's empathic aura in that moment. It had seemed different somehow, almost displaced. "I think he—"

Troi never got to finish the sentence. The door to the quarters opened and Riker filled the entrance. He held a phaser in one hand, and a humming tricorder in the other. She saw Lieutenant sh'Aqabaa out past him in the corridor, the female Andorian security officer's antennae raised in alarm.

"Wait outside, Pava," said Riker, his face stone hard. Jamming the phaser into the holster, Troi's husband stepped into the room and the door closed them in.

"Will . . ." She raised a hand to halt him, but he ignored her.

"How did you know?" said Picard, at length.

"I know how you think," replied Riker. "So I was watching for any signs of systems intrusion. When I detected an unscheduled, heavily encoded holo-signal, it didn't take long for me to figure out what you were up to." He scanned Picard's hologram with the tricorder. "I expected better, Captain. This kind of subterfuge is beneath you."

"You didn't leave me with much choice, Admiral," Picard said levelly.

"So you try to drive a wedge between me and my wife?" Riker's voice rose into a near snarl. "What's happened to you, Jean-Luc?"

For a moment, Troi thought Picard was going to strike back with an angry retort, but that emotion faded from his features. *"I saw the end of everything, Will. I'll sacrifice all I am to prevent that."*

"You already have," Riker shot back. "Mutiny, theft, conspiracy, insubordination, reckless endangerment . . ." He ticked off the charges one by one. "You'll never sit in a captain's chair again, do you realize that? And Worf, Bowers, and the rest? You've damned them along with you, all because the great Jean-Luc Picard thinks he knows what's best. There won't be a second chance this time. You're *done*."

"*As I said a moment ago . . .*" Picard gave a heavy sigh, and his image distorted and shimmered. "*There was no other choice.*"

"No." Troi stepped forward. "I'm not going to listen to you both turn this into a zero-sum game. We can't let this go on!" She gave Riker an imploring look. "There has to be another way! I know you don't want this!" She took her husband's hand, searching his gaze for the man she knew she loved.

He drew back, letting Troi's hand drop away. "Captain Picard," Riker said formally. "Out of respect for our friendship and for your service to the Federation, I've kept Admiral Idyn at bay while he petitioned Akaar to send the whole fleet after you. But that can't continue." He looked back at the flickering hologram. "Right now, I'm allowing this conversation to happen because I have one final offer to make."

Picard listened intently. "*Go on.*"

"Give yourself up. Send me the *Aventine*'s coordinates and I promise you I will shield the others as best I can from the consequences of this. You'll have to take the fall, Jean-Luc. But Beverly and your son will walk away."

"*That's a generous proposal,*" said Picard. "*Which I am afraid I have to decline.*" His tone shifted, becoming urgent. "*Will, I know what's wrong! I know what you are going through, what you see in the dark—*"

Riker's finger touched a tab on the open tricorder, and the hologram vanished instantly.

Christine Vale's voice filtered in over the intercom. "*Bridge to Riker. Sir, that signal just died on us.*"

"I know," he replied, turning back to Troi. "Did Pazlar get anything?"

"Admiral, Commander Sarai here." Vale's first officer broke in. *"We were unable to read any of the signal's content, but trace decay on the transmission narrows it down to an origin point somewhere in the Bajor Sector. If we'd had more time . . ."*

"That'll be enough. I'll be there in a few minutes. Riker out." He kept his gaze on his wife. "What did he ask you?"

"He's worried about you."

"Is that how he framed it?" Troi's husband spoke quietly. "I know this hasn't been easy for any of us. But while Jean-Luc is trying to undermine me by suggesting I'm not in my right mind, take a moment to ask yourself if *his* behavior seems right to you. He is the one who broke protocol, not me." Riker sighed. "Think of everything he's gone through, time and again with the Borg, then recently with the Zife scandal and the Section 31 revelations, with what's happened to René . . . Admiral Idyn was right when he said Picard's the one showing signs of instability, and what's worse is he's drawing good people into this delusion along with him." Riker walked away, shaking his head. "I won't allow that to happen to you and our children, Deanna. *I won't.*"

"Our child," she said aloud as the door closed behind him. "We only have *one* child."

U.S.S. *Aventine* NCC-82602

Picard stepped out of the area marked by the edges of the holo-scanner in the captain's ready room, frowning as Wesley made a throat-cutting gesture.

"He pulled the plug at their end," said Wesley. "I don't think they managed to trace our exact location, but *Titan*'s crew is top-flight. We have to assume they have a lead on us now."

Worf stood nearby, studying the readout on a monitor with grave focus. "*Aventine*'s speed is only an advantage while we are on the move. The moment we reach our destination, that becomes irrelevant."

"Which was always the reality of it," replied Picard. "We've been on borrowed time since the moment we slipped the dock."

Wesley read the expression on his face. "Is Counselor Troi with us?"

"I can't be sure." Picard shook his head. "She knows something isn't right. But it's a lot to ask. She'll have to come to the truth on her own. I don't know what else we can do."

"Deanna is the most perceptive woman I have ever known," said Worf. "She will know what to do."

"I hope so." Picard walked out onto the *Aventine*'s bridge, with the others at his heels.

"Captain." Bowers threw him a nod from the command chair. "How did it go?"

Picard returned the gesture. "Not well, I'm afraid."

"Well, we knew it was a long shot, but we had to roll those dice." Bowers called out to Lieutenant Mirren at the ops console. "Oliana, what's our ETA?"

"Two minutes and fifteen seconds, sir," said the woman. "As instructed, I'm bringing her in on a wide approach, high over the plane of the ecliptic. If we slow to impulse, we should be able to get close in before we're detected."

Bowers gestured at the air. "Carry on." He looked back at Picard. "I hope you've got a good argument up your sleeve, sir. Otherwise, this is all going to be over very quickly."

"I'll improvise," offered Picard.

Bowers did not look convinced. "I hope that will be enough."

At the aft of the bridge, the turbolift doors slid open to allow Data and Spock to exit. Picard saw a glowing object floating in the air alongside them, moving as they moved, and he realized it was Wesley's Omnichron.

The device hummed to itself, turning gently inside an orb of holographic panes, then it seemed to become aware of the Traveler's presence. It floated across the room and settled into Wesley's hand, like an obedient pet. "Was it any help with the long-range scans?"

"Quite," Data affirmed. "Thank you, Wesley. Merging your device's isomorphic sensing matrix with the *Aventine*'s deflector dish enabled us to create a temporary quantum imaging framework. Ambassador Spock and I were able to update our intelligence on the Devidian incursions across all four galactic quadrants. Lal is currently sifting the information for any additional insights."

"I'll just nod and pretend I know what all of that means," said Bowers.

Worf folded his arms. "What have you learned?"

"The rate of incursion continues to grow exponentially," said Spock. "It appears that another large-scale event took place on the far side of the Delta Quadrant only a few hours ago."

"Define *event*," said Picard, but his wary tone suggested he already suspected what the android meant.

"A number of stars inside the borders of the Krenim Imperium passed through catastrophic forced aging," said Data. "From what we can determine, the heart of the Imperium's military was obliterated."

"The Krenim are an aggressively time-active species," noted Wesley. "Their temporal weapon ships are formidable. It makes sense the Devidians want to take them out of play."

Picard nodded. "Yes, I recall Admiral Janeway's logs detailing her encounters with them." He paused, thinking it through. "First the Devidians went after the Hirogen, now the Krenim. The two most belligerent races in the Delta Quadrant, hobbled and defanged."

"But not destroyed outright," Worf said, grim faced. "No mercy of a quick death. The Devidians want their victims alive to suffer through the end of this time stream, so they can feed off them when the final moment comes."

"I believe we are fast approaching a tipping point," said Spock. "When the Devidians determine they have neutralized all significant resistance, they will proceed to the terminal phase of their plans for our reality. The cull."

"If they trigger the collapse of this timeline, nothing we can do will stop them," Picard said firmly, taking in everyone on the *Aventine*'s bridge. "It cannot be stressed enough. We are in the fight of our lives. The future of all we know hangs in the balance."

"We're in this to the end, Captain," said Bowers. "Whatever it takes."

As Picard accepted that, Lieutenant Mirren called out from her station. "Exiting slipstream in three . . . two . . . *one*."

The tunnel of threaded starlight on the main viewscreen unfolded into the blackness of normal space, and immediately the bright yellow glow of the star B'hava'el became visible off the portside quadrant. *Aventine* had arrived high up over the Bajor system, and the view shifted as the ship pivoted; but then an unexpected tremor ran through the deck plates, quickly followed by the chimes of sensor warnings.

"Report!" Captain Bowers twisted in his chair to address his crew.

"We're detecting unusually high concentrations of charged verterons throughout the system, sir." Lieutenant Kedair's hands flashed across her station as she brought up the readings. "Subspace particle density is off the scale."

"Verterons are emitted by intense subspace phenomena," said Spock, glancing at a repeater screen. "Most notably, wormholes. But never in such great amounts."

"Captain, with your permission?" Picard shot Bowers a look, and the *Aventine*'s commander gestured for him to continue. "Lieutenant Mirren, bring us around. Turn us toward the Bajoran wormhole."

"Aye, sir." Mirren worked the helm and *Aventine* extended its slow turn, the image on the main viewer slowly changing from the deep ink-black of interplanetary space to a field of sparkling energetic particles that glowed a searing, toxic shade of emerald.

Picard had witnessed the opening of the gateway to the Gamma Quadrant in the past, and each time he had been awed by the incredible dance of exotic energies. The whirlpool of silver fire and pure, radiant blue was a sight that caught his breath. But what came into view before them was not that majestic spectacle.

It was the ruin of it.

Burning virulent green the shade of some alien ichor, a grotesque tear in the surface of space hung open, a vast rough maw exhaling streams of corrupted particles and deadly radiation.

The monstrous inversion of the graceful, beautiful phenomenon seemed to corrode everything around it, and part of Picard recoiled as some deep animal instinct screamed at him to flee.

"What the hell *is* that?" breathed Wesley.

"Medusa," muttered Bowers. "Look too long and you'll turn to stone."

"That," said Spock, into the shocked silence that followed, "is the Bajoran wormhole. The Celestial Temple of the Prophets. Or rather, that is what it has become."

"The entirety of the Denorios Belt surrounding it is in rapid plasma decay." Data joined Spock in following Lieutenant Kedair's sensor scans. "The altered wormhole's outpouring of energy appears to be consuming it."

"We're too late," said Picard. "The end has already begun."

PART III

ECLIPSE

12

Deep Space 9, Bajor System

The rematerialization took uncomfortably longer than Kira Nerys would have preferred. She felt the disembodied sensation of being cut off from her senses as the transporter beam was shunted through a masking filter to hide it from detection; and then at last it was over.

Dressed in a jacket that was a riot of purples and browns, Quark beckoned her sharply from the console next to the cargo transporter. "Step off, Colonel, as quick as you can. Unless you want the others to stay stuck in the pattern buffer."

"I haven't been *Colonel* Kira for a long time," she told the Ferengi, pulling her traveling robes close as she climbed off the pad. "You know that."

"Force of habit," Quark retorted, running the materialization cycle again. "I've been thinking about the good old days a lot recently, it's on my mind."

"Good old days," she repeated. "That's not how I remember the Cardassian Occupation."

"Which one?"

"Either. They were both equally unpleasant."

"You know what I mean." He showed his snaggle-toothed smile as Julian Bashir beamed into solidity. "Doctor! Welcome back to the land of the living!"

"Quark." Bashir stepped down, following Kira across the cluttered space of the storage bay. He looked around, taking in the cavernous compartment. "Where are we?"

"We're down in the main cargo hold." Kira answered first. "Below the main spindle."

"Ah." Bashir turned to watch the last member of their party beam in. "More roomy than the old DS9."

Kira nodded. "I can't believe I'm going to say this, but as good as this station is, it doesn't have the character of that iron-clad monstrosity we used to live on."

"Quite." Bashir rapped his knuckles on a tritanium support pillar.

Built after the original Cardassian *Nor*-class mining station had been destroyed by the Typhon Pact five years earlier, outwardly the new *Frontier*-class station recalled the design of its predecessor, but inwardly its lines were Starfleet smooth and well maintained.

"That's the Federation for you," grumbled Quark. "Eventually they knock the sharp corners off everything, and what does that leave you with? Just a lot of . . . round things."

Around them, the compartment creaked and hummed, metal ticking under the strain of intermittent gravity waves from the turbulent singularity out in space. Every few minutes, a tremor like a distant earthquake rumbled through the decking.

"That's been happening for a few weeks," Quark explained as he worked. "It's getting worse. Putting everyone on edge." He blinked as the third arrival solidified. "And here we are. That's three for three, all organs intact, all limbs in the right place. I believe I've earned my fee for bringing you aboard covertly."

"That you have." Benjamin Sisko, dressed in robes of similar cut to those worn by Kira and Bashir, stepped off the pad and fished a flip-grid communicator from his pocket. "Sisko to Nog."

"Nog here." The voice of Quark's nephew echoed off the stacks of cargo containers.

"Down and safe, Commander. Thank you again for your help."

"Not a problem, sir. The Saticoy *will be in the system for a few more days. I'm here if you need me. Nog out."*

"Starfleet is a terrible influence on that boy." Quark made a tutting noise under his breath. "I don't know what dismays me more.

That he didn't ask after his dear old uncle, or that he smuggled you up here for free."

"Unlike you," noted Bashir, "who charged us handsomely for the privilege of being beamed over through your . . . What did you call it, a side channel?" He eyed the cargo transporter coldly. The system wasn't supposed to be used on living beings, but Quark had apparently made some unofficial modifications in line with his less-than-legal business enterprises.

"You'd take advantage of a local entrepreneur and ask him to work without recompense?" Quark affected a wounded tone. "I'm just trying to get by! Business has been down. DS9 is a ghost town! People left the station in droves. They've all been frightened off by the erratic behavior of the wormhole, and my profits are suffering!" He removed a masking device from the transporter console and shut it down. "The only ones sticking around are a few fanatics awaiting some prophesized end of days, and let me tell you . . . they are *not* big tippers!"

Bashir raised a hand. "Fine, you've made your point." He reached into an inner pocket for the price of their passage—a few strips of gold-pressed latinum—but to the doctor's surprise, his pocket was already empty.

"Don't worry, I separated my fee from you while your matrix was in the pattern buffer," explained Quark. "Plus a standard gratuity, of course."

"Same old Quark," said Sisko with a dry smile.

"Same old Sisko," noted the Ferengi. "Whenever there's trouble, you're never far away." He jerked a thumb at the air. "That light show out in the Denorios Belt, that's new. You must know something about it, otherwise you wouldn't be sneaking up here." He looked between the three of them, his eyes narrowing.

"Perceptive as ever," said Bashir.

"*Paranoid* as ever," Quark corrected. "That's what keeps me solvent! If I still had my personal shuttle, I'd be gone."

He led them away, into an adjoining corridor that curved around the station's circumference, and Kira noticed the faint shimmer of green light reflecting through ports at the far end.

"I'll have to be satisfied taking pleasure in this moment," grinned the Ferengi, looking back at them. "The venerated heroes of Deep Space 9, reduced to skulking about on the lower decks and hiding out from the authorities. How shocking!"

"He's enjoying this entirely too much," Bashir said, glancing at Kira.

"Oh, undoubtedly," Quark shot back.

"I don't buy it." Sisko made a negative noise in the depths of his throat. "Like you said, if you valued your hide, you'd be gone already. No, you're here because of something else. Loyalty."

"You take that back," Quark sniffed. "I'm . . . I'm above such things." All at once, Kira saw that the Ferengi's glib manner was brittle and forced, covering over something deeper, sadder.

It was Bashir, as incisively observant as always, who cut to the quick. "Dax would have appreciated what you're doing for us."

Quark stiffened, halting in front of them. After a moment, he spoke again in a quiet voice. "It's not right, what happened to her. Not right at all." Then he took a shaky breath and carried on. "So now you're here, what are you going to do?"

"We're going to knock on the . . . the temple door . . ." Kira's words caught in her throat as she moved past a port in the exterior hull, and for the first time she was looking directly into the mass of the turbulent wormhole, with nothing but vacuum and a layer of transparent aluminum between her and it.

All the impetus went out of Kira's body. Her gaze was dragged, like light across the event horizon of a black hole, into the seething jade fire that burned in the heart of the Celestial Temple. She imagined she could feel the furious heat from the inferno, feel it seeping through her skin and into her bones.

Kira Nerys was no stranger to fear, but what she experienced now was something else, something so much larger than words like *dread* or *terror* could encompass. A creeping, insidious thought formed in her mind and took root there; it told her that this would not be a battle she could win, nor an enemy she could flee from. *There will be no escape.*

"No time," she whispered.

"Nerys." Sisko's hand was on her shoulder, his tone gentle. "Are you all right?"

She nodded, and with monumental effort, tore herself away from the terrible sight.

"I've seen that look before," said Quark, gesturing at Kira as he opened another hatchway. "With those doomsters. They stand up in the park or on the promenade, staring into that thing for hours, chanting like they think it's listening to them." He shook his head. "The only thing that scares me more than them is the thought that it might answer back."

The four passed into another cargo bay, this served by a large turbolift that ran the height of the station, providing access to the upper tiers.

"Is there a safe path to the runabout pads from here?" Sisko looked up the lift shaft. "Just give us the route, we'll do the rest."

Quark looked around nervously, his earlobes twitching. "Suppose I do. What do you expect to do when you get there?" He pointed at Sisko and Bashir. "I don't see Starfleet uniforms under those robes. You won't get very far. Laren keeps security tight."

Kira noted that Quark referred to DS9's commander Captain Ro by her personal name, not her rank or status. She was aware they had recently rekindled their relationship, but now she wondered how far it went.

"Security is not *that* tight," Bashir was saying, indicating the group. "Case in point."

"Ro doesn't have to be involved in this," said Sisko. "We'll borrow a ship, and head for the wormhole. As for what happens after, well . . ." He sighed. "That's in the hands of the Prophets."

"I knew this was a bad idea." Quark gave a bitter chuckle. "I should have listened to my wallet instead of my heart, and ignored you when you contacted me!" He prodded Sisko in the chest. "You go out there, you will die!"

"You don't know that," said Bashir.

Quark rounded on him. "Yes, Doctor, I do! Yesterday, a bunch of those Talnot believers flew a shuttle right into the wormhole! Do you know what happened? They were torn apart!" He panted, on the edge of open panic, turning to face Kira. "You're a vedek now, aren't you? So tell me the truth! Are those zealots actually *right*? Are these really the Final Days?"

Kira couldn't lie to him. "I think so," she said. "And not just for Bajor."

"Where's that communicator?" The Ferengi's broad lobes drained of color and he held out his hand to Sisko, making a clutching motion. "Give it to me! I want to talk to Nog! Tell him his uncle needs to get off this station and far away from here."

"Quark, calm down," began Bashir.

"I will not!" Quark's tone rose, turning shrill. "I absolutely refuse to!"

As the Ferengi ranted, Kira heard an odd noise from behind a nearby stack of cargo pods, like something heavy and organic striking the deck with a low thud.

Bashir heard it too, and he froze. "Captain, we have company."

"Oh, no." Quark's head drooped and he stared at the floor. "No, no, no. This can't get any worse."

"I beg to differ," said a stern, growling voice. From out of the dimness came an imposing figure in the sand-brown uniform of a Bajoran security officer, with a humanoid face rendered strangely featureless, yet instantly recognizable. "This can and will get much, much worse."

"Odo." For a moment, the dark mood that was shrouding Kira lifted as she saw the Changeling. It had been a long time since the two of them had shared each other's lives, but she could not deny that she still cared very deeply for him. In truth, Kira had hoped to avoid crossing paths with Odo on this journey, but that was more out of uncertainty as to how he might react to seeing her. Now he was here, and she wanted to tell him everything.

But the Changeling was, above all things, Deep Space 9's primary law officer, and it was in that capacity that he had appeared.

"Nerys," he replied, with a nod. "It's good to see you. Captain, Doctor, you too."

"Why don't I leave you to get reacquainted?" Quark started to move away, but Odo's right arm distended into a thin, liquid tentacle that shot across the distance between them, grabbing on to hold the Ferengi fast.

"No one is going anywhere," Odo said firmly. "I knew Quark was up to something. He's been more shifty than usual. But I admit I didn't expect this."

"I'm just working to make ends meet," protested the Ferengi.

"Really?" Odo scowled, then looked at the others. "You know that ship full of Bajorans he talked about, the one that blew up? Quark neglected to mention that it was *his* shuttle. He sold it to them, at a tidy markup. That's why he's stuck on the station!"

"How was I to know they were going to use it for a suicidal pilgrimage?" Quark struggled against Odo's arm, and at length the Changeling released him.

Odo came closer, ignoring his old foe for the moment, instead studying Bashir and Sisko intently. "You know, I heard rumors that the Emissary had been seen on Bajor, and a certain ex-Starfleet doctor was at large. It seems I was mistaken to think it was idle chatter."

"Think of everything else you could be mistaken about," said the Ferengi.

"Give it a rest, Quark," muttered Bashir.

Odo's penetrating gaze returned to Kira as he searched her expression for some hint of the truth. "Nerys, are you going to tell me what's going on here? The last I heard of it, you were in religious seclusion on Bajor."

"I didn't want to involve you," she said. There was no point in lying to him; they knew each other too well for anything other than the truth. "It's better you stay out of this. Turn your back and forget you saw us."

Odo cocked his head and sighed, disappointed. "Do you really believe I would ever do that? Even for you?"

"That's not who he is," Quark said quietly.

"Then let's take him with us," said Sisko. "Actually, let's take you *both* with us."

"*What?*" Odo and Quark chorused the reply, each shooting Sisko the same incredulous look. "*No!*"

"I don't want to die," added the Ferengi.

"And I won't be party to a hijacking," said the Changeling.

"Some things go beyond matters of rules and regulations," Sisko noted. "We wouldn't ask you to step aside if it wasn't important. If you won't join us, then please don't try to stop us." He glanced at Bashir. "Doctor, call the turbolift."

Bashir went to the call panel and frowned at it. "It's already on its way down."

"If you set foot inside that elevator car," intoned Odo, "this goes from being a minor transit violation to a criminal conspiracy. I will put all of you in the brig, if I have to. But frankly, Captain, with the tensions seething away here on the station, all that's needed is one incident for it to boil over."

"Such as arresting the Emissary and the Hand of the Prophets?" Bashir shook his head. "Not a good look."

Kira stepped forward and took Odo's hand. "We are here to save lives. Not just the lives of people on this station, or Bajor, or the other planets in this system. I'm talking about everyone and everything you and I have ever known."

"Did you pick up a messiah complex while you were in the monastery?" Odo tried to dismiss Kira's words with a cynical snort, but he was hard-pressed to ignore the absolute certainty in her tone. "Ever since you came back from your . . . time away, you've been different. Do you hear yourself? You sound like those Talnot devotees."

"She's telling the truth," said Sisko.

"I have no doubt she believes that, and maybe you do as well." Odo shook his head. "But the only thing I have ever taken on faith is justice. For anything else, I want to see hard evidence."

"Once, you had faith in me loving you," said Kira.

"Yes, I did. And I had proof of it too," said Odo.

"Enough." Bashir stepped away from the console. "He's made his point. That's on him." From beneath his robes, the doctor produced a small conical device and aimed it at the Changeling, his finger resting on an activation stud. "I'm sorry, Odo, but this is how it has to be."

"What is that, a weapon?" Kira was shocked.

"I would guess it's a quantum stasis projector," said Quark. "It constrains the abilities of shape-shifters. Apparently, the effect is very painful."

"That's an understatement," muttered Odo.

"It's something I cobbled together while we were on the *Saticoy*," said the doctor. "Just in case we ran into this situation."

"Julian, no!" Kira stepped between the two of them. "We're not doing this!"

"We are already doing *this*, Nerys!" Bashir's retort was hard and cold. "You know what is at stake. You know what we have already lost! We have to make tough choices; you of all people must appreciate that."

"I do." She held up her hands. "I had a lifetime of fighting in the resistance, a thousand hard decisions I've made and still regret! I don't want to anymore!"

Bashir took aim. "It's all right. I'll bear the burden, not you."

"No, Doctor." Sisko reached out and put his hand on the device. "This is not the way. This isn't who we are."

For a long moment, Kira was sure Bashir was about to pull the trigger, no matter what was said to him. But then he relented and let the device drop, turning a flint-eyed glare on the captain. "You're making a mistake."

Sisko's reply was cut short as the cargo turbolift dropped into view along the open shaft, settling to the deck with a hiss. The elevator doors opened, but the empty car wasn't empty after all.

Six figures in Starfleet uniforms surged out into the bay, and each one of them carried a phaser. Kira heard Quark give a groan as the security officers fanned out to cover all angles around the group, revealing the seventh person still standing on the threshold.

"So this is why you've been out of contact all day?" Captain Ro Laren stepped out and gave the Ferengi a shake of the head. "I wish I could say I was surprised . . ." Then she caught sight of the faces of the others and her expression changed. "Actually, belay that. Vedek Kira, Doctor Bashir . . . and Captain Sisko? Okay, I'm wrong. I *am* surprised."

"I'm handling this, Captain," began Odo. "You can carry on."

"Oh, I don't think so." Ro gestured to the security team to lower their weapons. "See, when the station's senior constable and the station's most notorious entrepreneur go off the grid at the same time during an ongoing crisis, that gets my attention. Then you add in some transporter irregularities and I get very interested."

"I thought you said they wouldn't detect the beam-in." Bashir gave Quark an accusing look. "I want my latinum back."

"No refunds!" Quark snapped. "And my system is foolproof!"

"It's not." Ro's lip curled. "You talk in your sleep."

"Captain, this is not what it looks like," began Sisko. "We came aboard in secret so as not to inflame the rhetoric about Talnot's prophecies."

"Really? Because what this looks like is two of my planet's most revered spiritual figures, and a doctor with more metaphorical baggage than a space liner, are trying to work something illicit right under my nose." Ro fixed Sisko with an uncompromising look. "I bet Miles knew about this, didn't he?" She shook her head. "I knew something was wrong. He's been morose ever since Keiko and Kirayoshi evacuated." Then she turned to Odo. "So when were you planning on alerting me to this, Constable?"

"Actually, I planned to get them off the station and not say anything to you at all," noted the Changeling.

Ro gave a snort. "The old DS9 crew covering for one another, eh?" She folded her arms and went back to Sisko. "Well, you're obviously at the helm of this little escapade, so I'll bite. What the *kosst* are you doing on my station, Captain?"

"Do you believe in the Prophets?" Sisko glanced at Ro's ear, noting the absence of the devotional earring worn by most Bajorans. "I mean, truly."

"That's a work in progress," she admitted.

"But you believe they exist, out in the wormhole."

"I believe *something* does." A frown passed over Ro's face. "And right now, it seems very unhappy." As if on cue, another sullen rumble of gravity waves vibrated through the station's superstructure. "See?" she added.

"The anomalies, the energy discharges, all that out there . . ." Sisko gestured with a hand. "We believe it's the Prophets, wormhole aliens, whatever you know them as, calling out for help."

"They're trying to warn us, Laren," said Kira. "Talnot's Prophecy of the Final Days is coming to pass. He talked about the unhallowed fire in the sky. The Celestial Temple wreathed in lightning."

"That's from the passage about the land being poisoned by great evil, and the stars going out, right?" Off Kira's nod, Ro went on. "Yes, I remember old Prylar Yilb drilling that story into us at school. Never paid much heed to it, I admit, but given current events, it does have the unpleasant ring of truth."

Quark raised his hand. "Can I just say, I would have taken no part in bringing them here if I'd known it was to tell us the end of the universe was nigh."

"What else does this Talnot fellow say?" Bashir looked at the two Bajorans. "What comes after the fire and the lightning?"

Monsters. Kira tried to say the word, but it caught in her throat.

When the alert sirens began to wail, she thought the sound was in her head, but the others reacted with the same shock. Captain Ro's security detail brought up their phasers to the ready once again, uncertain as to what would happen next.

"Is that for us?" said Quark.

"You don't rate a red alert," Odo snorted. "I warned you this day was going to get worse."

Ro tapped her combadge. "Ops, this is the captain, status report."

"O'Brien here, sir," came the reply. *"Is, uh, everything all right down there?"*

"You and I are going to have a serious talk about trust, Command Master Chief," she shot back, "but not right this second. Why are we on alert?"

"Verteron energy discharge from the wormhole, the most powerful one yet. Should be hitting our deflectors any second now—"

This time the tremor through Deep Space 9's decks was enough to rob Kira of her balance and she stumbled. Bashir was close by and he grabbed her, stopping them both from falling to the floor. Overhead, active electro-plasma conduits sparked and vented vapor, and a rolling power surge briefly dimmed the cargo bay consoles and lighting.

"That's new." Ro pushed away from the support pillar she had grabbed hold of, and made for the nearest station. "Chief, can you give me an exterior view? Pipe it down to this console."

"Stand by."

Kira, Sisko, and Bashir moved closer, each trying to see what the screen displayed. An image of the void outside quickly cycled from view to view until the tormented shape of the distended wormhole appeared.

Even on the small screen, the brilliant lances of harsh lightning spitting out of the wormhole's maw were a frightening sight. Kira estimated that each of them was longer than the height of DS9's core spindle from tip to tip. The amount of energy they contained would be staggering.

Sisko pointed at the display. "Do you see that? There, in the upper quadrant?"

Shapes were moving amid the greenish haze and flickering fires at the mouth of the phenomenon, shapes that reminded Kira of swift, lethal vipers.

"Magnify," ordered Ro. The image grew larger, it sharpened, and everyone watching fell silent.

Heavy, thick-formed leviathans swam in the spill of radiation pouring from the wormhole's tattered event horizon, pushing themselves out into full existence, gaining form and mass as the lightning lit the darkness. Horned heads twisted and unfurled glistening cilia, their sensory palps tasting the vacuum.

"Are those . . . ?" Bashir turned to Sisko, the question forming.

Sisko nodded. On the journey from Bajor, the captain had described in detail the *Robinson*'s deadly encounter in the Dorvan Sector, and these creatures could only be of the same origins. "But we only saw one of them."

"Sensors are picking up five distinct masses emerging from the wormhole," reported O'Brien. *"Cosmozoan life-forms. Their quantum signatures don't correspond with that of our dimension."* Kira could hear the confusion in the engineer's voice. *"It's like they're here and not here all at the same time."*

"Giant snakes." Quark gave a shudder. "The end of the universe is bad enough, do you have to bring gargantuan reptiles into it as well?"

Ro turned on Sisko. "You've seen these things before?"

"Fought one," he corrected. "And I nearly lost a *Galaxy*-class starship in the process."

"Well then, it's good we have you around." Ro looked away from the screen, finding Kira. "Vedek, you said the Prophets summoned you both here? Any chance you can ask them how to handle those creatures?"

"It's not that simple," said Kira.

Ro's lip curled. "Of course not. It never is." She tapped her combadge again. "Ops, this is the captain. Full power to the weapons grid and deflector array. If those things want DS9, we'll make them work for it."

"Captain," began O'Brien, *"the creatures are passing beyond the wormhole's accretion disk, but they're not moving in our direction. They're ignoring the station."*

On the screen, Kira saw the scanners track the gargantuan serpent-things as they writhed free of the Celestial Temple's gravity and twisted away on spiraling courses, following an invisible path across the edge of the Denorios Belt. She instinctively recognized the action of a hunting pack, following the trail of prey. "Where are they heading?"

"Baseras," said O'Brien, using the Bajoran name for the ninth planet in the system. *"Those things are moving at near-warp velocity . . ."*

Ro turned ashen. "There are four hundred thousand people on that planet. Sand miners and settlements full of Dominion refugees from the Gamma Quadrant."

Sisko considered that gravely. "Chief, where's the nearest vessel?"

"The U.S.S. Saticoy,*"* said O'Brien. *"They're on their way to Baseras right now, carrying supplies to one of the sanctuary colonies."*

"A single ship," muttered Odo. "It won't be enough."

"No," Sisko said grimly, "it won't."

U.S.S. *Saticoy* NCC-75404

The keening whine of an overstressed structural integrity field cut through Nog's skull like a drill into bone. He felt an ache across his lobes as he picked himself up off the floor of the bridge, testing his limbs for injuries.

A second earlier, and he would have been in his seat next to Captain Hautuk, but the spatial shockwave that had slammed into the *Saticoy* came from out of nowhere, knocking the small *California*-class cruiser off its axis.

He wasn't the only one who had been unceremoniously thrown to the deck. Elsa, the Tarlac ensign at the *Saticoy*'s conn station, scrambled back to her feet, her amber features turning a shade of russet as she berated herself under her breath.

"Need a hand?" Nog made the offer, but the ensign refused.

"I'm all right, sir."

"That makes one of us," boomed Hautuk, her loud voice cutting through the cry of the alert siren. The captain followed up with a hissed Gatherer curse in her native Acamarian that Nog didn't understand, but he got the sentiment.

"Status report!" Nog looked to the back of the bridge, where Lieutenant Zuenel's masked visage was bent low over the main science-sensors console.

Without looking up, the Zaranite woman raised a single finger to show she was still working. "Patience, sir," she said, the words muffled by her breather. "I will answer momentarily."

Nog's jaw set. Zuenel had a habit of appearing unhurried in even the direst of situations, and he forced himself to wait for the science officer's reply. Meanwhile, the captain was striding over to stand between Elsa and her counterpart at the ops station. "Lieutenant Ottaq, bring us to a stable attitude if you can."

"Already in progress, Captain." The long-limbed young Xindi-Arboreal bounced his wide hands over the ship's controls in big, swift gestures, righting the *Saticoy* with pulses from the thrusters. "We're a few thousand kilometers short of our entry point for orbit around Baseras. Shields took the brunt of that impact, but I'm reading intermittent power from the engine nacelles. Could be a shock effect?"

"Correct," offered Zuenel, looking up as she gave her report. "Shields are offline. Impulse efficiency is impaired. Warp drive nonoperational. Subspace communications inactive. Life-support adequate. Transporter systems inactive. Thirteen casualties reported, no fatalities."

"And the origin of that shockwave?" Nog blew out a breath and went on. "Do I even need to ask? The wormhole?"

"Correct," repeated the science officer. "Shockwave caused by high-order subspace pulse generated by unknown verteron effect. Connection to approaching spaceborne creatures is unknown."

"What did she say?" Hautuk pivoted back toward Nog.

"Elucidating," said the Zaranite. "On-screen."

The bridge's main monitor snapped to a stern view, over the *Saticoy*'s saucer-shaped primary hull and underslung warp nacelles. Nog immediately noted the wake of sparkling, energetic plasma gushing from the starboard intercooler, but of far greater concern were the fast-moving forms coming out of the darkness toward them.

The hulking, serpentine creatures triggered some primal fear reaction deep in the Ferengi's brain and he reflexively bared his teeth. Back home on Ferenginar, snakes and slugs and anything that squirmed were delicacies, but these gigantic things were far more likely to consume him and the ship in a single bite.

"Identify!" Hautuk barked the order, but Zuenel was already shaking her wide, bald head.

"Nothing in Starfleet records other than a log from the *Robinson*. Contents sealed by executive order."

"The *Robinson*?" Hautuk shot Nog a questioning look. "Benjamin Sisko's ship."

At once, Nog knew what they were looking at. Sisko had described the creatures he encountered in Cardassian space, and these could only be of the same origins.

"They're closing fast," said Elsa. "But they don't seem to be interested in us. Their path will take them straight to the planet."

The captain stepped up to Nog and leaned down to speak privately to him. Hautuk was twice his height, and her manner could be quite intimidating, but in this moment her intensity was directed elsewhere. "XO, does the appearance of those things have something to do with those guests you brought up from Bajor? The ones I pretended not to notice?"

Nog blinked, taking that in. "Yes, sir. I mean, I'm not certain, sir."

"I give you a lot of latitude because you're one of the most talented officers I've ever served with," Hautuk told him, "but now you need to speak plainly."

"They're aggressive, predatory chronovores." The reply spilled out of him. "They consume temporal energy and they warp local spacetime. A single one of them tore apart a Cardassian space station. If they're here, it's to destroy."

"That's enough to go on," said the captain with a brisk nod. "Divert power to weapons and shields!" Her voice resumed its normal booming resonance. "Lieutenant Zuenel, contact Baseras and tell them to initiate immediate evacuation procedures! Lieutenant Ottaq, Ensign Elsa, put the ship in the path of the intruders, we'll try to distract them!"

"Captain, we can't hope to defeat those things," Nog said quietly.

"I know that," replied Hautuk. "Still, we have to try, though."

"Weapons active," called Elsa.

"Give me a wall of fire right in their path," said the captain. "Now!"

The viewscreen returned to standard setting as the *Saticoy* moved into a head-on aspect, bow toward the oncoming creatures. The bright flares of photon torpedoes scattered out ahead of the ship, bracketed with a sweep of phaser beams from the main collimator ring.

The breath Nog held in his throat turned into a choke as the serpents passed through the salvo as if it were mist, hurtling by the starship without slowing.

"No effect on targets," said Zuenel, just to hammer the point home. "The creatures are ignoring us."

"Rude," snarled the captain. "Elsa, take us in after them!"

"They're not slowing." Ottaq's dismay turned to alarm. "Captain, the creatures are entering the atmosphere of Baseras. They're diving toward the surface!"

Nog went to one of the secondary stations and brought up the sensor feed. The Xindi was right. Wreathed in the fires of reentry, the monstrous beasts plummeted toward the planet, radiating intense chronometric energy. As they fell, the air itself began to decay around them.

The sandstone-colored orb of the planet hove into view on the main screen. Nog saw darts of silver rising, most likely shuttlecraft filled with as many people as possible, the lucky few heeding the *Saticoy*'s warning to escape. But many more settlers were spread out across the surface of Baseras, and their lives hung in the balance.

"Attention." Zuenel spoke up again, and this time the Zaranite's usual terse diction was marked by genuine dismay. "Scans of the zone where the creatures made planetfall are showing . . ." She trailed off, her head tilting in confusion. "This must be an error."

"Lieutenant, what do you see?" The captain demanded a response.

"The planet is undergoing a massive tectonic shift. Its structure appears to be breaking down at an accelerating rate."

Nog's lobes stiffened and he felt ice form in his belly. "They're *aging* it."

"Why?" Hautuk snapped out the word. "There's nothing down there but civilians and refugees! What possible value could destroying it have?"

"I don't think they're doing it because they *need* to," said Nog, his throat tightening as he imagined the fear spreading through those down on the surface. "They're doing it because they *can*."

"Could we beam those people out? Some of them, at least?" Ottaq's plea echoed the desperation in the minds of the *Saticoy*'s bridge crew.

"Transporter systems are still down," said Zuenel. "We cannot assist them."

"That won't do." Nog shook his head, thinking back over what Sisko had told him about the *Robinson*'s encounter with the serpents. "Captain, request permission to modify and deploy a quantum torpedo."

Hautuk gestured at the planet. "Against them? You want to fire a quantum weapon at a populated world?"

"It might be enough to draw those things off," he shot back. "Even if it's only for a moment, it means more shuttles can get away."

The Acamarian woman's lined face creased in a deep frown, and she nodded. "Do what you have to, XO."

Nog dashed to a console and followed the same tactics that Sisko had used at Dorvan, remotely refitting a quantum torpedo with an anti-tachyon generator. Hautuk hovered nearby, watching him closely.

After a moment, Ensign Elsa called out from her station. "Torpedo at ready status. Clear to fire."

"Can you get a lock on one of the serpents?"

"Confirmed, sir. There's one in the upper atmosphere, loitering over the attack site." The Tarlac gave a curt nod. "Just say the word."

"Send it." As Nog gave the command, he felt a twist of tension in his leg, deep down in the meat of the bio-replacement limb. It was the ghost of his old wound, a remnant of those terrible days on AR-558 during the Dominion War, when he believed he might never see home again. He felt that same fear now, potent and strong.

"The creature is rising to meet the attack," reported the science officer. "It is aware of the incoming torpedo. Heading toward it."

Nog moved to stand between the conn and ops stations, staring into the main viewer, willing the bright flare of the torpedo to find its mark.

"Detonation!" Zuenel called it a split second before the weapon discharged in a ball of white fire.

"Magnify, that quadrant," he ordered. "Did it work . . . ?"

The surface of Baseras expanded to fill the viewscreen, and Nog found the expanding halo of agitated anti-tachyons from the torpedo. At the heart of the detonation, he saw the writhing form of one of the serpent-things, wounded and bleeding emerald fire; but the creature shrugged off the force of the blast and turned toward the *Saticoy*, pushing against the crumbling planet's gravity as it hurled itself upward.

"I think we've just made it angry," breathed Elsa. "It's on an intercept course."

"No." Nog clutched at the air, infuriated and confused. "It

should be gone. It worked before, Captain Sisko told me . . ." He ran out of breath.

"Like the Borg, perhaps these life-forms can adapt," said Zuenel.

"We took our shot," said the captain, "and it wasn't enough. Helm, get us away from here while we can."

"The creature is still coming," warned Ottaq. "We can't outrun it without warp drive!"

"Fire everything we have," snapped Nog. "Impulse power—"

He was cut off as the ship bucked under him once again, and this time the Ferengi felt his body rise and then lurch to one side as the *Saticoy* was struck by the full mass of the creature. The bridge spun around him and he crashed into Zuenel, the two of them collapsing in a heap.

The stink of burning polymers stung his nostrils and a horrible, low-frequency howl from damaged EPS conduits rose to a screech. Nog tasted rich blood in his mouth where a cut on his face leaked across his lips. Ignoring the searing pain, he rolled over and found the Zaranite nearby, gasping and choking.

Zuenel's atmospheric breather had been dislodged during the impact, and her hairless face shaded purple as she clawed at her throat. Nog snatched up the fallen mask and pushed it back into place, fumbling with the feeder tubules. With a hiss, they reconnected and the science officer broke into a shuddering cough as she gulped in a desperate lungful of vital gases.

Swaying, he staggered to his feet and pulled himself past fallen stanchions and blown-out EPS conduits toward the command station. Waving away a haze of acrid smoke with one hand, he found Captain Hautuk hunched over a repeater console.

"Sir, it blew right through our deflectors." Nog reached for her shoulder when she didn't respond. "Captain?"

The Acamarian slumped back at his touch, and he recoiled. The console had overloaded, blasting out shards of screen like shrapnel. Hautuk was dead, a dagger of debris buried in the dark mass of her hair.

"Baseras has entered a terminal implosive state." From behind him, Zuenel's dispassionate report seemed to reach Nog from a great distance away. "The planet's disintegration is complete."

"The creature is turning back," called Elsa. "Sir, it's going to finish us."

What do I do? The question tolled in Nog's thoughts like a death knell. *Can't fight. Can't run.* He looked back at Hautuk's body. He was in command now. The responsibility fell to him.

Nog tore his gaze away from the captain and spoke up. "Put me on intraship." He took a deep breath. "All hands, this is the first officer." The next words curdled in his throat. *Abandon ship. Say it, Nog. Say it!*

Then, without warning, a blinding wall of white fire cut across the *Saticoy*'s bow, slashing the returning serpent and cleaving it in two. The creature did not perish, instead discorporating into hundreds of smaller, identical forms that twisted away into space.

The *Saticoy* shook as the ship began to move, lurching out of the gravity well of the imploding planet.

"We've been captured by a tractor beam," said Ottaq, his eyes wide with amazement. "Another ship came in at high warp, and they're pulling us away."

Nog held on to his chair as they turned into the shimmering wake of the other vessel, and ahead on the viewscreen he saw a familiar, elegant form carrying them to safety. Despite the fear running through him, he managed a crooked smile.

"Incoming hail," said Zuenel.

"Let's hear it." Breathing hard, Nog collapsed back into his seat, and a voice he knew only from Academy lecture tapes and historical records sounded around him.

"*Saticoy, this is Captain Jean-Luc Picard aboard the* Starship Aventine. *Stand by.*"

13

Ashalla Starport, Lonar Province, Bajor

The sun was high over the landing fields, blazing out of a cloudless sky, and across the thermocrete expanse of the starport apron, there was barely any cover from the heat. Hundreds of desperate people had spilled out of the port terminal, across the taxiways, until they pressed up against the safety fences that walled off the shuttle pads.

Jake Sisko adjusted the makeshift hood around his head, wiping a film of sweat from his face as he picked his way back through the crowd to where he had left his wife. The people around him were almost all Bajorans, but on his way he had seen a couple of other humans, a lone Vulcan woman, and as he passed, he spotted the blue skins of a Bolian family huddled together by an abandoned grav-lifter.

An elderly male, perhaps the clan patriarch, looked up and caught his eye. "Do you know what is going on?" he called. "Have they said anything?"

Jake shook his head. "The replicators are broken. There's no more water, so conserve what you have." His words sent a ripple of concern through everyone who heard him, so he tried to find something positive to add. "The Port Authority said the next ships would be departing soon."

"They said that five hours ago!" A skinny Bajoran man pink with sunburn shot him a venomous glare. "Meanwhile, I see shuttles coming in and none of us are moving! Who are they for? Not us!"

Angry mutters of assent followed the man's outburst. These people were afraid, and that fear was hardening into fury. Jake looked to where the gateway in the fence was blocked by a force-field barrier. Men from the City Guard were up on watch platforms, fingering their rifles as they looked out over the throng, and they heard every hissed curse, just as Jake did.

Close by, a Bajoran woman sat atop a torn-open suitcase, likely abandoned by some previous evacuee, rocking back and forth as she recited line after line from the Prophecy of Talnot. Despite the oppressive heat, Jake shuddered and he had to force himself not to look up into the sky, where the burning halo of the wormhole was clearly visible.

"I'm sorry," he said, to no one in particular, and he pressed on, searching for Korena.

His wife saw him coming and beckoned. She was closer to the gate, near the lines of collapsible emergency barriers that had been hastily erected in the last few days, sheltering as best she could in the shade of a discarded cargo module. Two humans were with her, who hadn't been there when he left to go searching for food and water—and to Jake's surprise, he recognized them.

"Keiko? Yoshi?"

"Oh, Jake." Keiko O'Brien gave him a weary smile and they embraced. "It's good to see another friendly face."

"I spotted them in the crowd," said Korena. "I thought we should stick together."

"Good idea." Taking care to conceal his actions from the others around them, Jake produced the two packets of drinking water he had been able to salvage from the main terminal. "Here, take these, share them between you." He felt guilty keeping the water for his family and friends, but the circumstances were forcing him to make some hard choices.

The four of them sat and took turns taking sips. Keiko's son gave Jake a mournful glance. "Did you see anyone from Starfleet?" The teenager's question was anxious and sullen all at once.

Jake shook his head. He didn't add what he suspected: that if Starfleet were not around to assist in the evacuation, it was because something worse was happening elsewhere. He kept turning his father's words over in his mind, ruminating on what the elder Sisko had said. On the strength of that warning, Jake and Korena had set off to leave Bajor, but they had not reckoned with the surge of panic that swept over the planet.

Now it seemed that everyone on Bajor was falling into two distinct camps: those afraid for their lives and desperate to flee, and those who had resigned themselves to the end of their world.

"We were supposed to transfer directly to an outbound ship," Keiko was saying. "Miles arranged it. But then when we got here, the Bajoran Space Guard commandeered the transport and they put us off." She blinked away tears. "It was all so sudden . . . He told us we had to leave, find Molly back on Earth . . ."

"The Bajoran Militia have instituted martial law," said Jake. He'd been able to get some information from a worried trooper after showing his old Federation News Service accreditation, but little more than that.

"What? Why?" Keiko was aghast.

Korena nodded at the crowd. "There's been unrest in the cities. Clashes with Talnot Adherents. It's getting ugly." She sighed. "People look up and see the Temple on fire. Everyone is afraid."

Jake scanned the space beyond the fences as she spoke. He could see a pair of heavy cargo barges parked on a pad, their hatches open and their interiors empty. But no one was being loaded aboard the ships, and the guards nearby moved uncertainly, as if waiting for something.

"So we just sit here?" Yoshi stared at the ground. "For how long?" He grabbed for his mother's hand.

Jake didn't have a reply for the youth. As far as he knew, every warp-capable ship was being packed to the bulkheads with panicked people anxious to escape before Talnot's Prophecy reached its doomsday. What had once been an overlooked, discredited piece of Bajoran religious minutiae was now on everyone's lips, and for all intents it seemed to be coming true.

Jake had a journalist's instinct for skepticism, to question any fact put before him, but even he could not deny the change that had come over his wife—and Bajor—in the past few days. Azeni Korena's beliefs, while not fervent, were deep-rooted, and her husband could sense the fear she was holding in check.

On impulse, he drew her close. "We'll get through this," he told her.

"I want to believe that," she said.

"No! No! *Baseras!*" A shout went up from across the concourse, and everyone turned as a ragged-looking Bajoran man rose unsteadily to his feet. Jake saw he had what appeared to be a military communicator in his hand, and the man's expression was wide-eyed with panic. "Baseras is gone! They're saying it's been destroyed!" His claim was picked up and echoed across the crowd in moments.

"The ninth planet?" Keiko shook her head. "That can't be right."

Some of the evacuees were saying the same thing, but the man with the communicator was on the move now, pushing toward the shimmering force barrier. He jabbed a finger at the closest guard on the far side of the gateway. "You know, don't you? We have to get away from here!" He turned back, imploring the people in the crowd who had followed him. "Do you hear? Bajor will be next!"

Jake rose to see more clearly, stepping in front of Korena and the others. He felt the reaction of the evacuees like a palpable force, seeking a point of release.

It didn't matter if it was true about Baseras or not. Their fears and fury had been simmering in silence since dawn, and now that bottled-up emotion was about to explode.

"Why are you keeping us out?" yelled the man with the communicator.

"Those ships are empty!" A woman at his side pointed at the cargo barges. "They've been sitting there for hours! Let us on board! We need to go!"

"Step back from the barrier," said the guard, pointing with his phaser rifle. "We're . . . We've been ordered to hold those ships. For priority cargo."

It was exactly the wrong thing to have said. All at once, the people at the front of the crowd were yelling, voices crossing over one another in angry confusion.

"*Cargo?*" cried one man. "Wraiths take you, I've been out here for two days!"

"Talnot was right!" called another. "This is written! This is the end!"

"They're keeping those ships for the rich and powerful to use!" yelled the woman. "The rest of us are going to be left here to perish!"

"You're supposed to be on our side!" A young man in the robes of a novice prylar bent and grabbed a loose object from the ground, then threw it into the force field with a cry of rage.

The crackling barrier gave off a buzzing shower of sparks and the noise brought the crowd to its feet. In seconds, the mass of people were hurling abuse and other makeshift missiles at the security fence and the barrier.

They surged forward like a tide, and even though he was behind the force field, the guard backed away, raising his rifle to a ready position. Other Guard troopers drew their weapons, aiming but hesitating to shoot.

"Back off, or we open fire!" the guard yelled. "We are authorized to use force!"

Jake acted without hesitation. He grabbed the side of the empty cargo pod and pulled himself up on it, until he was standing level with the top of the gateway. One of the guards saw him moving and turned to aim a rifle in his direction.

But he couldn't stop now. He had to intervene, and there was only one way he could do that.

The scarf around his head came off with a single pull and Jake threw it away. Standing tall, he filled his lungs and then shouted with all the force he could muster.

"*Stop!*" His cry resonated over the landing pads and everyone heard it. Faces turned in his direction, and in the distance he heard someone whisper his name.

He locked eyes with the armed guard and called out again. "Do you know who I am? My name is Jake Sisko! *I am the son of the Emissary!*"

Emissary. Emissary. Emissary. The word rippled out over the crowd, momentarily damping down the fire of resentment. Recognition bloomed on the guard's face and he went pale; but the rifle remained steady.

"This has gone on long enough." Jake reached deep inside, remembering the examples his father had set, the lessons learned from him. "If you believe in the Prophets . . . Even if you don't! Open the gate. Let these people through!"

"We have our orders!" retorted the guard. "W-we'll fire if we have to!"

Jake dropped down from the cargo module and strode forward, through the gathered evacuees, until he was right in front of the force barrier. Every gun was on him now, and he spread his arms wide.

"If you're going to shoot these people, start with me." Up close, he could see the guard was about his age, and he noted that the man had a similar style of devotional earring to his wife. A connection passed between them, a shared moment of dread and uncertainty. "Whatever you believe," Jake told him, "you know this is wrong. *You know it.*"

"I . . . I . . ." Jake steeled himself for the phaser shot he feared would come; but then the guard let the rifle muzzle drop, overwhelmed by his own guilt and sorrow. "I know it," he breathed. Slowly, the Bajoran walked to the gateway, then put his hand on the switch that deactivated the force field. He tapped his communicator and spoke into it. "We're letting them through. *Kosst* the orders! Get the ships ready to lift off."

The crackling barrier dissipated, and silence fell. Jake walked to the gate, then turned back, looking out over the crowd.

No one spoke. Every face was watching him, waiting for his word. He found Korena nearby with Keiko and Yoshi, and his wife gave him an encouraging nod.

"We are leaving," Jake told the crowd, then nodded to the guard and the other Militia members. "Every last one of us."

Deep Space 9, Bajor System

The circular hatch opened like an iris and the two captains stepped out of the *Aventine*'s airlock, and onto Deep Space 9. An automated voice ordered them to stand by while a security scan took place.

Picard exuded a commander's confidence in a way that Sam Bowers envied. *In the midst of all this insanity, he always seems to know what he's doing.* A wry smile pulled at the younger captain's lips. *I've got to ask him how he does that.*

If Picard noticed his attention, he didn't remark on it. The older man walked to an observation window and peered out. Over his shoulder, Bowers saw the length of the *Aventine*'s hull extending away from the docking pylon, and a few hundred meters away, the disc of the *Saticoy* moving to lock on to the next pylon along.

"We were lucky," said Picard, indicating the damage visible on the smaller ship. "A minute later and we would have lost them."

Bowers nodded, but he couldn't help but think about the other ships that had tried to escape the destruction of Baseras. Had any of them made it to safety? It hadn't been possible for the *Aventine* to rescue everyone, and no matter how you cut it, the death toll had been terrible.

He shuddered to think what might happen when the Devidians' Nagas turned their attention toward the other, more heavily populated planets in the system. Bajor had billions of inhabitants; every ship from light-years around could come to help and it still wouldn't be enough to evacuate them all.

At length, the opposite hatch slid open, presenting a trio of figures in Bajoran security uniforms. Standing so he blocked the way forward was a being Bowers had not laid eyes on for some time, but the look in the Changeling's hooded gaze told him that Odo had not forgotten him.

"Commander Bowers."

"It's, uh, captain now," he noted. "A pleasure to see you, Constable."

"Is it?" Odo gave a noncommittal grunt. He glanced at Picard, looking him up and down. "And as for you . . . Well, you're about the last person I expected to turn up here. You do know there's a priority warrant for your apprehension?"

"I'm aware, Mister . . . Odo, is it?"

"Yes." The shape-shifter stepped into the vestibule, coming uncomfortably close to both men, studying them warily. "You'll forgive me if I'm thorough about vetting you before I let you aboard. These are strange days. One can't be too careful."

Picard held up his hands, wrist to wrist. "Do you intend to place us under arrest? If so, I ask only that—"

"If you're on this station, I have my eye on you," Odo replied. "For most intents and purposes, that's as good as having you in a cell anywhere else. Nothing happens on DS9 without me being aware of it." He made a grumbling noise and directed the two guards to move on. "For now, I'm your escort. Follow them."

Picard walked on, but before Bowers could take two steps, Odo had put out a hand and halted the younger man in his tracks.

Odo leaned in. His expression shifted, the stony aspect fading briefly. "Ezri," he said, saying her name gently. "Were you there when it happened?"

Bowers returned a solemn nod, forcing himself not to slip back into the memory of the moment. "It was quick."

Odo made the noise in his throat again. "That doesn't count for much."

"No," admitted Bowers. "It doesn't."

They rode the turbolift down-station in silence, and all Bowers could think of was how little this new place was like the old Cardassian heap. He didn't miss serving on Terok Nor, though—in fact, the best parts of his previous assignment had been serving aboard the *Starship Defiant*, DS9's attached cruiser. Even bunking in that ship's cramped fleet-issue quarters had been better than living with a Cardassian's idea of what constituted comfort.

They arrived on the conference levels, and the moment their group stepped out of the lift car, the sound of raised voices reached them. Bowers immediately picked out the low rumble of Benjamin Sisko's bass tones, counterpointed by Ro Laren's whip-crack retorts. Plainly, the two officers were at loggerheads over the situation at hand.

"In there," said Odo, waving them toward a briefing room. "I'll be waiting for you when you're done."

The way the shape-shifter said that last sentence seemed to suggest that he already had a nice lockup all picked out for Bowers and Picard, should they try anything foolish.

As they entered, they found Ro standing before a tactical plot of the burning wormhole, her hand jabbing at the ragged maw of the phenomenon. "Nothing has survived transit from the Gamma Quadrant, and every vessel that has gotten close to the event horizon at this end has been ripped apart by gravimetric shear," she was saying. "The *Defiant* is a tough ship, but you're dreaming if you believe I'll let you take her in there!"

"If you don't want to risk *Defiant*, then give me a runabout. A shuttlepod. *Anything*," Sisko retorted. He sat on the edge of the briefing room's table, leaning forward into the argument. "I don't need a crew. I'll fly it."

"And Vedek Kira?"

"She comes with me."

"The Emissary of the Prophets and the Hand of the Prophets, sailing into the fires of the End Time?" Ro made an exasperated sound. "And then what? More destruction? Plagues and rains of blood?"

"It's the only thing we can do."

"Not true." Ro looked up, briefly eyeing Bowers and Picard. "We have an unknown number of dimensionally unstable hostiles at large in our space, we can't just ignore that! We need to neutralize them before they do any more damage."

Sisko pivoted, glancing at the other commanders. "Care to weigh in?"

Bowers inclined his head, tacitly allowing Picard to take the lead. After a moment, the other captain cleared his throat. "I assume Captain Sisko and Vedek Kira intend to seek an audience with the beings known as the Prophets?"

"That's the idea," said Sisko.

"What guarantee do you have they will grant it?" Before Sisko could reply, Picard pressed on with a second question. "Moreover, how can you be certain they are still there to answer you?"

Ro looked back at the tactical plot. "Given the state of the wormhole, they might be dead . . . or whatever their equivalent of that is."

Sisko shook his head. "I don't believe so."

"What are you basing that on?" Bowers shot him a questioning look.

"Faith," said the other man.

"With all due respect," said Bowers, "I don't know if that's sufficient."

Picard approached the tactical plot, grimacing at the tortured shape of the wormhole. "Our people aboard the *Aventine* have concluded that the creatures that attacked the ninth planet and the other locations are indeed extratemporal in origin. They are forcing their way into our universe where the barriers between dimensions are porous." He pointed at the image. "If you are asking for my opinion, I agree with Captain Sisko that the status of the wormhole . . . the Celestial Temple . . . is a grave concern. But I must accede to Captain Ro's insistence that the most immediate threat is to the civilian population of this system."

"I know the dangers," Sisko rumbled. "My son and daughter-in-law are out there with those evacuees."

"Then help us keep them safe," insisted Ro. "Ben, I need you with me on this. Help me fight these things and I'll give you whatever you need to reach the Prophets."

"The Nagas won't stop with Baseras," said Picard. "They're attacking the planets in this system for a reason."

"Nagas?" Ro raised an eyebrow.

"That's what we've been calling them," noted Bowers. "After a mythic snake monster from old Earth history."

Sisko regarded Bowers. "You rescued the *Saticoy* from them. How did you accomplish that?"

Bowers folded his arms. "Since we, uh, made our unscheduled departure from Earth, we've picked up a few additions along the way." He explained about the impromptu brain trust that was at work on the *Aventine*—Spock of Vulcan, the android Data and his daughter Lal, Geordi La Forge and Wesley Crusher—and of their collaboration against the threat of the Nagas and their Devidian masters. "We were able to generate a transphasic pulse through *Aventine*'s main deflector that proved effective in negating one of the creatures."

"Despite our attack, the creature still survived, albeit in a changed form," noted Picard. "I fear the Devidians are improving their design with each subsequent Naga incursion."

Ro frowned at that. "But those things are living beings, aren't they?"

Picard nodded. "The Devidians are capable of manipulating certain organic forms as their tools, like the smaller ophidians they deploy in their feeding excursions. The Nagas are the same, writ larger."

"There are others," added Bowers. "Humanoid avatars, like handlers for the beasts. But we haven't seen any of them in the recent attacks. They're mixing up their tactics."

The Bajoran woman let out a low murmur of dismay, and walked away from the holographic screen, processing the information. "You know, Starfleet wants your heads on pikes," she said, after a moment. "Right now, I should be securing your vessel and letting Odo lock you up."

"The constable seems quite willing to do so," said Picard.

"I haven't reported your arrival to Starfleet Command," Ro admitted. "It's only a matter of time until they find out, but I don't have the luxury of caring about that."

She tapped the interface on the briefing room table and the image of the wormhole disappeared, to be replaced by a new graphic listing all combat-capable vessels in the system. Alongside the *Defiant* and various short-range defensive ships belonging to the Bajoran Space Guard were the *Aventine* and the *Saticoy*.

She went on, "Right now, the Bajor system is under attack, and having a *Vesta*-class starship to help defend it is more important than some difference of opinion with Starfleet Command. On my authority you can all consider yourselves on attached duty to DS9 until I say otherwise. Understood?"

"Whatever you say, Captain," said Bowers.

Ro let out a sigh. "I'll deal with the consequences later. If there *is* a later."

The conference center's doors opened once more, and Bowers saw that Odo was still out there, true to his word about keeping watch. A shorter figure drew past him, a Ferengi male in a Starfleet uniform sporting a commander's pins. He looked haggard and weary.

"Nog." Sisko put a hand out and the new arrival shook it. "You made it."

"Barely," he replied, nodding a greeting to Ro before finding Bowers and Picard. "Sirs, thank you for coming to our aid. My crew owe you their lives."

They all picked up on the unspoken part of that statement, and it was Ro who gave it voice. "Captain Hautuk?"

"Killed in action," Nog said stiffly. "As of now, I'm the *Saticoy*'s ranking officer."

Bowers felt himself tense, and he gave the Ferengi a grim nod of solidarity. He knew exactly what the other officer was feeling.

Ro took that in, glancing back at the screen showing the ship status list. "Can you fight?"

Nog's jaw set in a hard line. "With some help, we can punch above our weight."

Into the silence that followed, Ro gave them a measuring look before she spoke again. "Captain Sisko will join me at tactical on board the *Defiant*. Captain Bowers, Captain Picard, you'll link with our element, engaging the Nagas directly from the *Aventine*. Captain Nog and the *Saticoy* will support elements from the Space Guard screening any civilian ships in the engagement zone. I'll inform Command Master Chief O'Brien he'll be in operational control of DS9 until relieved."

"That transphasic pulse," said Sisko, "we'll need it up and running on all ships."

"I'll see the details are at hand," agreed Picard.

"Then let's get to it." Ro pushed away from the wall. "We deploy in twenty minutes."

"Aye, aye." Picard and the other officers chorused the affirmation, but as Ro, Nog, and Sisko walked away, the *Aventine*'s captain leaned close to speak privately to him.

"Sir," began Bowers, "what about . . . what we discussed before?"

Picard knew what he meant before he said another word. Data's fateful conclusion that the Bajoran wormhole had to be collapsed permanently was inescapable, but to bring it to the table in the midst of this would only serve to sow dissent.

"We have to tell Sisko and Ro," Bowers said quietly.

"And we will," Picard insisted. "But first, we must deal with the problem in front of us."

"Time to go back to your ship," Odo called out from the doorway. "Consider yourselves fortunate. Captain Ro is more magnanimous than I."

"A moment, please, Constable?" He tapped his communicator. "Picard to Spock."

"Spock here."

"Ambassador," replied Picard. "Circumstances have changed. I need Data, Lal, and yourself to transfer immediately to Deep Space 9. Chief O'Brien will be able to find you a workspace on the station. Take whatever you need from the *Aventine* and continue your preparation for . . ." He paused, faltering over his next words. "The contingency."

"Understood," said the Vulcan. *"By your tone, may I assume that the details of the . . . contingency . . . have yet to be widely disclosed?"*

"You are correct." Picard looked up and saw the Changeling's patience was at an end. Odo advanced into the room, making it clear he would haul the two men out if they didn't move of their own accord. "For now, let us keep it that way."

U.S.S. *Aventine* NCC-82602

Strange, thought Wesley, *how* right *this feels.*

Many years had passed since he had been on the bridge of a starship, to stand a post and be part of a working crew. In other timelines he had glimpsed on his journeys, Wesley knew there were versions of him that embraced the life of a Starfleet officer, but that had never been his personal destiny. Still, it was not until this moment that he realized how much he had actually missed the camaraderie, and the sense of being part of something greater.

He glanced at Lieutenant Kedair, sharing the *Aventine*'s wide command station with her. The Takaran was absorbed by the scanner readings coming in from near-Bajor space, busily feeding that data to the *Saticoy* and the *Defiant* running in formation with them. For his part, Wesley was finishing up the final adjustments to the transphasic pulse generator program, simultaneously co-ordinating with chief engineer Mikaela Leishman below decks and her counterparts on the other ships.

"Two minutes out." Picard called the time from his place at the first officer's station at midbridge. It was odd to see the *Enterprise*'s captain acting as *Aventine*'s de facto first officer, but by unspoken agreement it had become the working arrangement, with Sam Bowers remaining in the center seat. Of course Wesley's stepfather had the seniority, but this was still Bowers's ship to command, and Picard slipped into the role with practiced ease.

Indicators winked on across Wesley's station, showing ready on the other ships in the formation. "*Defiant* and *Saticoy* report ready," he announced.

"Acknowledged," said Bowers. "What about the Space Guard ships?"

"I have them," said Kedair. "A wing of six *Perikian*-class impulse interceptors, bearing two-six-zero mark one. They're moving into screen formation around the transport flotilla in sector bravo."

"Show me." Bowers gestured at the main viewscreen, and Wesley saw the display snap to a view of the bat-like interceptors powering up from Bajor's lower atmosphere. Ahead of them, cargo barges wallowed in the gravity wells of the planet's moons, making slow progress toward open space.

The Militia vessels had only limited range and capability, primarily operating close to home port, but with those ships on one flank and the Starfleet group on the other, the hope was that they could block the advance of the Naga invaders and drive them back from their inexorable approach to Bajor.

"Those civilian freighters are too close," said Picard with a frown. "They should be well away from here by now."

"Some problem down on the surface delayed their departure," noted Kedair. "Too late to send them back, sir."

"*Saticoy to all vessels.*" Captain Nog's voice issued out over the intership. *"We're moving to join up with the Bajorans. Good luck, and good hunting."*

"Aventine concurs," said Bowers. On the screen, the other starship banked away from the group and dropped out of view as the *Defiant* hove closer, the smallest of the flotilla leading the way toward the engagement zone.

A strident warning tone sounded from the tactical station, where Worf stood silent and aloof, his gaze fixed on the ship's threat display. "Five Nagas have entered sensor range." Over the past few days, the Klingon warrior had been dealing with his own inner demons, and Wesley knew it had shaken him to his core, but none of that was visible here. Worf was stone-faced and determined, with any suggestion of hesitation or misgivings entirely absent.

Bowers threw Worf a look. "Projected heading?"

"If they do not deviate from their current course, it will take them past the Endalla moon and then directly toward Bajor, through the middle of the civilian formation."

"Not today," Bowers said firmly. "Helm, stay with *Defiant* and take us in."

Picard gave a nod. "Battle stations," he ordered, "all decks to red alert!"

The *Aventine* surged forward, streaking by Endalla on a close pass and around into the *Defiant*'s impulse wake. Revealed before them, the twisting forms of the giant space snakes coiled around one another as they arrowed toward Bajor. Somehow, the Nagas were able to cruise through the void using a biological form of warp-field displacement, affecting the gradient of gravity to effectively fall from one location to another, moving at speeds that could approach light velocity.

Not for the first time, Wesley wondered what the Nagas must have been like in their natural forms before the Devidians had altered their physiology and transformed them into living weapons. He would never know. The work of the Devidian gene forges had consumed the entire species, dooming them to this monstrous existence.

Sensing the oncoming starships, the serpents burst apart in a flash of radiation discharge, chronometric fields pushing at one another as they took off on different vectors.

"Defiant *is engaging.*" Captain Ro picked the closest one and her ship banked hard, shedding speed as an explosion of pulse-phaser blasts streamed through the dark around a Naga beast with distinctive scarring across its bony skull.

The creature desynchronized itself, parts of its body phasing out of line with the quantum state of this reality. The instinctive reaction was exactly as expected, and *Aventine* took the advantage.

Bowers gave the order. "Transphasic pulse, fire!"

Worf released the surge of raw anti-tachyon energy from the ship's main deflector, and it caught the Naga with full force. The beast buckled and its fanged maw opened in a silent bellow of agony.

Once more, Wesley felt the sting of dismay at being forced to inflict such pain on an animal, but there was no other way. The Devidians had stripped out all but the Naga's innate savagery in their remaking of the creatures, and there was no way to undo the damage done.

Jaws snapping viciously at nothing, the serpent writhed and its tentacle-like cilia extended out and raked the *Aventine*'s deflectors. The ship shuddered as power overloads shocked through the space-frame, and for a moment Wesley feared that the wounded beast would strike back at them twice as hard.

Then the *Defiant* swooped into the fray once again, blazing a brilliant white pulse of its own from the ship's bow deflector. Wreathed in streaks of glowing light, the Naga twitched and burst apart into a tide of energized particles.

A shockwave pummeled the two ships and knocked them off course, forcing everyone to cling to their stations as *Aventine* rolled like a dinghy in a storm-tossed ocean.

Bowers's crew were quick to right the ship and bring them back to battle ready. But, the other three Nagas had already swept past, leaving the fourth to die while they dove toward the Endalla moon.

Worf growled, the light of fury kindling in his dark eyes. "If one can be killed, they all can be killed."

"This isn't about revenge." Wesley gave voice to the thought before he was even aware of it. If the Klingon heard him, he gave no sign.

U.S.S. *Defiant* NX-74205

"*Aventine* took the brunt of that," said Ro, gripping the captain's chair as if she could will the *Defiant* to fly faster. "Weapons status?"

"Transphasic pulse is recharging," reported Sisko, from his post at the tactical station. "All other weapons ready."

"Then let's keep up the momentum." Ro nodded to the woman at the conn. "Lieutenant Tenmei, give me a pursuit course. We need to keep harrying those creatures until we piss them off enough to come back at us."

"I'm more than accomplished at pissing people off, Captain," said Tenmei, her gaze fixed on the main viewscreen. "Leave it to me."

Sisko had to resist the urge to spring to his feet, the churning energy of the fight fizzing in his limbs. So many times, it had been him commanding the *Defiant* as it raced into battle, and he'd forgotten what it was like to sit in the cramped confines of the vessel's bridge. Compared to the open space of the *Robinson*'s command deck, *Defiant*'s was akin to being crammed into a photon torpedo tube.

He concentrated on the targeting scanners, trying to lock on to the fast-moving shapes of the racing serpent creatures, but it was difficult to zero in on the Nagas, as the chronometric radiation coming off them in waves fogged the sensors.

All Sisko could be sure of was their course and speed—directly at Endalla, moving too fast to pull away from the small moon's gravity.

"What are they doing?" Ro voiced the question.

"They're accelerating!" Tenmei's surprise was evident in her tone. "Captain, at this speed they're going to crash into the lunar surface!"

"That doesn't make any sense."

"Break off," snapped Sisko as he suddenly saw what would come next. "Laren, listen to me!"

To her credit, the Bajoran didn't question him. "Helm, hard to starboard."

But even as Ro gave the order, the serpents were glowing with new surges of radiation, putting out pulses that reflected and reinforced one another. Sisko saw the spike in chronometric particles climb to the top of the scanner's scale, and ahead of the ship, a shimmering flash broke across the curvature of Endalla's dusky landscape.

"Oh, Prophets, no . . ." Ro said quietly as giant, jagged cracks raced out over Endalla's surface from the impact point where the Naga pack had struck it.

Distorted tides of gravity reached up to swat at the *Defiant* as its impulse grids glowed orange, thrusters firing hard to pull away. It was not enough.

On Sisko's screen, a torrent of conflicting sensor readings told the tale. The Devidians' creatures repeated the same assault they had inflicted on the planet Baseras, but with the Endalla moon's smaller mass, it unfolded in a fraction of the time.

Phasing through the solid matter of the lunar crust and into the heart of the rocky satellite, the Nagas dragged waves of weaponized time in their wake. Endalla came apart from the inside out, the structure aged billions, even trillions, of years in a matter of minutes. Robbed of its inner strength, the moon broke apart, crumbling like a decayed moba fruit.

"We're too close!" shouted Tenmei. "I can't pull away!"

"Then take us through!" Ro called back.

Sisko rocked back in his seat as city-sized lumps of stone tumbled past, surrounded by storms of fragments and glowing streams of magmatic ejecta. He jabbed at the phasers, sending out spears of fire to blast anything that came too close, but even as he did, the *Defiant*'s shield envelope shaded cherry red as remnants of the dying moon raked over it.

Tenmei flew the vessel like a starfighter, skipping over the burning debris, inverting and rolling across the ship's axis until finally, mercifully, they burst through the expanding cloud of dust and fire.

"Well done, Prynn!" Sisko punched the air, relief flooding through him as they made it into clear space. But the moment was fleeting.

The scanners cleared as the *Defiant* left the ruins of Endalla behind, lighting up with the returns from the Nagas. The creatures had slowed as they cut through the moon, consuming some of its mass along the way, perhaps to nourish and restore themselves, and now they were rushing ahead again.

Ice formed around Benjamin Sisko's heart as he saw the next prey for the Nagas, ahead on the viewscreen. The *Saticoy*, the interceptors, and beyond them, the evacuee barges.

"There are thousands of civilians on board those ships," whispered Tenmei, aghast at the thought of what destruction the serpents could bring to them.

Sisko nodded grimly. "My son is among them."

14

U.S.S. *Saticoy* NCC-75404

"The Nagas are making another pass," reported Zuenel, the Zaranite's matter-of-fact delivery at odds with the wailing of the *Saticoy*'s alert sirens. "Closing on the interceptors."

"I need that transphasic pulse!" Nog leaned forward in the captain's chair, jabbing at the controls at his side. He wanted to be down in main engineering, rerouting the power himself, but his duty was to command. The Ferengi pushed away the steady drumbeat of fear that sounded in his ears and bared his teeth. His instincts warred with his obligations, but he could not falter. More lives were on the line than just his—the civilians on the cargo barges, and countless more on Bajor—and he had to hold the line.

"Pulse still recharging," said Ensign Elsa, without looking up from the conn station. "Estimate 130 seconds to full power."

A bright flash of nuclear fire on the main viewscreen made Nog flinch as he saw one of the Bajoran impulse interceptors disintegrate into fragments of glowing metal. The other ships in the Space Guard flight strafed the closest of the Naga creatures, but their weapons seemed to do little damage, and in return the serpents writhed, striking out with lashing hits from the barbed cilia along their flanks. A second interceptor took a bad hit that sheared off its portside wing, and the craft went spiraling out of view, trailing flames.

"Bring us about," Nog ordered.

The *Saticoy* pivoted and drifted sideways across the engagement zone, framed by the expanding cloud of gas and dust that had been the Endalla moon. Phasers lanced out, hitting their targets, but the Nagas shrugged off the damage.

Turning, the monstrous creatures struck back toward the fast-moving interceptors and snapped at them. Two serpents came at one ship from opposite sides, and like predators diving on an avian, each bit into a wing and shook their carapace skulls. The luckless crew of the interceptor perished as the Nagas ripped the vessel in half, feasting on the wreckage.

Nog heard Lieutenant Ottaq voice a Xindi war curse as the arboreal's wide jaw dropped open in shock. "Those poor souls."

The Bajoran ship ruined, Nog expected the Nagas to move on to their next target, but they tarried with the burning interceptor, battering it with their armored heads.

"What are they doing?" said Elsa, the Tarlac woman's large eyes shimmering.

"The behavior pattern suggests they are toying with their prey," offered Zuenel. "Confidence is high they will attack the civilian ships next."

"No." Nog straightened. "We're not letting that happen." He pointed. "Helm, put us directly between the barges and the Nagas."

"We are no match for them," said the Zaranite. "We should fall back and regroup with the *Defiant* and the *Aventine*. There is no shame in retreat."

"Were my orders unclear, Lieutenant?" Nog twisted in his seat to look back at Zuenel, fighting to keep his voice level.

The Zaranite paused, as if about to speak, then she thought better of it and shook her head. "No, sir. Quite clear."

He knew what she was thinking, what they all were thinking. The last time they had faced these things, the Nagas had claimed the lives of Captain Hautuk and a dozen more of their crewmates. How would this be any different?

"We will not retreat," Nog said aloud.

A Ferengi who does not run in the face of certain death. The words echoed in his thoughts. *Uncle Quark would tell me I'm insane.*

S.S. *Syjin's Folly* NAR-66012

The deck shook and Jake Sisko fell against the inner wall of the barge's hull, catching himself against a support stanchion before he went down. He rebounded off a screen and clung on to it as the helmsman tried to turn the lumbering vessel away from the expanding wall of ash and fire that had been Endalla.

The evacuees crammed into the cavernous cargo bay held on to one another as shock after shock pummeled the slow-moving ship. At first, after reaching orbit, there had been a halfhearted choir as the Bajorans sung hymnals to lift their spirits, but now that was a chorus of weeping and screams as the ship trembled.

Jake looked through a slit of a port and out into the void beyond.

What he saw robbed him of his voice. A moon of Bajor had become a ruin of dust and stone, a great muddy smear drawn out across the black sky above the planet. Before it raged monstrous things that seemed to have escaped from a mad dream.

Horned serpents better suited to tales of ancient folklore thrashed and turned in the melee, savaging the ships sent to defend the barges. Ethereal fires burning in their throats, the creatures chewed on the wreckage of the interceptors, before slowly turning their attentions in the direction of the cargo ships.

Jake saw the black pits of eyespots surveying the barges, and he felt the predators considering them. There was nothing in that alien gaze that he could read, nothing beyond pure animus and destructive need.

"Husband." Korena's hand reached for his and took hold of it. "Don't look." She pulled him away from the port, to where Keiko sat against a storage pod with her son in a silent embrace. Korena pressed her palms to Jake's cheeks, turning his face to hers. "Just be with me."

"Always," he said, and his breath caught as the glittering fires in the void burned brighter.

U.S.S. Aventine NCC-82602

"We're pushing through . . ." As Captain Bowers spoke, Wesley looked up, across the *Aventine*'s bridge, in time to see the haze clear as the starship passed through the Endalla dust cloud.

Even from this distance, Wesley could see that the flight of Bajoran interceptors had been destroyed. *And the* Saticoy *will be next.*

His mouth compressed to a thin line. In fight after fight, he had watched the Nagas and their Devidian masters wreak havoc and destroy innocent lives. The burden of it weighed more heavily on him than anything he had ever known. Each engagement was a retreat, every combat a desperate attempt to stop from losing ground. And each time, on some level, he had failed. Each time, he had been forced to run.

He could predict how this battle would play out. First the *Saticoy* would perish, then the civilian vessels, and if *Aventine* and *Defiant* did not flee, those ships too would be destroyed.

And even if we disengage right now, what would that gain us? The question lay heavy in his thoughts. *A few more hours or days? And in the meantime, Bajor will be sacrificed.*

Wesley shook his head. "No," he said quietly.

"Mister Crusher?" At his side, Lieutenant Kedair gave him a curious look.

"Take over," he told the woman, then stepped away from the console, down to the command tier. "Captain Bowers, Captain Picard. This isn't going to work."

Picard frowned. "Wesley, I don't—"

He pressed on. "Just listen to me, sir. I thought we might be able to give those things a bloody nose in a straight-up fight, but I was wrong. We need to get them away from Bajor, before they start to feed in earnest."

"We're open to suggestions," Bowers said briskly. "Just make it quick."

"Let me take a shuttle out there." He nodded toward the screen. "I'll draw the Nagas off. I'll make them come after me."

"How can one man in a shuttlecraft do that?" said Bowers.

Picard rose to his feet, his face falling. "Wesley, no . . ." His stepfather was a perceptive man, and he had immediately understood.

Wesley held up a hand and allowed a brief flicker of neurochronal energy to crackle between his fingertips. It was a clever trick the Travelers of Tau Alpha C had taught him, showing him how to tap into the deep, secret streams of power that underpinned the universe. Correctly manipulated, one could use it to detach from the bonds of reality and shift across distance, dimension, even time itself.

"I have something they want. Just like they changed the ophidians into their tools, the Devidians biologically programmed the Nagas to be their hunters. They're attracted to sources of potential temporal energy. It's why they are driven to destroy any time-active artifacts, and why they attacked races like the Vorgons and the Krenim. I can tap into that same potential, in a small way."

"You'll make them believe you are a full-blooded Traveler," said Picard. "Turn yourself into a living lure."

Wesley nodded. "They won't be able to ignore it. They'll come after me," he said. "It's the only thing I can think of that will save Bajor. But it'll take a few moments for me to prepare. I need to get moving right *now*."

"You could die out there," said Picard.

"I don't intend to," Wesley shot back. "Believe me, I haven't been in this fight for this long just to give up now. I'll draw them away, then regroup with you back on DS9."

Bowers nodded. "Take the *Azetbur*, the captain's yacht. It's fast as all get-out. Just try to keep it in one piece, Mister Crusher."

"I'll do my best."

"Wesley . . ." Picard approached him as he moved toward the turbolift, his voice falling to a low murmur. "Come back."

He gave the other man a brief smile. "I will. I have a reason to."

U.S.S. *Saticoy* NCC-75404

Two of the Nagas came hunting for the *Saticoy*, winding through the darkness, bending gravity to their will to propel themselves forward.

Nog rose to his feet, his hands tightening into fists. The sound of his blood thundering through the lobes of his ears was so loud, he would have sworn he could hear it echoing off the walls of the bridge.

"Are we ready to fire?" he called out to Elsa, his voice threatening to crack under the strain.

"Transphasic pulse charging . . . and ready!" The Tarlac bobbed her head.

"Angle us so the discharge from the deflector will strike both incoming targets," ordered Nog, gesturing at the screen. "We need to make this count!"

The ship turned into the path of the oncoming serpents, yawing to starboard to bring the *Saticoy*'s deflector pod to bear. Slung beneath the main, saucer-shaped hull, the glowing pod sat on spars between the warp nacelles, and now it crackled with overbleed from the energy coiled inside it. The pulse was a makeshift weapon, but so far it had been the best response to the Nagas' attacks, and Nog could not deny that he wanted to make sure the creatures would not take any more innocent lives.

"Contact imminent," said Zuenel. "Commander, pulse discharge ready to deploy on your word."

For a second, Nog's gaze dropped back to the center seat, where Captain Hautuk had died. The Acamarian woman's blood was still visible as a dark pattern on the material of the chair.

Is this the price of that seat? The question pressed at him. *Where does it end?*

He tore his eyes away. "Execute!"

The *Saticoy* shuddered as a crackling span of white light burst from the deflector array and caught the oncoming Nagas full force. For a split second, the energy effect overloaded the main viewer's filters and the glow turned the bridge into a stage of stark, knife-edged shadows.

Nog raised one hand to shield his eyes, ignoring the stabs of pain from his optic nerves. Then as quickly as it had lit up the void, the pulse effect faded, and the Ferengi blinked away the purple afterimages seared onto his retinas.

He took a few steps forward, blinking furiously and peering out into space through the viewscreen.

A line of black, depthless eyepits stared back at him from along the ridges of a scarred carapace, the bony exo-skull as broad as the *Saticoy*'s saucer. Ash and tatters of space-hardened epidermis flaked away from the Naga creature, burned off by the transphasic pulse. Adrift, but still very much alive, the thing and its monstrous companion hung in the vacuum before them.

"It didn't work . . ." Lieutenant Ottaq's broad, simian hands grasped the top of his station as he rocked forward in his seat. "How can that be? How did it not work?!"

"Analyzing," said Zuenel in a dead voice. "It appears the creatures altered their quantum phase state at the moment of discharge, avoiding the full force of the pulse." She hissed behind her breather mask. "They've learned. They adapted."

The Naga closest to the ship shook off its moment of lethargy and swam past the *Saticoy*, giving the vessel a vicious strike with the prow of its head. Razor-tipped cilia scraped over the hull, sending wild surges of lethal radiation into the spaceframe and ripping away great chunks of metal. The second beast fell in behind, flanks grinding over the starship's impulse grid and tearing through it as it rolled past.

Crimson warnings flooded the bridge as dozens of systems went down across the vessel, and Nog struggled to keep his footing.

It was all going wrong. The brave defense he had hoped to mount was crumbling around him. The trust that Captain Hautuk had placed in Nog, then bequeathed to the Ferengi with her death, was slipping through his fingers.

The Nagas shook off their injuries and wound slowly toward the fleeing civilian ships, two of them advancing on the barges while the other pair off to starboard continued to devour the wreckage of the Bajoran interceptors.

Shame filled Nog's heart. He had failed to stop the creatures, inflicting so little damage upon them that the monstrous predators did not even consider the *Saticoy* worth destroying. The barges were a far richer prize for them, packed with ten times the number of living beings, all gripped by abject terror.

He pulled himself to the nearest console and grimly surveyed the damage done to the ship. The warp drive, barely repaired from the last engagement, was offline and showed no signs of reactivating. Power systems were critically mauled. Life-support was failing, the heat and air bleeding out into the cold vacuum of space.

As a doctor might study a patient's vitals and know that death was close at hand, so the engineer in Nog knew that he was looking at a dying starship. The *Saticoy*'s end would not come in an explosive burst of fire, but slowly and painfully, her crew suffocating, freezing, or perishing from radiation poisoning.

Unless her commander challenges that fate.

Nog pushed away from the console and gave a shout. "All hands, this is . . . the captain! The order is, abandon ship! Everyone to the escape pods!" When Zuenel and the others hesitated, he called out again. "Go now!"

A new siren tone echoed through the decks of the starship, and within moments Nog saw the hexagonal shapes of lifeboat modules streaming away from the dorsal and ventral hull as his crew obeyed the order.

Elsa, Zuenel, and Ottaq left their posts behind and made for the turbolift, and the Tarlac woman hesitated on the threshold. "Sir? Sir!"

Nog ignored her. He halted at Elsa's station and input a command string. The *Saticoy*'s remaining thrusters fired, and the ship turned to move after the scarred Naga.

He mirrored the ship's warp-core control system to the console, his mind racing as a flurry of warning lights blazed before him. "They adapted to the pulse," said Nog, thinking out loud. "Because it was a controlled resonance burst. But an *uncontrolled* discharge . . . They can't anticipate that and phase through. A massive chroniton particle surge will do it."

"You're talking about a warp-core detonation."

Nog turned. Elsa had stepped back out of the turbolift, with Zuenel and Ottaq at her side. "Yes." He shook his head. "I gave you a direct order. Why are you still here?"

Ottaq pushed past him, back to his post, peering at his screen. "You can't fly this ship and jettison the core at the same time. That needs more than one person."

"Correction, we cannot jettison the warp core *at all*," Zuenel pronounced. "Damage to the ejection system has rendered that action impossible."

"The pods are away," said Elsa. "Sir, it's just us now." She looked to her colleagues, and the Xindi and the Zaranite both gave her a nod of agreement. "If you're staying, we're staying."

Nog choked off a gasp. "I can't ask you—"

"Please get out of my seat, sir," said Elsa, and she pushed Nog away, taking her post once again. At her side, Ottaq was already reconfiguring his console for operations.

"You will need to operate the engineering station, sir." Zuenel pointed at the relevant console, before striding back to her science station. "Release of the warp core's interlocks must be done manually." Her bald head bobbed. "We are with you, Captain Nog."

He walked to the station, each step taking an eternity. Around him, the *Saticoy* trembled and groaned, and he imagined it was alive, that it could sense the end approaching.

Is it better to do this? he wondered. *Give our all, and hope it counts?*

Unbidden, Nog's fingers reached up and he traced the delta shape of the Starfleet insignia on his chest.

It was just a piece of metal, a common device plated with gold and silver. It was also a symbol, an emblem of everything that Starfleet stood for. Every deed and word devoted to liberty, every struggle to preserve life and push back against the darkness.

"This is our duty," he said to himself. "This is how we make a difference."

Nog brought the console online and, one by one, he deactivated the safety mechanisms that would prevent the *Saticoy*'s warp core from destroying itself *in situ*.

From across the bridge, Zuenel reported that the scarred Naga and its hunting partner were fast approaching the cargo barges. Elsa and Ottaq guided the ship in, aiming them like an arrow into the midst of the pair.

The creatures sensed the starship closing in, and turned back to meet it. Their motions were first quizzical, then feral.

"Get us clear of the escape pods and set collision course," called Nog, giving his last command as he stared into the face of the monsters. "Maximum speed!"

U.S.S. *Defiant* NX-74205

"Oh, no." The fear in Tenmei's voice drew Sisko's attention, and once he saw what she had seen, he could not look away.

Framed in the middle of the *Defiant*'s main viewer, the *Saticoy* slammed into the flank of the scarred Naga, causing starship and cosmozoan to tangle around each other. The vessel careened on and collided with the second creature close by, the impact tearing away its portside warp nacelle, releasing a jet of plasma fire into the void.

Then a new sun was briefly born in the midst of the chaos. A searing fireball of matter and antimatter annihilation blossomed inside the *Saticoy*, consuming the ship and two of the vicious Nagas in the blink of an eye.

The leading edge of the blast wave from the detonation shunted

Defiant off course and Sisko fell against his console, but he felt nothing. He was numbed by shock and a cold understanding.

"Nog . . ." A memory flashed in Sisko's mind, of the determined Ferengi teenager who had first come to him seeking his endorsement to attend Starfleet Academy. Gone now, wiped from the universe in an instant.

Sisko's hand went to his face, and suddenly his flesh felt like fire. His heartbeat throbbed in his ears and his chest tightened.

"He blew up his ship," said Ro, her voice thick with emotion. "To save those transports."

"There's still another two of them out there," said Tenmei, gesturing at her monitor. "If the transphasic pulse isn't affecting them anymore . . . ?" She didn't need to finish. They all knew the question that followed.

Do we have to do the same?

Sisko rose to his feet, but it was a monumental effort, as if the bridge's gravity settings had increased tenfold. He opened his mouth to speak, but no words emerged. Ro, Tenmei, and the other bridge officers didn't seem to notice, all of them firmly focused on their own duties.

"Sensors indicate an auxiliary craft detaching from the *Aventine*," said one of the crew. "It's the captain's yacht, with a single life sign aboard."

Sisko couldn't connect the voice to a name. It was hard to think straight. He felt as if his mind were becoming untethered from his physical form. His flesh was vague and distant, registering only as the echo of an awful, sickening stress inside his thoughts.

He forced himself to form speech, but the meat and matter of him was too far away, moving farther beyond his grasp with every second. Sisko looked past Ro and Tenmei, seeing hazy aurorae around them, colored with emotions and moments yet to happen.

"Captain?" Ro turned to him, concern rising. "Are you all right?"

But he could not answer her. His senses were blinded, overloaded with input his human mind could not assimilate. And the worst of it was, Sisko knew this sensation *all too well.*

A searing flood of nothingness broke over him, and he surrendered to it, knowing that there was no other path open to him.

He fell into the vision.

"No time," said a woman's voice, from across an impossible distance. His mother's voice.

An infinite cascade of events surrounded him, pulling his consciousness in incalculable directions at once. They were trying to make him see, trying to show him their nonlinear understanding all at once, despite the impossibility of it.

There was no time, *only an endless ocean of simultaneous existence. He saw everything in shards of continuity, glimpsing brief pieces of the people he knew and loved as they swept past his consciousness.*

Jake and Korena, huddled together in the hold of a cargo barge, desperate to live; Kira praying at the shrine on Deep Space 9 for a deliverance she did not want; Julian in the sickbay, grasping the blade of a knife just to feel something; Nog's last thoughts and regrets as the fires swallowed him.

And then Sisko's mind expanded, becoming diffuse as the Prophets gave him, however briefly, an instant to know the universe as they did.

It was hard to hold on to his self, but he struggled and fought. What they had to show him was too important to miss.

"No time," said the voice.

He saw anti-life, as if it were a force of nature like the lines of a magnetic field. Thick streams of ethereal energy, solid threads of living terror drained from the minds of the living, plunging out of this reality and flooding toward a billion open jaws that could never be filled.

In a place outside time, horrors dwelled, so immense that they defied reason. Horrors that fed on raw fear. Horrors that could endure only by destroying life in unimaginable quantities.

Gripped by panic, Sisko became afraid he might be driven mad by the truth the Prophets were showing him; but then they offered a measure of hope. One tiny candle in the infinite darkness. A solution.

They showed him the Celestial Temple in the sky, burning and toxic, before it collapsed in on itself, never to have existed. They showed him the sacrifice that had to be made.

"No time," said the voice. "For us."

S.S. *Syjin's Folly* NAR-66012

"Dad . . . ?"

For a moment, Jake was certain that he heard his father's voice amid the noise of the people in the cargo bay, calling out to him through the weeping and the desperate entreaties to the Prophets.

"We're picking up speed," said Yoshi, pressing his hand to the deck plates. "I can feel it. That vibration is the warp engines spooling up to power."

Jake didn't doubt what the teenager was telling him. Kirayoshi O'Brien was the son of one of the best engineers in Starfleet, and he imagined the boy had picked up some knowledge from his father along the way. At length, Jake rose to his feet and went back to the port.

They had witnessed the inferno that consumed the *Saticoy* and the serpent creatures menacing the civilian ships. Korena tried to comfort Jake when the barges picked up the starship's scattered escape pods and rescued the surviving crew, insisting that his old friend might have lived.

Jake loved her for that, for his wife's ability to reach for hope and light even in the darkest of times. But he knew, as surely as if he had seen it with his own eyes, that Nog was gone. He felt the certainty as an empty space in his heart.

"What can you see?" said Keiko. "Are we going to make it?"

Through the mess of wreckage and debris, Jake found monstrous shapes prowling ever nearer, closing on the slow and ponderous barges. To escape to warp speed and flee the system, the elderly transports with their temperamental drives needed to get out of the mass shadow cast by Bajor and its system of close-orbiting moons, but until that moment, they were vulnerable. The destruction of Endalla and the *Saticoy* would only have made that worse, salting local space with energy distortions and debris.

None of which would slow the serpents. The giant predators moved easily through the sea of remains with mouths open wide, sifting the spoil for sustenance. In moments, they would be upon the barges, and there was nothing to stop them from destroying every living thing aboard.

Keiko called him again. "Jake, what's out there?"

"Nothing," he lied. "Just the stars—"

The comforting deceit faded on his lips as a small ship flashed past the barge at close quarters. Jake got the impression of a Starfleet craft, a hull with an arrowhead configuration, but that was pushed aside by the strange aura that shimmered around the vessel.

It wasn't a warp-field effect, or anything like Jake had ever seen before, but it lit up the dust clouds and debris field with reflected light. He pressed his hand to the portal slit. He wanted to cry out and warn the pilot.

Didn't they realize? Couldn't they see them? The serpents were out there in the haze, hunting for prey, and they turned sharply to race after the little ship's impulse wake.

Then all too suddenly, Jake understood. Whoever it was out there was finishing the job that Nog had started, saving the lives of the people on the barge flotilla. The gigantic snake creatures flared their colossal hoods and warped gravity to glide swiftly up and away, pursuing the vessel until they and the glowing craft were lost to his sight.

"Attention, everyone," said a female voice from an overhead speaker grille. *"We're almost clear. Going to warp any moment, so hang on. This will be rough."*

A ragged, tearful cheer went up from the gathered evacuees, and

Jake felt Korena's arms slide around him, pulling her body to his. "We're going to make it," she said. "Jake, we're safe."

"I hope so." His reply was lost in the rising wail of the barge's engines as the ship teetered briefly on the edge of warp velocity.

In that final moment before they leaped to light speed, Jake saw another ship out there, a battered form with a bullet prow and a muscular silhouette: the *Defiant*.

Good luck, Dad, he said silently as they shot away. *I love you.*

Deep Space 9, Bajor System

The corridors of the station were empty, echoing to the sound of Picard's footfalls as he followed the Changeling to the operations hub.

"Are we all that's left?" He ventured the question, having noted the last few freighters making their hasty departure as the *Aventine* and the *Defiant* docked.

Odo gave a brisk shake of the head. "There are a hundred or so Bajorans who have barricaded themselves inside the park. They refuse to leave." He snorted. "They have transporter inhibitors to stop them from being beamed out."

"Adherents of Talnot, I take it?" Picard had learned of the ancient vedek and his predictions in the interim. "They must know their lives are in grave danger."

"Oh, they know, all right," said Odo. "It's the reason they're here. It's what they want, to die in some grandiose religious rapture." He grunted. "*Solids*. Sometimes I wonder if your minds operate wholly on delusion."

"Belief can be a very powerful force," Picard noted.

"I know," Odo shot back. "I've seen enough beings who considered themselves good and decent do terrible things, all because some 'belief' led them to it." He snorted again. "Ought to be illegal."

They reached their destination, and Odo gestured for Picard to enter. Inside the large, circular space, a ring of consoles surrounded a holographic situation table in the lower pit, where the station's commander, Captain Ro, was already at work setting up a tactical plot of local space.

"Stay out of trouble," said Odo, in a way that made it clear he was leaving Picard to his own devices. The Changeling made his way over to where the Bajoran vedek, Kira Nerys, stood alone, staring into nothing. Picard observed the two of them, then thought better of it. It was clear from the constable's shift in comportment, and his halting manner toward the woman, that there was an intimacy between them. Picard looked away, having no desire to invade what was clearly a private moment.

He saw Sam Bowers in conversation with Worf at the tactical station and threw the two men a terse nod before taking in the rest of the command hub. Gathered around the science station on the other side of the hub, Data and Ambassador Spock were deep in an intense discussion, animated only by brief motions of Data's hands. The android's daughter, Lal, had already returned to the *Aventine*, to assist La Forge with repairs to the ship.

Benjamin Sisko sat alone, feigning interest in a screen, but his eyes told the lie of it. Sisko was lost in some inner reverie, and Picard recalled what he had shared with Bowers.

The thousand-yard stare. He sighed. *It is upon us all now.*

"Captain?"

Picard turned to find a familiar face coming his way.

"I'm glad you're here."

"Miles." Picard managed a wan smile. Despite the circumstances, it pleased him to see his former transporter chief. "I believe it's Command Master Chief now, yes?"

O'Brien nodded. "Captain Ro keeps telling me to take the officer's candidacy exam, but I'm content as a noncom."

"You prefer to work for a living, I understand." The old joke widened the smile into something genuine, and the brief moment was a welcome one. "It fits you well."

"I'm feeling the weight of it today," admitted the other man, touching his collar where the new rank insignia lay.

Picard mirrored the gesture without thinking, then shifted back to the business at hand. "Any developments to report?"

O'Brien's brow furrowed. "Energy output from the wormhole is all over the place, sir. I've never seen anything like it in all the years I've been here."

"The end of existence doesn't happen every day."

Picard turned toward the new voice, and realized that he had missed another person standing in the shadows. Although they had never met, he recognized the slight, bearded man with the intense gaze.

"Doctor Bashir, I presume?"

Bashir inclined his head. "Captain Picard." His pronunciation was metered and careful, almost as if he was out of practice. "Are you here to halt the end, or to hasten it?"

Picard chose not to reply to the question. What he knew of Bashir was a mishmash of rumors—the man had been illegally genetically engineered as a child, and his career in the top percentile of Federation medicine had been cut short by his violation of orders during the Andorian reproductive crisis. The darker rumors said that Bashir had been part of the clandestine group Section 31, and that it was because of him that S31's guiding artificial intelligence, Control, had ultimately been unmasked. Picard knew that Data and Lal had also played a part in Control's demise, but once again the details were murky. For the *Enterprise*'s captain, the only certainty was how the doctor's career had become entangled in that situation, and the fallout that followed. He wondered what might be revealed if he and Bashir compared notes.

Another time, he decided. *We have more pressing concerns.*

A signal chimed from a nearby comm, and Bashir reached for it, opening the channel. "DS9."

"*This is the* Azetbur." The sound of Wesley's voice served to ease

Picard's concerns by a few degrees. *"I'm on approach. Start without me, I'll be there as soon as I can."*

"Where are those snake creatures?" said Bashir.

"I took them on a wild ride through a solar promontory," he replied. *"They're still following my energy trail, but they can't keep up with this boat. They're maybe an hour behind me, no more than that."*

"We had better begin, then," Bashir went on, fixing Picard with a hard look as he signed off. "I imagine you didn't cross the quadrant in a stolen Starfleet vessel just to lend us a hand at the eleventh hour."

"As always, the doctor makes a cogent point." Sisko broke his silence, stepping into the hub's mid-tier. "Bajor has a stay of execution, thanks to Captain Nog's sacrifice and Mister Crusher's intervention. But we're not out of the woods yet. Two of those Naga creatures are still at large."

"There are far more than that," said Data. "Based on scans conducted by Ambassador Spock and myself, it is likely that the Naga life-forms are actually displaced temporal alternates of the same single being, plucked from various points in different time streams by the Devidians."

"Potentially, there may be an infinite number of them," said Spock. "It is quite fascinating."

"Cut down one and two more rise in its place," said Bowers. "I'd call that *alarming*."

Worf folded his arms and went straight to the most direct solution. "How do we kill them?"

"Nog already answered that question for us," said Ro. The Bajoran woman ran a hand through her unkempt hair. "But if Data is right, we'll run out of starships and exploding warp cores long before they run out of vipers."

It wasn't lost on Picard that Ro used the word *viper* to describe the Devidian war-creatures. The same term appeared over and over in Talnot's apocalyptic prophecy. He saw his moment and spoke up. "It won't just be Bajor they destroy. This is the point of invasion, you see, their portal into our time stream. From here, they can venture out across the galaxy and beyond. Undermining the foundations of our very dimension. Preparing it for destruction . . . and consumption."

"Well, that doesn't sound like a buffet I want to cater." Everyone's attention went to the new arrival standing by the main doors, an overdressed Ferengi with deep-set eyes, who scanned the room reproachfully. "What are you going to do about it?"

"Quark." Constable Odo growled his name and marched toward him. "Get out! You're not supposed to be in here."

"He's not even supposed to be on the station," insisted Ro, glaring at him. "I got you a berth on the last transport out; you should be halfway to Vega by now!"

Quark edged around the perimeter of the hub, keeping as far away from Odo as he could. "Do I look like a fool to you? I'm not just going to up and leave my bar behind! All that inventory, all that value? Ridiculous!" He waved at the air. "And considering my lauded status as one of the most important figures on the station, I thought it only fitting I be here to participate in this, uh, conversation!"

"I wanted you gone." Ro sighed. "*Safe.*"

"Yes, well." The Ferengi's practiced bluster faltered, and Picard sensed what was truly motivating the barkeep. "I suppose it's Nog's fault. That foolish . . . That brave young idiot. His predilection for making poor choices has obviously rubbed off on me."

Odo finally managed to lay a hand on Quark's shoulder, but Ro waved him off. Glowering, the constable released the Ferengi, who in turn made a show of straightening his jacket.

"Captains, assembled beings," began Spock, "in the interest of alacrity, I will clarify the circumstances at hand." The elderly Vulcan stepped down to the situation table, taking control of the holographic projector as Ro moved aside. "As Captain Picard has made clear, our universe faces a dire existential threat. No matter how many of them we destroy, the Nagas will continue to invade this dimension, guided by their Devidian masters from the safety of the region known as 'intertime.' Their ultimate goal is to trigger the collapse of this time stream in a single, catastrophic act. The only hope of forestalling that eventuality is to prevent further incursions."

"They're using the Celestial Temple." Vedek Kira spoke up, her voice dry and broken, as if she had been crying. "The wormhole. Crossing the barriers between realities where it is thinnest."

Sisko's eyes widened. "Nerys, how do you know that?"

They shared a look that Picard couldn't read. "Because I saw it, Ben. After you went out to fight them, I went to the station shrine."

"To pray," said Sisko. "To look for deliverance."

"The Prophets showed me another vision," she breathed. "Like the one I had in the Perikian Monastery, but much more intense." The vedek pointed toward the holograph hanging in the air above Spock. "The Nagas have breached the walls of the Celestial Temple. It's their gateway."

"Vedek Kira's description is accurate," said the Vulcan. "The Bajoran wormhole is a unique phenomenon that exists in all quantum realities, and through it, the Devidians have been able to dispatch their attackers. In order to stop their advance, that point of entry must be closed."

"Collapse it?" O'Brien leaned forward. "Well, it's been done before."

"Not in the manner that we propose," offered Data. "To be clear, the wormhole must be *destroyed*, beyond all possibility of reconstitution."

Ro shook her head, her eyes shining. "No. That's not possible. It can't be done."

"I'm afraid it is," Picard said gently. "And it must, if we are to succeed."

"How?" said Sisko, in a near whisper.

Spock indicated the hologram, which illustrated his words as he went on. "Deep Space 9 would cross the Bajoran wormhole's event horizon and initiate an overload of its matter/antimatter core at a predetermined locus." Amid the rendering of the lightning-wreathed wormhole, a small spindle glowing blue moved into the infernal maw. "Once in place, the station's self-destruction will release enough energy to permanently disperse the verteron nodes inside the phenomenon." The hologram flared white and vanished. "The wormhole will then cease to exist," concluded the ambassador.

"Are you out of your Vulcan mind?" Quark spat the retort across the room. "Do you realize what you're asking?" He jabbed a finger in the direction of Ro and Kira. "You're telling them to kill the Prophets! Blow up their gods!"

"Didn't think you believed in that sort of thing," said Bashir.

"I don't!" Quark shot back. "But Ro does! And I am pretty certain that the interdimensional beings living out there will have something to say about it!"

"They do," said Kira quietly. "They did."

Ro composed herself, putting aside her shock as she turned toward Sisko. "You're the Emissary, Benjamin. Could you sanction this?"

"I do." Sisko gave a slow nod. "Out there, when Endalla was destroyed, the Prophets reached into my mind. Like Nerys, they spoke to me." The hub fell silent as the words poured out of Sisko's mouth, as he described the vision that had been granted to him. "They told me those creatures, the Devidians, they are a force of *anti-life*. The Prophets have to die to stop them."

"Is everyone trying to be a martyr?" Quark muttered the question bitterly, turning his face to hide himself wiping a tear from his cheek.

"We have to put this to a vote," said Bowers. "It can't just be an order."

Worf nodded grimly. "It must be unanimous. The consequences are too grave for one person to make the decision alone."

Spock raised his hand. "I concur."

"As do I." Data mirrored the gesture. Worf and Bowers followed on, and as Picard watched, a silent communication passed between Bashir and O'Brien before they too raised their hands.

Picard took a breath, and spoke to Ro, Kira, and Sisko. "Everyone in this room understands the profound impact this act will have on Bajor and her people. But the alternative is nothing but an infinity of death and ruin." He raised his hand.

Sisko did the same. "We have no choice," he said.

"You don't have to agree to this." Odo went to Kira's side. "Nerys. If you say no, we can find another way."

"He's right." Quark spoke directly to Ro. "Everyone agrees or no one agrees. These humans don't get the right to decide for you!"

"I saw what the Emissary saw," said Kira. "The apocalypse that Talnot predicted. If we can stop that from coming to pass, whatever the price is—"

"It has to be paid," concluded Ro.

Slowly, the two Bajoran women raised their hands. Odo and Quark were the last to do the same, each of them grim faced with acceptance.

The hub fell quiet once more as the immensity of their shared choice settled in upon the gathered group. Picard searched himself for something to say, some words of encouragement, but he found himself wanting. The enormity of the moment robbed him of his voice.

At length, Kira broke the silence. "When it is done, when the station goes up . . . It will be me who makes the final commitment. The ultimate responsibility is mine."

"You don't have to carry that burden," began Sisko, but Kira waved him to silence.

"It must be me. I am the Hand of the Prophets." She took a shuddering breath and drew upward, steeling herself. "This is the role they chose me for."

15

Deep Space 9, Bajor System

The decision made, the group broke into teams and set to their assigned roles.

Alongside Captain Bowers, Picard joined Data to board the *Aventine*, where Geordi La Forge was already preparing the ship for departure. As with the android's daughter, Lal, Picard's wife and son were also aboard the starship, and he swallowed a pang of fear as he thought of the danger he was about to put them in. But the unpleasant reality was clear to him. Nowhere was truly safe from the predations of the Devidians and their monsters. No world, no starship, lay beyond their reach.

Better that we stay close to the ones we love, he thought. *If the moment comes, at least we'll have one another.*

At the docking ring, before the group separated, Picard went to Sisko and the two men shook hands solemnly. "I'm sorry that this is what has brought us together after so many years," he began. "What there is between you and I . . . I would have liked the opportunity to know you better."

"I feel the same." Sisko's dark eyes bored into his. "When you and I first crossed paths, we were both very different men."

"Agreed." He didn't need to reiterate the details. Sisko had fought Picard while he was Locutus, under the control of the Borg at Wolf 359. Later, they had met again when Sisko assumed command of Deep Space 9, and in the years since, the tension between them had eventually turned into a mutual respect.

"Something I've come to accept," Sisko went on, "is that we all have our roles to play. What we do with them is up to us, but the universe has its intention. We can only decide if we will follow along with it, or go off the page."

"I have to say," added Picard, "I'm not much for ideas of fate, predestination, and the like . . ."

"It's more complex than that." Sisko smiled briefly. "Perhaps we can have that conversation after this is all over."

The other captain nodded to the crew he had chosen for the *Defiant*, and Bashir returned the gesture before making for the airlock leading to the smaller ship. Ambassador Spock followed the doctor without comment, along with Odo, recruited to take a post. The Changeling had accepted the role grudgingly, clearly unwilling to leave Vedek Kira on DS9 with Captain Ro, O'Brien, and Quark.

"Good luck, Jean-Luc," concluded Sisko, and he strode away.

Picard turned to Worf, who stood silently waiting. "Commander?"

"I am going with the *Defiant*," said the Klingon, without meeting his gaze. "Captain Sisko requires a first officer with extensive combat experience aboard that class of vessel. I believe I will serve the operation better there than aboard the *Aventine*."

"Very well." It wasn't what Picard had expected to hear, and he felt he could not ask Worf to reconsider. "And Alexander?"

"He is an accomplished tactical officer," Worf said stiffly. "He will perform well under your command."

Picard recalled his own musing on family. "I don't doubt it. Perhaps he would be better suited to the *Defiant*. I'll see that he is beamed over."

"Thank you, sir," Worf said quietly.

Picard was silent for a moment. "Commander, this decision, I hope it is not rooted in the conversation we had after leaving Omicron Theta. I want you to know that I have complete trust in you."

"That means a great deal to me, Captain," Worf replied. "But I have learned from you that we must place ourselves where we can do the most good. In this instance, for me that is the bridge of the *Defiant*."

Picard nodded, accepting the other man's words. "Fight well, Number One. Today is a good day to live."

When he was alone, Picard took a last, long breath of the station's air. Once he stepped through the airlock and back aboard the *Aventine*, he would never return.

No one would; if the plan worked, in a matter of hours Deep Space 9 would be nothing but a memory.

His musings were broken as a secondary hatch hissed open and a figure in a dark jacket dashed out, searching the deck. "Damn," muttered Wesley. "Was I too late for the big farewell?"

"I'm afraid so," said Picard.

"Did you give a speech? I miss hearing those."

He shook his head. "There wasn't time. And besides, I think this is a moment where everyone involved knows the stakes. Nothing more needed to be said."

"True enough." Wesley started toward the far side of the docking ring, to where a ramp led up to DS9's runabout hangar.

"You're not joining us on the *Aventine*?"

Wesley halted. "No." He jerked a thumb at the airlock he had just exited. "I docked the *Azetbur* for Captain Ro and the others to use as their ride out of here. But I figure that every other ship we can field against the Nagas will help, right?"

"You're taking a runabout."

"Actually, we're taking *all* of them," said an identical voice. Picard turned back to the open hatch to see Wesley arrive for a second time. This version was identical to the first, except that his jacket was worn closed instead of open. "There's still four ships parked up there after the evacuation; we can bring them along."

"I'll fly the *Rio Grande*, you take the *Tiber*," said the first Wesley.

"Got it." The second incarnation jogged past Picard with a brisk nod, and carried on to the upper level.

The first Wesley gave a sheepish smile. "So, about him, let me explain—"

"We're all Wesley Crusher," said a third incarnation as he

emerged from the airlock, closely followed by a fourth. "Just at different moments."

The third and fourth Wesleys both went without the jacket, but other than that, they appeared identical. "He pulled us out of a few alternate time streams so we could all work together," said the last one. "To be honest, I was wondering what took me so long."

"Well, you know it's risky," offered the third.

"You two take the *Glyrhond* and the *Tecyr*," said the first. "We'll rendezvous with the *Aventine* after lift-off."

"Okay," the third and fourth incarnations replied as one, then followed in the footsteps of their duplicate.

Picard watched them go, holding back his amazement. "I wasn't aware you could do that."

"It's not something I can make a habit of," admitted Wesley. "Manipulating your own life path is a massive violation of the Temporal Prime Directive. Timefleet and the DTI would pitch a fit if they knew, but I figured right now we're operating without a net, so . . ." He trailed off into a shrug.

"We need all the help we can get," concluded Picard.

Wesley nodded and smiled once again. "I'll see you out there, Captain."

U.S.S. *Aventine* NCC-82602

"We're free of all moorings," said Lieutenant Mirren. "Maneuvering to attack posture."

"Sound battle stations throughout the ship." Bowers pulled himself ramrod straight against the back of the command chair as he gave the order. Immediately, the bridge was lit by crimson flashes as red-alert warnings blinked into life at every station. "Here we go again," he added, almost to himself.

It seemed like there had barely been a moment to breathe between the confrontations that had come over the past few days. His captaincy, such as it was, had quickly become a litany of battles and near-death escapes, with each new danger coming ever faster on the heels of the last.

Samaritan Bowers had always envisaged himself eventually commanding a starship. He expected to follow the traditional path, serving as first officer to the big chair aboard a smaller vessel, maybe a science vessel or a light cruiser, nothing too intimidating, and work his way up to a capital ship.

Fate had a different idea. It gave him his dream post, captaining one of the most advanced vessels in the fleet. And to put Bowers there, it killed a dear friend and plunged him into what was, quite literally, the fight of their lives.

It was impossible for him to want this and to hate this any more than he did.

How do I make it work, Ezri? Bowers wished that he could turn his head and lean in to quietly ask her the question, just as he had on dozens of other missions, on countless other days. *I need you here right now, Dax. More than I ever did before, today I need your wisdom.*

"Captain?" It took a second for the word to break through his reverie, and Bowers looked up to see that Picard had arrived on the bridge, with the android Data at his side. "With your permission?"

Bowers nodded. "Stations, please."

Picard stepped up to the tactical console. The veteran officer looked troubled, but only for a moment, shutting down whatever fears he might have had in order to do the duty before him.

He makes it look easy, thought Bowers. *But it isn't. Every step is a struggle to make the right choice. Every decision has the seed of failure in it.*

"Offensive and defensive systems optimal," reported Picard. "Ready at your discretion, Captain."

"Sensors have picked up the remaining Nagas," added Data, working with Kedair at the science stations. "They are heading directly toward Deep Space 9."

"If the transphasic pulse is now ineffective," began Kedair, "and damage inflicted by the chroniton charges is negligible, may I ask exactly how we intend to deter these creatures?"

"I would suggest we remove all phase-state inhibitor modules from every photon and quantum torpedo warhead aboard ship," offered the android.

"That will render those munitions critically unstable," said Picard. "A single error could cause them to detonate prematurely."

"Correct," said Data, "but that inherent instability will also prevent the Nagas from predicting and phasing through any impact event. They cannot avoid the blast entirely."

"That is risky in the extreme!" snapped Kedair.

The seed of failure, thought Bowers as he frowned. *But to avoid the risk will virtually guarantee it.* "Captain Picard, please execute Mister Data's recommendations." He turned toward Lieutenant Mirren. "Helm, close to attack range."

U.S.S. *Defiant* NX-74205

"*Aventine* is taking the lead on target alpha," said Worf, tracking the movement of the oncoming Naga creatures.

"Understood," said Sisko. "Commander, plot me a sweeping run at target beta. We'll draw them apart. Divide and conquer."

Worf did as he was ordered, losing himself in the work. He was grateful for it. The business of tactics and combat came as easily to the Klingon as breathing, and it gave him something to concentrate on, away from darker musings.

After a moment, he was done, and he forwarded the course to Tenmei at the helm. Worf looked up and found Alexander watching him.

"What is it?"

His son smiled slightly. "I can't tell you how many times I dreamed of something like this when I was a boy. You and I, father and son, standing shoulder to shoulder on the bridge of a warship, fighting a relentless foe."

Worf allowed a thin smile. "How does the reality compare to the fantasy?"

"Favorably." Alexander gestured at the walls around them. "Although I don't remember it being quite this cramped."

"You become accustomed to it."

In fact, for Worf, being on the *Defiant* was like being home. The *Enterprise* would always be the most impressive ship he had ever served aboard, but *Defiant* was like an old battle comrade. Worf had shed blood on these decks, fought almost to the death on more than one occasion. It felt *correct* to be here, considering the severity of the foe they were facing.

"Closing on target designated beta," said Odo, working a sensor console. He glared at the display, absorbing the readouts. "Someone going to tell me how we destroy this monster?"

Sisko replied with orders. "Tenmei, take us past the target at maximum impulse, as close as you dare. Tactical, fire phasers at will."

"Captain, phaser hits will not be enough." Worf voiced his concern even as he powered the weapons. On the viewscreen, the twisting form of the Naga grew large, radiating waves of chronometric radiation. The first searing lances of energy from the phasers shot out of the *Defiant*, and where they hit home the Naga trembled, but it rode out the damage.

Sisko turned to Odo. "Constable, stand by to vent warp plasma . . . Now!"

"Venting!" The Changeling tapped the control and Worf felt the ship tremble as a gusher of gaseous material ejected into space.

The Naga recoiled, spinning about and attempting to lash out at the swift little ship as it raced along the length of the gigantic serpent's flank. Trailing behind the *Defiant* in a thick, shimmering cloud, the expelled energetic plasma enveloped the creature, crackling where it interacted with the Naga's innate warp field.

For an instant, the alien creature was caught in the toxic haze, its space-hardened flesh seared by the touch of it. As the *Defiant* accelerated away, Worf realized how Sisko's tactic was about to play out.

"Aft torpedo," called the captain, "fire into the warp plasma, proximity detonation!"

"Torpedo away!" Worf slammed his hand down on the launch control and heard the thud of release through the deck. "Brace for effect!"

Alexander's eyes widened as he caught up to the plan. "Oh."

Before the Naga could writhe away, the photon torpedo exploded at the edge of the plasma cloud, and the gaseous material instantly transformed into a screaming inferno. Like tossing a lit taper into a lake of oil, a wall of fire expanded to consume the plasma and torch the serpent still moving inside the cloud.

The Naga's jaws opened in a silent shriek of agony that echoed into subspace, briefly overwhelming communications channels. Worf watched as the great beast coiled tightly into a quivering knot, mortally wounded by the *Defiant*'s attack.

"Did we kill it?" Tenmei stared at the viewer, at once elated and horrified.

Worf opened his mouth to give voice to a victory shout; but the cry died in his throat when the Naga's vibrating form *exploded*.

The eruption came with a lightning flare of power, and the creature discorporated, coming apart in a torrent of pieces. It reminded him of a seed pod ejecting kernels into the wind, but here the Naga was transforming itself even as it perished. Great chunks of dermis burned into ashy masses, but death did not end the creature's lethality. Every fleshy fragment ripped open and disgorged a swarm of smaller versions from within. The Naga's huge leviathan form was one beast, of one mind and purpose, but by dying, it hatched hundreds of quivering, eyeless spawn in a final act of aggression.

The main mass of the newborn swarm hurtled across the *Defiant*'s bow, following the same path as the creature that had birthed them. Falling in a glistening rain, the Naga spawn hurtled toward Deep Space 9.

Worf opened fire into the mass, but there were so many of them that the phasers could only reduce their numbers by a minuscule amount.

"Warn DS9!" bellowed Odo. "Those things will destroy the station!"

But with subspace channels still echoing with the death scream of the Naga giant, the crew of the *Defiant* could do nothing but steel themselves as another sinuous cluster of spawn-creatures slammed into the ship's hull, and began to bite and claw at it.

Deep Space 9, Bajor System

Captain Ro watched the progress of the station, as DS9 moved slowly in deep space and on to the fatal trajectory that would take it into the mouth of the burning wormhole.

Thrusters along the support pillars and docking ring flared blue white, and the station's entire spaceframe creaked gently as it began its final journey. Ro placed her hand on a panel, feeling the vibrations through the metal.

How did we come to this? She closed her eyes and looked inward, searching for an answer she knew she would not find. *Even if we succeed, we fail.*

In her thoughts, Ro pictured the Celestial Temple as she wanted to remember it, as a shimmering beacon in the sky, and a symbol for her people. Her own relationship with the Prophets was, to put it bluntly, *complex.* But she respected what those beings meant to her fellow Bajorans, and even if she didn't consider them deities, she valued their existence.

But now I'm leading a mission to destroy them in order to save ourselves. Even if, as Sisko and Kira had said, the Prophets had accepted their fate, Ro remained conflicted. *When this is done, what will be said of us? Whatever happens today, the world will end for someone.*

A warning tone reached her and Ro's eyes snapped open, her

moment of introspection put aside. On the readout before her, one of the primary sensor arrays lit up as it detected a brief energy spike.

"What was that?" said O'Brien, throwing her a questioning look.

"Radiation surge from the engagement zone," she reported. "It's hard to get a clear image."

"The *Defiant* hit its target," added Kira, from a nearby station.

"Hurray for our side!" Quark gave a halfhearted cheer and a shake of the fist, faltering when no one else joined in. "Isn't that a good thing?"

"What the hell?" O'Brien tapped angrily at his screen. "Captain, we're reading multiple incoming objects on approach, vector two-two mark six."

"Organic material," added Kira, then her eyes widened. "Correction, those are *living* organic forms."

"Show me." Ro went to the situation table, pushing Quark aside as the holographic display pinged into life. An image of nearby space appeared, captured by sensors, and in the middle of the frame, a squirming mass of thick-bodied, maggot-like forms tumbled past.

"Those are Nagas," said O'Brien. "Different from the big ones, but they're still dangerous." The color drained from his face. "Captain, they just phased right through our deflectors like they weren't there—!"

The master chief's words were cut short by the dull, resonating echo of something striking the station's outer hull. The noise was irregular, and it came from everywhere, vibrating through the stanchions and the decking.

A new cascade of alert sigils blinked on along Kira's console. "Multiple hull breaches detected. Level two, level eight, nine and ten, fourteen and seventeen . . ." She halted, unable to keep up with the cascade of new warnings. "They're inside the station."

"Ro," said Quark in a worried voice. "You'd better take a look at this." The Ferengi pointed at the console before him, where internal security sensors showed a mosaic of views from different sections of DS9. Some screens within the screen were already dark, but on many others the shadowy forms of the Naga-spawn were spilling down corridors and across the empty atriums on the habitation decks.

"Chief, can we get a transporter lock on those things?" Ro called out to O'Brien. "Beam them back out into space?"

"Negative," he said, frowning. "Their bodies are in a constant state of temporal flux, the scanner can't track them."

"Are they here for us?" Quark grimaced at the thought.

"They're here for everyone," said Ro, catching sight of the station's parkland on one of the displays. There, captured at the corner of the image, were the group of Talnot Adherents who had refused to leave DS9. Their prayer circle became a chaotic tangle of panicked bodies as a horde of the Nagas thrashed across the grass toward them, leaving blackened and aged earth in their wakes. Sickened, Ro looked away as the believers fell to the beasts.

"You couldn't have saved them," Quark said quietly. "They didn't *want* to be saved."

"They'll come for us next." Kira looked up, sparing each of them a glance. "The vipers of the prophecy. *The destroyers and the eaters of flesh.*"

Despite herself, Ro shuddered to hear the ominous words uttered by the vedek, and for an instant she was the little orphan girl in school once again, listening to the nightmarish oratory of a grim-faced teacher.

She shook off the moment and went to a weapons locker on the wall of the hub. "Then we'll have to hold them off until the station is in position." Ro drew a compact phaser pistol for herself, and then tossed another to Quark.

The Ferengi caught the weapon awkwardly. "Wait, what? *We* will hold them off? Don't I get a say in this?"

Ro found a pack of photonic grenades and weighed them in her hands before deciding to take them too. "O'Brien, I'm transferring command of DS9 to you." She turned to face him. "You know what to do, Miles."

O'Brien nodded once, as the weight of that settled in on him. "Aye, Captain."

"Nerys." Ro went to the other Bajoran and placed a hand on her shoulder. "We'll buy you the time you need to finish this."

"Laren." Kira looked deep into her eyes. "If you wish for absolution, I can give it." Her hand reached up to touch Ro's ear, to the place where Bajorans believed the spiritual energy of their people was strongest—but Ro stopped her.

"It's all right," she said, a sad smile forming on her lips. "I have everything I need."

As Ro walked out into the corridor beyond the hub, Quark reluctantly fell in step with her. "You know, it's very presumptuous of you to assume that I'd just go along with this, without complaint." He kneaded the grip of the phaser, shaking his head.

From a few levels below, the sound of tearing metal reached them. She leaned in and planted a kiss on Quark's cheek. "I never assumed you wouldn't complain."

U.S.S. *Aventine* NCC-82602

The darkness became infernal.

Picard willed himself to be still in the midst of the battle, walling off his emotional responses to the fury and destruction, narrowing his concentration down to the moment directly at hand. His world contracted to the tactical display in front of him as he placed shot after shot into the flanks of the gigantic Naga.

The *Aventine*'s torpedoes detonated in chain-fire loops, each bombardment knocking back the alien creature with powerful concussive blasts, but every time the starship scored a hit, the Naga came back at them twice as hard.

Piercing the wall of the opening salvo, the thing had already scored a devastating hit on the port side, turning a swath of the primary hull's saucer section into a rusting, decaying ruin.

Picard was thankful that the *Aventine* was operating with a skeleton crew, for although it made the vessel respond slower, it meant that those damaged sections were empty. He loathed to imagine what might have befallen people on those decks, had it been otherwise. The effect of the Devidian weapons was not just violence, but *spite*. Everything in their gene-engineered arsenal was built around inflicting cruelty on those they considered their prey.

He looked up as a wing of runabouts raced past on the viewscreen, each one dropping microtorpedoes in streamers of crimson, and at the apex of their attack run, the smaller ships broke formation, streaking off in four different directions.

"Maintain fire," called Bowers as the *Aventine* rocked under another collision impact. "Throw everything we have at it!"

"Chronometric particle levels are off the scale," called Kedair. "It's starting to warp local spacetime . . ."

Picard hissed through his teeth and fired again as doubt crept in. "Captain, we're making no headway. This has become a standoff."

Bowers nodded grimly, seeing the truth of it. "Sisko's trick with the warp plasma, can we do the same?"

Data turned from the science station to give a reply. "I do not—"

He never finished the sentence. The deck suddenly fell out from underneath everyone on the bridge, and Picard felt himself propelled upward by an impact so powerful it put a savage twist on the starship's spaceframe. *Aventine*'s structural integrity fields struggled to compensate as artificial gravity went into flux, and for an instant the craft teetered on the brink of breaking apart. Stressed to its limits and beyond as the Naga slammed itself into the hull, *Aventine* tumbled away, trailing a comet tail of debris.

Picard reconnected with the deck and the blow knocked the air out of his lungs. Tasting blood in his mouth, he sucked in a shaky breath and pulled himself back to the tactical station.

Blinking through smoke from fused circuits, Picard refocused on the viewscreen in the exact instant the runabout *Glyrhond* was bifurcated by the falling slash of one of the Naga's spear-shaped cilia.

The craft vanished in a ball of fire, taking Wesley Crusher—or, at least, *one* of him—with it.

Deep Space 9, Bajor System

Quark yelled at the top of his lungs, wordlessly screaming at the serpents crowding the corridor as he fired into the last of them.

He remembered seeing Worf do something similar—some kind of battle cry—during a fight with Jem'Hadar, but what had bolstered the Klingon warrior's spirits seemed more like an inadequate wail from the mouth of a Ferengi.

The phaser ran hot in his clammy grip, the weapon just short of overloading after Ro had made some quick battlefield modifications. She had altered the emitter to fire beams that shifted frequency at random, and it worked against the Naga-spawn, at least for the moment.

The first group that had come boiling up the deck toward the hub level lay in heaps of sizzling meat and disintegrating ash, and the stink of them lingered in Quark's nostrils. The smell reminded him of boiled *gree* worms, and perversely, it made him hungry.

At his side, Ro coughed and sagged against a wall. Like him, she had taken a near hit when they met the attack. That perfect face that Quark loved to look at had grown drawn and gaunt, and her auburn hair was heavily streaked with silver gray. All this had happened in a millisecond, when a Naga tried to bite her throat and perished in the attempt.

Does she know that thing stole a dozen years from her? Does she feel it?

Ro gave him a sideways look. "You look pale," she said briskly. "Wrinkly."

"What?" Quark ran a hand over his face and found deep lines

that hadn't been there an hour earlier. He found a screen on one wall and peered at his reflection in it, dismayed by what he saw. It was clear that the Nagas had taken a decade from him as well. "My boyish good looks are ruined."

"You look distinguished." Ro fiddled with the phaser in her hand, and then cursed. "*Kosst.* The emitter is fused." She tossed the weapon away. "Useless."

Below them, the decking trembled, and Quark heard the sound of movement. Another horde of the Naga-spawn were coming, and by the sound of it, there were many more than they could hope to stop.

It didn't need to be said. Ro and Quark had that kind of friendship, where the unspoken could ring as loud and as clear as anything given voice. The Bajoran and the Ferengi both understood that the invaders could not be allowed to get past them.

Ro dug into the pack she had brought, producing a handful of cylindrical photon grenades. As Quark watched, she unscrewed the caps and worked at the circuits inside.

"Do I want to ask what it is you're doing?"

"No." The Bajoran looked up, past the ramp leading back to the hub on the deck above them. Two sets of heavy doors, bolstered by a force field, blocked off the command center from the corridor. "It's a surprise," she chuckled.

Quark couldn't stop himself from mirroring her. Ro could always do that to him, reach in and pull out the emotions he tried to hide with just a smile or a word. And then he blinked, the brief laughter merging with a jolt of deep sorrow. He palmed a tear away from his cheek, thinking of his nephew, Nog, his brother, Rom, his mother, and a thousand things left unsaid.

Ro looked up. "I really wish you were not here," she said, her voice thickening. "You should have gone."

"I would never leave behind the most precious thing I have." He shook his head, making a show of checking his phaser. The gun's charge was close to spent, so he put it down.

"You really love that bar."

"I meant something better." He sighed. "Remember that time I drank too much tulaberry wine, and I confessed to how besotted I am with you?"

"I remember." She nodded, activating the grenade's charges. "I think what you actually said was, *Ro Laren, I want us to grow old together.*"

He nodded firmly. From the corner of his eye, he could see shapes were moving at the mouth of the corridor. The Nagas would be upon them in moments.

"I did say that," he admitted, reaching up to run his fingers over the new age lines on her cheek. "This isn't what I had in mind."

"Trust me." Ro took Quark's hand in hers, and as he lost himself in her eyes, they placed their fingers on the grenade cluster's trigger pad. "We'll stay handsome and beautiful forever."

U.S.S. *Aventine* NCC-82602

Over the open communications channel, Picard could hear Wesley Crusher conversing with himself, the voices broadcast from the runabouts *Tiber* and *Tecyr*.

"*Where's our third?*" said one.

"*Not seeing him,*" said another. "*I can barely read anything on these sensors, we're swimming in charged verteron particles out here!*"

Picard had to agree. The bleed of exotic radiation spilling from the disturbed wormhole blanketed every scanner on the ship with a seething hail of interference. Combined with the slick of wreckage from *Aventine*'s hits and the destruction of the *Glyrhond*, the battle zone was a mess of gases, debris, and danger.

"*Anything on visual?*"

"*Just the station,*" came the reply. "*Deep Space 9 is in position at the wormhole's event horizon.*"

"*Aventine, do you have the* Defiant *on your screens?*" One of the

Wesleys called out the question and Picard heard Data's clipped response.

"Negative. Tracking of the *Defiant* was lost after the discorporation of target beta. It may be masked by radiation effects, or . . ." He trailed off.

"Let's not count them out yet," Picard insisted. "The other runabout, the *Rio Grande*, it could be with Sisko's ship, perhaps we can't detect them."

"I hope that's true." Bowers spoke up from the captain's chair. "But we can't wait. We have to operate with what we have." He looked up at the tactical station, finding Picard. "Status on quantum torpedoes?"

"Loaded and ready to fire," he replied. "But we already know they will be ineffective."

"Lieutenant Kedair has a notion," said Bowers. "We're going for it."

"Very well." Picard steeled himself for what was to come. "On your mark, Captain."

"My mark, aye." As the wounded starship made a wallowing turn, Bowers tapped the intercom. "*Tiber*, *Tecyr*. Come to zero-eight-zero mark two. Put all power to your tractor beams, set them to modulated pulse, and throw a line on that thing."

On the main viewer, the Naga designated target alpha drifted into sight. Its massive jaws were open, sifting the wreckage like some marine mammal filtering krill from an ocean current.

"*Aventine*, *say again? You want us to tractor the Naga?*"

"And hold it steady," said Bowers. "While we get our licks in."

"Ah." Data's head bobbed. "Ingenious. A modulated tractor beam will impede the creature's ability to phase, at least to some extent."

Picard suspected the android's assessment was an overly hopeful one. This was where they were now, reduced to making dangerous choices and choosing the riskiest of options.

He shut down his misgivings before they could bed in, and

tapped out a firing solution as the *Aventine* and the runabouts closed the distance.

Deep Space 9, Bajor System

The explosion threw O'Brien and Kira into their consoles, and the engineer hung on for dear life as a grinding aftershock resonated through the station's hull. Supports twisted, deck plates crumpled, and conduits blew in gouts of searing white sparks. Alert icons on his station warned of a sudden, massive hull breach on the deck below them, but unlike the others caused by the Nagas chewing their way inside, this had been a detonation from *within*.

A chunk of superstructure had vaporized, taking with it a huge pack of the creatures. Now the damage was spreading into secondary effects, shutting down vital systems.

"Captain Ro? Do you read me?" Kira called into the intercom. "Quark? Are you there?"

O'Brien bit down on the grim certainty borne out by the silence that followed her words. His gaze went to the holo floating over the situation table. The hazy storm of virulent emerald lightning filled the view as the station fell into the bruised, burning nimbus of the wormhole.

"We're out of time," he told her. "We have to do this now." O'Brien went to the master systems control, where the safety interlocks for DS9's reactor core had already been disengaged. Forcing himself to ignore the portent of his actions, the engineer concentrated on deactivating the last few mechanisms that could stop the station from destroying itself.

Kira picked her way through the debris littering the hub to O'Brien's side. "They're gone," she said quietly.

"I know." He stopped and they shared a look. "Are you ready?"

"No," she admitted. From beneath them, broken metal clanged and ground against itself. They both knew what that meant. The

Nagas were still out there, and they would not stop coming until every living being on DS9 was ashes. "Begin," Kira told him.

O'Brien gave the station computer his identity code. Ro's input had been made, giving the chief the sad duty of initiating the command string. With a few keystrokes, it was ready. A crimson COMMIT tab blinked on.

"That's it," he told her. "Point of no return. Like Captain Sisko said, you should be the one to give the final order. Just press that and the whole station will—"

Kira slammed the heel of her hand into the tab before he could finish.

"Attention. Emergency." The synthetic voice of the station computer sounded from speakers overhead, and O'Brien could hear the echo of it being broadcast on every deck of DS9. *"All personnel must evacuate immediately. You now have ten minutes to reach minimum safe distance."*

"That's it," said Kira, turning her hand to study it, as if it belonged to someone else. "Prophecy fulfilled."

"We have to get out of here. We can't go that way." O'Brien jerked his thumb at the doors that Ro and Quark had left through, now permanently closed.

He stooped to pull aside a piece of wreckage, uncovering a hatch set into the deck. After he flicked up the manual releases, it took all his effort to work it open; the hatch's frame had bent, compromising the seal around its edges. Beneath was a poorly lit shaft descending to the station's lower levels.

"Here," he said, "follow this down, it leads straight to the runabout pads."

Kira was half over the lip of the open hatch when another crash of noise sounded, and a shudder knocked O'Brien into a stumble.

The Bajoran lost her grip and she slipped into the shaft. For a second, Kira's eyes widened in panic as she expected to plummet into the dimness, but instead she drifted, falling slowly.

"There's no gravity in there," O'Brien called after her. "Push off with your arms, you can float all the way down."

"You could have warned me!" she shot back.

The crashing sound grew louder, and O'Brien looked up, finding the source of it. Through overhead windows, he could make out the shimmering aurorae surrounding a dozen of the smaller Nagas. They were biting and tearing into the hub by a different path, this time trying to breach it from the outside.

Then he heard the fateful sound that all spacers dreaded: the high-pitched whistling of escaping atmosphere.

Kira must have caught it too, and she shouted back up the shaft to him. "Miles! Come on! They're getting in!"

"I know." An icy calm washed over O'Brien, a sudden and inescapable realization forming in his mind. He saw what was coming, and forced himself to think of it as just another engineering problem.

There was a solution, a simple and effective one. The *only* solution.

He snatched up a tool case from nearby, plucked a microwelder from inside, and fired it up. "Nerys," he shouted. "Give my wife and kids a kiss from me when you see them, will you?"

His hands began to move almost of their own accord, dragging the damaged hatch across. This was the right thing to do. Someone had to survive. And for that to happen, someone had to stay behind, on this side.

"Miles, no!" Kira was still descending, unable to haul herself back up toward him. He couldn't see her anymore, just a vague shadow growing smaller. "Please, don't!"

The whistling air leak became a shriek, and he pushed the hatch back into place as far as it would go. The gap wouldn't close completely, exposing the shaft and anyone in it to the inexorable drag of decompression. The only way to save Kira's life was to weld the hatch shut, so he set to work. A hurricane roared around him and he felt the air in his chest being forced from his lungs, the terrible cold leaching in as the hull plates above buckled and tore.

Miles O'Brien ignored the burning pain on his bare flesh and kept on working, fighting the violent shivering in his limbs, the blindness that took his eyesight, until he couldn't do any more.

His last conscious thoughts were five words. *Yoshi. Molly. Keiko. I'm sorry.*

U.S.S. *Aventine* NCC-82602

The shimmering tractor beams from the two runabouts flashed into existence and enveloped the Naga's great bony carapace, causing the creature to rear up and writhe against the force projected against it.

Picard watched the beast's furious movements, and silently cursed the Devidians once again for forcing this action on them. The Nagas were impressive life-forms, even magnificent in some senses; he wished that he could have met the cosmozoans in some other setting, as explorer and starfarer rather than enemies bent on destruction. *One more crime for the Devidians to answer for,* he thought, *along with all the others.*

"Tractors are locked on and holding," said Data. "The target is attempting to alter its quantum phase signature without success."

"We've got him!" Bowers punched the air. "Engineering, Commander La Forge?"

"La Forge here." Geordi's harried tones filtered up through the intercom.

"I need full shields," said the captain.

"You have them," came the reply, *"at least for the next five minutes. After that, all bets are off."*

"Good enough." Bowers closed the channel and shot Picard a glance. "He's a miracle worker, all right."

"Today, each of us are going above and beyond the call," he replied. As the *Aventine* made its approach, Picard recalculated the torpedo solutions programmed into the tactical station, shaving off seconds here and degrees there, seeking the best angle of attack. "Captain Bowers, we may not be able to make another pass."

"I concur, Captain Picard." Bowers took a long breath. "So we make it count. We finish this."

"If we can," muttered Kedair.

"Helm, take us in," said Bowers, tensed forward in his chair like a runner on the starting line.

Aventine surged forward with a jerk, trembling as the wounded vessel closed the distance to optimum range.

"*Tiber* here, *I'm getting dropout on my tractor beam.*" The voice from the runabout sounded over the open comm channel.

"*Same,*" called the other Wesley. "*It's adapting again! Hurry this up!*"

"Fire when ready," said Bowers.

Picard nodded, hesitating over the tab that would release the torpedoes. The targeting sensors were damaged, forcing him to go with a best guess.

"Captain?" Bowers pressed him.

"Firing." Picard tapped the control and a low rumble signaled a successful launch. "Torpedoes away and running."

"*Aventine, I'm losing it!*" He couldn't be sure which of Wesley's time-displaced incarnations had spoken, but when Picard looked up at the screen, he saw the tractor beams on both runabouts flickering wildly.

Then the Naga tossed its head and a pulse of lethal chroniton radiation bloomed from its cracked and pitted skull, moving through the void like a sonic shock through water.

Closest to the creature, the *Tecyr* and the *Tiber* were hit first. The runabouts came apart under the impact of a wave of accelerated time, becoming papery fragments and dust that dissipated into nothing.

Then the pulse struck the oncoming salvo of quantum torpedoes. The reaction between the collision of exotic particles and the chained energies inside the warheads became a sheet of blinding flame reflecting back at the *Aventine*.

"Evasive!" Someone bellowed the order—it might even have been Picard himself—and then the freakish effect enveloped the ship, draining every iota of power from it.

The same mutated emerald lightning that even now consumed Bajor's Celestial Temple clawed for purchase around the *Aventine*'s quaking deflector bubble, and in the moment it buckled, Picard stared into the face of death.

This cannot be the end, he told himself. *Not here! Not yet!*

Every station, every screen on the bridge went dark, each fading to black one after another as all power on the starship ceased. Picard felt the pull of gravity lessen and he grabbed the edge of the tactical station in front of him to keep himself in place.

The only illumination was from the clear crystal dome that capped the *Aventine*'s bridge, the toxic green glow emanating from the wormhole turning the space into a mass of shade. Every face turned to look upward as something huge and dreadful moved past, briefly eclipsing the sickly illumination.

The Naga creature swam past the powerless starship, flanks carelessly scraping across the edge of the long, elliptical saucer section, tearing great divots out of the hull. Its tail caught the tip of a warp nacelle and crushed it.

The impact put the *Aventine* into a slow roll, and the view through the dome shifted. Fascinated and terrified, Picard continued to look on as the Naga left the ship behind and wound slowly away, toward the seething mass of the wormhole.

"It let us live," said Kedair, her words husky with fear. "W-why did it let us live?"

"We are no longer a threat," said Data.

"It's more than that," noted Picard. "The Devidians like the taste of terror. They want us to live to see our end coming."

A figure moved close by, revealing itself as Mirren, the lieutenant from the ops station. "It's heading for DS9. We can't stop it."

"Yes." The word escaped Picard's mouth in a puff of vapor. With life-support offline, the ship's atmosphere was chilling rapidly. But the cold seemed a distant, unimportant concern.

He could not look away from the tormented maelstrom hanging in the wreckage-strewn blackness. Past the silhouette of the space station, he glimpsed serpentine shapes moving in the storm of gelid light.

Caught in the twitching, shivering membrane of the wormhole, Picard could see more Nagas struggling past one another, a nest of hundreds of them. Slashing and ripping, trying to force their way out and into this reality.

16

Kira choked off a sob and pulled herself along the narrow access way from the drop shaft, toward the hatch that led to the runabout pads.

The station trembled around her, every surface vibrating with the pulsing throb of energy from the tempestuous wormhole. She forced herself not to dwell on the fates of Miles O'Brien, Ro Laren, Quark, and the luckless Adherents, all of whom had ultimately fallen to the predations of the Nagas swarming through DS9. Kira had the very real sense that she was the last humanoid alive aboard the station, feeling the terror of that reality as a bleak shroud drawing close, suffocating her.

She took a breath and steeled herself, refusing to submit to the desolate thought. If the end truly was at hand, Kira Nerys would meet it as she had every other challenge in her life, with fortitude and defiance. To do any less would be an insult to the lost.

With a swift motion, she kicked open the hatch and bright, gold light flooded into the passage. Kira squeezed through, expecting to drop out onto the deck near the runabout pads.

But her boots scuffed against flagstones and she felt gravity shift around her. Blinking against the brightness, Kira's eyes adjusted and the first thing she saw were the lines of nyawood pews and the curving pillars supporting an arched roof. The light was coming through stained-glass windows depicting devotional scenes and religious iconography.

The station's shrine. Kira turned in place, fighting off a sudden bout of dizziness. *That's not possible. The shaft doesn't lead there, it's on the opposite side of DS9!*

There was no sign of the hatch she had come through, no visible means that could have brought her to this place.

Then she heard footfalls behind her, the quiet pad of sandals approaching. Kira turned and found a woman in a veiled, flowing dress standing between the pews. The woman held a bundle wrapped in swaddling, cradling it like a newborn.

The woman smiled at Kira from behind the veil. She had her mother's face, the same face Kira had glimpsed in the cloister of the Perikian Monastery days before.

She wanted more than anything for this to be real, for the person before her to be the true Kira Meru—but Kira Nerys's mother was long dead, and this ghost was only a being who wore her aspect. She was looking into the eyes of a Prophet.

"No time," said the apparition.

"I don't understand." Kira forced out the words. "Did I fail you? Do you want me to stop this?"

"No." Her mother shook her head sadly. Then she offered Kira the shrouded bundle. "Don't be afraid. Take this."

Kira accepted the burden. It was strangely light, but a warmth flowed from it that felt like sunshine. In the act of acceptance, Kira's fingertips brushed the skin of her mother's hands and a surge of emotion rolled through her. It was a potent amalgam of happiness and sorrow, so strong that it made her gasp.

"Take it and go." The Prophet led Kira to the doorway of the shrine and opened it. "Keep it safe."

Kira started walking, compelled to obey. She looked down at the bundle as she crossed the shrine's threshold. "I am sorry," she managed. "Will you forgive me?"

"Kira—"

Her mother's whisper was lost in the howl of the alert sirens, and Kira stumbled, falling against the frame of the airlock as the exterior hatch sealed behind her.

Startled, she jerked away, the transition shocking her. The shift from the tranquil, dreamlike space of the shrine to the reality of the ship's cabin was seamless.

Kira found herself standing in the vestibule connecting to the *Azetbur*'s cockpit. The displays on the control panels of the captain's yacht blinked warnings as a countdown to automatic launch neared zero.

Clutching the bundle to her, Kira raced to the pilot's station, finding a place to secure her precious cargo on the copilot's chair. Out through the *Azetbur*'s canopy, she saw the runabout pad drop down to reveal the raging vista beyond.

A sky that should have been sapphire and darkness was a wall of nauseating emerald, shot through with sickly yellow lightning. The poisoned aura of the wormhole churned around the station, spitting out eye-searing sparks of lambent energy, and for Kira, the sight was abhorrent.

To the very core of her spirit, the corruption of the Celestial Temple was sacrilege. The heart of her people's most deeply held beliefs had become an atrocity, suborned by the Devidians for their apocalyptic obsession. Kira stared into it, equally terrified and revolted. There, thrashing in the nimbus of the light storm, she saw dozens, perhaps hundreds, of the gigantic Nagas, struggling violently to breach the barriers between dimensions and flood into this reality.

Then the yacht blasted free of Deep Space 9, impulse engines howling as it veered away from the doomed station. Navigation scanners were virtually useless, but the *Azetbur*'s previous pilot had been careful enough to program in an escape route away from the mouth of the defiled wormhole to safety. Kira confirmed the course and came about, increasing power to the engines to squeeze as much speed as possible from them.

As the yacht turned, the station came into view again through the starboard canopy. Framed against the viridian madness of the fiery Temple, DS9 was a black shadow, a shape of curves and spires that reminded her once more of her mother. Kira Meru had once owned a delicate locket, a gift from Nerys's father, a finely tooled piece of volcanic glass that shone brightly when the light struck it. She had wept when it broke, and nothing Nerys or her brothers could do that day to cheer her had worked.

Kira touched her face and felt tears of her own there as the station fell slowly across the turbulent event horizon.

"What have I done?" She spoke the question aloud, knowing the damning answer. Kira Nerys, the Hand of the Prophets, had signed the death warrant of her gods, and now she was condemned to bear witness to their end.

She looked down at the bundle on the seat beside her, and, unbidden, she unwrapped the layers of soft swaddling. The burden revealed, light bloomed inside the cabin, bringing with it the same intangible aura Kira had experienced in the shrine.

Nestled against the common cloth was the rough-hewn crystal hourglass of the Orb of Time, its gentle magenta glow shimmering through the tears that misted Kira's eyes.

U.S.S. *Aventine* NCC-82602

Picard suppressed a shiver and pulled the survival jacket closer over his shoulders. Kedair and Data had been able to restore gravity to the wounded *Aventine*, but lighting and heating were still offline, and the chill throughout the bridge had already fallen to sub-zero temperatures. While Bowers distributed gear from the emergency locker, Picard tried in vain to get power to the ship's internal sensors. He scowled at the open panel in front of him and reluctantly admitted defeat.

"No good?" Bowers approached.

"I'm afraid not," he replied. "I managed to get the main viewscreen operable, but little else."

"That's something." Bowers looked back at the screen, the image flickering and cracked. "We've got a ringside seat for the big show." Adrift and unable to maneuver, *Aventine* floated at the edge of the Denorios Belt, bathed in the ill light from the despoiled wormhole.

"How long do we have?" Lieutenant Mirren stood close by, hugging herself for warmth.

Picard followed Bowers's gaze. "Any moment." He searched the void for any sign of other vessels, the *Defiant* or the last surviving runabout, finding nothing.

Silence fell as the skeleton crew paused in their labors, all eyes turning to the dreadful vista before them. At this range, Deep Space 9 was visible as a comma of black cutting across the entrance to the wormhole. It seemed so infinitely small against the storm of emerald fire consuming it, a match head tossed into an inferno.

The captain was gripped by a moment of clarity, a true reckoning of perspective forming in his mind as Picard considered the scale of the station and the ship before the Celestial Temple and the cosmic maelstrom of the wormhole.

The universe was a place of such incredible majesty and infinite wonders, but its vastness could make a mere human feel insignificant. To challenge that, to know that the tiny spark lit in this moment might alter the arc of history for an entire reality, was almost too much to grasp.

"Time," said Data, his voice carrying.

An instant later, the brief dawning of a new star occurred, right in the heart of the wormhole. Running out of control, Deep Space 9's matter/antimatter reactor core consumed itself in a release of energies as powerful as the primal forces of creation.

Picard raised a hand to shield his eyes, but the brilliant disc of light had already seared a purple afterimage on his retinas.

The station's mass transformed in the spherical shockwave propagating out from the heart of the detonation. Thousands of metric tons of metal and polymer, organic and inorganic material, all became liberated particles and radiation. DS9 ceased to exist, but in its death throes the station's fiery obliteration expanded to engulf the extradimensional structure of the wormhole surrounding it.

The complex web of verteron nodes throughout the phenomenon broke apart under the strain, invisible lines of force crackling, allowing energy from subspace domains to leak through and corrode them. Caught in the cascading collapse effect, the multitude of half-formed, phase-shifted Nagas and their surviving pathfinder were dragged inexorably back into the crumbling singularity. Subjected to forces impossible to measure, their screeching forms were crushed by quantum imbalances as the universe rejected their presence.

Awed by the sight, Picard could only watch in silence as the burning Celestial Temple buckled and dwindled. Like the wilting of a great flower, the kilometers-long petals of green plasma fire and lightning folded in on themselves, decaying and shrinking. The collapse dragged in everything within range—dust and fragments from the inner rings of the Denorios Belt, debris and wreckage from the battle with the Nagas—and Picard felt the *Aventine* tremble under the brief, distant pull of hypergravity.

But the moment was already at an end. With a final shimmering glint, the point of light that marked the death of Deep Space 9 faded to nothing, taking the wormhole with it and erasing the Celestial Temple from existence.

Kedair spoke up from one of the consoles. "External sensors are back online. Readings are sporadic, but I find no sign of Naga biosignatures in any phase state."

"They're gone." Mirren was the next to speak. "We stopped them." Then she repeated her words in a shout: "*We stopped them!*"

A ragged cheer went up around the *Aventine*'s bridge, shot through with exhaustion and elation in equal measure, but Picard could not join in. He walked to the main viewer, until he was close enough to place his hand on the display, as if he could reach through it and grasp the stars beyond.

"*Mon dieu*," he whispered, "what have we done?"

"What we have always strived to do, Captain." Data stood behind him, speaking quietly so his words would not carry. "Defy the odds, and go on in the face of the impossible."

"But the cost . . ." Picard stared into the darkness. "I fear the price of this ordeal will be everything we have. Everything we are."

"I have never lied to you," said the android. "I will not begin today." He paused, framing his words. "What you believe is true. The price paid by you, your family, by Worf and his son, Bowers and his people, Sisko and all of Bajor . . . That will not be the sum total of it."

"This isn't over." Picard acknowledged the bleak reality.

"We have not ended the Devidian threat," continued Data. "We have merely set back their plans. They may no longer be able to deploy the Nagas into this timeline, but they remain whole and active in the zone between dimensional realms."

"Intertime." Picard recalled the term that Wesley had used to describe the nonspace where the Devidians hid, and he felt a pang of worry as to the fate of his stepson. "If we can be sure of anything, it is that these beings are persistent. They won't be easily dissuaded from their plans for temporal genocide."

Years ago—centuries ago, if he were to be accurate—Picard had looked one of them in the eye and challenged their predation. The response had been direct and unequivocal. *We need your energy.* Even when he had offered to find some solution that might allow peaceful coexistence, the Devidian's intention had been clear. *We must continue.* They would not countenance anything else.

"We have bought ourselves time," Data concluded. "We cannot waste a moment of it."

As Picard weighed his reply, Lieutenant Kedair called out from the upper bridge. "I have detected a vessel on approach . . . It's the *Azetbur*! Badly damaged but still operational!"

Bowers spoke up. "Life signs?"

Kedair's triumphant tone faltered. "Only one."

The *Aventine*'s captain nodded. "Reroute power to the shuttle-bay."

The doors to the shuttlebay half opened and then stalled, forcing Beverly Crusher to push her medkit through the gap and then squeeze herself through after it.

Inside, the *Aventine*'s landing zone was a mess, where cargo modules had come free to scatter their contents across the deck, and shuttles and workbees had crashed into one another as the starship took a beating. Crusher scrambled over the broken nacelle of a ruined shuttlepod as the aft doors parted, revealing the *Azetbur* on automated approach.

She found Geordi La Forge already at work at a control console, deftly manipulating a single tractor beam to bring home the captain's yacht. "Any communication from the survivor on board?"

La Forge shook his head but didn't look up from the screen in front of him. "Not a word," he confirmed. "I don't like it."

Crusher said nothing, watching as the yacht made a shaky descent to the deck. One single person escaping the destruction of Deep Space 9 was a grim statistic, and the doctor could only wonder who had not made it out in time. At the back of her mind was the fear for the fate of her firstborn son, lost in the chaos. She took cold comfort in the knowledge that Wesley's Traveler abilities gave him an edge on survival, but until she could see him again, and hold him in her arms, the doubts and the apprehension gnawed at her.

La Forge tapped the controls with a flourish, sealing the bay doors as the *Azetbur* settled heavily to the deck. "Secured!"

The yacht seemed to sag, like a long-distance runner faltering past the finish line, the damage across its hull starkly visible. As Crusher moved around to the airlock, she could see swaths of the fuselage melted by energy strikes, missing panels, and other evidence of structural damage. It was a miracle the ship had made it back to the *Aventine*.

La Forge came with her, and he worked the hatch controls to no avail. "It's fused. I'll have to cut my way in."

As the orange-white beam from La Forge's phaser burned into the metal, Crusher put down her medkit and pulled herself up so she could peer in through a port. Inside, the yacht's cabin was hazy, but she spotted a humanoid figure, bent over something she couldn't see.

She banged a fist on the transparent panel. "Hello! Can you hear me? Can you open the hatch?" When the figure didn't respond, she pulled her tricorder out and activated it.

The readout told her little. *One humanoid, species Bajoran, life signs depressed but stable.* She looked closer, and made out what could only be monastic robes pooled around the unmoving figure.

Kira Nerys. It has to be her. Although the two women had never met, the doctor had heard much about the hero of the Bajoran resistance during her brief stint as chief medical officer aboard Deep Space 9.

"Doctor!" La Forge called out as the *Azetbur*'s hatch gave way, allowing acrid gray vapor to billow out into the shuttlebay. She quickly followed the engineer inside, into the cockpit.

The Bajoran sat near a flickering command console, a disconsolate and distant expression on her face. She stared into nothing, her ash-smeared cheeks marked with the tracks of tears. As La Forge shut down the damaged ship's systems, Crusher dropped into a crouch and put a gentle hand on Kira's shoulder.

"Vedek? Are you all right?"

Kira did not reply, or show any reaction at all. Crusher felt an involuntary shudder, as if it were an empathic reaction to the woman's visible despair. She had seen this kind of behavior before, from people who had suffered a traumatic experience so severe it forced them into a kind of mental paralysis. Knowing the terrible price the Bajoran had paid to endure this ordeal, Crusher could only feel sadness for her.

"You're safe now," continued the doctor. "It's over . . ."

Her words seemed to penetrate Kira's malaise and she blinked. It was then that Crusher realized the woman was holding a rough cloth bundle in her hands.

"What is that?" said La Forge as the doctor guided Kira shakily to her feet.

Crusher tried to take Kira's burden from her, but the Bajoran held on to it tightly, the action dislodging the covering.

Inside the bundle was an object she did not recognize, a thing in the shape of a crude hourglass, as if hacked out of smoky quartz. It was dark and cold, giving off a lifeless aura so strong that she instinctively backed away.

"It's dead," said Kira. "They're all dead."

The hours stretched on as the *Aventine* limped back from the shattered ring of the Denorios Belt toward Bajor.

With its quantum slipstream drives damaged beyond repair by the Naga attacks, a flight that should have taken a few seconds became a slow, hesitant crawl at low impulse power. They lost the better part of a day in the journey, but despite his exhaustion, Jean-Luc Picard could not rest. In the end, he had managed a few hours of blank torpor, but it barely affected the fatigue that had settled in his bones.

Determined to make himself useful, he walked the ship, eventually returning to the bridge and the captain's ready room. He found Samaritan Bowers in much the same state.

"Captain." He gave Bowers a weary nod.

"Captain." The younger man was in the process of cleaning up the cabin, damaged during the engagement with the Devidian creatures. He put books and broken ornaments into a storage case, an eclectic collection of items that didn't seem to tally with what Picard knew of the man.

Then he understood. "These are Ezri Dax's personal effects."

"Yes." Bowers turned a small geode over in his hands. "This is from one of the digs on New Sydney, where she grew up. Her family runs a big mining concern there." Carefully, he placed it in the case, atop a bound collection of Klingon folktales in the original language. "I'd been putting it off, securing all her stuff. Then things started to happen and there wasn't time." He sighed. "This is all that is left of her now. Relics. But no body to bury, nothing but a memory to mourn."

"And she is just one of many." Picard knew where the other man's grief stemmed from. "A high price paid."

Bowers looked up at him. "Tell me this will be the end of it, sir. Please."

"If only I could." Picard sighed. "Believe me, I want nothing more. But the fight isn't over."

Bowers let out a long breath, and before Picard's eyes he changed, shuttering away the fear and despair, reassuming the firmness and the strength that was needed to command. "All right. We go on. We'll go on until we can't go any farther."

Dax chose her crew well, thought Picard. He handed Bowers the padd he was carrying, becoming businesslike. "A complete damage report, compiled with the assistance of Mister Data. He and his daughter have been able to bring the life-support system back to full operational capacity, along with short-range communications, but Lal informs me that the slipstream drive may be permanently out of action."

Bowers looked over the text, his dark brow furrowing. "Not good. We'll have to figure out an alternative. Starfleet must be on the way to the Bajor system by now; what happened here can't have escaped their notice." He paused, considering their options. "What about the *Defiant* and the *Rio Grande*? Any trace of them?"

"Nothing," said Picard. "But that doesn't mean they didn't survive the . . . the collapse. The *Azetbur* managed to escape, and I have faith in the abilities of Mister Crusher and Captain Sisko."

"I hope you're right," said Bowers. "Speaking of the *Azetbur*, how's our guest?"

"Vedek Kira is in sickbay. She remains uncommunicative," he noted. "The object she brought with her resembles one of the sacred Orbs of the Prophets, but it exhibits none of the properties usually associated with those artifacts. It appears to be nothing but inert matter . . . But despite that, she refuses to part with it."

Neither of them spoke, both considering what the presence of an inert Orb might mean. Then the familiar three tones of a bosun's whistle sounded from the intercom on the captain's desk, and Bowers gestured for Picard to answer it.

"This is Captain Picard, go ahead."

"Kedair here, sir. We have detected a Starfleet warp signature closing on our position, from orbit of Bajor. They'll be in communications range in a few moments."

"Sisko?" Bowers said hopefully.

"Negative, Captain. Sensor returns are too large. This is something else."

The two men exchanged a wary glance, and together they moved to the portal looking out from the ready room and into the darkness of space. Picard's keen eye soon picked out the shape of the approaching vessel and he pointed. "There."

With a flash of deceleration, the distinctive, rugged configuration of a *Luna*-class starship dropped out of warp and heeled around, slowing to a halt directly across the *Aventine*'s course.

"It's the *Titan*," hissed Bowers. "Damn Riker, does he never give up?"

"Never," noted Picard. "He must have been waiting for us in Bajor's magnetosphere. We wouldn't have detected him until he was right on top of us."

Bowers drew himself up, straightening his uniform tunic with a tug on the hem. "Well. I'm game to bluff our way through this if you are. Unless, of course, you've got a Plan B up your sleeve that I don't know about?"

Picard avoided the question, and answered with one of his own. "Do you recall what you told my wife when we first set out on this endeavor?"

"Whatever you need, we are here," Bowers replied without hesitation. "That offer still stands."

"Thank you, Sam," said Picard. "That means a great deal."

"It's the least I can do . . . Jean-Luc."

The intercom sounded again, and this time Kedair's tone was tight with anxiety. *"Captains, the* Titan *has locked weapons on us. Admiral Riker is demanding to speak with you directly. If we refuse, they'll board us by force."*

Bowers moved to stand shoulder to shoulder with Picard. "All right, Lonnoc. Open a secure channel. Let's hear the man out."

With a crackle of photons, a projector in the ceiling of the ready room activated, sketching in a holographic avatar of William Riker. The admiral's expression was a haggard mask, with all the telltale signs of a man who had not rested in days. Riker met Picard's gaze and the warmth that usually lived behind those eyes was noticeably absent.

"Do you have any idea what you have done?" He stood ramrod straight, stiff and angry. *"It's not enough for you to disobey the direct orders of the Federation president, steal a Starfleet vessel, and suborn other officers into your schemes? You colluded to destroy Deep Space 9 and obliterate the Bajoran wormhole, you cut off countless ships and colonies in the Gamma Quadrant, jeopardized thousands of lives!"*

"I regret the choices that were required," began Picard. "But I would make them again in the same circumstances." He paused, and tried a different tack. "Will, please, listen to me. I know what you must be experiencing, the mental turmoil, the . . . the *shadows.* We've been able to understand it, it is part of all this—"

"Stop!" Riker bellowed the word. *"Just stop!* You *listen to* me, *Jean-Luc! This is over. You are finished. I am in charge here."* He strode forward, as if to menace them with his presence. *"You left me with no alternative! After the Borg took you, I had to take over . . ."*

He faltered for a second, as if lost in that memory, then quickly regained his impetus. *"And this is the same! You've let us all down, with your hubris and your blind conceit. This is where it ends."*

"You didn't see what we saw in that future," Bowers shot back. "You were not there, Admiral! You can't possibly understand what is at stake!"

"I understand enough," said Riker, matching the other man's icy tone. *"A first officer unprepared for the burden of command, traumatized by the loss of his friend and captain?* I know that full well. *I lived it."* Before Bowers could respond, the admiral switched his ire back to Picard. *"You will stand down. Every person aboard the* Aventine *is under arrest on the charges of mutiny, gross insubordination, and actions jeopardizing the safety of the Federation and its citizens. You and your coconspirators will be brought before a full Starfleet court-martial and you will answer for what you have done."* His rage ebbed for a moment, turning regretful. *"You forced me into this, Jean-Luc. When you put the future and my family at risk."*

At length, Picard gave a solemn nod. "Very well. I take full responsibility—"

"No." Riker refused to let him finish. *"That ship has sailed. I warned you that you would drag these people down with you. Now you'll carry that along with everything else."* He let his words hang in the air for a moment before he went on. *"Captain Bowers, if you don't have Picard beamed over to my ship in the next five minutes, I swear to you I will cut the* Aventine *in half and haul him out myself. Am I clear?"*

Bowers looked away. "Clear, Admiral."

Riker's image dissipated, leaving the two of them alone once more.

U.S.S. *Titan* NCC-80102

"He's going to try something," said the admiral, speaking directly to Commander Tuvok as the Vulcan led the way along the corridor. "He's Jean-Luc Picard. He doesn't give up without a fight."

Tuvok said nothing, but the brief look he sent in Captain Vale's direction spoke volumes. Her second officer's expression remained inscrutable, but she knew him well enough to sense his discomfort. They were on their way to metaphorically clap one of Starfleet's most decorated captains in irons, for the most serious of crimes. That was something that hadn't happened since the days of Kelvar Garth.

"I want triple security on him at all times," Riker went on. "And his coconspirators are to be held in isolation from one another, once we have the *Aventine* in tow."

"That seems like overkill," ventured Vale.

Riker fixed her with a hard gaze. "We have no way of knowing exactly how compromised Picard is," he insisted. "This is more than some lapse of judgment on his part. He may be under a malign influence. It's happened to him before, more than once."

I could say the same thing about you. Vale bit down on the reply before she could utter it, but Riker had to know what she was thinking.

He held up a hand in front of her, halting Vale in the middle of the corridor. "Tuvok, prepare the transporter room to receive the prisoners. We'll be with you in a moment."

"Aye, sir." The Vulcan gave Vale another questioning look, then went on his way.

Riker's hand fell and so did his tone. "If you have something to get off your chest, Christine, now's the time."

"You're damn right I do," she replied.

Since the Starfleet Command briefing, Riker had become more and more distracted, his usual outgoing manner turned sullen and inward looking. At first, Vale had thought it was the stress of the situation, but she was afraid it was more than that. Riker had ducked every attempt she made to talk to him until this moment, and now she feared it was too late.

"This whole thing is a blasted mess, and we should be trying to hold it in check. But I just had to listen to you threaten to destroy another Starfleet vessel and intimidate men and women that I consider my friends. Where is this going to end, Admiral? Picard's not the only one crossing a line."

"What did my wife say to you?" It wasn't the response that Vale expected, and when she hesitated in her reply, Riker pressed on. "You realize that Picard tried to win her over to his point of view, right? Do you think that a man who sows dissent like that can still be considered a friend?"

Vale found her voice again. "Deanna is concerned." There was a lot more to it than that, but Vale was wary of stoking the admiral's ire. "We all are. How many people on this ship have served on the *Enterprise*, or alongside Jean-Luc Picard, over the years? He inspires loyalty. People are conflicted."

"And where are your loyalties, Captain?" Riker said quietly.

"How can you even ask that?" Vale's color rose in her cheeks. "My loyalty is to my crew, my ship, my oath. That's never altered."

"Good." Riker folded his arms. "Because that oath is to Starfleet, and here and now, I am the representation of it." He let that statement hang, then looked away. "Captain, if it troubles you, you're free to step aside."

"No, sir," Vale said firmly. "If this has to happen on my ship, I will see that it is done by the book."

"Agreed." Riker started after Tuvok, and Vale reluctantly fell in step behind him.

The Vulcan was already at the control console as they entered the transporter room, and along with Tuvok, *Titan*'s chief of security, Lieutenant Commander Keru, was present, standing guard with a phaser at his hip.

"The *Aventine* signals they are ready to transport Captain Picard," said Tuvok.

"Energize." Vale took up a position in front of the empty transporter platform.

A column of flickering white light formed, but within a few

moments the tension in the room jumped. It was taking longer than it should to beam Picard aboard.

"Something wrong?" Keru glanced at Tuvok.

"A slight loss of signal," said the Vulcan. "I am compensating."

Riker's hand tightened into a fist. "What is he doing? Tuvok, I want him on this ship! Do not let him escape!"

"It appears to be nothing more than a minor pattern shift," Tuvok replied. "Likely a result of ambient radiation effects in local space from the collapse of the wormhole." He paused. "If you wish, I can shunt the captain's pattern to a buffer and hold him there."

"No." Riker gestured for Keru to draw his weapon, and he stepped up to the foot of the transporter platform. "Beam him aboard."

Tuvok worked the matter alignment controls and the column of light solidified into a recognizable face and form. The glow dissipated to reveal Picard, dressed in a simple civilian tunic and trousers, his hands clasped behind his back.

He ignored Riker, finding Vale. "Permission to come aboard, Captain?"

"Granted, Captain," she replied. "I regret it is under these circumstances."

"You gave up the right to be called captain the moment you fled," insisted Riker, glaring at his former commander. "My only regret is that I allowed our friendship to cloud my judgment."

Picard seemed unfazed by the bitterness in Riker's tone. "In my experience, justice rises above such things."

Something in Picard's manner rang a wrong note with Vale. It seemed off, but in a way she couldn't quite articulate.

The admiral didn't seem to notice. "This is the last time you'll do this. I won't allow you to abandon your crew again, to put everything we have in danger! You are under arrest, and I will make sure you answer for all you have done."

"As you wish." Picard held up his hands, showing the wrists, as if waiting for manacles to be placed around them.

"Bridge to Captain Vale!" Commander Sarai's voice issued out of the air, with an urgency that was unusual for the typically stoic Efrosian woman.

The captain tapped her combadge. "This is Vale, go ahead."

"Captain, the admiral asked to be informed of any irregular activity. We've just had a transient sensor return off the starboard bow. It only lasted a half second, but I thought you should be alerted."

"What kind of return?" demanded Riker.

"A neutrino pulse."

Tuvok raised an eyebrow. "That is a trace factor common to the operation of a cloaking device."

"Commander, go to red alert!" Riker barked, before anyone else could react. "Do it now! I want a full-power sensor sweep of the area!"

Vale noted the slight upward quirk of Picard's mouth. It wasn't quite a smile, but it was close enough. At her side, Tuvok had drawn a tricorder from an opening on the console and was using it to run a high-order scan on the captain.

"Curious," he muttered as he scrutinized the readings.

Picard sighed and raised his hands. "Shall we do away with the charade?"

Vale's jaw dropped open in shock as the man standing on the transporter platform *transformed*, briefly becoming a shimmering mass of copper-hued liquid that remade itself into a different, less-defined humanoid form.

She reacted with immediate muscle memory, going on the defensive. Vale had faced Changelings in the past, during the war with the Dominion. One of them had tried to kill her while she was serving aboard the *O'Keefe*, and the recollection of that moment was hard to shake off.

But the being before her wore a Bajoran militia uniform and a benign—*if smug*—expression. He made no attempt to attack.

"Constable Odo." Riker fairly spat the shape-shifter's name. "Where is Picard?"

"Oh, I'm afraid he will be long gone by now," the Changeling said, cool and unruffled in the face of the admiral's indignation. "I believe the captain has other business to attend to."

U.S.S. *Defiant* NX-74205

In the capture of the beam, time passed in moments for Jean-Luc Picard.

His final view of the *Aventine* was the worried expression on the face of Lonnoc Kedair as the young officer sent him into the non-existence of transportation. He didn't regret making the journey; events had overtaken him. The hand Picard held was nothing but poor cards, but he would play what he had been dealt.

When the effect of the transporter dissipated and he was whole and present again, Picard knew at once that something unexpected had happened. Through force of habit, he took a deep breath and checked himself over.

No pain, no difficulty breathing. He had rematerialized without harm, but clearly not on the *Titan*.

"All right!" An exultant shout drew his attention. "We got him! Well done!"

"Team effort," said another voice.

Picard blinked and stepped forward, out of the dazzle of the pad's lights and into the low-ceilinged confines of a cargo bay. Close at hand, Geordi La Forge and Wesley Crusher shared a smile at their accomplishment.

"Gentlemen," he said warily. "If I am here, then can I correctly assume that our fail-safe was a success?"

"It worked," said Wesley, producing a medical tricorder to scan the new arrival. "I won't lie to you, sir, it was touch and go. But here you are"—he smiled at the tricorder's readings—"safe and sound."

"I told you we could do it," said La Forge. "A former *Enterprise* engineer gave me the lowdown on adapting transporter buffers for nonstandard operations. I just improved on his process."

"Wesley." Picard was still taking it all in, but for a moment he allowed himself to be relieved by his stepson's presence. "When we lost track of the *Rio Grande*, your mother and I . . ."

"It blew up," admitted Wesley, taking Picard's offered hand. "But I managed to make it across to the *Defiant* before, you know." He pulled a face. "The effort took it out of me, I have to say."

Picard looked around, taking in the compartment. "But Geordi, you were still on the *Aventine* when I beamed out."

"You're a few hours out of synch." Wesley gestured at the console as La Forge powered it down. "You've been in there for nearly a day, sir." He let that sink in. "The *Defiant* was damaged by the wormhole's collapse and it took us time to get her back up and running. We were closing in on the *Aventine* when the *Titan* appeared, so we cloaked . . . And then initiated Plan B."

"I take it Mister Odo had no problem impersonating me?"

"He was up for it." Wesley nodded. "I intercepted your matter stream from the *Aventine*, diverted it here, and replaced it with Odo's. It was tough to match the exact frequency on the fly, but I managed."

"That's not all he did," noted La Forge. "He pulled six other people off the *Aventine* and hid us in the transporter buffer while the *Defiant* made a run for it."

Wesley's expression shifted. "I'm sorry, Captain. I couldn't get more than that. The buffer was at full capacity. I had to leave Captain Bowers and his crew behind."

"Your mother? And René?"

"They're both here," said Wesley. "And Data and Lal, along with Geordi."

"It's quite the reunion," said another voice. "A big group for a small ship." Picard turned to see Benjamin Sisko enter, and the man's wary manner was unchanged from their last meeting. "I have Mister Crusher to thank for rescuing Vedek Kira along with the others. I greatly appreciate the care your wife has given her."

"And I appreciate all you have sacrificed to bring us to this moment," said Picard, with feeling. "But I fear I must demand more from you. From all of us. There is still much to be done, if we are to end the Devidian threat."

"We've come this far," noted Sisko. He gestured at the walls around them. "My crew evaded the *Titan*'s pursuit and got us into interstellar space. Thanks to Ambassador Spock's input, we've been able to avoid detection so far, but the net is closing."

La Forge gave a nod. "Starfleet has every ship in the quadrant looking for us. Admiral Riker has declared the *Defiant* renegade and disavowed us to the Klingons, the Romulans, the Typhon Pact, everyone."

"We will follow you, Picard," Sisko said firmly, "but we have to have a plan. We can't just react to what the Devidians are doing. We have to take the fight to them. And for that, we need allies. A safe place where we can lick our wounds and regroup."

Picard was silent for a long moment as he considered the hostile reality they now faced. *If half the galaxy is hunting us, where can we turn for help?*

"I have a suggestion." A shape detached from one of the gloomy corners of the room, becoming a tawny-skinned man with a ragged beard and bright, searching eyes. Julian Bashir stepped into the light, studying Picard and the others with an intense focus that bordered on unsettling. "But you're not going to like it."

"How long have you been over there eavesdropping?" Wesley looked him up and down.

"Long enough."

"Doctor, at this point we're willing to entertain any option," said Sisko.

Bashir smiled, a wild light in his eyes. "It's only when you have nothing left to lose that you can truly know yourself. And here we are." He spread his hands. "There is somewhere we can go where Riker won't follow." His smile grew into a feral grin. "Beyond all this . . . and into the mirror."

EPILOGUE

Somewhen

The weight of a thousand years rested in the old man, heavy like lead.

Humans were not meant to live as long as he had, to venture where he had and see what he had seen. His kind were only meant to encompass a brief candle of existence, but he had defied evolution and history. He had *Traveled*.

But his time, for as much as he had been able to extend it and defy expectations, was running short.

He walked, leaving footprints in the deep ash of the dead world, advancing on the horror rising before him. He had to see it, before the end. To look upon the danger with his own eyes and know for certain before he took that final step. The one that would kill him.

There was no name for this place, so he had christened it *intertime*, amusing himself with the term. The whole notion of it, of a reality that could exist between the passings of seconds, seemed like madness. But he had lived a very long while and he had seen things that many sentients would think insanity.

Across uncanny, inexplicable realms, peering into *what was*, *what might have been*, and *what must never be*, he had caught fleeting glimpses of the complex machinery of the infinite. He was a flea, walking over the cogs of a gigantic chronometer, knowing only enough to understand how *little* he understood.

But death, though. He knew that.

How many times had he cheated it? He no longer recalled the exact count. He had wriggled free of it by dint of his intelligence and cunning, employing powers no human should ever have wielded. And now, as the darkness drew closer, he understood why.

Every choice he had made, every road taken, they were bound to bring him inexorably to this wasteland.

He marched woodenly up the blackened ridge, over the crumbling and lifeless rock, toward the roar of the culling, and into the horror's pestilent aura.

There was so much death and despair in this place that the magnitude of it had transgressed physical reality. It was in the air. He took it in with every breath, dense and cloying, filling his lungs. It tasted like powdered bone and acrid smoke. The renderings of an apocalypse, clogging his pores, burning his eyes.

Reaching the highest point of the ridge, on a jagged spear tip of black obsidian extending out over a bottomless crater, he dared to walk to the edge.

He removed the battered breather mask and optic rig over his head, baring his face for the first time in days. His craggy, age-lined aspect was framed by white-gray hair and a dirty, unkempt beard.

But his eyes; they had never aged. They were still those of a young man thrilled by the immensity of the universe and driven by the need to know it.

He removed a small device from his belt, opened it, and allowed it to record the view before them. He looked up, into the blackness, and saw the horror in full for the first time.

Beneath a beheaded mountain of rock and metals fused with arcane biotechnology, the vast bowl of a deep caldera dozens of kilometers in diameter faced an eternal night sky. Lambent flashes of energy seethed around its edges, illuminating a mass of millions of shimmering forms within.

White fire in crackling profusion fell from a great mechanism drifting in the darkness high above, a huge orbital platform of eerie, alien dimension. Captured by the construct, drawn in and condensed until it screamed, every particle of that light represented the pain and anguish of some living being, murdered to feed an abhorrent and unending appetite.

Neural energy, richly marbled with agony and misery, found its way down and down until it reached the hungering masses gathered at its base.

Surrounded by a host of their Naga weapon-creatures and pools filled with languid ophidians, the last throng of a dying, parasitic species ate their fill.

This great arena was just one of countless others scattered over the surface of the dead world. Amid the silvery rivers of light, the Devidians seemed like poor examples of destroyers. In their immense numbers, the spindly, emaciated beings sat listlessly, barely moving as the open scars of their feeding maws yawned to suck in packets of refined neural energy. The falling, sparking embers glistened like poisonous snowflakes, and not a single morsel escaped consumption.

The old man stared up at the impossible geometry and soul-crushing dreadfulness of the gargantuan orbital construct, this thing built solely to destroy on a near-unimaginable scale. With every new influx, he was witnessing the harvest of the fear-energy of countless beings, perishing in abject terror each time the Devidians collapsed a timeline.

I can't stop them alone. He might have spoken the words or held them in his thoughts. The truth was undeniable. For all the power he had, it would not be enough.

And slowly, he accepted the realization. *The only way to end this is to risk the lives of everyone I have ever loved. My friends. My family.*

Down in the crater, some of the wraith-like Devidian avatars began to stir. They sensed his intrusion, and it angered them. They had been trying to destroy him for thousands of years of their subjective time, and almost succeeded.

To fight them now would be death, but to flee would end him too.

Propelled by shimmering gusts of force, a cohort of avatars came racing toward him, death-energy crackling around the tips of their spidery, outstretched fingers. He heard them howling, heard the desperate greed in their screams.

Wesley folded shut the Omnichron device and pocketed it, closing his eyes as he summoned every last iota of potential the Travelers had granted him. He knew, even as he gathered the power to him, that this jump would be his last. It would kill him to project his body out of the intertime realm, back and back into the past—but there was no other way to end this.

He could not hope to win this battle alone; and so he would fling himself through time and space, across the distance to carry a warning to the only people he trusted.

As his body began to fade, he no longer heard the howling of his enemies. His only thought was of a word that could encapsulate a place, a moment, a feeling—that ephemeral *somewhere* in which he would be content to die, knowing that the fight would carry on without him.

Wesley reached out across the infinite, and he found—

—*Enterprise.*

END OF BOOK II

will conclude in

BOOK III

OBLIVION'S GATE

AFTERWORD

So here we are.

You and me, author and reader, at the edge of the end. *Don't look down.*

If you've come this far, I hope you might recall what my esteemed colleague Dayton Ward wrote in his comprehensive afterword for *Moments Asunder*, the book that precedes this one—and if you haven't read the first volume of our *Coda* miniseries before you got to this page, *wow*, you must be *extremely* confused.

I'm not going to reiterate all of what Dayton said, because he summed it up succinctly (feel free to go back and reread what he wrote before you carry on here, I'll wait), but if you'll indulge me, I will touch on some of the same points.

The *Coda* series is a waypoint for something unprecedented in the world of tie-in fiction. *Star Trek*, along with a small handful of intellectual properties like *Star Wars*, *Doctor Who*, *Warhammer*, and a few others, is in the privileged position of having an ongoing literary component that parallels the source material, building out the world and adding new stories to the great tapestry of its imagined universe.

For people who want to go deeper into that world, to see other shades of their favorite characters, or just keep the fun going, we've got you covered.

Over the years, writers like me have been allowed to play with *Star Trek*'s vast toy box. It's no lie to say we helped keep the flame burning when there were no new TV episodes to watch and no movies to thrill to. A responsibility we relished, let me tell you.

With the future of *Star Trek* unwritten, we stepped in to map the uncharted regions where untold adventures were waiting. We picked up the baton from the creators of our favorite *Star Trek* shows when those narratives ended, and we kept running. We kept writing. And the good folks like you, our dedicated readers, came along for the ride.

But *All Good Things . . . something something something,* as they say.

Set into the work of being a tie-in writer is an unspoken Sword of Damocles that hangs over every tale we tell. There is always the possibility that our stories will be invalidated by new developments in the source material, if someone chooses to take the characters or the narrative in a different direction on the big or small screen. It is part and parcel of the gig, the price of admission for getting our hands on that toy box I mentioned.

In the fallow seasons where new content is thin on the ground, it's not an issue. But recently, as the pendulum swung back toward *Star Trek* making its return to television, we knew the days of the *Star Trek* literary universe were numbered.

I sensed that sword looming when my colleague Kirsten Beyer recruited me in 2019 to write *The Dark Veil,* a tie-in to the *Star Trek: Picard* television series. *Picard* would be set beyond the era in which we were currently telling *Trek*-lit tales, but it couldn't be reasonably expected to follow the direction laid down in the novels.

In the books we've done a lot of . . . let's call it *remodeling* . . . including such big swings as doing away with the Borg, blowing up Deep Space 9 (the first one), marrying Jean-Luc Picard to Beverly Crusher and giving them a son, sending Will Riker and Deanna Troi off on their own series of adventures, killing then resurrecting Kathryn Janeway, and lots more.

And while our longtime readers have followed along, it's unfair to expect new television viewers to understand all that continuity. Only a small percentage of the people who would watch *Star Trek: Picard* would even be aware that our novels existed. The new TV show would pick up where the last piece of screen *Trek* narrative had left off—from the end of the 2002 movie *Star Trek Nemesis*.

Down came the blade. When writing *The Dark Veil* I found myself in the odd position of working in a continuity where the last two decades of *Trek* fiction hadn't happened, in a time stream where everything old was new again.

But the "lit-verse" (as some readers christened it) was still out there, with stories unresolved and questions unanswered. Our friends over in the Galaxy Far, Far Away had gone through a similar thing when the return of the *Star Wars* saga signaled the end of that franchise's expanded universe, with their prose stories literally becoming "Legends."

Rather than follow that model, we chose to do something different on the Final Frontier. We would write a conclusion—a *Coda*, if you will—to bring down the curtain on the stories we had been telling, and reset the clock.

And I have to say, when I was approached to join my colleagues Dayton Ward and David Mack in this monumental endeavor, my first reaction was to refuse. The part of me that will forever be a fanboy hated the idea of turning out the lights on the lit-verse, on a continuity that I had not only read and enjoyed, but personally helped to build.

But, over beers and barbecue on a clammy Fourth of July, Dave talked me around.

"If we don't do this, who will?" he said. We owed it to our readers to go big and give the novels the heroic send-off they deserved, and damn it, he was right.

Swansong, *Reset*, and *Long Goodbye* were all code names for this project in the early days, but it was *Wormhole Death Canon* that became our working title and ersatz band name (*yes*, that is the correct spelling, and *yes*, we'll probably have T-shirts made). And like a bunch of loud nerds jamming in a garage, Dayton, Dave, and I riffed on how best to both burn down the house *and* test our cast of characters in the most epic way possible.

I'm fond of thinking of *Star Trek* stories as the equivalent of heroic myths for the modern age, so we worked on creating something that lived up to that theme and scale.

For all of us, *Coda* has been a unique and challenging project. My part, writing this middle movement of the symphony, involves dialing up the tension, shifting stuff around, introducing new players, and the aforementioned setting-fire-to-things, as well as plumbing the depths of the building drama.

Along with Dayton and David, I've done my best to reach back into all that has come before, in the hopes of acknowledging the work of my predecessors and the stories they have told.

Know that these books come from a place of love, and even if our narrative has its bleak and desolate moments, it is at its heart a story about carrying light through the darkness.

Some choices we've made will be welcomed, and others will not—but like with all great disaster-adventure tales, *you'll laugh, you'll cry, but you don't know who'll die.*

I'll sign off here with a final observation. My first ever piece of *Star Trek* prose writing was a short story for *Distant Shores*, a *Voyager* anthology; the title of that work was "Closure," and it was about the act of letting go of things lost and embracing the future. I can't help but smile at the circularity of this, with my final work for this incarnation of the lit-verse being the book you hold in your hands, this *Coda*.

And as to where we go from here?

Keep reading. The tale's not told yet.

James Swallow
London
April 2021

ACKNOWLEDGMENTS

First and foremost, I salute my esteemed colleagues Dayton Ward and David Mack, without whom the *Coda* project could not have happened; thank you, lads, for your focus, your insights, and your comradeship. As always, it's been a blast working with you.

I must also show my appreciation for those who provided support for this particular novel in manners editorial, authorial, educational, and inspirational—Margaret Clark, Ed Schlesinger, Kirsten Beyer, Keith R. A. DeCandido, Glenn Hauman, Scott Pearson, John Van Citters, Mark Rademaker, and John M. Ford.

Beyond this work, along with those aforementioned, I'd like to thank some of the *Star Trek* authors from whom I've had the honor to learn, and to work alongside, over the years—Vonda N. McIntyre, Diane Duane, Peter Morwood, Una McCormack, Kevin Dilmore, Geoffrey Thorne, A. C. Crispin, Greg Cox, Alan Dean Foster, David R. George III, John Jackson Miller, Marco Palmieri, and Andrew Robinson.

And finally, with much love in this and every other reality, to Mandy Mills.

ABOUT THE AUTHOR

James Swallow is a BAFTA-nominated, *New York Times* and *Sunday Times* bestselling author. Swallow is proud to be the only British writer to have worked on a *Star Trek* television series, creating the original story concepts for the *Star Trek: Voyager* episodes "One" and "Memorial."

His *Star Trek* writing includes *The Dark Veil*, *Fear Itself*, *The Latter Fire*, *Sight Unseen*, *The Poisoned Chalice*, *Cast No Shadow*, *Synthesis*, the Scribe award winner *Day of the Vipers*; the novellas *The Stuff of Dreams* and *Seeds of Dissent*; the short stories "The Slow Knife," "The Black Flag," "Ordinary Days," and "Closure" for the anthologies *Seven Deadly Sins*, *Shards and Shadows*, *The Sky's the Limit*, and *Distant Shores*; scripting the videogame *Star Trek Invasion*; and over four hundred articles in thirteen different *Star Trek* magazines around the world.

James is the author of the internationally bestselling Marc Dane thrillers *Nomad*, *Exile*, *Ghost*, *Shadow*, and *Rogue*, the *Sundowners* steampunk westerns, and novels from the worlds of *24*, *Doctor Who*, *Warhammer 40,000*, *Stargate*, *2000AD*, and more.

His other credits include scripts for videogames and audio dramas, including *The Division 2*, *Ghost Recon Wildlands*, the *Deus Ex* series, *Disney Infinity*, *No Man's Sky*, *Fable: The Journey*, *Battlestar Galactica*, and *Blake's 7*.

He lives in London, and is currently working on his next book. Find him at his official website at **jswallow.com** or on Twitter @jmswallow.